SUMMONS TO MURDER

Charles Dickens Investigations
Book Nine

J C Briggs

SAPERE
BOOKS

SUMMONS TO MURDER

Published by Sapere Books.

20 Windermere Drive, Leeds, England, LS17 7UZ,
United Kingdom

saperebooks.com

ISBN: 978-1-80055-485-6

For Tom, as always.

'Hope, Joy, Youth, Peace, Rest, Life, Dust, Ashes, Waste, Want, Ruin, Despair, Madness, Death, Cunning, Folly, Words, Wigs, Rags...'

— *Bleak House* by Charles Dickens

'All men are fortune hunters ... the law, the church, the court, the camp — see how they are all crowded with fortune hunters ... every man has the right to make himself as comfortable as he can, or he is an unnatural scoundrel.'

— *Barnaby Rudge* by Charles Dickens

CHARACTERS

Charles Dickens
Catherine, his wife
Georgina, his sister-in-law
Superintendent Sam Jones of Bow Street
Elizabeth, his wife
Eleanor and Tom Brim, their adopted children
Scrap, messenger boy and amateur detective
Sergeant Alf Rogers
Mollie, his wife, formerly Mollie Spoon
Constables Stemp, Feak and Semple
Inspector Grove
Inspector Bold of the River Police
Constable John Gaunt of the Thames River Police
Doctor Woodhall of King's College Hospital

Members of Dickens's Circle in Real Life:
William Thackeray, novelist
Annie and Minnie, his daughters
Augustus Egg, artist
Henry Egg, gunsmith, Augustus's brother
Frank Stone, artist
Thomas Beard, journalist
Thomas Talfourd, judge and poet
Gilbert À Beckett, lawyer and playwright
Henry Austin, architect and Dickens's brother-in-law
Bryan Procter, Commissioner of Lunacy and playwright
Doctor John Elliotson
Pegasus (Francis Clarke), racing correspondent for *Bell's Life in London, and Sporting Chronicle*

The Fictional Characters:

The Mallory Family:
Pierce Mallory, journalist
Carr Mallory, his brother
Mrs Volumnia Mallory, their mother
Miss Emmeline Leaf, her companion

The Ellis Family:
Stephen Ellis, journalist
Mrs Esther Ellis, his estranged wife
Mr Castle, her father
Mr Arthur Ellis, Stephen's father
Mrs Ellis, his mother

The Dax Family:
Caroline Dax, former mistress of Pierce Mallory, mistress of Solomon Wigge
Barnaby Dax, her father
Alfred, her son

The Lawyers:
Nathaniel Snee, friend of Pierce Mallory
Montague Wildgoose, at Doctors' Commons
Matthew Guard, at Doctors' Commons
Solomon Wigge, legal adviser
Richard Nimmo, formerly at Middle Temple, missing for six years
Frederick Estcourt, former lawyer at Middle Temple
Sir Mordaunt Quist, Q.C., at Middle Temple
Micah Reed, his clerk
Mordaunt Purefoy, in Ireland

Herbert Wing, at Lincoln's Inn
Dermot Barbary, former colleague of Quist's
Queeley O'Shea, of Bolton Street
Mr Speed, the coroner

The Doctors:
Doctor Ebenezer Garland
Doctor Sir James Savage, neighbour of Sir Mordaunt Quist

The Racing World:
Captain Bone, former racing partner of Frederick Estcourt

The Pub Workers:
Mr Lion, landlord at The Lion and Lamb
Mary Goody, servant at The Lion and Lamb
Mr Daniel Stagg at The Old Ship Tavern
James and Dolly Wildgoose at The World's End

Servants:
Simon Jarvis, Head Waiter at The Athenaeum Club
Betsey Ogle, servant to Caroline Dax
Mrs Crutch, charwoman at Middle Temple

Extras:
Fanny Hatton, once betrothed to Richard Nimmo
Lady Primrose Quist, wife of Sir Mordaunt
Constable Doublett, new to Bow Street
Roland Graveson, an undertaker
Mrs Flax, a landlady
Jem Batty, a coal heaver
Mr Lobbs, a carpenter at Tavistock House
Tramper, a tramp, who brings news of a ghostly kind

PROLOGUE

London, 1851

A night of bitter chill. The moon is up, lighting the way along a path to a little stone arch tucked away down a nondescript lane where nobody ever comes. The arch leads to a little courtyard where there are only two houses, and they are in darkness. It is almost midnight. In the distance, cheerful voices fade. A cab rolls away down a nearby street. Footsteps come along the lane.

There are three steps down into the courtyard on which the man stumbles. He is not drunk, though he has dined well and heartily on beef and good claret. Not that he paid. He never does. His feet scrape on stone, but he steadies himself. The night is still and very silent now. He looks up at the moon, which seems particularly bright and large. Like a face looking down at him — expressionless, though. His mother's face was often like that. He always wondered how an expressionless face could contrive at the same time to convey distaste. Some twist about the lips, he thought. He supposed the blankness of the eyes was studied. "I don't know you. You are not my son."

Well, the moon doesn't know him, either. It can go hang for all he cares. So can his mother. No one knows him. No one knows anybody, really. Those good fellows who have just gone off in the cab, they think they do. They'd say they do. Women would say they do. Their faces would not be blank. Disapproving; hurt, probably; jealous, certainly. He doesn't care much just now. He'd be glad to be out of it. If only he didn't feel so damnably ill. Perhaps he should see that doctor

Thackeray recommended. No use. Better to see one in Paris — they understand these things.

He should wait for Carr, though. He owes him that much. Carr hasn't abandoned him — but that business seems hopeless, too. Like everything else in this benighted city. Nothing will come of it because nothing ever comes of anything in the money way. Money and power — dangerous things.

He feels the cold suddenly and flings the butt of his cigar across the yard, watching the red pinpoint arc and fall into a dark corner. His shaking hand fumbles for the keys.

A clock strikes the hour and several more bells echo through the stillness. The door closes. The pinpoint of red goes out. Silent stars blink and the moon stares at the door. The red point flares again, vanishes, flares again, and is gone. A wavering light shows briefly at a window.

The night goes on. The clocks strike two, the sounds reverberating across the dead night of the silent city, across the spires and the domes and the bridges, and across the black river where the ships lie motionless, their great sails furled, and faraway down to the empty sea. Clouds steal in to cover the face of the expressionless moon and the winking stars. The darkness thickens. Somewhere a hoarse voice sings, out of tune, but melancholy and hopeless. No one hears, not even the girl the singer left behind him. She is long gone — to the arms of another, perhaps.

The clocks strike three and the air moves. Shadows shift in the courtyard and settle again. The night waits, scarcely breathing.

Then a little light peeps through a chink in the closed shutter, a sly little eye staring into the listening night. The stillness holds. The world is motionless yet, paused in that time before and after. Not dawn, not night, not morning. An empty time, that sickening void between past and future in which sleepers turn on their restless pillows; dreamers wake to cry again; discarded lovers reach for vacant air; and dying men wake alone in the blank dark for the last time.

What's that? A sound cracks the air. The silence stirs as if a wind has passed; a sleeper turns in his makeshift bed; a child cries out and is soothed; an old woman wakes at her window and snores again; the last few leaves fall from the old mulberry tree in the garden beyond; the clouds shift from the face of the moon. The moon looks down on the empty court.

The moon and stars begin to fade. Darkness thins. The clocks strike eight and cold light begins to filter into the courtyard. Nothing has changed there. But a man lies dead in an upper room where a candle still burns.

1: BITTERNESS

One month later

A careless — reckless, even — good-humoured, genial man. A good companion in good times. Not there in bad, however, or not often. He'd send a note assuring you of his sympathy in your distress. Quarrel, failure, bankruptcy, bereavement — all the same to him. He'd do a disappearing act to Paris, Athens, Constantinople, anywhere. His wife had given up on him years ago. She was in Ireland with the children he never saw — or thought about, Dickens realised now. He never spoke of them. And now he was dead and had left nothing, which was why Caroline Dax — not his wife or widow — was looking at Dickens with an expression he could not quite fathom. A cold look, certainly. Calculating, too.

He would not have known her if he had seen her in the street. She had been a remarkably pretty young woman. She was only about twenty-five, he knew that, but in the dim room she looked older, her mouth just a thin line, and her once bright eyes were hard and dry. She had not wept. She was a girl who had sparkled in the good times when she had been flattered and indulged, but in misfortune she had become sullen. The room felt stale; he could smell drink and the fumes of the oil lamps whose wicks had not been trimmed. There was something suffocating in the atmosphere. He felt that he couldn't breathe easily, but that might be because of the hostility he sensed coming from her, which made the back of his neck tingle. The words of comfort had died on his lips.

'You and your lot are his friends. Are you to leave me in poverty with his child?'

The child, a boy of about three years, seemed to pick up a note in his mother's voice and looked up from his toys, a little sob escaping from his lips. He had been playing so quietly that Dickens had hardly been aware of him. The child was looking at his mother, an expression half-scared, half entreating on his little white face. Perhaps her black dress frightened him, made his mother a stranger.

'Come here,' she said. There was no tenderness in her tone. It was a command. The child came to stand by her, but she didn't touch him. 'This is Mr Dickens — a very rich man — Papa's dear friend who is to ask Papa's other dear friends to look after us.'

The boy looked at Dickens, puzzled and anxious. So much coldness and sarcasm in the words "dear" and "Papa" — the boy sensed it. Dickens smiled at him. 'What is your name?'

'Alfred.'

'Oh, I have a boy with that name — a little older than you, and he likes —'

He was going to say "toy soldiers", but Caroline continued as if the exchange had not occurred, 'For we are very poor now that Papa has left us. We shall end up in the workhouse, and you and I shall wear rags and eat only bread. You shall be a little vagabond or a little robber —'

The boy looked at her, uncomprehending. Dickens thought of the echoes of those words — words he'd used about his child self, the labourer in the blacking factory, cast upon the streets to make his own way. He'd understood, even then, what it meant to be cast away, but this little fellow could not.

Caroline Dax was still speaking. 'Perhaps I must go about the streets in rags to ply my trade — I have nothing else to sell — except...' She pushed the child away. 'Go back to your toys. Enjoy them before they are sold.'

Alfred went back to his toy soldiers. Out of the corner of his eye, Dickens saw the boy pick up one of the little figures and hold it very tightly, his face pinched with anxiety. He thought of his own stocky, rosy-faced Alfred playing with his soldiers and his laughter when he shouted, "All fall down." Caroline was very bitter, he thought, and he partly sympathised, but her treatment of the child was chilling. She was punishing him for the sins of his father. An unwanted burden. Pierce Mallory had said something similar. Mallory had not been able to desert her entirely, but he hadn't lived with her. And she was trapped — a discarded mistress with a bastard child.

She was looking at him with hard eyes, waiting for the help she had promised the child. Why couldn't she just ask? Why this performance?

'I will certainly do everything in my power to help and so will Pierce's friends, I'm sure. Have you any relations who might —'

'I hardly think so, Mr Dickens. I am ruined in my father's eyes. Perhaps you will offer me a place in your home for fallen women — have I not fallen as far as a woman can go?'

'The young women at my home are not at all like you. They have often been in prison; they come from orphanages or the workhouse. They have not —'

'Been kept by an irresponsible, heartless, selfish man.'

Dear Lord, Dickens thought, *I can't stand this.* Pierce Mallory had escaped her by his death and his friends must be punished. He stood up. He would help, but he would not come again. He dared not look at the child or he would make a promise he could not bear to keep.

Caroline Dax stood, too. 'I hope I may count on you and his other friends for my immediate wants. I should not like to make a public appeal for charity.'

'You may, of course.' Dickens realised that she was asking for money. 'Perhaps I can help now.'

She was not at all embarrassed and took the sovereigns he offered without a word. He didn't even know how many there were.

In the street, he was glad to breathe. Why was it he thought he was somehow being blackmailed? "A public appeal for charity." It was a kind of blackmail. No doubt, Mallory's friends — "your lot"— would be exposed as letting her starve. He supposed the name "Charles Dickens" would be at the top of the list. He hardly knew her, but, of course he had accepted Mallory's account of himself. He'd dined with the man, drunk with him, laughed with him, and shaken his head with others about Mallory's reputation. Laughed about it. He felt guilty now that he had seen Caroline Dax and her child. It was true — she might face the workhouse.

Thackeray knew Pierce Mallory better — had been at Cambridge with him, admitted he was shocking about women. Edward Fitzgerald called Mallory "My wild Irishman". He recalled a carriage ride with Thackeray, Fitzgerald and Tennyson years ago — he couldn't remember where they were going or had been — but Fitzgerald had talked of Pierce Mallory, who had not long been married. He had wondered if it would last.

It hadn't — the man was incapable of fidelity. And now, he, Charles Dickens, had been chosen to raise money for the man's mistress. And what about his wife and those other children? Being taken care of in Ireland, he hoped. He'd better see Thackeray. He hailed a cab to number thirteen Young Street.

2: FOLLY

Thackeray's two daughters, Annie and Minnie, were in the hall making ready to go out with their governess. They greeted Dickens as an old friend. He admired the new ribbons on their bonnets and saluted the old cat, Nicholas Nickleby — or was it Barnaby Rudge? Nickleby, he remembered — a grey tabby and of large proportions. Minnie scooped up the cat and thrust him into Dickens's arms. The little girl had complete faith in Mr Dickens's passion for all creatures — great and small, as the Sunday school hymn had it. She had the same faith in Papa — not entirely well-founded in either case. The cat gave him a look of one whose patience was sorely tried. Dickens stroked his head.

Thackeray's great height loomed into view at the bottom of the stairs. What offence had he given now, he wondered, remembering a recent quarrel with John Forster, Dickens's close friend. People were always gossiping. A stray word repeated and then fireworks. But Dickens looked his usual cheerful self. Planning a new best-seller, no doubt. Thackeray had been at dinner with Dickens in June to celebrate the publication of *David Copperfield* in volume form. Thackeray had praised the book for its sweetness and freshness, so things had been all right then, but Dickens rarely called at Young Street. However, Thackeray smiled and stepped forward to take Nicholas Nickleby from his guest's arms and deposit him on the stairs, from which he hissed bad-temperedly. Preferred Dickens, of course. Thackeray bade farewell to his daughters and invited Dickens into his study.

'Something up?' he asked, noting the change in Dickens's face. He looked worried.

'I've been to see Caroline Dax — just come from there.'

'Oh, Lord, Pierce Mallory — what did she want?'

'She wrote to me. She wants money. Needs it, I think. I'm to ask his friends — "your lot", she called us — for hand-outs. She doesn't want to have to make a public appeal for charity — those were her words.'

'Oh, dear — thought you were a soft touch, I suppose. Easy to write to the papers if you refused. And some of 'em will print anything against us.'

'I know, I thought of it. There was something unpleasant about the whole episode. Somehow, she doesn't invite pity, though she thinks she deserves it. By God, Thackeray, she's very bitter, and quite changed. You wouldn't know her. Drink, I suspect.'

'Pretty girl she was — bit of a spitfire — that's what Mallory liked — for a time. His wife is a lady. Then he left the girl, of course. That's what he always does — did. Lusted and left — his wife, too. And there was a young woman, Fanny somebody — some young lawyer's girl he abandoned, though that was a long time ago.'

'There's the child, though, now. A little boy about three years old, I guess. She says she has nothing. Her family don't want to know her — fallen woman and all that.'

'I thought he was supporting the child.'

'She said — and in front of the child — that she'd have to go on the streets. I gave her something to tide her over. I couldn't see her starve.'

'It's just like Mallory. He was a careless devil. He'll have put them out of his mind. Too busy fighting duels in Paris.'

'Yes, I met him earlier in the year. He told me about his row with some fellow over a woman. The duel didn't actually come off, though.'

'James Wildgoose, his name was, and true, there was no shooting, but they were all there, principals and seconds in some Paris woods, choosing their weapons —'

'Pistols at dawn.'

'They were persuaded to give it up. Mallory had risked it before — in Paris again — over that dancer Lola Montez. Duelled with Count Roger de Beauvoir, who'd insulted her or something.'

'You'd think Miss Montez would be used to that — she's not exactly pure as the driven. The list of her lovers is a very long one. What happened to James Wildgoose?'

'Last I heard of him he was listed as an insolvent debtor — in the King's Bench by now, I suppose. Good family, too. Father a squire, uncle a lawyer in Doctors' Commons — folly —' Thackeray sighed.

'What is it, I wonder, that drives these promising young men to their own destruction? Everything before them and —'

'Too much, too soon — I wasted a fortune —'

It was true, Thackeray had inherited money and spent it, but Dickens only said, 'And you worked to recover yourself.'

'Wife, children — responsibilities.'

'Mallory had those —' it was Dickens's turn to sigh — 'and now he's shot himself — with a duelling pistol, I suppose.'

Thackeray's face changed from the half-cynical, half-serious expression it had showed until Dickens's words seemed to shake him. And behind his spectacles his large eyes were troubled. 'Yes, Fitz and I were there at Duke Street where he was living. A policeman came here to find me in the late morning. A girl had gone to give him breakfast — some arrangement he had with a local inn. The policeman found my name and address. We identified him. Fitz recognised the gun because he gave the pair to him — years ago. Mallory was a good shot. They used to shoot at oak trees from ten yards. Fitz always missed, but Mallory never ... not this time, anyway... Valuable things, those duelling pistols, made by Joseph Egg —'

'Egg's father.' Augustus Egg was a painter, a mutual friend.

'Beautiful things — in their way — until you see what damage they can do... I shall not forget the sight of his face and head as long as I live. Fitz was shattered. We gave evidence at the inquest.'

'Yes, you dined with him that night at The Athenaeum with Edward Fitzgerald and Nathaniel Snee. I read it in the papers.'

'He was just the same. He was going to Constantinople via Paris. There was a lady —'

'Another?'

'I'm afraid so. Married, too.'

'Complicated. All too much for him?'

'You know about Ellis's wife? That he'd had an affair with her?'

'Everybody does — including Ellis, I imagine. I knew him slightly through Tom Beard on *The Morning Herald.*'

'Ellis's wife told him. It's actually worse than you think. Mrs Ellis told her husband that their last baby was Mallory's, not his. That's why Mallory was going to Constantinople. He left his job on *The Daily News.*'

'Lord, what a web of intrigue: Caroline Dax and her child, Mrs Ellis and hers, his own wife and hers, and the usual money troubles, I expect. When I saw him I gave him some money — bought a sketch from him. He wanted cash. I thought he looked a bit ragged round the edges. Do you think he felt it all — even after dining? Or especially after dining. I mean, you other three — not without means, and Fitzgerald, especially. Mallory alone in cheap lodgings, nothing much in his pockets, ashes in the grate —'

'There were ashes, in fact. He'd burnt some letters. From his various ladies, I suppose, but there was an envelope addressed to Fitz. We wondered if it was a plea for money. Fitz has money to burn and he'd not turn Mallory down — friends for years. Cambridge.'

'But it's corroding to the soul, always having to ask — for some, anyway —' Dickens thought of his brother, Fred, whose soul seemed to be entirely untouched by constant borrowing. Perhaps it was different for a brother — not a matter of self-respect when you'd seen your lender in a sailor suit, spinning a top in a muddy puddle. Cambridge, though… 'Might he have written the letter, been overcome by a fit of self-disgust — shame?'

'I don't think he knew what shame was. He was in good form at the dinner — a new post in Constantinople — correspondent for *The Morning Herald*. There's a great to-do there between the Turks and the Egyptians. Snee got it for him — Mallory was in Constantinople in 1846.'

'I know. I sent him when I edited *The Daily News*. That's how I knew him.'

'So you did. He was glad to be leaving everything behind. The new lady in Paris was just a dalliance, I think.'

'Why did he come to London — not straight to Turkey?'

'I assumed to see Snee — Mallory didn't say anything about it.'

'Was he drunk at your dinner?'

'No, none of us was. We left him about midnight. Just in high good humour — that's why I was so shocked. I tell you, Dickens, it's damn well out of character. And that verdict —

the coroner directed the jury to return the fact of the cause of death and to leave the state of mind an open question. I suppose I felt it wasn't satisfactory.'

'I don't suppose anyone can really say what another man might feel or do in the cold and dismal wastes before dawn.'

'No, you're right —' Thackeray knew what he meant — 'we've all been awake at that time when the future seems a blank.'

'And the past, perhaps —' Dickens hurried on, in time remembering Thackeray's mad wife who did not know him anymore — 'in his case.'

'Yes, his past — those children in Dublin. I suppose there was a hardness in him. He did just what he wanted. Fitz called him the wild Irishman. You half-admired him for it... He didn't care what anyone thought. What about Caroline Dax, then? Do you want me to write to Fitz? He's gone home to Woodbridge, but he'll do something. He's helped before. In the meantime, I'll give you a cheque — no, this is not your responsibility. I'll deal with it. I'll see *The Daily News* folk and get them to stump up. Where is she?'

Dickens was glad to give him the address and rose to go. He had a thought. 'He wasn't ill, was he? I thought he looked out of sorts when I saw him.'

'Oh, you mean the old complaint — he did look a bit peaky, but laughed it off as he usually did. When he was last in London, when you saw him, he did have trouble — some infection. He led such a rackety life in Paris. I suggested he see Doctor Elliotson on the quiet.'

'Might have been serious — he might have thought of a future with that disease racking him.'

'He didn't see Elliotson. I asked.'

'Still, a man knows.'

'He used to say, "when I die, may I die solvent".'

'And he didn't.'

They were silent for a while. Thackeray was looking at his hands. Brooding, Dickens thought. Then he looked up — something troubled in his eyes. Dickens knew what he was thinking and began, 'You don't think…'

'I don't know what to think, except I wonder … if it wasn't suicide, then —'

'Accident?' Dickens tested. It was unlikely. A man didn't hold a gun to his head by accident; neither did he come back from a congenial dinner and begin to play games with his guns.

Thackeray gave him a half smile. 'You know all about the other thing. Your friend, the good Superintendent, might you consult him? I'm uneasy, Dickens. Fitz went off to the country, Snee was quite satisfied, but then he's a lawyer and on the dry side, but now I've talked about it, I realise —'

'You're not convinced. I'll see Superintendent Jones — put the matter to him. See what he thinks. I don't know what he could do, but I can ask.'

Dickens thought about it all on his way to keep an appointment with his brother-in-law: Mallory had debts; troubles with his women; possibly facing a dread disease; unable to sleep, possibly seized by a fit of despair, the gun to hand — the duelling pistol. Somehow fitting. Perhaps Mallory thought that. Yet to set against all that: a new dalliance in Paris and a new posting to Constantinople. And no shame. Enemies, he supposed — enraged husbands, fathers, even. Enraged creditors. Impossible to say, he thought. An open verdict on his state of mind. But Thackeray — something in that troubled expression. He could talk to Superintendent Jones. He'd know about it. Two of his men had given evidence.

3: DOUBT

Henry Austin, Dickens's brother-in-law and superintendent of works at Dickens's new house just off Tavistock Square, had bustled away with his instructions, leaving Dickens to contemplate the unfinished state of the house. It was consuming money like some hoary old monster of the deep, and it looked, he reflected gloomily, like the wreck of a ship from that same deep. Ladders, trestles, dust, collapsed shelves, fallen doors, dust, paint cans, a dilapidated bow window that might have come from Nelson's cabin, dust, broken chairs, and improbably a broken birdcage. Parrot flown over the seas, perhaps. More dust.

This room would be the drawing room — he hoped. Some day — when the seas ran dry. He could see it in the eye of his fancy. Green wallpaper, a looking glass over the mantel, a connecting door to his study with sham bookshelves to disguise it and sham book covers. *Jonah's Account of the Whale* was one he'd invented. Very apt, if depressing. And no study. And ideas about a new book whirling about his brain. Would he ever sit at his desk in that study and take up his pen? He looked at the remains of his neighbour's studio. Frank Stone, the artist, had lived in this part of the house. Dickens was taking over the whole of it and Stone was moving next door. Dickens wondered if he still needed the bird cage.

He heard voices from downstairs. Stone — on cue, which he had never been on stage. Frank Stone had been one of the actors in Dickens's amateur theatricals earlier in the year.

'All aboard the Wreck of the Hesperus — heading for the rocks,' he called as he went down to the hall to see Stone and his fellow artist, Augustus Egg. Now that was propitious.

'Captain — how's the wind?' Stone joked.

'In the wrong direction — drains, Stone, trouble me.'

'We saw Austin hurrying away — not deserted, I hope?'

Dickens grinned. 'I wish your friend the rat — and his family — would. Leave by the way they came in. Under the kitchen sink — aptly.'

'Send for Browning,' Egg joined in.

'We came to offer a lifeline. A chop, perhaps.'

'Alas, I cannot. *Household Words* demands my attention and I dare not say no, but, Egg, I should like to talk to you if you'll walk with me.'

Dickens locked the door, they bade farewell to Stone and went out into Tavistock Square where Dickens asked Egg to stop a moment in the gardens. 'You heard about Pierce Mallory?'

'I did. Last man I'd have thought. Devil-may-care type.'

'Thackeray said the same. I've been to see Caroline Dax. You remember, the woman he lived with for a time.'

'There's a child, I believe.'

'She's in want of money. Thackeray's getting up a fund.'

'Mallory had friends — Fitzgerald's not short of money. He and Thackeray were called to see the body, I read.'

'Yes, Thackeray's very cut up about it. He and Fitzgerald were at Cambridge with Mallory. Fitzgerald had given him the pistols.'

'The flintlock,' Egg said, 'one of my father's — cased presentation duelling set signed on the locks: *Joseph Egg*. My brother, Henry, was surprised at his using one of those —'

'But it would do the job?'

'Oh, yes, but it's a business, you know, getting out the case, choosing the pistol, pouring the black powder from the flask, putting a quantity down the barrel, tamping it, moulding the bullet, putting powder in the pan, testing the flints, and you'd want to check it was all working, so open up the lock —'

'I see what you're getting at. Not a matter of impulse — a pistol lying on the desk just ready to snatch up.'

'It's a question of balance, too. It's not like holding a pocket pistol to your head — handy and light — or a percussion gun, which is quicker. Your hand shakes —'

'Especially if you're about to shoot yourself —'

'Exactly. It's heavy, but of course, he knew about duelling, so I suppose he'd know that precise moment when the gun is perfectly balanced and ready to fire, but that's when you're twenty paces from your opponent.'

Dickens thought about it. 'But still, I wonder … having made the decision, you are entirely bent on it. Peculiar state of mind — almost automatic. You've decided, so you prepare the weapon as you've done before. Same with hanging yourself — you've to think about how you'll do it. Find the rope, or belt, or whatever, put the stool or chair in place; or even if you decide to drown yourself, you've to get to the water. Think of all those folk who go off to some remote spot —'

'I'd rather not.' Egg was a sensitive soul.

'He just didn't have another gun.'

'I suppose that makes sense. Do you know what's happened to the guns?'

'No, why?'

'My brothers would like to buy them back — signed by our father, as I said. They shouldn't just go into a job lot of Mallory's effects. They are works of art, you know.'

'Matter for the lawyers — I'll bet Thackeray is an executor, along with Fitzgerald. Perhaps he'll be getting the guns back.'

'Mallory used them in his duels?'

'I don't know, but he certainly used one of them to kill himself. Thackeray and Fitzgerald saw it by the body.'

Egg gave him a meaningful look. 'The police would still have that one.'

'Oh, all right, I'll ask the superintendent. He'll know whether and when it can be returned to whoever. I'll let you know.'

'Pierce Mallory,' Dickens said after Superintendent Sam Jones had welcomed him into his office at Bow Street.

Jones looked at him suspiciously. 'Suicide. Inspector Grove was on the case, and Constable Feak. The gun was right there on the floor beside him. You knew him, I suppose.'

'I did. I was surprised. In fact, I was more flabbergasted by his death than by his life — even his liaison with Lola Montez.'

Jones smiled. 'The stories you bring me. Charged with bigamy, she was, as I recall a few years back.'

'Sensation in court — she said she thought she'd been divorced. I suppose she might have been under some other name — she has plenty.'

'I thought she was a countess —'

'Oh, yes, alias the Countess of Landsfeld, or Mrs Heald, or Mrs James, or Maria Torres, or Rosanna, formerly Gilbert — maybe — stage name Lola — take your pick. She changes her name as often as her dress. Anyhow, Mallory fought a duel over her in Paris with a Count —'

'Of Monte Cristo?'

Dickens grinned. 'Alexander Dumas had a dalliance with her, too, and Liszt, but no, it was with Count Roger de something or other — poet.'

'Ah,' said Jones as if that explained everything. 'Mallory was familiar with guns — knew what he was about.'

'He did, though his friends are much surprised — last man to do it and all that.'

'Not pertinent, the coroner said. Impossible to know a man's state of mind. You know that. How many times have I heard the tale? "He was in good spirits the last time I saw him," etcetera.'

'True, my sage. I saw Thackeray, who knew him well. Debts, entanglements with women, possibly seriously ill —'

'There you are, then. Anything else? You're too late to assist me in the Witham case.'

'Oh, the fraud. I read about it. Got your man?'

'We have. So what's your interest in this suicide?'

'The gun — the fatal weapon, as the newspapers say — my friend, Augustus Egg, son of Joseph, he who —'

'Made the duelling pistols, I know, number one Piccadilly.'

'Augustus Egg tells me his brothers, Henry and Charles, want to buy back the pair, case and all. Family and all that. Remembrance of their father.'

'Matter for the lawyers — presumably after the funeral. He made a will, I imagine. You can find out from Mr Thackeray.'

'I can. Is the gun he used still here?'

'The case is here with all its accoutrements. It was shown in evidence at the inquest. Mr Fitzgerald identified the gun found by the body as one of the pair he'd given to the deceased. It'll be sent to the lawyer. Do you want to see it?'

'Not exactly.'

Jones looked at him very closely indeed. 'So what do you want?'

'There was something about Thackeray's face.'

Jones didn't comment on that. 'Well, find out if he knows the lawyer and ask if the guns can be viewed by Mr Charles or Mr Henry Egg.'

'But I don't want Mr Charles or Mr Henry —'

Jones was laughing at him. 'I know that. You want to see the crime scene and you want me to come with you because like Mr Thackeray, you are uneasy.'

'You read my mind — which is rather alarming, now I think of it. I never believed in telepathy —'

'Until now.'

'Go on then, what do you think?'

'I think I don't want to find that Inspector Grove was wrong, but at the same time, if there is a possibility of something other than suicide, then I'm bound to take another look.'

'Now?'

'You'll not want to wait, I know you. We have the keys to the house. It's all locked up, waiting for the lawyer or the family — they're coming from Dublin, I believe. They'll want to collect his belongings. I'll bring the guns.'

4: WASTE

Duke Street was a narrow lane off Seymour Street where the cab had stopped on the night of Pierce Mallory's death. It went through a wilderness of warehouses and works to do with nearby Euston Station and Mallory had lodged in one of two houses left standing, reached by a sharp corner leading to a bit of forgotten lane which now led nowhere. They found themselves staring at a blank wall. Constable Feak, whom Superintendent Jones had enlisted, turned back and found the archway through which he had been led by the girl who had discovered Mallory's body. Feak knew better than to ask his chief the reason for their presence in Duke Street. Superintendent Jones had not consulted Inspector Grove, but he had brought the gun case with him.

'Bit out of the way for a gentleman,' observed Jones, halting for a moment at the archway.

'Hiding from his creditors, I daresay.'

'You don't know when he came from Paris to London?'

'No, I didn't think to ask Thackeray.'

'It might be useful to know what he was doing in the days before the suicide.'

'Or —'

Jones indicated Feak, who was at the door of the shabby little house. 'Let's not — '

'Jump the gun, so to speak.'

They went into the little courtyard. It was enclosed by high walls above which they could see the looming warehouses. The winter's day was fading and the courtyard was filling up with shadows.

Feak's bull's-eye lantern showed them the way into an empty hall. Feak pointed up the bare staircase. 'He was up there — he only used the one room. The other room's empty. It's ter be demolished by the railway company.'

'What was Mr Mallory doing here?'

'Used ter own the house, sir, that's what was said at the inquest.'

Mallory was hiding, then, Dickens thought. *Not just from his creditors?*

'What's through that door?' Jones asked.

'A scullery — just a sink and tap and a door leading to a bit of a yard and a privy, but there's no way out. Nothing behind this 'ouse but a wall, and above that the workshops — fer the railway.'

'Right, show me, Feak, while Mr Dickens goes upstairs. Give him your lamp. I have mine.'

'Is there something wrong, sir, about Mr Mallory?' Feak's thin face looked worried.

'It's all right, Feak, Mr Dickens knew Mr Mallory. He just wants to see.'

Dickens stood outside the room and closed the shutter on the lamp. Then he stepped in to breathe in the dusty staleness and feel the chill of the darkness envelop him. The very stillness of death. He might have been in a tomb. *You knew it,* he thought. Something dreadful had happened here.

He slid the shutter of the lamp and the flickering light revealed the sordidness of the room: the battered velvet chair beside the tiny fireplace — where the letters had been burnt. Pity, that. On the hearth was an opened bottle of brandy and one glass. Half of the bottle had been consumed. A threadbare rug lay before the hearth. There was no other floor covering. There was a tattered velvet couch with a couple of cushions and a blanket, a wash stand with jug and bowl in a corner by an old chest, and a table under the window, on which were a tray with a teapot, plate and cup, an old tin candlestick, a few books, a quill pen and ink, and an open newspaper.

The light extinguished, the deserted seat, the closed book, the unfinished occupation — all images of death. The stopped life, the broken thread — snapped by Mallory's own hand, or another's? And the stain there in the centre of the room where his blood had run out onto the bare boards. That would never come out until the house was demolished by the railway company and the boards burnt. Blood into smoke spiralling into the empty air, Mallory Pierce and his dreadful death forgotten.

What a place to end. He thought of Mallory as he'd been in life: tall, handsome with his thick brown hair, his clear hazel eyes and neat beard. Something of a dandy — always spruce with his white cuffs and silk cravats and his waistcoats with the heavy gold chain. And he saw him that last time — the frayed cuffs when he had given him the money for the drawing. Dickens had offered him a cheque, but Mallory had laughed and asked for cash — he was on his way to Paris, he had said. Talented, too, as an artist and writer — and a lover.

What had brought him to this waste?

Jones and Constable Feak came in. 'It's as you remember?' Jones asked Feak, adding his light to the lamp held by Dickens.

'Yes, sir, the shutters was closed, but there was a candle still burning on the table there. The tray with the teapot an' that was on the floor outside the door. I put it on the table out o' the way.'

'You snuffed the candle out?'

'Yes, sir, an' I opened the shutters so I could see more clearly. The girl from the pub — you know, The Lion an'

Lamb, where they 'ad the inquest — down Drummond Street — she'd seen 'im lyin' on the floor just there and the gun beside 'im.'

Jones went over to the table. The candle was not a tallow one, as might be expected by the poverty of the room. It was wax and about two thirds burnt down. By the candlestick was the stub of an old candle. And there were some black powder grains scattered on paper. It looked as though Mallory — or someone else — had lit a fresh candle at some time. How long it had taken the second candle to burn its two thirds down would give some idea of the time of death, Jones thought. He had been found at about nine o'clock in the morning, quite cold. Yet the candle was still burning. Might be something in that.

'I wonder when he changed the candle?' Dickens was beside him. 'To write the letter to Fitzgerald, perhaps —'

'Or load the gun — he'd want light for that.'

Dickens picked up the newspaper, *The Morning Herald*, opened at a report from Constantinople. 'He was going to Constantinople to write for this paper — he was interested enough then to find out what was going on there.'

'Could be telling. The gun case, Feak, it was here on the table — open or closed?' Jones put the case down.

'Just by the candlestick, sir, and closed — the gentleman, Mr Fitzgerald, confirmed it was Mr Mallory's and that he'd given Mr Mallory the guns about fifteen years ago.'

Jones opened the fine mahogany case to reveal a green baize-lined interior in which the pistols lay snugly fitted into their recesses. Beautiful things, certainly, with their cross-hatched walnut stocks and shining steel mountings. Signed, too, by Joseph Egg. Expensive gift. Not meant to kill the recipient. Other sections contained the paraphernalia needed to prepare the guns: the red leather-covered powder flask, the turnkey for removing the lock, the ramrod, a small brass-lidded box, a little fine-haired brush and a scissor-like device which he knew was for moulding bullets. There were two baize-lidded compartments at diagonal corners. They could be opened with little ivory turned knobs, but he didn't touch anything in the case. He'd let the gun-maker do that.

'Which gun was used by Mr Mallory?' Jones asked.

Feak came over with his lamp and pointed to the gun in the lower recess. 'Cold, o' course, sir, but there was black powder — see the marks there.' Feak lowered his lamp.

Dickens and Jones looked at the gun. Tell-tale black powder marks and evidence of burning at the end of the muzzle.

'Where was the gun in relation to the body?'

'By 'is hand, sir, woulda dropped it as 'e fell.'

'The shock of the recoil, I would think. Powerful things, these,' Dickens observed. 'Thackeray said he would never forget the sight of Mallory's face.'

'It looked bad, sir,' Feak said. 'Good thing the girl didn't see that.'

'How did she get in?' Jones asked.

'The door was open, but that wasn't unusual, she said.'

'And the keys?'

'Just on the 'all table, sir, as if he'd just dropped 'em there.'

'He'd been out to dine — had a drink or two and forgot the door,' Dickens mused.

'How did the breakfast arrangement come about?' asked Jones.

'She said Mr Mallory just come inter the pub an' asked if breakfast an' tea could be brought ter the 'ouse fer as long as 'e needed. 'E'd been 'ere about a week, she said.'

'Did she get any impression of the man — what he was like with her and so on?'

'Not much, sir, she ain't the sort — not a thinkin' sort, if you see what I mean. Gen'rally she'd knock an' if the door was open, she'd call out an' just go upstairs with it. If 'e came down, she just 'anded it over.'

'All right, Feak. I'll lock up. You get back to Bow Street.'

Feak hovered, looking from Jones to Dickens and back again. 'I didn't do anything wrong, sir?'

'Not at all, and neither did Inspector Grove. One of Mr Mallory's friends is not convinced that he killed himself. I said I'd have a look —'

'But the inquest, sir —'

'I know, and there is nothing in the world for you to worry about. You gave your evidence — you told exactly what you did and saw, as did Inspector Grove. The jury decided on the clear evidence you gave and the doctor's evidence.'

Feak's face cleared and off he went, a happier man. Whether Superintendent Jones was quite so happy, Dickens could not tell.

'As long as needed, Sam — surely, until he was going back to Paris on his way to Constantinople.'

'Could have changed his mind — this place would drive anyone to despair. He was used to better things.'

'But, why here? In a place he no longer owned. A place so out of the way. Even if he was broke, he had friends — someone would have put him up.'

'This was where he decided he would end his life? Now, look, there's no point in our going round in circles. We don't know anything yet, but let's get these guns looked at. I am curious about what your friend, Augustus Egg, said about the preparations for firing.'

'Ah, the superintendent is uneasy,' Dickens teased.

'Curious, certainly. Why would a man bent on suicide put back all the bits and pieces he'd used and close the lid of the gun case? Tidy, eh?' The two men started down the stairs.

At the bottom of the stairs, Dickens looked round at the door. 'Find anything out there?'

'A wall — brick.'

Jones locked the front door and they stood looking about the little courtyard and at the boarded-up house across the way.

'Demolition as well, I should think, for the railway company.' Dickens thought about the bloodstain on the bare boards.

They went across to look. The door was locked. 'Who owned this one?' Jones wondered.

'We could ask at The Lion and Lamb — ask to see the girl. Just in case she remembers something now that the shock's worn off.'

'Not the thoughtful sort, Feak said — still, it's on our way.'

'Drummond Street, where I spent some of my misspent youth — on the way home from school, begging from old ladies, I recall, on the grounds that we schoolboys needed charity.'

'Make any money?'

'Not a bean — one old dame told us she had no money for beggar boys.'

If Mary Goody was the lamb, then the landlord was certainly the lion — a big, tawny-haired, thick-necked man who looked as if he could have eaten little Miss Goody had he a mind to in a hungry moment. He bore a remarkable resemblance to the lordly brute occupying the sign outside — or rather, the lion's face was as near a counterpart to the landlord's as it was possible for the artist to have rendered. The painted lamb bore no resemblance to very much except a blur of now dirty white. On second thoughts, Miss Goody possessed that quality, too. Strong yellow teeth, as well, Mr Lion, but his smile was amiable enough when the policeman from Bow Street introduced himself and asked about Mr Pierce Mallory.

'Bad business, sir. Mary was that shocked. I doubt she can tell you any more than what she said at the inquest.'

Jones turned to Mary Goody. She looked frightened. 'You told my constable that Mr Mallory just came in and asked for his breakfast to be sent. Is that right, Mary?'

Mary nodded and the landlord added, 'So he did, but I knew him, see — the houses off Duke Street, he owned 'em once. Sold 'em to the railway. They're to be pulled down, but Mr Mallory said he was only in town for a short time so he'd camp there — I got the impression that he wasn't wantin' to spend money. Said he was off to Turkey or some such foreign place for a new job.'

'Who lived there before they were sold?'

'Oh, he let 'em — some old cove lived in the little house where Mr Mallory was found — for a long time. Moved on, I suppose, when the place was sold, and there was a woman lived in the opposite one — young woman with a little lad —'

'Did you know her name?'

'Mrs Dax, but she moved on — don't know where to. Friend o' Mr Mallory's — that's the impression I got. That was a year or two back — Mr Mallory used to order a dinner for two sometimes.'

'That kind of friend,' Dickens observed.

The landlord's big teeth showed in a hearty smile. 'Not for me to say, sir — she wasn't his wife, I do know that.'

'His suicide — what did you think about it?'

'Knowed him, did you, sir?'

'I did — very well at one time, but I never thought —'

'No more did I — but then you never knows a man's heart as someone once — wait a minute, you're him — ain't you —' looking at Dickens closely — 'I seen you alonga this very street. You are, ain't you?'

'I think I might be.' It was true. Dickens did walk down Drummond Street occasionally — for old times' sake. He'd put a milliner, Miss Amelia Martin, at number forty-seven and he looked at it sometimes, remembering a thin, pale young woman he had seen once coming from the house. He had never seen her again, but he had made a life for her — a disappointed one. Looking at the landlord, he wondered who exactly he was going to be.

'I knowed you was —' a triumphant smile — 'burn me, I knowed. Human heart, eh? You knows about that, all right. Burn me.'

'Who?' asked Jones mischievously. 'Who do you think he is?'

The landlord looked at the policeman doubtfully for a moment. 'Well, he ain't no copper. Knowed that. I'll tell you who he is — he's that Mr Charles Dickens —' as if Dickens were not there — 'him what writes the books and the newspaper —' looking from Dickens back to Jones — 'go on, admit it — he is, ain't he?'

Superintendent Jones was forced to confess it. The subject of the discourse looked suitably bashful as the landlord wrung his hand in his lion's paw — and forbore to flinch.

'He'll take a drink, won't he?' the landlord asked. Dickens wondered if he thought Jones were his keeper — writers, perhaps, being regarded as unfit to be out alone. 'An' you too, Mr Superintendent from Bow Street?'

Jones and 'he' professed their gratitude and in that sudden atmosphere of conviviality, the superintendent was able to ask if Mr Mallory had ever brought anyone with him to The Lion and Lamb. 'Say, in the days before he died?'

'He did come in — 'twas the Thursday afore it happened. We was busy so I didn't have a word, but I saw 'em at that corner table. Now, there was a gent sittin' at the table, but I can't say if he came in with Mr Mallory.'

'Did they leave together?'

'Dunno, sir — my boy mighta seen. He knows Mr Mallory — an' he'd have served 'em most like an' cleared the table.'

Mary Goody faded away from her place behind the bar. A tow-haired lion cub replaced her, and he did remember cos, o' course, he knew Mr Mallory. He was very sorry about the shootin'. Oh, the other cove — not much ter say — jest a gent. Dark hair, dark clothes, jest ordin'ry.

'Did they seem friendly?' Dickens asked.

The boy looked surprised. 'Funny you should say that, sir, Mr Mallory wasn't himself. Not laughin' as he usually was. Dunno — jest annoyed, I thinks. Didn't leave a tip like he usually did.'

'Did they go out together?'

'Didn't see, sir, but they was gone when I goes to clean the table.'

'What did they drink?'

'Brandy, sir, an' a deal of it. Saw Mr Mallory go out to the privy at the back — stumbled a bit.'

'And the other man?'

'Watched him.'

And with those artless final words — rather sinister, Dickens thought — the lion cub was sent off with a friendly cuff from his senior. Dickens and Jones went out into the dark, warmed by the landlord's brandy. They walked down by Euston Station towards Tavistock Square.

'Anything in it?' Dickens asked.

'Not much, except that he met someone in a pub and they didn't seem to be getting on very well.'

'Someone who didn't like him.'

'How do you make that out?'

'Watched him, the lad said.'

'Hm — now you say it, it does sound a bit menacing — but then you're saying it. Makes a difference.'

Dickens grinned at the superintendent. 'Sounded sinister to me, yer honour. Anyway, what about the gunsmiths?'

'Too late now; we'll go tomorrow morning. You can write to Mr Thackeray about the lawyer. Pick me up at Bow Street at nine o'clock.'

5: WAX

They set off from Bow Street to walk to the corner of Piccadilly and Haymarket where the two brothers, Henry and Charles Egg, ran their very prosperous gun shop and manufactory.

'Why is your friend, Mr Egg, not in the gun making line?'

'Ah, well, apart from the fact that he wanted to be an artist, he's a delicate fellow, weak about the chest. A gentle, sensitive soul, thoroughly good-hearted. Painted my portrait and a very charming little picture of my sister-in-law, Georgina, for whom — speaking of hearts and weaknesses — he harbours a tender feeling.'

'Anything come of it?' Jones had met Miss Hogarth and had noted her devotion to Dickens.

Dickens tapped his nose. 'There are strings in the human heart, Mr Jones, which had better not be vibrated. I think poor Egg is to be disappointed — in love at any rate — which is the way of things in this unhappy wale o' tears,' he added in the manner of Mrs Gamp, whose maunderings on the subject of the vale of life were familiar to Superintendent Jones.

They passed into Coventry Street, from where they could see the handsome building at number one Piccadilly which bore high up the simple legend: "Egg".

'And of guns and their makers, my ancient, Joseph Egg had four sons — all his eggs in one basket — so no doubt he could spare his young Augustus for the world of art. Now, before we enter, I take it I am to say to Mr Charles or Mr Henry that Mr Augustus has told me — a friend of the late Mr Mallory — that they would like to purchase the guns, and that you,

43

Superintendent Jones of Bow Street, having charge of said weapons, has consented — etcetera.'

'By all means, your tame policeman. Lead me on.'

Mr Henry Egg came out to meet them in the shop part of the premises. The workshops were behind. He looked at the case while Dickens explained the purpose of their visit. Henry Egg would be very pleased to buy them back, as they were made by his father — and, he added, in the tragic circumstances — a bow to Mr Dickens — he, Mr Egg, and his brother, should hate the pistols to be sold with a kind of notoriety attached to them. They were works of art, made by a master, and should be appreciated as such. Turning to the superintendent, he enquired whether he might contact Mr Mallory's lawyer.

'I am sure that will be possible, Mr Egg. Mr Dickens will find out his name. You might enquire after the funeral. I wonder if you would oblige me by looking inside the case to see that everything is in order.'

Henry Egg put on a pair of cotton gloves and opened the case. 'It is complete. One would hardly think it has been touched since Mr Edward Fitzgerald bought them. Our ledger tells me it is fifteen years ago.' He took out the powder flask. 'I shouldn't think this — you did say that Mr Mallory shot himself with one of these pistols?'

'This one —' Dickens pointed — 'there are powder and scorch marks.'

Mr Egg continued to open and close the powder flask and then he picked up the bullet making mould and examined that. 'This has not been used recently — there's not a mark on it.' He opened one of the little compartments with the ivory knobs. 'Linen patches for wrapping the bullet to make sure it stays in place —' he opened the second compartment — 'no bullets.'

'But these pistols fire only one?' asked Dickens.

'That is so, Mr Dickens.' Henry Egg picked up the gun.

Dickens saw that Jones was looking intently at it. 'What about the pistol, Mr Egg?'

Egg took up a magnifying glass and examined the end of the barrel, after which he slid the ramrod down and withdrew it and looked at carefully. 'This pistol has not been fired recently — if ever at all. Furthermore, the powder here has been smeared by a finger and the scorch marks have been made by a candle flame. Mr Mallory did not use this pistol to kill himself.'

'You are certain?' Jones asked.

'Superintendent Jones, I have worked with these guns for more than twenty years. I know the difference between a scorch mark made by gunpowder and one made by a candle flame. In any case, if you use my glass you will see that there are two pinpoints of wax at the end of the barrel.'

Jones looked and handed the glass to Dickens. The wax was there and you wouldn't have seen it without magnification. And a candle left burning in Mallory's room. Pierce Mallory dozing, perhaps, having drunk his brandy. That bottle had been half empty. The door downstairs open. And a man who watched him again? A man with a gun of his own?

'I beg your pardon, Mr Egg —' Jones was apologising for asking if Henry Egg was certain — 'but I had to be sure. There was no other gun found in Mr Mallory's room. May I ask for your discretion on this matter? You will understand that I must make further enquiries about Mr Mallory's death. I must keep the gun case, but you will be able to approach Mr Mallory's lawyer in time.'

Henry Egg assured them of his discretion, though he looked rather wistfully at the case as Jones picked it up.

They didn't speak until they were standing on the steps. 'Murder,' Jones said.

'As sure as Egg is Egg.'

'Very funny — I should have known the moment you said "Pierce Mallory".'

'What see'st thou now in thy crystal ball?'

'We need a doctor,' said Jones. Then, as they walked away, 'I should have known. I thought of you when I read the report about the inquest. The doctor's name was — is, I should say — Garland. Fate at work — against me. The Ghost of Christmas Yet To Come. And in you came. And it's not Christmas.'

'Which doctor?'

'Oh, very funny — the one who was called to Mallory's house. Mr Ebenezer — I should have known — Garland, surgeon, of number five Euston Grove.'

'And thither to his bower we are proceeding?'

'We are. I want to know about the bullet. Did he take it out? They don't always, but if he did where is it?'

'And what sort of gun did it come from, if not from the duelling pistol?'

They got out of their cab at Euston Square from where it was but a step up Euston Grove to the terrace of fine houses where the surgeon lived.

According to the scrap of a maid, who looked as though she might benefit from a doctor's tonic, Doctor Ebenezer Garland was at home. They waited in his cavernous hall, a chamber more suited to an ogre's castle, Dickens thought, examining the pictures on the wall — a series of anatomical engravings.

Skeletons in various contortions: alone, in pairs, or even groups, seemingly rattling their bones in some hideous dance of death; skulls laughing at their own jokes; skeletal hands in imploring attitudes; and feet savagely lopped off at the ankle. Parts of human bodies that he could not identify — nor did he wish to. A turbaned man whose skin was opened like the pages of a very large book to reveal a nightmarish tangle of intestines and organs. He caught Jones's eye and they both started to laugh. 'Reassuring, ain't it?' Dickens spluttered. A door opened and they adopted looks of serious attention. Doctor Garland came down the corridor.

Not unlike Mr Scrooge — a somewhat cadaverous individual, and as unlike Dickens's genial Doctor Garland as it was possible to be. A long chin very like a spade, or an axe head, perhaps, a nose expressly formed to hang your coat on, and uncomfortably piercing dark eyes under thick black brows of a decidedly Coriolanian nature. You might not mind much if he were digging his long fingers into your mortal remains, but you would hardly wish to consult him about the mysterious pain in your abdominal regions which was keeping you awake at night. He would undoubtedly exclaim —

'Foolery —' this to Superintendent Jones's explanation about the doubts cast on the verdict of suicide in the case of Pierce Mallory — 'arrant nonsense —' he turned his glare on Dickens — 'humbug, sir, humbug —' His words seemed to pepper the air like grapeshot. Dickens restrained an urge to duck.

Jones exercised his well-honed patience. Doctors never liked to be wrong. 'I am afraid evidence has come to light —' he began.

'Stuff. Nonsense, Superintendent, the gun was there and a hole as big as a crater in his head. Gunpowder on his fingers. Lived alone; some kind of scribbler; debts, they said; drank like a fish; bad liver; duels in Paris; fool about women — not a well man — no wonder he killed himself. No doubt about it.'

'Mr Egg, whose father made the guns, tells me that it had not been fired recently — if ever at all.'

'Well, somebody fired a bullet into him.'

'I don't dispute it — and if somebody did, then they fired a different gun and it will have to be investigated. What happened to the bullet?'

'Still in him. The coroner was quite satisfied that the circumstances pointed to suicide. The gun was there beside him. Didn't ask me to go pokin' about the brains for a bullet.'

'No, indeed, I see that, and I see how the assumption was made. However, Mr Henry Egg found traces of candle wax on the barrel of the gun. It is his view that whoever killed Mr Mallory scorched the barrel with a candle flame and smeared the gunpowder on it —'

'To make it look like suicide. Damned cunning. What do you want me to do about it?'

Jones took the abrasive route. 'Get the bullet for me — now. I will take it to Mr Egg. If the bullet is from another gun entirely, then that will confirm that a murder has been committed.'

'Body's at the Free Hospital — waitin' for the undertaker who's waitin' for the family — comin' from Ireland, I'm told. Won't be a pretty sight. Hope you've a strong stomach.'

Doctor Garland did not wait for a reply, snatched up his bag, bustled them from the room as if they were keeping him waiting, seized a coat from a peg, jammed a top hat on his large head, and they were out into the street and striding towards Gray's Inn Road before they had time to draw breath.

Dickens wasn't surprised by how at home the doctor seemed in the mortuary of the Free Hospital. In the freezing little cave of a room with icicles on the wall, he whipped off the sheet like some diabolical conjuror to show the mangled head of Pierce Mallory. Dickens remained by the door — the brief glimpse of the head in the light of the very little mortuary attendant's lamp was enough. Jones had to go nearer to see it all done, as a witness for the prosecution.

The doctor opened his case and brought out a devilishly sharp-looking scalpel. Dickens watched his shadow on the wall fold itself over the corpse and the long black hand plunge the weapon downwards as if the shadow were to murder him all over again. The goblin attendant raised the lamp. Dickens didn't look again until he heard the sound of something metallic drop into something made of china.

'There,' said Doctor Garland, 'satisfied, Superintendent? Do you want it cleaned, or do you need the evidence of brain matter and blood?'

The goblin grinned, but Jones was cool as Mrs Gamp's cucumber. 'No evidence of a linen patch about the bullet? Or in the head?'

Doctor Garland returned to his patient and worked his scalpel again. 'No. Will that be all?'

'I shall have to call you and your attendant as witnesses to the extraction of the bullet, should it prove not to have come from the duelling pistol. There'll have to be a new inquest. Wrap it in some paper, if you will.'

The attendant did that. Jones thanked the doctor and he and Dickens were out of the door before he could respond even with a "Bah humbug".

'Devilish cool, Mr Jones,' Dickens observed.

Jones chuckled. 'Mr Egg again now — he's all the lunch I can take at the moment.'

'Liver?'

An hour later, however, they were seated in a quiet nook by a cheerful fire in The Old Ship Tavern not far from Lincoln's Inn Fields where the landlord, Daniel Stagg, could be relied on for his steak and kidney puddings. Now that the subject of brains and blood was out of the way and the smell of the mortuary dispersed by a bitter east wind, they felt they could address the pudding — liver was out of the question — and the matter of murder with some equanimity.

While they waited and drank a pale ale apiece, Jones rolled the bullet, now perfectly clean, between his fingers. 'This is too small, Mr Egg tells us. Could not have been fired from either of the duelling pistols, which are too big at three point eight calibre. A pocket pistol or what they call a muff pistol, point two-five calibre, two inch barrel.'

'But it could pack quite a punch at such close range.'

'And the pocket pistol could have been a percussion pistol —'

'Which the murderer took away with him — or her.'

'Her?'

'A pistol in a lady's muff, worn on a cold winter's night — Mrs Caroline Dax, perhaps. The lady I told you about — the one that our leonine friend said lived in the bigger house. The one Pierce Mallory had loved and left — with a little boy. The one who asked me for money. The one who hated him.'

'She'll have to be questioned, but not before I speak to Inspector Grove and Constable Feak. It will upset them. I'll have to see the coroner about a second inquest. Mr Speed presided over the first. He won't like it because he's inclined to be in a hurry. Lives up to his name.'

'Wanted his luncheon, perhaps,' Dickens said, the smell of hot pie wafting towards them with Mr Stagg and his tray.

The table set, the napkins unfolded, knives and forks taken, and the pie deemed splendid for the sake of Mr Stagg's vanity, they set to and didn't speak until a pause was called for.

'I was at one of Speed's inquests on a young lawyer found dead in his chambers,' Jones resumed. 'I must say it was all very cursory. The doctor attended and found that the deceased had cut his throat. Suicide. It was over before you could say knife. Grove and Feak reported what they saw at Mallory's lodgings, as did our friend, Doctor Garland.'

'And it did look as though the gun had been fired.'

'And the evidence that Mallory had fought one duel at least. Gunpowder on his fingers, too.'

'Damned cunning, so said the doctor, and it is. Someone knew what he — or she — was doing.'

'A woman who owned a pistol would know what to do — cool, though. And premeditated, perhaps, the pistol primed and ready to go,' Jones wondered.

'Caroline Dax wanted money. Perhaps she just meant to threaten Mallory —'

'How come she was holding a gun to his temple?'

'Oh, yes — she'd have to be very close to him — a last embrace and she takes the gun from her pocket. Mind, she didn't look particularly embraceable when I saw her —'

'We'll have to wait and see what she has to say. In the meantime, detective, who else is on your list of suspects? You knew the man.'

'There was a Mrs Ellis in Paris, who told her husband that the father of her latest born child was Pierce Mallory. Thackeray told me that's why he was going to Constantinople.'

'And the wronged husband?'

'Still in Paris, I assume — works for *The Morning Herald* there. Journalist friend of Mallory's.'

'No cause to love him.'

'My friend, Tom Beard, you remember him — he gave me all the stuff about that actress, Kitty Lovell, in the Mornay case — he's at *The Herald*. I'll go and see him.'

'Anyone else?'

'Some young woman he stole from a lawyer. Thackeray remembered the name Fanny, that's all, but it was years back. Mallory left his wife and children before that even, and she's in Ireland with her children. Didn't Doctor Garland say the family is coming from Ireland?'

'He did. You'd better ask Mr Thackeray about family — any avenging father or brother on the warpath. Anyone else?'

'The man who watched.'

'That reminds me: we didn't question little Miss Mary Goody properly, as Mr Lion — can that really be his name? — was so busy recognising you. She did take Mallory his breakfast for several days. She might have noticed someone even if she didn't think about it. You go and see your Mr Beard and I'll get off to see Grove and Feak to reassure them that the evidence seemed clear enough, and I'll see the coroner, too.'

They looked at the black lead globe on the table — a little world that had contained a man's life.

Jones drank the last of his ale. 'He — or she — made mistakes, though. Too clever, by half.'

6: CONVERSATION

Dickens watched Mr Simon Jarvis bustle about the cupboard making preparations for their confidential meeting. He removed a stack of aprons from a chair, dusted it down with a linen napkin and invited his guest to sit down, gazing at him with an air of innocent expectation. Simon Jarvis, head waiter at The Athenaeum Club, preserved an air of hopeful innocence at all times. Some people had that, Dickens reflected, making himself comfortable — despite the cruelty and harshness of the world, despite the vicissitudes with which life tormented them, and Simon Jarvis, a man whom he would trust with untold gold, had endured a good deal before he had reached his present eminence.

They were in a store room of the club somewhere about the kitchen regions, as the smell of onions and gravy attested. It was little more than a cupboard. Mr Jarvis had taken the notion of discretion to a very great length. Dickens felt the hard edge of something poke him in the back, but he replied that he was perfectly comfortable when his host asked him solicitously if he were "comfy".

'On the quiet, you said. I thought, sir, that you might want something for your magazine — stories from behind the scenes —'

'Not quite.' What Dickens wanted was an account of Thackeray's dinner with Pierce Mallory. What he wanted was to know if anything untoward had occurred during the evening. For example, had Mr Mallory met anyone else? Dickens had deliberately come early to The Athenaeum before dining with Tom Beard. The club was always quiet between three o'clock and about four-thirty, when the evening newspapers were brought in and members would come to read before dining. However, before he could approach that delicate subject, Simon Jarvis was pursuing his theme.

'Life in the kitchen, a waiter's life — that sort of thing. I've made a few notes. What do you think, Mr Dickens? Born to Wait or The Sole of Discretion — s-o-l-e, you see, sir,' he explained anxiously, seeing Dickens's bemused expression.

'Oh, I do —'

'You see, sir, a waiter — if he wants to get on — has to preserve his silence. No gossip about the gentlemen.'

Which is just what I want, Dickens thought, as Jarvis fumbled in his pockets for his notes. However, he said, 'Oh, I'd certainly like to see your ideas, but —'

'There you are — in my own fair hand.'

Dickens took the proffered papers, noting with mingled surprise and dread that the 'notes' comprised several sheets of closely written script. Oh, Lor, a would-be writer. 'Now, Mr Jarvis, I am sure this will be most interesting. Of course, your name would not — could not — appear. Your position, you know.'

Simon Jarvis's kindly moon face crumpled a little. 'I had hoped —'

'I never publish the names of my writers. Our readers know only that *Household Words* is conducted by Charles Dickens.'

'Ah, then — they might think that you had written — oh, dear, Mr Dickens — that would be unfortunate. They might think you had — well — betrayed The Athenaeum — there are some humorous touches — I say, modestly, some very pretty touches about some of the characters I meet.'

'Indeed, I'm sure, but what I suggest is that you work on it to make certain that no one can suspect me — or you.'

'Me — oh, dear, no.'

'Perhaps it might be more suitable for *Punch*.'

Mr Jarvis beamed, moon turning to sun. 'Mr Lemon, you think — a very humorous gentleman.'

'He is — sent anonymously, of course — to the editor. Mr Lemon might make something of it.' Dickens metaphorically crossed his fingers. Passing it on to Mark Lemon, talk about betrayal. Still, the editor of *Punch* received all kinds of eccentric and anonymous communications — which usually went in the waste basket. Ah, well… His complacency was soon dashed.

'You'll mention my name?'

'Very discreetly, Mr Jarvis — just a whisper.'

'Thank you, sir.' Simon Jarvis rose to go.

'Just one more thing, Mr Jarvis, if you will. Another matter of discretion — it concerns Mr Mallory.'

Simon Jarvis sat down on his large hamper and looked at Dickens in innocent anticipation.

Dickens was forced to skulk in an alcove in the South Library to wait for Thomas Beard. Silence prevailed here. The newspapers were read and chatted over in the morning room. Many of Dickens's closest friends were members of The Athenaeum and he did not want to meet any of them — certainly not Thackeray, not yet at any rate.

He looked at the desks with their inkwells and stationery and thought about what Simon Jarvis had told him about the stranger who had asked for Pierce Mallory on the evening of the dinner with Thackeray and Fitzgerald. Mr Mallory had been in the library — where gentlemen often went to write their letters, and to read, of course. Mr Jarvis, who had been passing between the coffee room and the morning room across the great hall had seen the porter follow the gentleman in — the porter was remonstrating with the stranger. Members' guests were always to wait in what was called the strangers' room off the lobby beyond the glazed doors of the hall. The porters were always under strict instructions — no moneylenders, no creditors, no inquiring lawyers — and certainly no wives. The commotion had attracted Jarvis's attention, for the stranger was shouting that he would see Mr Pierce Mallory — and be damned to him — the porter — as Jarvis helpfully elucidated. Mr Mallory was coming down the stairs and seemed about to turn back, but the stranger called out to him angrily — using words which Mr Jarvis observed piously were certainly not fit for the ears of the Bishop of Winchester, who had just come in.

The scene had come to an end when Pierce Mallory had taken his unwanted guest out into the lobby, where Mr Jarvis could see them arguing. The stranger went away and Mr Mallory came back, looking rather ruffled, but he had put on a cheerful face and vanished up the stairs again. Simon Jarvis saw him next at the table with Mr Thackeray and Mr Fitzgerald, by which time Mr Mallory was in good humour again. Naturally, it was not for the head waiter to refer to the scene which had occurred. Such things did happen occasionally to the best of gentlemen.

So, thought Dickens, *could the stranger be the man in The Lion and Lamb?* Was he pursuing Pierce Mallory for money, or was it about a woman? Stephen Ellis for instance. Tom Beard should be able to tell him if Ellis were still in Paris.

He spent a fruitless further half hour browsing the shelves. It was said that The Athenaeum library held thirty-thousand books — *a good many of them unreadable*, he thought, contemplating the works of John Francis Davis, whose *Chinese Novels Translated* came in at eight volumes. No one had read them. A Mr Hall — whoever he was — offered *A Peep at China*. You wouldn't see much of it.

The Miseries of Human Life in two volumes — *only two?* Dickens thought. He looked inside to see what the reverend author, Mr Beresford, had to say. Oh, a satire — illustrated, too. A ruined man in blank despair, ankle-deep in a quagmire. He closed the book. You couldn't have blamed poor old Mallory for going back to that miserable room to shoot himself if he'd seen that. Except that he hadn't.

Dickens was always glad to see one of his oldest friends. Tom Beard had been best man at his wedding all those years ago and knew everything there was to know about Dickens's father and his debts. He had helped out the young Dickens on many occasions and Dickens had never forgotten that help. Beard was a loyal, modest, self-effacing bachelor, a little older than Dickens. They had been reporters together a long time ago on *The Morning Chronicle*. Tom would know all about Pierce Mallory, who was to have taken up his post for *The Morning Herald* in Constantinople — and Stephen Ellis in Paris. It would be quite natural for Dickens to ask about the matter — and he wouldn't have to send Beard's comic writings to *Punch* or anywhere else. Not that Beard went in for comedy for *The Morning Herald*. His editor had not much sense of humour.

They went into the dining room, known as the coffee room at The Athenaeum, and Simon Jarvis materialised. *Doppelganger*, thought Dickens. Would he ever shake him off? However, Mr Jarvis's face was neutrality incarnate as he took their order, as befitted the head waiter of this august establishment. Exchanges about family life took Dickens and Beard through the soup: Beard's sister very well; his younger brother, Frank, a doctor, thriving in his practice. Mrs Dickens blooming in Broadstairs with a company of lesser blooms running races on the sands and treasure hunting for pirate bones and stolen stashes of gold. When was Tom going to come down for a breath of pure air? Steamer to Ramsgate — put him off for a boat to Broadstairs. The sail would do him good. Yes, Charley, Beard's godson, Dickens's eldest son, was in fine twig — winning prizes at Eton.

The works at Tavistock House took them through the roast beef — *a bit on the tough side*, Dickens thought. He entertained Beard with his account of the chiselling, sawing, puttying, chinking and hammering, apparently with few results, and of the philosophical workmen sat atop of ladders like Diogenes, gazing at the heavens, and never coming down again. And the Inimitable flitting bat-like through the rooms to the tune of whistling carpenters.

The day's news from Paris about the election of Louis Napoleon led to pudding and to Pierce Mallory and Dickens's adroit question about what Beard's editor thought about losing his potential correspondent.

'Somewhat red about the gills, I daresay?' Edward Baldwin, editor and proprietor of *The Morning Herald*, had an irascible reputation.

Beard laughed. 'He is. Bad business, though — I'd not have thought Mallory was the type —'

'So everyone says.' Dickens went on to tell Beard all that had happened. He didn't need to stress the importance of secrecy. Tom Beard had met Superintendent Jones.

'Ellis?' Beard said. 'Oh, Lord, yes. I must say that I wasn't too keen on engaging Mallory, given the gossip about him and Ellis's wife — I mean Ellis working for us, too. But business is business for Baldwin, and we needed someone fast because of all that's going on with the Egyptians and the Turks. Our other man's gone down with a fever and had to come home.'

'Is Ellis still in Paris?'

'As far as I know — good Lord, you don't think —'

Dickens lowered his voice. 'Someone did for him — no doubt about it.'

7: MEMORY

It was Drummond Street of which Dickens was thinking when he went back to his rooms at the office of *Household Words* in Wellington Street, where he had set up what he called his gypsy tent while Tavistock House was being renovated. He took up his pen and wrote a title: "Our School" — now there was a pretty subject for *Household Words*. That memory of begging from old ladies had prompted memories of his old school, Wellington House Academy, now gone to make room for the railway. White mice trained to run up ladders, turn wheels — the one that drowned in an inkpot. And slate pencils — the Latin master with a crutch — the fat dancing master — the headmaster with his bloated mahogany ruler smiting the unwary palms of offenders — the boys — the one who came from some mysterious part of the earth where his parents rolled in gold, whose father was rumoured to be a pirate and was shot dead — and the boy who was supposed to have been the son of a viscount who had deserted his mother. The mother who had sworn that she would shoot her errant husband if she met him again, shoot him with a silver pistol she always carried...

Dickens put down his pen. Caroline Dax. "Bit of a spitfire", Thackeray had said. Could she have shot Pierce Mallory? A woman? In cold blood? He thought of Dora Copperfield and her little dog, Jip, and her curls and her artlessness. She couldn't, but Rosa Dartle could. She would have been capable of shooting Steerforth. She had been wronged — the scar on her lip, her badge of suffering. Her love and hate for Steerforth in perpetual conflict so that she was burnt away from within.

No more bitter enemy than the one you had loved who had cast you away. Caroline Dax could — she despised the man she had once loved. He thought of her hard eyes and her sullen mouth. She hated them all — Mallory's friends, too — just as Rosa Dartle hated David Copperfield.

In hot blood or cold? She could have killed him in a rage at being abandoned and having heard, maybe, of Mrs Ellis and her child. She could have planned it. A gun had been taken there. She would have known where Mallory might be. She had lived in that other house. And she had lived with Mallory. She would have known about his pistols. It was not uncommon for women to use guns — there were stories of highway robbers and burglars with their female accomplices.

And last year they had covered a story from Devon in the *Household Narrative of Current Events*, the news supplement to *Household Words*. A girl of fourteen had armed herself with two pistols and shot at some burglars who had broken into the house. She had jumped out of the parlour window to pursue them. She knew how the pistols worked — and at only fourteen.

Caroline Dax visiting Mallory? He thought about that little tucked away house where no one lived but Pierce Mallory. He felt the stillness of the night around him here in his own room, the moon shining through the window and on the river, quiet now, but flowing ever onward, the tide on the ebb, a scarcely breathing night. The steeples and towers, and the one great dome, now more ethereal; the smoky housetops losing their grossness in the pale effulgence. The noises that arise from the pavement outside becoming fewer until no one passes by. A night in waiting.

And still he sat on, picturing the scene — a scene in which murder has been done. On such a night, a man walks alone

61

into the dark court. Somewhere a clock tells the hour, but there is not a voice within a mile of him to whisper, "Don't go home!"

What's that? Who fired a gun or a pistol? But no one hears. On such a night a heavily veiled woman slips in and out of that lonely house. No one to see her; no one to hear her; but after she has gone, a man lies dead in a room where there is a bottle and a glass, and a candle sending its faint light into the darkened world.

He thought of Caroline Dax's hard stare and bitter words. Cold blood. She wouldn't confess, and they certainly wouldn't find a gun. There was no evidence unless little Mary Goody had seen her at any time and thought nothing of it. No use him going round to Lancaster Place to see Caroline Dax, even under the pretext of taking her some money. Lancaster Place — now that was interesting. He wondered who owned the house she lived in now. Had Mallory installed her there? And then stopped paying the rent? And, he remembered now, there had been a servant to let him in. He hadn't paid much attention, and she had not been there when he let himself out. But, she might be there tomorrow.

He went back to his work, the memories of those far-off schooldays spilling from his pen. And at the end he thought of the school, swallowed up by the railway now:

So fades and languishes, grows dim and dies,
All that this world is proud of

— and is not proud of, too. He thought of Pierce Mallory. The candle guttered and went out.

8: BREAKING AND ENTERING

Superintendent Jones was keen to visit The Lion and Lamb as early as possible, and to revisit the scene of the crime. Now he knew it was murder, he wished to see if anything had been missed. He was waiting for Dickens to come to his house in Norfolk Street, from where it was no distance to Drummond Street.

He had endured a meeting with Mr Speed, the coroner, who had not been particularly speedy in accepting this new turn in the open-and-shut case he thought he had already dealt with. However, he accepted the new evidence and the necessity of a second inquest. Jones had also endured a rather uncomfortable meeting with the Commissioner, Mr Richard Mayne, to tell him that a murder investigation was underway into the death of Mr Pierce Mallory. New evidence had come to light, he had explained without mentioning Charles Dickens, of whom Mr Mayne tended to be somewhat suspicious. Hence the superintendent's discomfort. However, he did mention the name of Mr Thackeray and his misgivings about the case, which had prompted Superintendent Jones to make enquiries — as a favour to Mr Thackeray.

Mr Mayne had raised his eyebrows — Superintendent Jones seemed to have some rather influential friends in the literary world. Thackeray, indeed. Cambridge man — as he was himself. Jones's wife was a lady, it was said. Perhaps that was it. He expressed himself satisfied in his rather haughty way, and Superintendent Jones had gone on his way with a feeling of relief.

Dickens arrived with his usual promptness and they set off for Drummond Street, where they found Mary Goody raking the ashes from the inn's parlour fire. Mr Lion was nowhere to be seen, for which Jones was grateful. Mary Goody looked from one to the other nervously, her little face streaked with soot and her hands filthy with ash. She wiped them on her already dirty apron as she stood up. The taller man was a policeman — Mr Lion said — an' 'e looked a bit fierce. She'd told the truth at the inquest about what she'd seen. Mr Lion said she was a good girl an' give 'er sixpence after it was over. She couldn't understand what they wanted — she 'adn't told no lies, she 'adn't.

Dickens saw the tears spring to her eyes and took the lead, sitting her down and taking a chair next to her. He asked her gently if she would mind talking about Mr Mallory. He knew she'd had a shock, but he, a friend of the poor gentleman, wanted to know a bit more about his life at the house, whether any friends had called to see him, for example.

Mary Goody's grubby hands continued to smooth down the apron, but she looked at his kind eyes and felt reassured. She didn't know of any visitors — not in the mornings when she took the breakfast.

'And you never saw anyone about the court, or in the lane, who might have been going to Mr Mallory's house, or coming from it?'

'No, sir, niver saw nobody, only Tramper, but 'e want comin' or goin'.'

'Who is Tramper?'

'Just Tramper, sir, I don't know, 'e eats the crumbs an' 'as the leaves.'

'Is Tramper a man?' Dickens wondered if he might be a dog, or a bird, even. Mary Goody had a very literal turn of mind, it seemed.

'Oh, 'e's a man, sir, wot eats the crumbs an' bits of bread — 'ungry, see.'

'A tramp?'

Mary Goody considered this question. 'I calls 'im Tramper cos I thinks 'e must be. 'Is boots is all broken. Lives in the other 'ouse sometimes an' sometimes 'e asks for a bit o' bread. 'E's got a tin cup on 'is belt an' 'e 'as the tea from the pot wot Mr Mallory didn't finish. Says I'm a kind girl —' she looked anxiously at the policeman and back to Dickens — 'I give 'im the tealeaves sometimes. Did I done wrong, sir?'

'Not at all, Mary, my dear, you did right for poor Tramper. You are a very good and kind girl. Now tell me, was Tramper there on the morning when you found Mr Mallory?'

'Don't know, sir, niver thought about it — I jest runs fer Mr Lion an' I ain't been back since, not even fer the tray. I jest put it down by the door — should I —'

'No, no, Mary, don't you worry about that. Mr Jones, here, will bring it back for you — he won't mind. Policemen are very good about finding lost property — that's their job, you see.'

Mary found the policeman's smile reassuring and became instantly more loquacious. 'Mr Lion'll want it, I'll bet, an' the teapot. It woz a nice one fer Mr Mallory, 'im bein' a gentleman, an' 'e woz, sir — ter me. Give me a penny, sometimes, an' 'e give Tramper one, too. Said ter Tramper that 'e 'adn't much, but 'e could spare somethin' fer a...'

'What, Mary?'

'An Irishman, that's wot 'e called Tramper, but they wozn't friends, I don't think — a feller, 'e said, I remembers — a feller Irishman —'

Dickens thanked her and gave her a sixpence. 'One more question, Mary,' he said as he stood up, 'Mr Jones would like to know — is Lion really Mr Lion's name?'

"Is name, sir? Mr Lion is Mr Lion, sir — it's what they calls 'im. It's 'im on the sign, see — Mr Lion.'

Unenlightened, at least as far as Mr Lion was concerned, they left Mary Goody with her reward and made their way up to Duke Street.

'Somebody had Pierce Mallory's breakfast,' Jones said. 'I remember the tray and the teapot, but there was no uneaten food.'

'Tramper,' Dickens said, 'the funeral baked meats, as it were.'

The second house was boarded up, the front door crossed with unbroken planks, the windows completely obscured. There was a very narrow passage running between the house and the wall, over which loomed more warehouses, but Jones could see that there was a tree, a branch of which bent over the wall. An old garden, perhaps.

'Take your sylph-like self down there. See if you can find a way in.'

'And if I find someone pointing a pocket pistol at me?' said Dickens. 'I only ask for information.'

'Duck.' Jones took Dickens's hat in exchange for his bull's eye lamp.

Dickens squeezed into the space. The wall, he judged, had been built later than the house, by the railway people, probably. He manoeuvred his way along and almost had an eye poked out by the overhanging branch. He did duck and found himself almost on his hands and knees. Someone had been here before. He could tell from the way in which the dead leaves had been kicked aside. He crouched down where the muddy

66

earth was bare and he saw — hard to tell in the gloom — part of a boot print. A man's?

A sharp left turn where a rusty drainpipe dug him in the ribs brought him to the back of the house, where again about a foot separated house and wall and a sturdy branch rested there. Handy escape route, perhaps? Something white caught his eye and he crouched again — a broken bit of bread. Tramper, surely. He hoped.

The back door was boarded up, but he tested the boards on the windows. Two of them on one of the windows were loose and easily moved aside to reveal just an open space where the window frame and glass had been, and, conveniently, there was an old crate ready to give someone a step up. Dickens climbed through the space to find himself in the back scullery. There was no water in the sink and the single tap felt rusty. He didn't suppose Tramper would mind that; he'd simply be glad of a dry place to sleep. A few steps took him into another room in which he could make out an upturned table on which were piled what looked like old blankets. There were crumbs on a tin plate and the burnt-out end of a cigar.

He went into the hall and up the stairs into one of the bedrooms, where he saw that the boards were loose. Again there was no sash window, just an empty space through which he put his head and saw Jones's top hat below. He resisted the temptation to throw down a few coins, and called out, 'Up here.'

Jones looked up. 'Any sign of life?'

'Makeshift bed, bit of bread and a cigar butt.'

'Mary Goody's tramp.'

'Probably.'

'Do I need to look?'

'No, pray spare yourself, Superintendent. I shall come down.'

'Does it look as though he'll be back?'

'I should say so. It's all very cosy.'

'Good, I'll go and fetch Stemp and Feak. We need to search the other house as well.'

'And while this is happening?'

'Ah, I thought you might wait. We don't want to miss him.'

Dickens went downstairs to the kitchen and sat on a three-legged stool and contemplated the cigar butt — Tramper had picked it up outside, he supposed, wondering if Mallory had thrown it away on the night of the murder.

The lamplight cast shadows over the kitchen. He could hear faint rustlings, as of mice — or rats. He hoped not the latter. Where Caroline Dax had lived with Pierce Mallory, where, perhaps, they had laughed, quarrelled, loved, where she had given birth to that poor little boy which event had hastened Mallory's departure. The house had not been empty for so long, but it might as well have been years, so abandoned did it seem, the rooms upstairs forlorn, not even a window left through which Caroline might have watched for her lover — and then he went away to Paris. Had she come back in that still night?

He heard a noise, the scrape of a foot on the window ledge. A voice called out, 'Who's there?' Irish Tramper.

'A traveller,' Dickens called back. He had acquired a quantity of dust and cobwebs in his exploration of the house, mud on his boots, and a few old leaves in his hair. His face was probably dirty, too. He might pass.

'Stand and show ye'self. Black'll be the white of your eye if ye try anythin'.'

Oh, Lord, a pugilist. He had a thought. 'I'm not armed.' The tramp may well have heard the shot. He heard a shuffling and held up the lamp.

A very ancient and fish-like smell wafted in. A bundle of old clothes materialised, tied up with string like a badly-made parcel which had been sent years ago and was not much wanted when it arrived. A good deal of matted beard and hair, a dirty face, a crushed hat like a fallen chimney. And the broken boots. Dickens could have knocked him down with a goose quill feather.

'Your makin' very free with my household, whoever ye are. How d'ye get in?'

'Same way you did.'

'Plannin' on stayin'? Only that's my bed, and I don't like to be sharin' with strangers.'

'No, just passing.'

'Oh.' Tramper was somewhat nonplussed by his visitor's coolness.

'A drink, perhaps?' Dickens took his flask from his pocket.

'Well, I don't mind if I do. Sure ye're a friend to a poor man.' Tramper untied his tin cup from his string belt. 'A gentleman, ye are. Down on your luck?'

'Not exactly.' Dickens poured a generous measure of brandy into the tin cup.

Tramper drank a great gulp, spluttered, wiped his eyes and mouth with a grimy hand, smiled at Dickens, revealing the black remnants of his teeth, and said with satisfaction, 'Bless yer honour for that,' and held out the cup again. Dickens poured a smaller measure this time.

'I came about your neighbour.'

'The divil you did — an' what's he to you, Mister Traveller?'

'A friend — did you know him?'

'Talked to him a few times — a gentleman, to be sure, an Irish gentleman from Dublin like meself. Down on his luck, too, though generous. Gave me a penny or two an' to the little

girl from the pub. She's a good girl. He used to own these houses, but he didn't mind me dossin' here. Go back to the ould country, I told him, but there was nothin' for him there, he said. Off to foreign parts, he said. I can't understand him —
'

'Did you hear the shot?'

'Now that's a question, sir — I don't exactly know. I sees him come in that night. I picks up his cigar and then I came to me bed an' slept the sleep of the dead until somethin' woke me — I remember thinkin' mebbe someone was after comin' in, but then there was nothin'. Off I goes again till mornin', when I hears the girl scream and run away. I sees him laid out up there. Sure, there was nothin' to be done, but I says the rosary for him. I couldn't be part of it, see — not with the polis.'

Dickens didn't ask about the breakfast. 'I do see. Did anyone visit while he was here?'

Tramper's eyes twinkled in the lamplight. He took another swig of the brandy. ''Tis the lady, you mean.'

'I think I do.'

'He was not for answering the door, and she was not for givin' up — shoutin' like an ould banshee an' throwin' stones at the windows. She'd a temper on her, all right.'

'When was this?'

'Not the night he died. Day or two before.'

'Did he let her in?'

'He did — I heard her screamin' blue murder, but then it was all quiet —' Tramper chuckled — 'made it up, I'd guess. She was up there a while.'

'Could you recognise her again?'

'No, sir, she was wearin' a dark veil. Lookin' like Deirdre of the Sorrows.'

'You didn't see anyone on the night he died?'

'No, sir — someone shot him, you think?'

'It's possible. Now, Mr...?'

'Just Tramper, sir. 'Tis what the girl calls me. Sure, 'tis good enough for me.'

'Well, if I give you some money, would you go and find some food? There'll be a policeman along very soon, and I rather think you might wish to be out of the way.'

'To be sure, I'd rayther not meet the polis. They've an ungentlemanly way of movin' a poor soul on. Murder, then, ye think, an' me away with the blessed angels. Poor divil — the woman, mebbe? They can be the very divil when they're crossed. Sure, don't I know that.'

'Perhaps.' Dickens gave him a sixpence and Tramper went out, reminding Dickens not to let the "polis" go pokin' about his household goods. A man had his pride.

9: WANT

Jones came back with his constables. Dickens told him what Tramper had said and that he had let him go. 'He wasn't too keen on meeting you. I gave him a sixpence to get him out of the way.'

Dickens and Jones left Constables Stemp and Feak to search Tramper's house while they went over to the other house. Jones thought of Caroline Dax's possible visit to Mallory. Had she left anything? Had the murderer left anything? Doubtful, but it was as well to be sure.

Jones opened the shutters to let in what light there still was, and he had brought with him another lamp and some candles. He removed the stub of candle from the tin candlestick and lit a fresh one. He wanted to know how long it would take to burn down to the part where Pierce's fresh candle had burnt. That would give an idea of when he was killed, because Feak had said that he had blown out the candle in the morning.

'Wax,' he said, looking at the table, 'and gunpowder. He — or she — sat here and set the scene for a murder. Cool as you like.'

'I was thinking about the body. Feak said he was found on the floor, so he fell from where he was standing. Now, if we exclude Caroline Dax for the moment, who got so close to him that they could shoot him in the temple? And I thought the other day about that half-empty brandy bottle by the fire and the one glass.'

'You think it might have been done when he was asleep by the fire and the body moved?' Jones contemplated the shabby old armchair on the right side of the hearth. 'Let's have a look.'

He went to stand behind the chair. 'Sit in it for a moment, lean back towards me and close your eyes.'

Dickens did as he was told and lay back in the chair, his head resting on the back. Jones looked at him. 'Lean a bit to the left.' Dickens did so and felt Jones's finger at his right temple. 'He was shot in the right temple, probably by a right-handed person who simply came in, saw that he was asleep and crept up on him. It was easy. But there must be some blood.'

Dickens leapt up. 'Not on me, I hope.'

'Dried now.' The armchair was a very dirty velvet, a maroon colour and very much worn to black in parts and very stained. The blood wouldn't have been noticed and no one was looking anyway. Jones went to wet his handkerchief at the washstand and rubbed it on the worn velvet where Dickens's head had rested. The handkerchief showed pink under the light of the lamp. He trained the lamp over the floor from the chair to the spot where Feak had indicated that the body had lain. There were marks of blood on the wooden floor, but, again, the significance would not have been realised, and if they had been noticed then the conclusion would have been spatter from the shooting.

'I wonder if Caroline Dax could have moved him?' Dickens mused.

'Possible. There was no hurry. Now let's have a look around. See if there's anything. You look through the books while I see if — where are his clothes? He can't only have had the suit he was wearing to dine out.'

They looked around the room. 'In the chest?' Dickens pointed.

Jones opened it and began to lift out the shirts and underwear and a pair of checked trousers while Dickens leafed through the books, but there was nothing, no notes, papers or letters. He looked again at the newspaper which had been opened at the news from Constantinople, but there was nothing of interest until Jones called out, 'There are some letters here at the bottom of the trunk. We'll have a look while we are waiting for the candle to burn down.'

'Candle?'

Jones showed him the one he'd taken from the candlestick. 'There's about two inches left of this. We think the murderer lit the new candle after he had shot Mallory so that he could see what he was doing with the pistol case. He left it alight when he left — or she — so I'd like an idea of when he was here, as your Mr Tramper can't help us.'

Neither of them fancied sitting in the armchair, so Dickens sat on the table and Jones took the couch so that they could look at the letters. There were not many, but Dickens felt a twinge of uneasiness when he came across one from Mrs Ellis. He scanned it, getting the gist of her importunings, then Jones interrupted.

'Paris,' he said, 'must be something in the air. This is from Ellis, wanting satisfaction from Mallory —'

'Pistols at — oh, Lord, Sam, I wonder if — but Tom Beard said he was still in Paris — or so he thought.'

'Can he find out?'

'I daresay — I'll send him a note. This is from Mrs Ellis — painful reading — she wants to leave her husband. She is begging Mallory not to abandon her. She also says that he, Mallory, knows how cruel Ellis was.'

'I wonder if that's true. He threatens to horsewhip Mallory here.'

'Perhaps he was the man at The Athenaeum. Anything else of interest?'

Jones was looking at an envelope. 'Writing to his brother, perhaps, a Mr Carr Mallory — at a poste restante address in Dublin. Oh, no — the letter inside is from Mr Carr Mallory of Rosemount, Kiltiernan, Dublin County. I wonder why Pierce Mallory didn't write to him there.'

'What does it say?'

'He mentions Constantinople and Mallory's wife and children, who are well, and a mother who — have a look —'

Dickens read aloud: '*I need not tell you that Mama was not at all interested when I tried to tell her about your appointment in Constantinople. I'm afraid, my dear Pierce, that it's no go there. The purse strings, as you know, are very tightly strung, and she will not forgive you for deserting Cecilia and the children, but you know all that. I'm sorry to say that Michael is now of an age to ask questions about Papa and the answers are not very favourable to you. Cecilia has been told very emphatically that the children must not be contaminated and that it is her duty to teach them that you are dead to them from henceforth. She has Cecilia very firmly in her claws. And my own poor wife — not that she says much about anything. Petticoat rule, eh? At least you have your freedom. And it's worth having, as I know very well.*

'*Of course, they heard about all that duelling business in Paris, and news of your affair with Mrs Ellis — and the child — has filtered through. No use coming here, dear boy, or writing. They won't answer. However, I know you are in want of cash, so I have sent some money for any immediate expenses. You know it is all I can spare at the moment — though things will surely improve when I come to London. All our fingers crossed. I shall be very glad if you can prepare the way — carefully, mind.*

Think of Fagin's kitchen! In the meantime, I have sent a banker's draft to Mr Irwin at Gray's Inn. He will give you cash.

Ever affectionately,

Your brother,

Carr Mallory

'Well, that's clear enough,' said Dickens, 'the black sheep — perhaps that's why Pierce Mallory didn't write to him at home. It's interesting about the money — some secret dealing. I wonder what way Pierce Mallory was preparing, and what's it to do with Fagin's kitchen?'

'Stolen goods? Somebody stole something from Carr Mallory? I'll ask him when he arrives. What do you know about the family?'

'Substantial, I remember, land-owning somewhere near Dublin. That's all about I do know. I've no idea where Kiltiernan is. I'll have to see Thackeray. And what about the funeral — I mean, now we know it's murder?'

'After the second inquest. The jury will have to view the body at the Free Hospital and Old Scrooge can give his evidence about taking the bullet out. I'll have to call Mr Henry Egg about the guns. The verdict ought to be the usual — murder by person or persons unknown and the police will continue their enquiries.'

'When will the inquest be?'

'When I've informed the family — to which end, we have the name of Mr Irwin, who was to receive the banker's draft. Solicitor, I presume, at Gray's Inn. I'll go there after we've finished here while you go to tell Mr Thackeray and ask about the family.'

'I'll need to go back to Wellington Street first, and I'll send to Thackeray and ask to meet him.'

'Now, before we go, let's contemplate this candle. We've been here about an hour. I should say it's burnt down about an inch.' Jones went over to the table and picked up one of the fresh candles. 'About nine inches — two inches remaining of the one the murderer left, so seven inches burnt down. Pierce Mallory was found at nine o'clock in the morning, which tells us that whoever fired that shot was here at, say, two to three o'clock this morning. I want to know if anyone saw him —'

'Or her.' Dickens thought of Caroline Dax, heavily veiled, slipping out into the courtyard on that moonlit night.

10: MADNESS

Constables Feak and Stemp had found nothing of interest in Tramper's house. They were instructed to try the few remaining houses in Duke Street and the warehouses. Superintendent Jones was thinking of night watchmen, and he thought of the beat constables on that night. Inspector Grove would know who they were.

He and Dickens went away down into Tavistock Square. Dickens resisted the temptation to look in, and they parted at High Holborn from where Dickens went back to Wellington Street, where he found a note from Thomas Beard informing him that he had heard that Mrs Ellis had returned from Paris and was living in lodgings in Montague Street at number fifteen. That gave him pause. He knew that house, those lodgings, where had lived a young man called Felix Gresham who had been murdered. Well, well, a coincidence, indeed, but coincidences were always happening to him. The world, he always said, was so much smaller than we thought, and London especially, where so often, even in those crowds, someone you knew brushed your shoulder, or passed you in an omnibus, or greeted you from across the street. Someone you did not wish to meet brought close by the inscrutable decrees of fate — that fate which was taking him to Montague Street in the very next few minutes.

He wrote his note to Thackeray to tell him that he had news about Mallory and asking him to dine at The Old Cheshire Cheese in Fleet Street, one of Thackeray's favourites.

He took his hat and stick, slipped down the stairs to avoid his sub-editor, Harry Wills, his conscience salved by having told Wills that he had finished his piece entitled *Our School*, and made his way up to Montague Street. Mrs Flax was the landlady, he remembered, but he hadn't met her, which was probably a good thing. Landladies, in his experience, were never keen on lady guests associated with scandal, or murder for that matter.

A girl answered the door and pointed upstairs to where Mrs Ellis had her rooms. He heard sounds of weeping and knocked gently on the door, but there was no answer. It wasn't locked, so he pushed it open and saw her sitting by the fire in an attitude of the utmost dejection. There was a cradle beside the table — the baby, he supposed, Pierce Mallory's baby.

He stood by the door and knocked again, a bit more loudly, and she turned round. Her anguished face with its red and swollen eyes shocked him, but she just stared past him as if she thought someone else might be coming. He wondered if anyone was looking after her. Sam Jones's Sergeant Rogers had described Mrs Flax as a good-natured sort of body who had been fond of her young lodger, Mr Gresham.

He stepped in and told her who he was, but she made no response

'I have come to ask if you need any help. I knew Mr Mallory and —'

'Everyone knows. It is my fault. I told Stephen that I loved Pierce and that the baby was his. I wrote to Pierce. I told him what I had done — I begged him to take me away. I knew he was going to Constantinople — but he went away — he did not write back — I killed him —'

She didn't mean that, Dickens thought, he hoped.

'Stephen said he would kill him — it is my fault —'

'Where is Mr Ellis now?'

'I don't know — I don't know —' her voice rose — 'I thought he would kill me — he was so angry. He said I was a — a disgrace. I am — I am — his people came to Paris to care for the children — Stephen's children. They said I must come home. My father is coming here to take me to Cheshire with the baby. They say I am ill — that I cannot look after my children. I am to see doctors —' she looked at him with terror in her eyes — 'I know what it means — they will lock me away —'

She pulled the lace cap from her head, tore at her hair, and then covered her face with her hands, which looked as transparent as paper and as thin. Dickens saw that there was water in a carafe on the table. He took her hands gently from her face and held the glass to her lips. 'Drink some of this, Mrs Ellis. It will calm you. I will do whatever I can to help.' Though what help he would be, he had no idea.

She obeyed him and was calmer, but still her voice broke. 'I will never see my children again. They will forget me — and it is better so — better that I died. But no one knew but Pierce how cruel Stephen was. He did not love me. How could I help it?' She pleaded now. 'How could I? Pierce loved me — was kind to me — and now he is dead — and it is my doing. I drove him to it because I told Stephen. Stephen wanted to kill me — he'd rather I was dead —'

'Could your husband have come to London?'

'I don't know — you mean to see Pierce, and Pierce killed himself because of Stephen. It is my fault — I shouldn't have — I don't know why I —'

He couldn't tell her. Not while she was in such distress. She could not bear it. 'When does your father come?'

'Today, I think. I cannot remember. He will put me away. He is ashamed of me. I have disgraced them all. There is nothing left —' And she sobbed, rocking herself back and forth. The baby started to cry, but she paid no attention.

Dickens went to the cradle and looked down at the crumpled face. Nothing more pitiable than a child in distress. He lifted the baby from the cot. She stopped crying and looked at him with round, blue, innocent eyes. The last baby he had held had been his own little Dora, who had died in April. He thought of her in her cot — her convulsions, her little delicate, bewildered face like this one. The baby looked at her mother, but Mrs Ellis was beyond reach.

The girl downstairs, he thought. He looked back at the weeping woman. He couldn't see anything with which she might harm herself and went out and down with the baby in his arms. He couldn't help smiling as she looked about with wondering eyes. He could have walked out of the house and she would not have stirred. At that moment, the front door opened and a lady came in. A lady with a kindly face under a brown bonnet decorated with a red flower.

'Are you Mrs Flax?'

She looked at him, astonished. 'That is Mrs Ellis's baby. What are you doing with her?'

'Looking for help — Mrs Ellis is in great distress. The child was crying so I came to find your girl.'

'Give her to me — we'll look after her.' Mrs Flax took the baby, but she looked at him suspiciously. 'I know you —'

Before she had a chance to finish, the front door was pushed open and in barged a gentleman — obviously in a hurry. His face was red and he was breathing heavily.

Seeing Dickens, he cried out angrily, 'Who the devil are you? That blackguard is dead — another lover, are you — another of those journalist blackguards? By God, you deserve a whipping, all of you — scum —' he advanced threateningly, his face turning purple with rage — 'you damned swine —'

Mrs Flax stood between them and the baby began to scream, at which point the servant girl came rushing from the corridor, which must have led to the kitchen.

'And you,' the stranger roared, 'a brothel, is it, that you have here? She receives her callers here, I suppose.'

Mrs Flax did not turn a hair. 'Take her downstairs,' she ordered the girl. The baby was speedily removed, though they could still hear her screams until a door slammed shut. Then there was quiet, apart from the heavy breathing of the stranger. But Mrs Flax had a dangerous light in her eye now. Dickens guessed that this must be Mrs Ellis's father. Time to put matters right.

'Mrs Flax, I am Charles Dickens, and this gentleman, I presume, is Mrs Ellis's father. May I suggest that you go upstairs to attend to Mrs Ellis while I speak to Mr...?'

Mrs Flax had known who he was, of course, but she only said, 'Yes, sir,' and with a look of profound contempt for the gentleman, she went upstairs.

The red-faced man did not answer, but simply gaped at Dickens, who continued coldly, 'You mistake me, sir. I have never met your daughter before. All I know is that she is beside herself up there. I brought her child down so that Mrs Flax's servant could look after her. I am going away now, but I shall be returning with a policeman.'

The man was less sure of himself now. 'What for? What has all this to do with the police?'

'You have insulted Mrs Flax and me, but of more importance is the fact that the police are investigating a murder — the murder of Mr Pierce Mallory. I should not think of going anywhere, if I were you.' Dickens made to push past him.

'Wait, I — I — beg your pardon. You cannot think that I — I have only just come from Cheshire.'

'Go up to your daughter, sir, and try to show her some compassion.'

Dickens side-stepped the bulky man and went out through the open door. He hoped Sam was back at Bow Street. Still, he could bring Sergeant Rogers. Mr whoever-he-was needed a sharp lesson in manners. That poor young woman, though, completely deserted, and thrown onto the mercies of a father who clearly thought she was nothing better than a prostitute.

Jones was coming out of Bow Street police station when he caught sight of Dickens marching towards him at his usual brisk pace.

'I was just coming to see you about the solicitor — what's happened?'

'Beard sent me word that Mrs Ellis is in London — at fifteen Montague Street.'

'Mrs Flax's.'

'Yes, I've seen her. I want you to come with me. I'll tell you on the way.'

Mrs Flax looked anxious as she opened the door. 'Oh, I thought you were the doctor. I've sent the girl and I've got the baby — oh —' She caught sight of Jones.

'I am Superintendent Jones of Bow Street. You remember me from the case of Mr Gresham?'

'I do, sir. Oh, what a coil is here. She's gone quite mad, sir — ' this to Dickens — 'she screamed the place down when her father — Mr Castle, he is — came in. He wasn't very gentle with her — she keeps saying she's murdered Mr Mallory.'

'Could you send Mr Castle down to see me, Mrs Flax, and might we use your parlour? Could you stay with Mrs Ellis until the doctor comes?'

'What about the baby?'

'Where is she?' asked Dickens.

'In the kitchen, sir — asleep.'

'Mr Dickens will watch her while you wait with Mrs Ellis,' said Jones. 'He's plenty of experience.' He shot Dickens an amused glance and told Mrs Flax, 'I'll wait here.'

Dickens went into the kitchen. *Left holding the baby*, he thought, looking down at the baby sleeping in a nest of cushions on an armchair. What on earth would happen to the little thing? Mrs Ellis was in no fit state to look after her. She might have to be confined — and her father? He could hardly imagine that purple-faced gentleman wanting to take charge of the child.

He heard heavy footsteps come down the stairs and then the front door opened and there were voices. Mr Castle shouting, a stranger's voice trying to calm, the voice of Superintendent Jones, authoritative, and then footsteps hurrying upstairs. Another set of lighter footsteps coming down and along the corridor. The girl appeared at the door.

'That's all right, sir, I'll look to her now.'

Dickens hesitated at the parlour door. He could hear Mr Castle still ranting with the rusty screeching of an old saw. The voice of a man who always fancied himself injured, but who generally meted out injury himself. 'I thank God that my wife is dead. That she did not have to witness this ruin. Ruin, I say — my daughter has brought ruin — better she were dead, too—'

There were a great many people in this case, Dickens thought, who were very ready to wish themselves or others dead. His entrance stopped the flow of words and Mr Castle looked much put out at the appearance of Dickens.

'What's all this to do with him?' he asked of Jones. He was surly now.

'That is my business, Mr Castle, not yours. Yours is to answer my questions. I have told you that this is a case of murder and it is my duty to investigate it.' The superintendent's cool tone seemed to enrage Mr Castle further.

'I've told you I have just come from Cheshire. On the train, just now. Ellis's father wrote to tell me that Ellis was getting shot of her — why wouldn't he? They sent her with a servant who was to leave her here until I came to fetch her. I don't want her. Nobody wants her.'

'And where is Mr Ellis now?'

'In Paris, I suppose. How do I know? I wouldn't blame him if he had done for Mallory — his wife to tell him — a bastard child —' His fury rose again. His red-rimmed blue eyes seemed to boil. 'And she's mad — I want her put away —'

The doctor came in, a mild, sensitive young man with pity in his eyes. 'Well,' he said, 'you'll need another doctor to certify —'

Mr Castle stood up. 'Then get one — she's a madwoman — a lunatic —'

'Sit down, sir,' barked Jones, 'and listen to the man.'

The doctor looked from Mr Castle to the superintendent. He could hardly tell what was going on.

'What do you think, doctor?' asked Dickens.

'I have given her something to calm her, but she is very ill, I am afraid. I do think that it will be best to confine her for the time being. I cannot answer for her life. I must get a colleague to sign.' He turned to Mr Castle. 'Mrs Flax tells me that you are the lady's father. You will give your permission for her removal.'

'Take her to Bedlam for all I care.' Castle had sat down.

The doctor went without a reply, his face pale and his lips pursed.

'You had no connection with Mr Mallory before his death?' asked Jones.

'None at all. I knew nothing about him until that letter from old Ellis — and a damned self-righteous thing it was, too. As if it were my fault that my daughter is a —'

'Mr Castle, your daughter is a sick woman. Mr Mallory has been murdered and I am bound to question you about Mr Ellis. I should like you to tell me if you think he might have attempted to find Mr Mallory.'

'Served Mallory right if he did. I suppose he might — he'd not take the matter lightly.'

'Not enough that he discarded his wife and the child?' Dickens asked. He meant to provoke him.

'Why should it be? Ellis had a —'

'A what, Mr Castle?' asked Jones. 'You'd better tell me.'

'A temper.'

'And how do you know this?'

'My daughter mentioned it to her mother when they first married.'

'Which was when?'

'Eight years ago.'

'She wasn't happy?' asked Dickens, remembering Mrs Ellis saying that Ellis was cruel to her.

'I've no idea — my wife didn't tell me. She read the letters. I tell you, though, my daughter was a difficult girl — wilful. She needed discipline as a child. Ellis wouldn't stand any nonsense.

What did she want? He's not a poor man. Living in Paris, children — good God, sir, what more did she want?'

Superintendent Jones knew that they would get no further with the man. He probably didn't know Mallory. In any case, he was all bluster — not a man you'd imagine sneaking in at the dead of night. He might horsewhip a stable lad, he might beat his wife and daughter, but he was a coward at heart — just a bully. He'd find out where he was staying now and his address in Cheshire. Let him go back there. They could find him if he were wanted.

They heard the door open again and the young doctor came in with his colleague for Mr Castle's signature — which condemned his daughter to an asylum. Dickens could only hope that the young doctor would see that she was treated kindly. He felt he could not bear to be in the same room as Castle for any longer and he went out with the two doctors. He would have to ask Mrs Flax if she would keep the baby for a while at least.

It was very dreadful when they brought Mrs Ellis down. She was quite unresisting. Mrs Flax had put on Mrs Ellis's cloak and bonnet. Her face was perfectly blank — from the sedative, Dickens assumed — she was calm and her eyes expressionless as stones.

'You had better tell me where you are taking her,' he said to the young doctor.

'Guy's hospital — the asylum. There's a private wing, but if he won't pay —'

'He signed the paper — sue him.'

The doctor smiled faintly and they waited while Mrs Flax took a length of dark veil from her hall table and placed it over the bonnet so that Mrs Ellis's face became just a white blur. She was becoming invisible, he thought; she would be erased from her life and the lives of all her children. Then she was gone.

'I don't know what Mr Castle will do about the child,' Dickens said to the landlady.

'Nothing, I shouldn't think. Talk of madness — he was like a madman up there. I thought he was going to strike her. You want me to keep the baby, Mr Dickens? Poor little mite — Esther, she's called. I'll keep her until you can find who is to take her.'

'You are very good, Mrs Flax — shall you need any —'

'Goodness me, no, sir, for a little thing like that. Don't think of it. That poor girl — an unhappy creature, for all she did wrong. Still, we can't know, sir, can we, what trials some ladies have to endure?'

'Mr Ellis didn't come here, did he?'

'No, sir, no one came. Mind, she was only here a week —'

'She didn't go out at all?' Dickens thought of her telling her father that she had murdered Pierce Mallory. He knew she was just raving, but it was well to be sure.

'No, she wasn't fit to go anywhere. She was to wait for her father, the servant that brought her said.'

'Who was she?'

'She was maid to Mrs Ellis's father-in-law. She said Mrs Ellis was to go home because she'd not got well after the baby — she was to go to the country.'

'And was the maid to go back to Paris?'

'Oh no, sir, she said Mr and Mrs Ellis, the in-laws, were coming to London with Mrs Ellis's other children in a week or two.'

'She didn't say where?'

'Torrington Square, sir. I know their housekeeper. She recommended that Mrs Ellis come here.'

Jones came out of the parlour behind Mr Castle, at whom he looked with an expression of distaste. Mr Castle simply walked out of the house.

'Nothing about the child, sir?' Mrs Flax asked Jones.

'No, Mrs Flax — his view is that the child is legally the responsibility of Mr Ellis. He's a lawyer and the law says that every child born in lawful matrimony is considered to be the child of the husband. He was most eloquent on the subject — if she had half a dozen children by as many men, her husband must support them all — I beg your pardon, Mrs Flax —'

'Not to worry, sir. I heard enough up there and when you've had all sorts of lodgers, you hear things about life, sir.'

'You heard about Mr Mallory, I take it, and that poor baby,' Dickens added.

'I did, sir. And I'm that sorry Mrs Ellis saw the newspaper — I thought she'd die of hysterics. I put her to bed, but I knew she wasn't right. She never stopped crying, but I made out from what Mrs Ellis said that she and he — well, I'm not one to judge. Mr Dickens has asked me to look after the baby for now and I'm willing — poor mite. No one wants her, it seems, and such a good baby.'

'Thank you, Mrs Flax,' said Dickens. 'You won't see Mr Castle again.'

'Nor Mrs Ellis, I suppose. Well, I'll pack up her things and keep them until something is decided.'

'Send 'em to Torrington Square, Mrs Flax — let them deal with them.'

Mrs Flax smiled at him. 'So I will, Mr Dickens. What a good thing you were here.'

Outside in the street, Dickens asked Sam, 'Ellis, do you think?'

'Could be, from what we heard in there. I doubt it's Mr Castle — I can check that he's only just arrived. He's staying at the Euston Hotel. What about Mrs Ellis — killed him and turned mad?'

'I asked Mrs Flax — Mrs Ellis has been there a week and was not fit to go anywhere, especially after she'd read about Mallory's death.'

'Thank the Lord for that.'

'Torrington Square, then?'

'Let's get this inquest out of the way. I need a verdict and the coroner's direction that further investigation should be made; then my way is clear — to see Caroline Dax, too. We'll go to your office. I'll tell you about the solicitor on the way.'

At Wellington Street in Dickens's upstairs room, Dickens lit the fire and made tea.

'So, the Mallory family is due tonight and the inquest tomorrow.'

'After which, I'll talk to them. The mother and brother were coming for the funeral, but the solicitor will meet them to tell them of the new developments.'

'And Mallory has not been back to Ireland for years.'

'I spoke to the solicitor, Mr Irwin, about the brother's letter and he confirmed the estrangement from the mother — Mrs Volumnia Mallory —'

'Sounds formidable — of a Roman character, perhaps.'

Jones laughed. 'It's to do with Mallory's father's death, it seems. She blamed her son — Pierce is her elder son. Carr Mallory is the younger, his mother's favourite. Pierce was his father's favourite.'

'How did the father die?'

'Killed in an accident. Pierce Mallory was one of those lads who enjoyed danger —'

'He hadn't changed, then — Fitzgerald called him the wild Irishman. What happened?'

'Pierce Mallory insisted on riding a horse that was too much for him. The father let him ride it — only at a walk, but the lad used his whip and the horse took off. Father went after him on another mount. The gates were open, the father galloped after, tried to overtake by jumping a hedge and came off. Killed instantly, and Pierce — not a scratch. Mother never forgave him. He was sent to school in England — in the north somewhere —'

'I never knew that. I always had the impression that he was an Eton or Harrow man.'

'That was the brother — Carr Mallory went to Harrow. He was to be kept from Pierce Mallory's influence. He was sent up north and stayed there. Farmed out in the holidays.'

'Lord, Sam, no wonder he was so rootless. He could never settle.'

'And when he abandoned his wife and children, she cut him off without a penny and wrote him out of her will.'

'And the brother?'

'Runs the estate and slipped his brother money when he could, and, of course, received letters poste restante. Pierce Mallory's son will inherit if Carr Mallory doesn't have any children. His wife is an invalid, so the solicitor said.'

'Unlucky family. Am I to come with you to see them?'

'I don't see why not — they won't know how well you knew him.'

'I'm seeing Thackeray tonight. I'll tell him and I'll ask if he knows any more about the family or anyone Mallory knew. What about the inquest?'

'You come with Thackeray — it'll be in the papers, but if you are with Thackeray, there won't be anything singular about your presence. Perhaps Mr Beard would come. The family may see you and assume your friendship was more than it was. And Thackeray and Beard might see who's there and give us a name or two.'

'Cunning old fox, aren't you? I'll ask Beard.'

11: CRUELTY

Dickens waited for Thackeray at his usual table in The Old Cheshire Cheese. A good plain dinner was what was wanted — something to settle the spirits — and the stomach. Queasily, he wondered what to tell him about Mrs Ellis. Thackeray's wife had been confined in an asylum in France years back when the little girl, Minnie, was only a year old. Now she resided at Camberwell, looked after by some kind people. Thackeray rarely saw her, and he did not speak of her. Still, it would be a painful subject to bring up, but Thackeray would surely hear of it from someone else, and at least Dickens could tell the truth of it.

Thackeray arrived. His mood was hard to read. The news of the murder must have shocked him, even though he had half suspected that Pierce Mallory was not a suicide. Dickens told him what he and Superintendent Jones had discovered about the duelling pistol and Caroline Dax.

'Caroline Dax was there,' Thackeray repeated.

'Could have been — the tramp heard a row and saw a heavily veiled woman.'

'But not on the night of the murder?'

'No, but the superintendent will want to see her.'

'Do you think —'

'She was bitter enough — I suppose it's possible. Hell hath no fury and all that. The superintendent asks that you and Beard come with me to the second inquest — as friends of Pierce Mallory. Mr Jones would like to know if there is anyone there we might —'

'Draw his attention to? I suppose I owe him that — he's re-opened the case.'

'If you feel —'

'No, no. I started it and Mallory's been murdered. He didn't deserve that, even though he didn't care…' Thackeray looked suddenly shocked. 'You don't think Ellis —'

'I asked Beard to find out if he is still in Paris,' Dickens told him.

'He's abandoned his wife, I heard, sent her back to London with the baby. Mallory has left such a mess — I know I asked you — but — I wonder —'

'You wonder if you've started something more dreadful than you imagined?'

'It is dreadful, and — thinking of Ellis now — you can imagine a man so enraged that he might — you could understand —'

'But it wasn't rage. Jones and I went to Mallory's rooms. We think he might have been asleep. There was a half empty bottle of brandy. And the guns, Thackeray, to make it seem like suicide.'

'I see what you mean — premeditated, maybe. I was thinking about those left behind, too — Mrs Ellis, for instance, and his children. If he has done it, that would be a stain. I think of my daughters — and your children. Think what it would mean for them. It would be a tragedy for Ellis's children.'

'It is anyway. Mrs Ellis is not allowed to see her children by Ellis.'

'Dear Lord, that is cruel, but she'll be better off than Caroline Dax. Mrs Ellis's father is to take her to Cheshire.'

'I know. I saw her; I saw him. Beard told me where she was, so I went round to see if she knew where Ellis was.'

'What's the father like?'

'A brute —' that slipped out — 'I mean, not entirely sympathetic to his daughter.'

'He'll give her a home, though?'

'Not exactly —' he would have to say it — 'he has had her committed to an asylum.'

Thackeray ran his fingers through his hair — a habit that Dickens recognised. His large eyes closed briefly behind his spectacles and his mouth tightened. He had made the decision to commit his wife and Dickens knew that he felt the sharp stab of guilt. Thackeray gave him a half smile and asked, 'Is she — mad?'

'I am afraid so. The landlady sent for a doctor — he couldn't answer for her life. She broke down completely when I mentioned Ellis. She was terrified of her father, too — that he would lock her away. I dared not mention murder —'

'It never seems real when you read about it or talk about what's in the papers. Fitz is always interested in what murder reveals about the soul of the perpetrator — of course, he's disgusted by some brutal, commonplace murder by some ruffian, but now — it's not table talk, is it?'

'No, it's real enough — and it casts a long shadow across the lives of all those involved. It leaves a mark as indelible as a bloodstain.'

'But, Ellis?'

'Mrs Ellis said that Ellis threatened to kill Mallory. She didn't seem to know where he was, but I don't know if that was because she was so broken up and confused.'

'He could be in London, I suppose.'

'He could. Someone had a row with Pierce Mallory at The Athenaeum before your dinner, according to the head waiter, Jarvis — forced his way past the porter, but Jarvis didn't know who he was. That's a thought. Was Ellis a member?'

'No, they wouldn't know him.'

'Mrs Ellis said he threatened to kill her, and she said only Mallory knew how cruel Ellis was. Did he say anything to you about Ellis?'

'He — this is the devil of it — I don't want to put a noose around Ellis's neck — I saw enough at Courvoisier's hanging — as you did. That man's face stayed with me for an age, and Ketch, taking the rope from his pocket with as much ease as if it were his kerchief.'

'I know, it's brutal, and if it's someone you know, or you think it may be, then —'

'That happened to you?'

Dickens remembered a time when he had briefly considered a friend of Thackeray's as a possible murderer and the sense of betrayal he had felt when Thackeray had innocently given him details about the man's relationship with the victim. 'Only once,' he said, 'but when I talked with the suspected person, I knew, without a grain of a doubt, that he was innocent.'

'But, if he had been guilty…' Thackeray insisted.

'Then I would have to think which is the greater evil: that I should betray a friend or betray the innocent victim. I might know him or her, too. Mallory was your friend.'

'But not so innocent as Ellis's wife and children.'

'Then I won't ask what you know. But, you will come to the inquest?'

'I will. I hope it isn't Ellis, or Caroline Dax, for that matter — she has that little boy, Pierce's child. I hope it's someone none of us knows.'

'So do I,' Dickens answered, but he couldn't help thinking of those two who had reason to hate Pierce Mallory.

They went out into the cold night and walked to the nearby cab stand. Thackeray would take a cab back to Kensington. He made to get in and then turned back, his spectacles flashing briefly in the lamplight, making his expression unreadable. 'Ellis was a brute to his wife. Mallory said.'

Dickens walked back to Wellington Street, his thoughts on Mrs Ellis and madness — and Thackeray's wife. Did they remember at all, in however brief a flash of recollection, those whom once they had loved and who had loved them? Was it agony to them to remember? Or did they recall snatches of that other life and wonder what they meant? And return bewildered to the ignorant present, lost to their lives as irretrievably as if they were lying fathoms deep in the black river flowing under Waterloo Bridge?

12: ICE

The place still smelt of carbolic — and corruption, more noticeable this time. Pierce Mallory was decomposing.

The light was better, though. Doctor Garland had turned on the gas lamps — a courtesy he had not offered to Superintendent Jones and Mr Charles Dickens. Probably did that on purpose to revenge himself on the policeman who had dared to challenge his conclusion that the dead man had committed suicide.

Not that the gaslight rendered the scene any less macabre. The goblin attendant appeared even more imp-like in the bluish glare, and Doctor Garland's iron brows gave his face the look of an inquisitor about to turn the screws on the rack. His predatory gaze was directed to the jury of respectable householders summoned by the coroner Mr Speed to the hospital mortuary for the customary viewing of the remains. The doctor looked as though he might like to anatomise any one of his audience, some of whom looked a touch corpse-like in the shadows beyond the sickly light. They would attend the second inquest upstairs in the hospital after viewing the body and its injuries. Dickens thought that Mary Goody would be pleased that she wasn't required, though the amiable Mr Lion might have missed the custom the second inquest might have brought him.

Doctor Garland whipped off the sheet to reveal the mangled head. If he were to be judged by the melodrama of his performance, he was worth his fee — a guinea for the post-mortem and two more for his twice-told testimony. More than he could have got at Drury Lane. The jury shuffled forward and listened attentively as the doctor pointed out the wound made by the bullet which Superintendent Jones would show them later. Dickens looked at the jurors' faces, some well-fed with bulging eyes avid for the gruesome detail, a few gaunt ones, rather pale — one shrinking back with his hand over his mouth.

Doctor Garland stood aside while the goblin flourished the sheet back over the head — another with a flair for the dramatic. The respectable householders let out a collective sigh — of pity for the corpse or of disappointment that the show was over, Dickens could not tell, but as they began to turn away, he slipped out to lurk in the shadows while they made their way upstairs. He removed his spectacles, ran a comb through his hair, and took off the long coat he wore for camouflage purposes — he had not wanted to be recognised, but Sam Jones had wanted him there in case he saw anyone who knew Mallory or Stephen Ellis. A murderer, perhaps? His hands conveniently dyed red to advertise his grisly calling? No, there had been no one especially remarkable apart from Doctor Garland and his sorcerer's apprentice. He took his top hat from the convenient peg where he had left it. Superintendent Jones came round the corner and found the respectable Charles Dickens again.

'That man,' Dickens murmured, as they went upstairs, 'has dramatic powers that would do justice to Drury Lane. He could play Mephistopheles any day.'

Dickens found Thackeray and Beard and they went in to stand at the back of the room in which the coroner presided over the inquest. Superintendent Jones gave his evidence that new information had come to light which pointed to the murder of the deceased rather than his suicide. Mr Henry Egg gave particulars of the duelling pistols which had not been fired. He showed the jury the supposed suicide weapon with its candle grease; he showed the gun mould and the bullet he had made which fitted the muzzle of the duelling pistol. He demonstrated that the bullet found in the head of the dead man could not have been fired from the duelling pistol made by Joseph Egg. Doctor Garland, in his gunpowderous way, and his smirking imp, corroborated the superintendent's evidence that he had seen the bullet taken from the dead man's head.

Mr Speed was satisfied and precipitate; he explained to the jury that the police were making further enquiries, and directed them to bring in their verdict which was: *murder by person or persons unknown*.

Then they were out in the street, observing Thackeray speaking to a black-clad woman and a tall man who bore a resemblance to Pierce Mallory. Thackeray gestured to Jones and Dickens, and Tom Beard went over to be introduced. Carr Mallory was gravely friendly; the woman merely inclined her head, but Dickens felt a decidedly ghostly chill in the air about her — the effect of the black veil, he supposed. Close up he couldn't make much of her face, but he had an impression of disapproval which was not surprising after what the solicitor had told Sam Jones.

The superintendent was to accompany Mr Carr Mallory and his mother to the Euston Hotel, which was handy, Jones thought, as he could ask about Mr Castle as well as question Carr Mallory about his brother. Carr Mallory asked Thackeray and Dickens to go with them — he knew that Mr Thackeray had dined with his brother on the night of his death. Beard excused himself, but slipped a note to Dickens as he turned away. Mrs Mallory said nothing. Thackeray looked back at Dickens and Jones with a rather anguished expression as he was shepherded into the first cab after Mrs Mallory.

'Hamlet's aunt ain't very forthcoming, is she?' Dickens laughed, as his and Jones's cab moved off. 'Soliloquising to herself, I daresay.'

'You and Mr Thackeray can entertain her while I speak to Mr Carr Mallory. Tell her the one about —' Sam chuckled.

'Like making conversation with an iceberg.'

Mrs Volumnia Mallory did not thaw even though she was seated by a bright fire in the sitting room of the suite the family had hired. *Very comfortable*, Dickens thought, remembering Pierce Mallory's frayed cuffs and that dilapidated room where he had died. The Euston Hotel was for first class travellers — convenient for a quick getaway, too. He did not imagine Mrs Mallory wishing to remain in London to mourn over her son's grave.

Tea was brought and Mrs Mallory removed her veil and bonnet. *A handsome woman — and in the Roman fashion*, Dickens thought, contemplating her marble brow and high nose. She might have been a match for Doctor Garland. Her two sons were very like her, though the handsomeness sat more easily and genially on them. Her hair was silver grey and her skin had a curiously silver pallor as if she were dusted with frost. She sat very still and with so straight a back she might have been made wholly of marble. Her face was as unmoved as stone, the lines from nose to mouth set as in iron, but some twist about her mouth gave away her disdain, and her pale grey eyes remained as cold as rock crystal in response to Thackeray's tentative offering of sympathy.

'You knew my son, Mr Thackeray — and I take it you both —' her icy gaze swept to Dickens — 'knew of his disreputable life. And now his death is a disreputable one, too. I suppose the husband of his paramour has dealt him his just deserts.'

'We have no idea, madam. It is a matter for the police,' Dickens lied. 'Mr Thackeray and I attended the inquest out of respect for —'

'Respect, forsooth, my son did not deserve respect. He has ever been an irresponsible, reckless creature — and a selfish, debauched one. You expect me to feel sorry — I am not. Pierce Mallory has not been my son since he brought about the death of his father by his wild selfishness. At least his wife and children are free of him and the shadow of his degraded life.'

'The child of Mrs Ellis —' Dickens began. Thackeray seemed paralysed — probably frozen by that frosty glare.

'That child has nothing to do with me — Mr Ellis is by law the child's father. If he cannot keep his wife in order, then he must take the consequences. And now, I have nothing more to say on these matters. If the policeman must carry out his enquiry then he must, but it is nothing to do with me.'

She rose and swept away into another room before they had time to stand. She left them half out of their chairs, bent over like two cowering menials before the Snow Queen.

'I'm certain that's snow on the ground,' Dickens murmured, peering at the carpet.

Thackeray grinned and sat down again. 'I'm damn well having my tea — I need it hot — and one of those cakes.'

'The sins of the mother — you can see why Mallory was like he was. She'd be enough to drive any man wild.'

'You know about his father's death?'

'Yes, the solicitor told Superintendent Jones.'

'He mentioned it once. He was just a lad — foolish, reckless, yes, but —'

'Was he sorry?'

'I don't know, Dickens, you could never tell with him. He never mentioned his mother — or his wife, for that matter.

Still, the ice queen's treatment must have hardened him. Imagine a mother so unbending, so distant —' he smiled then — 'though I wish mine were a little more distant sometimes. It's seeing us in petticoats as makes 'em too fond.'

Dickens didn't answer that one. He never thought his own mother over fond of him — unless she wanted something. 'You didn't notice anyone at the inquest who —'

'Who might have murdered him?' Hot tea and sweet cake had cheered Thackeray up. 'Only some of the writers from *The Daily News*. I can't think of any one of those especially close to Mallory. Fitz was his oldest friend and he didn't do it. Remember, Mallory had been abroad for most of the time in the last couple of years.'

Carr Mallory and Jones came in. The superintendent was thanking him and telling him that he would keep in touch. Jones directed a meaning glance at Dickens, who stood. Carr Mallory asked Thackeray to stay and finish his tea.

'I'll see him again before he returns to Ireland. He has business with the solicitor,' Jones said as he and Dickens walked down the elegant staircase into the foyer of the hotel. 'Oblige me, will you, and ask at the hotel reception about Castle. They won't want enquiries from a policeman.'

Dickens came back to tell him that Mr Castle had arrived yesterday and had gone out.

'To visit his daughter, perhaps?' Jones speculated.

'To make sure they've thrown away the key.'

They made their way down Euston Grove, past the house of Doctor Ebenezer Garland, and walked into Tavistock Square, where Dickens saw that the gate to his house was closed. No workmen, then. Perhaps the rat and his family were not receiving. No use leaving his card.

He remembered Tom Beard's note and took it out, stopping to read it. Jones walked on, oblivious. Dickens caught him up. 'Sam, this is from Beard. He slipped it to me after the inquest. Ellis is not in Paris.'

'Where is he?'

'Beard doesn't say — just that he left suddenly a few days ago. Family emergency, he told another journalist friend.'

'We'd better go to Torrington Square.'

13: WISDOM

Torrington Square was an oblong really, with a narrow garden in the centre and rows of stucco and brick Georgian houses surrounding it. Here lived the surgeons, solicitors, barristers, bankers, clergymen, retired colonels and genteel ladies — widows and their spinster daughters. The Misses Tarte resided at number four, where a resplendent brass plate flourished forth the legend: *Seminary for Young Ladies. The Misses Tarte.* What Stephen Ellis's father did, Dickens had no idea — perhaps he was a gentleman of private means.

However, they were not to find out yet, for the maid at number thirty-six told them that Mr Ellis was not at home. Dickens asked if Mr Stephen Ellis were in, but was told that he was not at home, either. Now whether that meant that Mr Stephen Ellis was not actually in, or that he was simply not receiving, the well-trained maid's face did not reveal. Dickens asked whether the younger Mr Ellis might be at home in the evening. The maid repeated that the family was not at home. Would the gentleman care to leave a message? The gentleman would not. Dickens beat a hasty retreat and joined Jones just by the ladies' seminary.

'Ambiguous,' he said in answer to Jones's question, 'not at home. I asked if Mr Stephen Ellis might be back this evening. She did not say that he is abroad.'

'He could be there, I suppose, but we can't insist. I wonder if the senior Ellis — oh, wait, someone is arriving.'

Two carriages drew up outside the Ellis house and the front door opened to reveal an older woman, the housekeeper, presumably, the maid with whom Dickens had spoken, and a boy in a green apron. The man who stepped down from the first carriage helped a child down — a boy of about six or seven years who was followed by another, a little younger, and from the second carriage came an older woman and one younger with another child in her arms. The boy and the maid from the house began to unload luggage from the carriages.

'Mrs Ellis's children,' Dickens said. *Whom she will never likely see again*, he thought, *and who might never remember her.* They'd be told she was dead.

At that moment, the front door of the seminary opened and a maid came down the steps with a broom.

'Miss Tarte and Miss Janet beg to say that they would be pleased if the gentlemen would move along. The young ladies 'as not to be bothered. Miss Tarte begs to say further that she will fetch a constable if you won't go away.'

With a flourish of her broom, she was gone and the door shut emphatically. Dickens saw a curtain twitch and a sharp nose do likewise. Jones grabbed his arm and they were round the corner into Russell Square in a trice.

'Close shave,' grinned Dickens. 'We wos jest watchin' the gen'l'man, yer honour, fer Mr Jones o' Bow Street.'

'Give over, let's get back to the station.'

'Spare cell goin'?'

'What did Carr Mallory tell you?' Dickens asked when they were safely ensconced in Jones's office.

'Only that Pierce Mallory and his mother were estranged. He had hoped that Pierce would go to Constantinople and leave his women behind him. I told him about Mrs Ellis, but his opinion was the same as Mr Castle's — rather more delicately put — the child is Stephen Ellis's responsibility. He was sorry for the lady, of course, but —'

'Nothing to do with them. Same for Caroline Dax, I suppose.'

'Carr Mallory didn't know about the child. He wondered if the boy was his brother's after all. I got the impression that he didn't think much of Caroline Dax.'

'Ought we to see her? She was there before he was murdered. She might have been there again.'

Lancaster Place was another of those retired nooks where solicitors, clergymen and doctors came to roost. The brass knocker of number four was somewhat tarnished and there was a greenish coloured plate by the door on which some letters were now indecipherable. Let to lodgings now that the professional man had departed, Dickens supposed. He knocked, reflecting again on who paid for Caroline Dax's lodgings in this respectable house. The same servant he had seen before answered, but Mrs Dax was not at home. *Not again*, he thought, wishing people would be either in or out like good Christians instead of lurking in their bedrooms or drawing rooms, hiding their guilty secrets. However, he smiled benevolently on the square-shaped girl with the square jaw and very round brown eyes and asked if it were just that Mrs — that was the appellation she used — Dax was not receiving visitors.

'No, she ain't here, sir. You came the other day, I remember —' her brown eyes opened wide and her square jaw dropped — 'aren't you Mr Dickens? I've seen you in Wellington Street. Well, fancy — I've your paper in the kitchen. I was just going to —'

'I am he, and I am sorry to disturb you, Miss...?'

'Ogle, sir, Betsey.'

Dickens kept a straight face. 'I wonder, Miss Betsey, if I might come in with my friend.' He pointed to Jones, who was standing on the pavement. 'It's about Mr Mallory — has Mis— Mrs Dax said anything about him?'

Betsey Ogle smiled a knowing smile. 'Oh, yes, sir. She likes a drink, does Mrs Dax, an' she told me all about him — he was the father of that poor little boy an' he left her for someone else. Promised to marry her, she said, or she wouldn't have — well, you know.'

'I do, Miss Betsey. Mr Jones —' Jones had come up the steps — 'is a policeman. Mr Mallory has died suddenly and Mr Jones would like to ask some questions, if you would oblige us.'

Miss Betsey was all agog to know about Mr Mallory — she did not care overmuch for Mrs Dax, whom she suspected of not being very much above herself in station and who had a high-handed way about her and was inclined to be moody, confidential in drink, and coming the lady when sober. And as for that little boy — Mrs Dax was downright cruel at times.

They went into the kitchen where Miss Betsey, still talking, needed no encouragement to tell them further that Caroline Dax had taken her little boy on a visit — to her fancy man, most likely. The gentleman that came to see her at times — times when she, Betsey Ogle, was took advantage of to look after the little lad, while Mrs Dax went off to dine or to the theatre, or for a little trip away. Not that the little boy was any trouble — a nice little boy — very quiet —

Oh, Mr Wigge it was — a lawyer. Plenty of money and a very pleasant, good-humoured gentleman — very taken with Mrs Dax, who could do herself up very nicely for all that she could look very haggard at times — rouge, did they see? And Betsey Ogle, though she oughtn't to say it herself, was very good with the curling tongs — though what went on upstairs when she,

Betsey Ogle, was in the kitchen with the little lad — them curls didn't always stay in place — oh, Mrs Dax was very fond o' Mr Wigge — my Wisdom, she called him — her legal adviser, she said — though what advice —

Dickens took advantage of the breath he had hoped for. Betsey Ogle seemed not to need the air of mortals. He plunged. 'And Mr ... er —' he found himself hesitating over the name, and plunged again as Miss Ogle's mouth opened — 'Wigge — with an "e"?' he asked loudly to forestall her. He'd naturally thought of Tarte with an "e". Betsey Ogle nodded. Dickens hurried on. 'A generous man, is he?'

Dickens was asking the questions — his confidential manner always inspired loquaciousness in servants, who were sometimes inclined to be a bit tongue-tied in front of the superintendent. Not everyone possessed such a gift, Dickens would say, to which conceit Mr Jones would only smile and urge him "to get on with it" before the witness — usually female — fainted away in delirium.

'Oh, yes, sir, it was him as brought Mrs Dax — a widow lady, he said, who needed the rooms. An' Mrs Dax told me about her husband, Mr Dax, who died, and his family didn't want to know her — and all the money she should have got was took away. I mean, that was a shame.'

'Oh, it was. Now about Mr Mallory — do you know if Mrs Dax ever saw him?'

'She said he was in Paris with another lady and that she had no wish ever to see him again, an' though she ain't always as pleasant a lady as you could wish — gives herself too many airs — I think this Mr Mallory must 'ave been a cruel-hearted man to leave the little boy — though you say he's gone an' I shouldn't want to speak ill —'

'No, indeed —' *What next?* Dickens wondered, feeling as one in a labyrinth.

'And you, Miss Ogle —' Jones interrupted, sensing that she was now sufficiently off her guard to be confidential with him, and keeping a straight face, too — 'how came you to be Mrs Dax's —'

'Housekeeper,' Betsey replied with dignity. 'Mr Wigge offered me the post and he pays me a bit weekly and some extras for lookin' after the boy. Housekeeper was the word.'

'And where did you meet him?'

'Here, o' course. See, I was housekeeper to Doctor Sage, an' he went to live with his sister an' his rooms as he'd lived in was to let — off the hall is still the surgery — an' very gloomy rooms they are, sir. There's noises — ghosts of folk what in life was in pain, I daresay, lookin' for the doctor still. I don't like goin' in at all if I can help it. Doctor Sage is hopin' that his own son will take 'em up, so I'm paid to look after the rooms until —'

'And has Mrs Dax had any other visitors recently — a friend or two, perhaps?'

'Well, there was the gentleman who just came off the street. I was takin' the air with the little boy — the door was open and a man walked in, free as you please. When I went upstairs — well, there was a row. She sayin' she'd no idea where Mr Mallory was an' he had no business to force his way in — she had nothing to do with any other child — an' he sayin' she'd to tell him or —'

'Or what?'

'I don't know, sir, for little Alfred was shoutin' for me an' I had to go down. I heard the door slam. I didn't like to go upstairs, but Mrs Dax never said a word after about him.'

Having enjoined Miss Ogle to inform Mr Dickens at Wellington Street when Mrs Dax should return, he and Superintendent Jones left her to her copy of *Household Words*.

'In my wisdom,' Dickens began, 'and before we discuss such sagacious matters, and —' holding up an admonishing finger to his confederate, who seemed to be about to speak, he continued — 'as we are near the admirable Mr Simpson's Divan — the wind blows from the East, bringing dust and stinging sleet upon us — we shiver, we weary, we hunger — you are pale as old Hamlet's ghost — the roast beef of old England is needed — in short — luncheon. My treat. What have you to say?'

'Not a thing.'

Mr Simpson knew Mr Dickens, of course, having furnished him with meals from his tavern to the office of *Household Words* in Wellington Street. A quiet table was found; roast beef, roast potatoes, some greens, and a bottle of wine were ordered and two glasses of brandy and warm water were before them on the white cloth before Dickens said, 'In your wisdom?'

'Very droll,' said Jones. 'What do I think, you mean?'

'I do.' Dickens took some of his hot drink.

'Sounds like Ellis has been to see Caroline Dax. Therefore, he is here or hereabouts, and after this we will return to Torrington Square.'

'And Mistress Dax?'

Superintendent Jones, however, did not reply, his gaze turning to the waiter who had rolled up a trolley with a silver-covered dish aboard, under which must repose the good roast beef which Dickens had promised. The superintendent, unlike Dickens, did not dine from home very often, and certainly not in Mr Simpson's Cigar Divan and Tavern. The waiter lifted the silver cover and there it was, a great joint of meat as large as a portmanteau, brown on the outside and red in the middle, and gravy in a silver sauce boat, and crisp roast potatoes. Dickens did not interrupt, for Mr Jones was watching the waiter, who with the air of a great artist took up his great knife and fork and began to carve.

Nothing of wigs, or wisdom, or sages, or even onion, was said until beef was finished. *Better than The Athenaeum's beef*, Dickens thought. He had enjoyed his, but he enjoyed more the sight of Mr Jones's relish and the colour coming back into his face.

'Now you have addressed that beef with such courtesy, may we address the matter of Caroline Dax and her fancy man, Mr Wigge?'

'She asked you for money, and yet she has a new admirer.'

'Exactly.'

'Mr Wigge not so generous with his money as Miss Ogle believes? Don't,' he said, seeing Dickens's lips form the word "sweet" as if he were about to break into song. 'Sweet Betsey Ogle' was a favourite.

'Have it your own way, Mr Jones, though I concede she is not very sweet and neither is Caroline Dax. She wants as much as she can get — and thinks she deserves it — which she does, in a way. Pierce Mallory abandoned her and the child without a penny.'

'As far as you know. What happened to the money Carr Mallory sent his brother, I wonder?'

'Oh, I forgot that. How much was it?'

'Fifty pounds, and he had ten pounds in his pocket when he was found. He'd received the cash from the solicitor.'

'The murderer could have taken it.'

'And left a dead man ten pounds? Or Mallory could have given it to Caroline Dax on that night the tramp said she'd visited. If she did visit. We'll ask her when she comes back.'

'Anything from your men about the night of the murder?'

'A nightwatchman thought he heard something — couldn't be sure. Feak thought he was probably asleep on the job. A baby cried and was hushed to sleep again, and an old woman who swore she never sleeps heard nothing.'

'The beat constables?'

'One heard the shot at about three o'clock, as we surmised. Thought it came from the railway station. Of course, they made a search through the yards and sheds, and those alleys off Eversholt Street where the warehouses are, but found nothing.'

'And the murderer slips out unseen in his — or her — own time.'

'Quite. Now, I suppose we ought to make for Torrington Square, though after that meal, I feel as if I couldn't walk a step. And I thank you, Charles; it was a treat.'

Mr Arthur Ellis was not pleased to receive Mr Charles Dickens and even less pleased to receive Superintendent Jones of Bow Street. He regarded them both with irritation. A short, white-haired man, slenderer than Mr Castle and calmer, but equally contemptuous of Mrs Ellis. Acidulous about the cold blue eyes with a sour thin mouth that made Dickens think of lemons.

'My son's wife has forfeited all claims to this family. She is undoubtedly mad — as you say — that is the only explanation for her scandalous conduct,unless she is simply a woman of—'

'Where is your son?' Jones cut him off with such sharpness that Mr Ellis blinked in surprise.

'In Paris.'

'I have reason to believe that he has returned to England.'

'Why should you make enquiries about my son? He is not the guilty party in all this, and the fate of that disreputable creature's child is nothing to do with him.'

'The law says it is.' Jones repeated, with some satisfaction, though in a neutral tone, what Mr Castle had told them.

'Well, it will be up to my son to find someone to bring up the child. It can hardly be brought up with my son's legitimate children. It is out of the question. However, I do not see why a policeman comes here to question me or any of my family about that woman. I repeat: it has nothing to do with us. Now, I will bid you —'

'Mr Pierce Mallory —' Arthur Ellis looked furious at the name — 'has been murdered. A second inquest was held this morning. I am bound to make enquiries.'

'My son is in Paris — I cannot help you.'

'Very well. I shall make my enquiries elsewhere.'

Jones made to go. Dickens said, 'Mrs Flax is looking after the baby —' he used the word advisedly — 'for now. She will be safe in Montague Street until your son decides how she will be cared for in the future.'

Mr Arthur Ellis turned away. Just as Jones opened the door, a lady came in, preceded by a small woolly dog which she scooped up, saying, 'Oh, Arthur — I do beg your pardon, I didn't... Oh, Mr Dickens, how good of you to call. We met — rather a long time ago — at the house of Mr Lawson before — ' She faltered, remembering their mutual acquaintance Mr Lawson's tragedy; his wife had since died. 'You entertained us so wonderfully — it is so lovely to meet —'

Dickens realised that she had sensed the tension, for her husband had turned round and was looking at her, unsmiling. He said coldly, 'Mr Dickens and his friend are just leaving.'

'Yes, indeed, Mrs Ellis, so delighted to meet you again. Another time, perhaps,' he added, looking at Mr Ellis.

'What now?' Dickens asked as they crossed the road to walk by the gardens, thus avoiding the Misses Tarte's establishment.

'There are mews behind those houses — stables and so forth. Constable Stemp can do a bit of spying. Had reports of thieves in the area. It is true, actually — there was a break-in on Byng Place and in Gower Street North — two ladies robbed at number four. What?'

'Good Lord — when I was a boy, we rented that house and a gloomy place it was. A neighbourhood for ladies of straightened means, and of families equally unfortunate.'

'And thinking of ladies, Rogers can inveigle his way into the Misses Tarte's seminary on the same pretext — almost as good as you with the ladies. There'll be a groom, maids, a boot-boy — someone might say something. Can you remember what Stephen Ellis looked like?'

'Hunchback — dwarfish —' he saw Jones's face — 'no — all right — but he isn't very tall. Plump, dark curly hair, round face. Brown eyes. Jest ordin'ry, yer honour.'

'As Mr Lion's boy said. Still, it's something for Stemp to ask about.'

'Somebody might say, "Oh, that's Mr Stephen Ellis".'

'And I'm the Police Commissioner.'

'Some are born great, some have greatness and all that — yer niver knows. There's Beard, too — he'll let us know if he hears anything. There'll be a lot of gossip about Mallory and Stephen Ellis. Thackeray couldn't think of any of his journalist friends who might want to murder Mallory.'

'Carr Mallory gave me the names of people who knew his brother — there's a cousin in Chelsea; there's a lawyer at Gray's Inn, who was at Cambridge with him.'

'That'll be Nathaniel Snee, who was at the dinner with Thackeray.'

'So he was — it won't do any harm to talk to him. In the meantime —'

'Mr Sagacity.'

'Yes, let's do a bit of digging in the law directory.'

14: WIGS

There was no Wigge in the law directory, a fact to which Dickens responded with a gloomy, 'I always knew the law was an ass. T'ain't nat'ral. There should be, there ought to be, there must be a lawyer called Wigge.'

Superintendent Jones shrugged. 'But there isn't — no use wasting —'

Another name leapt out at Dickens — a name he had heard very recently from Thackeray. 'Wildgoose,' he said.

'Who's he?'

'James Wildgoose is one of those with whom Pierce Mallory intended a duel, according to Thackeray — over a woman, of course. They were persuaded to call it off. Thackeray told me that Wildgoose was last heard of in a list of insolvent debtors. Went to the bad, perhaps. Blamed Mallory?'

'Lord, another vengeful lover.'

'His uncle is a lawyer — it's not a common name.'

'What does it say?'

'Montague Wildgoose — a kind of monkish attorney to be found in that lazy old nook near St Paul's —'

'Doctors' Commons.'

'Thackeray did tell me that. Wives, wills and wrecks, as they say. Wills are Mr Wildgoose's work — and a lucrative business, too. The Prerogative Court is where we shall uncover him — where the resurrectionists dig about in the dust of ages in the unsure and uncertain hope that Great-uncle Jack Tar, whose wreck — investigated next door — has not been so untimely as to prevent his leaving his prize money to his undeserving kin, or whose bigamist crimes exclude his seven wives —'

'You know a deal about it.'

'Time, Mr Jones, that faithless spinner, turns her wheel backwards and upon it is bound a gay young sprig of eighteen or so, who took his place in a box there — more like a coffin than anything else — proficient in deadly shorthand, and sat down to report on the wives, the wills — and the wrecks. The Dean of the Peculiars is in charge there.'

'Peculiar what?'

'No one knows — or they're not telling.'

Doctors' Commons in Knightrider Court was David Copperfield's first foray into the working world, and it had not changed a bit since young Charles Dickens had reported there on matters matrimonial in the Court of Arches, on shipwrecks in the Admiralty Court, and on legacies in the Prerogative Court. The Prerogative Will Office declared itself by a legend carved in stone above an archway that led into a narrow court at the end of which were a few steps, and an oak door inside which a porter pointed to a harassed-looking, portly gentleman with a wig a little askew, a hot red face, and rather staring eyes of a decidedly gooseish character and the colour of unripe gooseberries. Like David Copperfield, though with more staying power, Mr Montague Wildgoose was a proctor — a kind of solicitor who acted for his clients in the court from which he had just come. Perhaps he had not been successful, for his ermine feathers were certainly ruffled and the wings of his black gown drooping.

He looked at his visitors with a bewildered air, for they did not look at all like his usual clients. Neither greedily asking for more — his mind somehow connected Oliver Twist with the smaller man — nor in such heart-breaking poverty that he felt them a burden to his conscience. He was their last hope, and they often said so.

'Mr Charles Dickens.' The smaller man offered his card. Mr Wildgoose's head cleared — he felt he understood his wandering thoughts now, but his brow creased when the other man said, 'And Superintendent Jones of Bow Street.'

'Bow Street,' he repeated, bewilderment increasing. Had Oliver Twist been brought up before the magistrate there?

'Yes,' Jones said, 'I should like to speak to you about your nephew, Mr James Wildgoose.'

'I must —' Montague Wildgoose turned, opened a door and darted through it, leaving them gaping at each other. Dickens stepped across the threshold into what seemed little more than a cupboard. It was crowded with papers stacked on shelves, crammed with black deed boxes, and massive volumes of mouldering leather were piled on the floor and on every other available surface, including the windowsill, where they formed a useful barrier to what was left of the daylight. Mr Wildgoose had removed his wig and was in the act of tossing it on his desk, where more papers and volumes were scattered along with quill pens, inkwells and sealing wax, wafers, pounce and parchment, and a top hat stuffed with paper rolls and one bread roll by the look of it. Dickens was astonished to see him at the washstand, where he plunged his head into a bowl and could be heard splashing about like a porpoise. He emerged, plunged again, and, snatching a metal jug up, poured a good deal of water over his head.

A vigorous towelling followed, and at last a damp face under a circlet of hair standing up like goosequills looked at them from under eyebrows that were triangular in shape and gave him a look of surprise. 'Dust,' he said, 'ashes, waste, want, ruin — madness. Do you ever think you are going mad?'

Dickens advanced into the room. 'I do — I find myself very often in a maze of bewilderment.'

Mr Wildgoose looked about his room as if he had never seen it before. 'I thought of Oliver Twist when I saw you. All these people asking for more, you see. Was he taken up at Bow Street?'

'No, before Mr Fang at Mutton Hill.'

'Then he —' pointing at Jones — 'really is a superintendent from Bow Street and not just a figment of —' He shook his head again and droplets of water scattered.

'I am,' Jones said, stepping in. *Mad?* he wondered mildly, never surprised at the odd people Dickens found as if a kind of magnetic force drew them to him.

'That's a relief, I can tell you. It all gets too much at times. It's living in the past that does it, and the dust. However, I am recovered — a good drenching and I am myself again. Do sit down. Something about a will, Mr Dickens? I do hope not — let it alone. Ruin — madness —'

Jones interrupted, 'I wanted to ask about your nephew, James Wildgoose.'

Mr Wildgoose sat down, too. 'I thought you said his name. Is he dead?'

'Why should he be?'

'Should he be? That is a question. He should be, he ought to be — I don't know. Duels in Paris —'

'That is it, exactly,' Dickens interposed, feeling that he was probably better-equipped to deal with mad persons than Superintendent Jones. Mr Wildgoose was perhaps only mad but north-north-west, but still, better to treat him as an ordinary mortal. 'Your nephew almost fought a duel with a man called Pierce Mallory, whose murder the superintendent is investigating.'

'My nephew has killed him?'

'No, no, we — simply —' not quite the word at the moment — 'want to know if your nephew had ever spoken to you of Mr Mallory — or if you knew him.'

'Knew my nephew — oh, yes, I did — my brother's son, you see. Pleasant as a child, but went to Paris. Lady in the case — I never married — never fought a duel over a lady.' He gave a little shudder — whether at the idea of a duel or the thought of marriage to a lady, Dickens couldn't tell.

'Do you know who the lady was?'

'Betrothed to James, I believe, in Paris — governess to an English family. Very pretty, but no family to speak of. My brother was not pleased, but then he never is. Keeps geese. Bad-tempered creatures.'

'And Mr Mallory?'

Mr Wildgoose wiped his face with the damp towel. Dickens hoped he would not plunge again, but he only shook his head as if to clear it. 'Ah, Mr Mallory — it seems that he had designs on the young lady and she broke away from James. After the duel —'

'Which did not actually take place.'

'No, but the young lady changed her mind and wished to — well, James had changed his mind, too, and did not wish to — his father was much relieved, until James returned and married — a barmaid. Dolly. She paid his debts. Dolly — the barmaid.' He shuddered again and a queer expression of fright crossed his face. It was marriage, then — or just the barmaid, perhaps.

'Oh, and he is —'

'Dead — dead to his father, that is. You'll find him — James, not his father, of course — at The World's End —' he saw their faces — 'a public house in Earl Street near Puddle Dock. I saw him not so long ago — a client of mine drowned and the inquest was held there — very dreadful. Poor fellow, and the will just found. He'd have had a fortune, but for a careless step. There's many a slip —'

'We are much obliged,' Jones interrupted hastily. For what they were obliged he wasn't at all sure, but he had no wish to hear Mr Wildgoose's ruminations on the vagaries of human fortune.

They left Mr Wildgoose apparently lost in philosophical musings, for he only acknowledged their departure with a vague wave of his towel.

'Lord, Charles Dickens, and I thought you made 'em up. Let's get out of here.'

'It's the law,' Dickens said, 'waste and ruin.' He guided Jones to a door with the words "Prerogative Office". 'Look in there and see for yourself what afflicts our Mr Wildebeest.'

Jones followed Dickens's pointing finger. There were long tables down the centre and at several there were figures poring over huge volumes. And all the figures had in common a dusty ancientness, as if they had been shut up there for years, searching and never finding their inheritance — never finding that death-bed promise of riches. A cadaverous man in a rusty black coat gnawed his lip over some yellowing parchment — food for misery, perhaps; a large woman in a bonnet the shape and colour of a turnip turned to a very little man beside her and shook him by seizing his cravat, as if she would strangle him. Disappointment there, too. But a sly leer on the face of a hard-featured old man who passed them, putting a notebook into his pocket with the air of a man who had found something to his advantage — cashing in on someone else's leavings. There were clerks in their wooden cubicles, busily copying or examining deeds, or lugging the huge volumes from shelves or lugging them back, and paying no attention at all to the treasure hunters.

'For the very reasonable price of a shilling, Mr Jones, you can ask to view Shakespeare's will.'

'Leave much?'

'A good deal of cash and lands, houses. Did well for himself.'

'Better than Pierce Mallory, I daresay.'

'Now here is wiglomeration in abundance,' Dickens said as they stepped outside, 'the Court of Arches is sitting, I see, or dining.'

A procession of crimson gowns and heavy wigs passed by, followed by black gowns and more ermine, and more wigs, and well-fed faces, gaunt faces, solemn faces, determined faces — on their way, perhaps, to decide the fate of some deserted wife, or widow, or jilted lady — or gentleman. That happened, sometimes.

'Think,' Dickens was saying, as they turned away, 'think of the inquest on poor Pierce Mallory in the smoky, ale-swilling, gin-smelling parlour of The Lion and Lamb. Think of anybody's inquest — at The Pig in a Poke, for example, but money, Mr Jones, now that needs robes and furred gowns, insignia, wigs —'

'Or at The World's End — worth a look?'

'I should very much like to see the prodigal, Mr James Wildgoose — and his Dolly Varden, for that matter.'

They went into Knightrider Street and passed the Horn Coffee House, from where Mr Pickwick had ordered several bottles of wine to be drunk in the debtors' prison where the law, as was its habit, had most unreasonably flung him, for Mr Pickwick had, according to the law, most unreasonably refused to pay the damages in a breach of promise case — a case for the

Court of Arches — the wives, not the wills or the wrecks, though Pickwick had been shipwrecked in a way — in the Fleet Prison. Then down Addle Hill — a name to conjure with, thought Dickens — and into Earl Street, just above Puddle Dock where, he observed to Sam Jones, Shakespeare had owned a house which he'd left to his daughter, Susannah. 'More salubrious two hundred years ago than now, I'll bet.'

'That's progress for you — watch out.'

Dickens dodged out of the way of some sheep driven their way by a man in a dirty smock. The sheep bleated plaintively and looked as though they would have liked to go another way, perhaps with Dickens and Jones to the pub, though they were probably bound for their own world's end at Smithfield. The man shooed them up St Andrew's Hill.

'We've enough black sheep to be going on with,' Jones said as the sheep made their sooty progress up the hill.

'The World's End, indeed,' Dickens said as they smelt their way past the vile, dirt-infested Puddle Dock and its companion, the unlovely Dung Wharf, whose smell proclaimed most accurately its purpose. Earl Street, named for the Earl of Chatham, had nothing very noble to offer now but warehouses, a few mean shops and houses, and almost by Blackfriars Bridge, the inn they sought which looked surprisingly prosperous, and where they found at the bar the object of James Wildgoose's desire.

She was undoubtedly a most attractive and buxom lady, tall with glossy black ringlets, warm and sparkling brown eyes, a high colour, and a clean white apron over a red tartan dress. Too old to be Dolly Varden of the Maypole Inn, but very comely.

'Mrs Dolly Wildgoose?' Jones asked.
'Yes.'

'I am Superintendent Jones of Bow Street. I should like to have a word with your husband.'

Mrs Wildgoose looked at Jones with narrowed eyes. 'What about?'

'An old acquaintance — Mr Pierce Mallory.'

Mrs Wildgoose laughed, a deep throaty chuckle which ripened into a ringing peal. Tears sprang to her eyes and the glossy ringlets shook. When she had finished, she wiped her eyes. 'That's the boy, is it? Away with your friend's wife, is he?' She looked at Dickens appraisingly. 'You're not bad looking, but Mr Mallory, now, he's what I'd call a handsome man and a great one for the ladies. It's the height, I daresay.'

Dickens felt a bit crushed by her verdict on him, though she might have crushed him to death in an amorous moment, he thought — her arms were decidedly beefy.

Sam Jones answered her, 'He is dead, Mrs Wildgoose. Murdered.'

Her be-ringed hand flew to her mouth. 'Dear God, you mean it. But he's in Paris. Oh, wait, wait, Mr Policeman, you're not thinking —'

'I am not thinking anything but that I need to talk to those who knew him, his old friends — from Paris.'

'You know about the duel, then?'

'I do.'

'Then you'd best come through to the parlour and have a talk with my boy.'

He was a boy — compared with the voluptuous Mrs Wildgoose, who must have been a good ten years older. James Wildgoose was in his shirtsleeves and waistcoat, and he looked the picture of a very happy and comfortable man at his table by a cheerful fire, where he was reading his sporting paper and eating a piece of pie at the same time. Still, many a murderer enjoyed his pie and potatoes without a qualm — even in Newgate, even before his hanging.

'Jimmy, love, these gents want to talk about Pierce Mallory.' Mrs Wildgoose went over to her boy and wrapped two strong protective arms about his neck. 'Now, don't take on, but Pierce is dead. Murdered, they say.'

'Good God, Dolly!' Jimmy put down his pie and took a gulp from the glass of red wine by his plate. 'In Paris?'

Jones introduced himself and Dickens, at which name husband and wife stared as if mesmerised. Jimmy took another hasty gulp and stood up. He was a handsome young man, too, tall and well-made with broad shoulders. Just what Dolly liked, no doubt.

'Charles Dickens at The World's End! Good Lord, Dolly, Charles Dickens.'

'I knew Pierce Mallory, you see,' explained Dickens, 'and Mr Jones is investigating. Mr Mallory died in London at his lodgings. He was shot.'

'Duel? Some outraged husband?'

'Not a duel, and we don't know yet. We have been to see Mr Montague Wildgoose — simply because your name was mentioned.'

The happy couple — for they clearly were — laughed like two children who knew a secret. 'Old Monty, eh? I suppose he thinks I did it.'

'No,' Jones reassured him, 'but he told us where to find you. Now, if you will oblige me, tell me about Mr Mallory.'

'You'd best sit down and take a glass,' Dolly offered.

When they were settled, Jimmy Wildgoose began by saying, 'I take it you know about the duel. I can tell you now, it was a blessing — and not just because it was called off. I saw the light about my young lady, over whose honour I was fool enough to try to fight Pierce. She only wanted me back when Pierce threw her over. I've no grudge against him. Never been happier — Dolly and me — well —' he gestured round the comfortable parlour — 'you can see for yourselves — and I don't care a fig for what my father says — or old Monty, for that matter. But, you want to know about Pierce. We met again and he came here sometimes when he was in London. He was in Paris, I thought.'

'When did you last see him?'

'Not for ages — he was like that, he'd turn up and then be off again.'

'Did he ever bring any friend here, or meet anyone?'

'Not as I remember — we get all sorts, a lot of wigs — and clerks — from Doctors' Commons of an evening. Pierce would talk to anyone, but I can't think of anyone in particular —'

'Caroline Dax,' Dolly interrupted, 'a lady he — er — knew.'

'I've met her,' Dickens said.

'Ah, you'll know, then. Left her with a child, but he told us he was supporting her — and so he ought, Mr Dickens. I liked Mr Mallory, but I didn't like his treatment of his ladies — even of Caroline Dax. I never liked her much, but there was a married lady in Paris after her.'

'How well do you know her?' Jones asked.

'He brought her here from time to time — not recently. But she has been here —'

'With a Mr Wigge, perhaps?'

'With an "e",' Dickens added.

Dolly and Jimmy burst out laughing again. 'Wigge — that's a good one,' Jimmy said.

'Who is he?'

'Well, his name ain't Wigge,' Dolly put in, 'or it wasn't when he was born.'

'He was a clerk up at the Commons — the Prerogative Wills office. You ought to ask old Monty about him — mind, he'd need to immerse himself in the Thames if you mentioned Solomon Wigge.'

'He did rather surprise us with his ablutions,' Dickens said, 'but tell us more about Mr Wigge —'

'His real name would be handy,' Jones added.

'Solly Wiggins — suppose he thought Solomon Wigge more distinguished — and then he might have thought he needed a change. Just a matter of dropping a few letters and there you are — a different man altogether. A man of mystery, is our Mr Wiggins. He is no longer with the wills — a little matter of fraud. People go to the Wills Office all the time — after money, property. But wills go missing — there was a to-do in the papers about it a few years ago. Let's say a man inherits an estate, the will proved, becomes a wealthy man, but there's a danger — another man starts looking for a rumoured second will which cancels the first. He thinks he's found it, but it vanishes.'

'You think Mr Wiggins — Wigge — was paid to dispose of wills?' Jones asked.

'That's what people said. Solly resigned his post, declared that he'd been falsely accused — by Uncle Monty in particular, who normally wouldn't say boo to a — well, obviously. Poor Monty — he hardly dares hold his head up before the clerks. Wiggins wasn't accused as such, but enquiries were set in motion.'

'And he has been here with Mrs Dax?'

'Yes, not so long ago,' Dolly said, 'they were in here with his pals — clerks from the Commons and young lawyers, all ready for a drink or two before going on to a club. They like their drink and their cards. He looked well set up, I must say — everybody's pal.'

'Quite the swell,' James Wildgoose said, 'Mr Solomon Wigge. Legal advisor, he calls himself — titled clients, they say. Quite the gentleman these days — you should hear him talking of the country houses, the fishing, the shooting —'

'Shooting?' asked Jones sharply.

'Oh, I see what you're getting at. I don't know — it was just gossip. I didn't believe half of it.'

'Describe him, will you? Mr Dickens and I haven't had the pleasure yet.'

Jimmy Wildgoose was not gifted with the power of description. 'Dark hair — er, smaller than me — er —'

Dickens turned to Dolly, who was laughing at Jimmy's difficulties. 'Ask a woman, sir — many's the time I've taken a few long looks at Solly Wiggins. 'Bout your height, Mr Dickens. Similar build. Black hair and eyes — very sharp eyes. Kind of glitter about them, when he's looking at someone else — calculating what he can get out of 'em, I'd say —' She gave them a knowing look and a smile. 'Not eyes you'd want to find on the pillow next to you — but all cats are grey in the dark, they say. Long about the nose. Bit pockmarked about the chin. Not bad looking, in his way, though. Caroline Dax seems to like him. Charming when it suits. Smooth tongue, too — ready with the compliments. A cat that got the cream. No whiskers, though.'

'What about Caroline Dax?'

'Oh, she looked pretty prosperous,' Dolly answered, 'nicely dressed. Looks like a lady — which she ain't. Out of the frying pan, though, I wondered, but she's a hard little piece. They don't spoil a pair.'

'Do you know anything about her family?'

'They don't want anything to do with her, she said. Respectable people and not short of money, she told me. In the clothes trade, I think — tailor's shop, maybe?'

They bade farewell to the happy pair, who promised to send a message if Wigge and Caroline Dax appeared again. Jones felt reasonably sure that Jimmy Wildgoose was not involved in the murder of Pierce Mallory, though he recognised that Dolly might be capable of anything to protect her "boy". However, Mr Solly Wiggins or Mr Solomon Wigge was very interesting indeed, as was his lady love, an observation he made to Dickens as they walked towards Fleet Street.

'What's she up to?' Dickens asked by way of reply.

15: RAGS

'That's right, sir, two suspicious persons, lurkin', they said, lurkin' was definitely the word, right outside the school.'

'And neither bore a resemblance to Mr Stephen Ellis?' Superintendent Jones asked neutrally. Sergeant Rogers was reporting on his morning encounter with the Misses Tarte at the seminary in Torrington Square.

'No, sir, though from the description — one burly, menacin' sort o' fellow, the other, a shifty-lookin' cove — well, sir, Sam Swidger an' his pal, Charlie Slyme, came to mind —' Rogers couldn't stop himself from grinning.

Jones grinned, too. 'All right, Sergeant, it's a fair cop, so to speak, Mr Dickens and I were moved on. I'll bet they didn't say "lurkin'" or "cove".' Rogers laughed. 'What about Ellis?'

'They don't miss much; one or the other's at the window and they see all the comin's and goin's — but they didn't recognise the description of Mr Ellis. I didn't dare mention the family.'

'No, you were right there. Stemp?' Jones saw a gleam in his constable's eye. Stemp didn't miss much, either.

Stemp had talked to a groom a few doors down from the Ellis house who had seen someone going into the mews behind the house, and he'd seen a light upstairs. Downstairs, the Ellises kept a carriage and a horse. There had been no sign of their groom.

'Must be a hayloft, sir. I just said that I'd speak ter the family. I 'ad a look, but the place was locked. I went back last night and sure enough there was a light, but I didn't linger in case anyone came from the house.'

'Mm — I don't want to go back to Torrington Square unless we have evidence that he is there. We'll send Constable Feak. See if he can get into conversation with a maid or someone. When Mr Ellis senior is out, though. I'll tell Feak to have a stroll about now — see who goes in and out.'

Dickens came in. 'News,' he said, 'Betsey Ogle has just been to see me. Caroline Dax didn't come back from her day trip.'

'No idea where she went?'

'No, she didn't tell Miss Betsey, but she thought we'd like to know. Did you consult the Trade Directory about her father?'

'I did. It's not a common name. I found an architect, a greengrocer, and a rag dealer in White's Alley, off Cutler Street. There's a shop, and since Mrs Wildgoose mentioned the clothes trade, it might be him. We've news, too. Stemp, here, tells me that someone may be using the loft over the stable behind the Ellis house. Stemp spoke to a neighbour's groom who noticed a light, and he saw it last night, but we can't go barging in. I'm sending Feak to have a look.'

'Anything from the Misses Tarte, or should that be Tartes?'

Rogers grinned. 'Tart's the word — pair o' sour pusses. Two suspicious men seen loitering — moved on quick when threatened with a constable.'

'Dear me, the rogues that lurk about respectable homes of genteel spinsters.'

'Oddly enough, I was able to identify them,' Jones said drily. 'I suppose we might as well go and loiter about Cutler Street for want of anything better.'

The Rag Fair in Cutler Street was one of the centres of the old clothes trade. A man or a woman could pick up an entire outfit for a few bob — that was if you had a few bob. Many didn't, but you could buy a third-, fourth-, even fifth-hand jacket for a few pence, a shirt if you felt it necessary, or a dress or shawl, or shoes for a penny. They might not fit, but they'd be better than going barefoot. And a bride could buy her wedding outfit for three shillings — white gloves and white stockings for twopence.

Not that dressing for the occasion was much in evidence here. Most people in London had a second-hand look, Dickens always thought, but fourth- or fifth-hand was the fashion hereabouts. The poorest of the poor rummaged the stalls for clothes, for household items, for food — pies on trays, biscuits three for a penny, oranges, pennyworths of oysters, chestnuts, walnuts and baked potatoes, and the place reeked of fried fish and unwashed humanity, and sounded with the tongues of many nations. Many Jews settled here and traded in old clothes. There were Italians, too, and others, all sorts of rootless souls who had been shipwrecked here — and no home flag on the horizon. Nor any star to guide them.

The street was packed and ankle-deep in mud — mud which clung to their boots as Dickens and Jones wove their way along to White's Alley where Mr Dax — who might or might not be Caroline Dax's respectable father — kept his shop. White's Alley was anything but, being a dank and gloomy place as packed with stalls as Cutler Street. Clothes of every type hung from the stalls. Some sold only hats — worn-out silk hats that had once adorned the heads of fine gentlemen, beaver hats, billycock hats, greasy caps, straw hats with broken brims, old cotton bonnets lying like rotting cabbages on the makeshift counter, poke bonnets which had gone out of fashion years before. Some sold only shoes and boots, others waistcoats and trousers, and some the most unappetising drawers and corsets — not to be dwelt on. Or smelt on. Few people washed hereabouts.

Mr Barnaby Dax's shop was at the end of the alley. An assortment of jackets, dresses, shirts and shawls hung from poles. In the window there was a picture of a red paper mill at which a cart was unloading a quantity of sacks of old rags. Inside, a man was showing the contents of a sack to the man behind the counter — a rag-picker, he'd be, Dickens knew. Rag-pickers made their living by scavenging in gutters, in the streets, in the waste heaps. A step up, perhaps, from the "pure-finders" collecting dog dung for the tanneries, though they earned a bit more. Rags thrown away were too far gone even for the poorest clad. They were bought by a dealer like Mr Barnaby Dax and sold to paper mills.

They waited while the proprietor weighed the contents of the sack on a one legged wooden scale hanging from the ceiling: tuppence for five pounds in weight; three farthings for a pound of canvas. The man took his money, his hooked stick, his sack, and slouched towards them.

'Mr Dax?' Dickens asked, stepping forward.

The ragged man stopped and Dickens caught a glimpse of a dirty face out of which shone two extraordinary eyes — just for a few seconds, but Dickens almost stepped back from the intensity of their suffering. Very pale eyes, perhaps blue or green, but with a ring of black round the iris. For a moment they might have been alone, the celebrated author and the pauper. Then he was gone.

Mr Dax, a large man with a benignly whiskered face, asked, 'From the paper mill, sirs?'

'No, I am Superintendent Jones from Bow Street and this is Mr Charles Dickens.'

Mr Dax turned to Dickens with a wide smile. 'Well, blow me down — a customer in a manner o' speakin', sir, a good customer in your way, sir — without my rags there'd be no paper for your journal or your books. Colleagues, in a way, sir, Mr Charles Dickens. How about that?'

'So we are — extraordinary to think —' he gestured at the rags on the counter and on the floor — 'that all this ends up as white paper.'

'There's no shortage o' rags in these parts.'

'Most people are wearing them,' observed Dickens.

'True, sir, an' every scrap worth somethin', specially these days with the paper tax. All the mills has ter pay a levy on the rags — even this bit o' lace collar. Where'd that come from, you wonder? A lady, perhaps — takin' her tea in her fine house in Belgrave Square, she didn't know the value of it when she cast it away to her servant an' she didn't know when she gave it to the charwoman who brought it to me — and then it makes a fine book for a gentleman who —'

'Rags to riches.' Dickens thought he had better interrupt the journey of the lace collar from Belgravia all the way to White's Alley.

'Or the other way round, sir; take that man what's just gone out. Rich man once, scholar from Cambridge University — university, sirs, on the way up and then come to this. Nimmo's his name.'

'A sad thing, Mr Dax,' said Sam, 'but we wanted to ask about your daughter, Caroline.'

Barnaby Dax looked at Jones rather less genially. 'What about her?'

'A gentleman she knew, Mr Pierce Mallory —'

'He should have married her — left her with that baby. I said she could come home, but she wouldn't stay. Lookin' for work, she said. Mallory left her nothing and now he's dead.'

Jones picked out the words "wouldn't stay" and asked, 'Your daughter has been here?'

'Came yesterday mornin' with the boy — her ma's glad to have him until she gets settled. What about Mallory, anyway? He committed suicide. Caroline said. She wasn't sorry — but I suppose, I can't blame her.'

'He was murdered, Mr Dax.'

Dax paled at that. 'You're not thinkin' that —'

'I have been making enquiries of people who knew him, that is all. Do you know where your daughter is living?'

'Lancaster Place, she said, for the time being — some friend's house. I don't know the name.'

'Why wouldn't she stay, Mr Dax?' Dickens asked. He was curious. Caroline Dax had created a very different father from the rag dealer.

'Rags, Mr Dickens, it's a dirty business. Caroline always wanted better. I gave her money until she got in with Pierce Mallory — engaged, she said, and then the child, and he was gone to Paris after a couple of years. They fell out, she said — his fault. He wouldn't marry her, so I supported her — the baby, see. They lived somewhere near Euston Station — not that we was ever invited — but she said Mallory had thrown her out. Come home, I said, but we wasn't good enough, I dare say. So I gave her money for new lodgings. Now, she says she wants ter work… I don't know.'

'You don't object to the child?'

'Look around you, Mr Dickens, those mothers, half-starved, buying a baby's dress for a penny. Do you think they care if Barney Dax's daughter has a bastard child? Bastard children are two a penny round here. Do you think I care about such things? Turn away my own flesh and blood when I see what I see every day? I make a livin' sellin' rags ter make paper — I've enough, and no one gives a damn whether I'm respectable or not. They care how much I'll pay fer their rags.'

'I see that, Mr Dax. Do you think Caroline will come back?'

'Fer the boy?' He looked at Dickens with saddened eyes. 'Truth to say, she didn't seem to care much, but we'll look after him until she decides what she wants.'

Mr Dax recommended they try Lancaster Place. They didn't enlighten him about their visit or about Wigge and left him as another ragged creature with sack and stick came in. Barney Dax was an honest man. He didn't know much about his daughter and he wouldn't know where she was. Dickens couldn't help thinking that she was unlikely to return for her child. Little Alfred would be better off. White's Alley was not Lancaster Place, but the child would be loved there, he was sure.

'A good man with a bad daughter,' he said to Jones. 'She's run off with Mr Wigge, I'll be bound. And abandoned that poor little boy. A good liar, though. She had me convinced that she might end up in the workhouse — or on the streets.'

Betsey Ogle was in a state of outraged indignation as she showed them the empty cupboards and drawers.

'Gone,' she said, 'an' not comin' back, an' not a word from either of 'em — the crafty, deceitful, thievin' —'

'Thieving?' Jones asked.

'Owed me wages.'

They looked through the rooms, but there was nothing — no papers, no letters, nothing. She'd planned this, Jones thought, though why she had approached Dickens for money was a mystery.

'What will you do?' asked Dickens.

'Doctor Sage's family'll let me stay on to look after the place. I get somethin' from them, but it was nice to have the extra from Mr Wigge.'

They didn't enlighten Betsey about Wigge. 'Nothing we can do now,' Jones said as they went back towards Wellington Street. 'Perhaps Wigge made her a better offer than you did.'

'She didn't trust me, maybe, and he offered to take her away — without the child. She didn't seem to care much about him.'

'We'll have to make enquiries about Wigge back at Doctors' Commons.'

'Poor old Wildgoose — his wings will be flapping. Tomorrow?'

Jones nodded. 'Yes, after the funeral. Now I'm going home. What about you?'

'Dining out with my brother-in-law, Mr Henry Austin, to sit upon the ground and talk of beds and baths, hot and cold, drains blocked and to be unblocked, and unwanted guests — rats.'

16: ECHOES

The matter of the shower for the bathroom at Tavistock House was agreed, the curtains thereof decided upon, the concealment of the water closet determined — Dickens explained to Henry Austin that he would be glad not to have it demonstrate itself obtrusively to the bather. 'Bowels,' he had said in a whisper so sepulchral that it might have emanated from a tomb. Henry had solemnly taken his notes and made promises about the drains. And with such dull sublunary matters finished, they had enjoyed their dinner at The Oriental Club where Austin always said the wine was very good. It was.

Bowels and baths and matters watery naturally led to Montague Wildgoose as Dickens made his way back to Wellington Street, and to that good-natured pair, Jimmy and Dolly, snugly tucked in at The World's End, and to rags.

And Nimmo — something had struck him powerfully about Mr Nimmo, more powerfully, he realised suddenly, than the murder of Pierce Mallory, about whom as a person he had not thought much, beyond the feeling of waste, and shock, of course, over the murder of a man he knew. He was intrigued by the matter of the duelling pistol, sorry for Mrs Ellis, curious about Caroline Dax, and always glad to be in the company of Superintendent Jones.

But it was Nimmo he thought of now. Those eyes meeting his for those few seconds. Nimmo — Nemo, perhaps — Mr Nobody at whom no-one looked because he meant nothing. He looked out of the window into the night and listened to the footsteps dying away, echoes coming back to him. Sometimes he imagined such sounds to be the echoes of all the footsteps

139

that were coming bye-and-bye into his life, unknown as yet. Nimmo had come as if from the grave in his rags and with his burning eyes in mute appeal.

A man in rags — rags — Caroline Dax's voice echoed. "Rags," she had said. He remembered bitterness in the word. A man in rags was nobody — no more than a beast — a poor bare forked animal, yet those eyes had something in them. What had been in that suffering gaze? Had it pleaded, "I am human"? Had Nimmo heard an echo, perhaps, of voices he had known? He had heard the voice of a gentleman and it had pained him? A Cambridge man to have sunk so low.

And an echo in his own mind — Nimmo — Italy — Genoa — a party — a dinner — some very fine whisky. *Got it.* John Nimmo, Ship and Insurance Broker, Genoa. John Nimmo had a brother, a wine and whisky merchant in London. A walk in the hills above Genoa, sunshine, the scent of flowers, a picnic, a man with an anguished face, a man with pale green eyes, ringed with black. A family tragedy. Lord, yes, he remembered now. He could conjure John Nimmo, and he remembered the story. Thomas Nimmo, another brother, a suicide years before. And he had left a wife and child — a son to be brought up by the whisky merchant. John Nimmo had said how the boy had prospered. Gone to Cambridge — an Apostle, so it seemed. And now studying for the bar.

And Pierce Mallory had been an Apostle. Clever fellows, they had to be if they belonged to that society. He knew that. *I wonder*, he thought. Impossible to tell how old ragged Nimmo had been, but those eyes were the eyes of a young man. Dickens had been in Italy seven years ago. He couldn't remember if John Nimmo had told him when the suicide happened. He couldn't remember the boy's name, either.

Was it folly to think that the rag-picker Nimmo had anything to do with the case? Yet, John Nimmo's eyes in Genoa. Cambridge. An Apostle. Pierce Mallory. Nimmo in Mr Dax's rag shop. Another coincidence? Fate weaving her net? Yesterday came back to tap the shoulder of the present and to point its wrinkled hand to the future. And footsteps echoed in the night. A pauper's footsteps had begun their journey towards him on a hot afternoon in Italy. A meeting foretold in the stars looking down on an Italian town. His pulse quickened and he felt a familiar pricking of the thumbs. He could go and buy some whisky.

The Trade Directory gave him Mr George Nimmo's address in Pentonville — Pentonville where Mr Micawber had taken lodgings at Windsor Terrace. Something would turn up.

17: RUIN

Dickens had time before the funeral in the afternoon. No sense in telling Sam Jones — unless Mr George Nimmo, the whisky man, knew anything about Mr Nimmo, the rag man. Wild goose chase, probably, he thought, laughing to himself. Wildgoose and Wigge were more likely leads, but he was in the cab now going towards Pentonville and the City Road, where the barrels of whisky and wine no doubt came from the docks into the canal basin for Mr Nimmo's business in York Place.

He had to be. Mr George Nimmo looked very like Mr John Nimmo of Genoa; his eyes were pale green, too, with that distinctive black ring round the iris. Their expression, however, was frank and genial. He looked very much the business man — a firm, straight mouth, lines deeply scored from nose to chin, very short, iron-grey hair; a commanding presence in his office, with its big mahogany desk stacked with folders and ledgers and its captain's chair by which reposed a handsome Newfoundland dog showing his age by the grey about his whiskers. All was very tidy and neat — a well-organised man, Dickens thought, who knew what he was about.

Of course, he greeted Mr Charles Dickens with great cordiality. He was honoured, most anxious to oblige with an order of wine — or perhaps whisky, which came from his cousin's distillery in Glasgow —

Dickens took his chance. 'I think I have tasted it — your brother — in Italy —'

'John — John, of course — he met you. Oh, he was full of it in his letters. Why, there was nothing for it but that we must read all your books — and we did. My word, we did —'

'How does he fare?'

'Well, very well, sir, still in Genoa. Loves the place, says he will live there forever — live forever — all that sunshine.'

'Yes, I remember he said he would not come back. Some painful memories, I think.'

Mr George Nimmo's face fell into sterner lines and his frank eyes clouded. 'I'm surprised he spoke of it — not something I wish to remember.'

'I understand, Mr Nimmo. It was just that your brother and I walked together and spoke of home and memory — of those who were long gone, but not forgotten. It happens sometimes that strangers are drawn together in a chance encounter to talk of things unspoken for many a year.'

George Nimmo looked at the pair of bright, searching eyes gazing at him kindly. 'I can tell from your face, Mr Dickens — not just from your books — that such things must happen to you very often. I expect people tell you things, but John didn't tell me. We never spoke much of what happened — for the boy's sake. I don't know now whether that was right. It is all wrong now — and will ever be wrong.'

'Mr Nimmo, I need to be frank with you. I saw a man yesterday — a man called Nimmo — a man with your eyes.'

'Richard? You saw him?'

'I do not know, but the name Nimmo reminded me of your brother in Genoa and the family tragedy he spoke of. Are you able to speak of it to me? It may help you to understand if the man I saw was Richard. It is he you mean when you say all is wrong?'

'It is. I have not seen him for six years. He simply vanished from my life — I thought he might have taken his life, but no news ever came. I made enquiries at his chambers, but no one could tell me where he was.'

'And you think his disappearance is to do with the tragedy?'

'I hardly know where to start — it is all so tangled in my mind, Mr Dickens. If I did not devote all my energy, my rational mind to my business, I sometimes think I should go mad.' His capable hand rubbed his face. The dog stood and came to lean against his master's leg. George Nimmo looked down fondly and stroked the woolly head. 'But you are a busy man. I cannot take up your time.'

Dickens sensed that the man wanted to tell him, but simultaneously wanted to retreat — to push it away and go back to his ledgers. There would be comfort in those ruled lines, in those neat columns of martial numbers, in the familiar rhythm of counting the casks as they came off the barges at the basin. He felt sympathy with that, but he wanted to know. 'Mr Nimmo, my coming here has pulled at a scar over which time has grown a carapace. Now it bleeds afresh. The telling of the story might — I only say might — ease that hurt and grief. Some good may come of it —'

'You would look for him again?'

'I would.'

'I must know about the man you saw — how he looked. What was his condition?'

'Very poor, I am sorry to say — but his eyes held mine for a few seconds, as if he and I were alone, as if he appealed to me in some way that I cannot fathom.'

'Where was he?'

'In White's Alley, off Cutler Street.'

'Rag Fair — in rags, was he?'

'I am afraid so. Now, tell me the story and we shall see if my Nimmo is yours.'

In answer, George Nimmo took some keys from his desk, opened a drawer, and took out a much worn leather folder from which he extracted what looked like newspaper cuttings. He held up one, saying, 'This is the story of my dear brother's suicide. You may take it away — I have plenty of other versions of the story, which gets no better for the reading. I don't do it now, but after Richard... Clues, I thought... After Thomas's death, I took his boy, then aged four years, named Thomas for his father. His second name was Richard after his grandfather, so I gave him that name. His mother went back to her own family in Scotland — she was not able to look after her child. After several years she married again — a prosperous merchant in Edinburgh. She had two sons — more than enough to compensate for the loss of that first child.'

'She did not want him?'

'Her new husband did not want him. I was glad. I loved him as my son — I have no children of my own, nor a wife. We never spoke of his parents. I thought it best for him to forget. A clever boy, my Richard, a fine scholar who in time went to Cambridge to study law. He became an Apostle — a grand thing for him, he told me — and then went to take his place at Middle Temple. All the world before him, Mr Dickens, and the prospect of marriage, too, to a young woman he loved, and then he vanished without trace.'

'And the young lady — she could not tell you anything?'

'I never spoke to her. I went to a house — in William Street near Regent's Park. Her guardian had no sympathy at all for my plight. He said that Miss Hatton wished to know nothing about Richard ever again — as if he had wronged her, but I don't know how. He loved her and he would not have betrayed her. Miss Hatton had gone to relatives. He shut the door in my face. The ruin of my hopes.'

'What was her Christian name?'

'Fanny Hatton. I don't know where she is now. I read of her guardian's death in the newspaper some years ago. Probably married someone else.'

'What was she like?'

'A pretty girl —' His eyes were hard suddenly.

'You didn't like her.'

'You are very quick, Mr Dickens. Let us say that I did not take to her. Something cold about her. Richard would be a wealthy man at my death. My will leaves everything to him — even now. I told him that he could sell the business or get a manager. It was all one to me — what use are riches in the grave? I wanted him to have the best in life — Fanny Hatton was not the best. But how will this help you find him?'

'Did he ever mention any Cambridge friends?'

'He told me once that he had met Mr Thackeray at a dinner. He had been at Cambridge before Richard — Richard left there in 1840, but whether they were friends, I don't know.'

'When was that?'

'About 1844, I think, for Richard had met Fanny Hatton by then. He disappeared a year later. A Mr Buller was at the dinner. I remember his name because he became an M.P. Oh, a Mr Estcourt — I remember that name, but whether he was at the dinner, I don't know. Fine acquaintances, I thought, who might have influence — help him, perhaps, in his ambitions.'

'I know Mr Thackeray very well. I can ask if he remembers Richard and any of his other acquaintances. I shall see him this very afternoon — a sad occasion — at the funeral of a mutual friend, a Mr Pierce Mallory.'

George Nimmo showed no recognition of the name. He only said, 'And Rag Fair — will I find him there?'

'There are thousands of ragged people there — let me find out what I can from Mr Thackeray. Be assured, I will do all in my power —'

'Why? Why should you do this for me — a stranger?'

'For that talk in the hills above Genoa — for a man who showed me his heart — and to whom I showed mine — and for a ragged young man whose anguished eyes — so like yours — looked into mine for a few seconds.'

People hurried to and fro along the City Road, all bent on their destination, some eyes down, others looking forward, striding on to meet those who were coming to meet them, from many strange places and by many strange roads. *And*, Dickens thought, *what it is set for us to do to those we meet, and what it is set to them to do to us, will all be done.* So Fate decreed. Richard Nimmo and he were destined to meet again. Of that, he was sure.

He stood, waiting to cross the road, the streams of people passing unheeding. They thought their purposes known and fixed. They were, in one sense — a sense they did not think of in the bustle and rush of life — for all those criss-cross journeys and meetings would lead finally to the place where he was going now.

18: FUNERAL

Highgate Cemetery — "that shrine of blighted hopes", as Dickens's friend, Douglas Jerrold had written. Dickens had made that journey up the Hampstead Road too often: for his sister three years since; for Mr Brim, father of Sam Jones's adopted children; for his father, only eighteen months ago, and for baby Dora last April. He had not wanted her under the ground or in a gloomy catacomb, but it had to be for the time being. One day he hoped to find a resting place for all his family in the free air. *Out of this darkness*, he thought. Looming clouds threatened rain in a sky darkening like a funeral pall.

Journey's end for Pierce Mallory. His heart felt leaden somehow, after all he had heard from George Nimmo. Fanny Hatton — Thackeray had mentioned a Fanny — another discarded mistress of Mallory's. A long time ago, Thackeray had said, and Richard Nimmo had vanished in 1845. But, there were plenty of girls named Fanny, his own dead sister included.

Granted, George Nimmo had not heard the name Pierce Mallory, but Richard Nimmo had dined with Thackeray and Mr Buller — Charles Buller was a friend of Thackeray's — dead now. Dickens didn't know who Mr Estcourt was. It was possible, surely, that Richard Nimmo had met Thackeray in the company of other Cambridge connections. Including Pierce Mallory? Both Apostles, too.

The cab dropped him at the grand Tudor-style entrance to the cemetery flanked by the mortuary chapels, Anglican on one side, the Dissenting chapel on the other. He thought of his sister, buried in the Dissenters' ground. The last time he had visited her grave was at the funeral of Mr Brim, dead of consumption, leaving his two children to the care of Sam Jones and his wife, Elizabeth. He wouldn't go to the graves today — too much sorrow to bear. He turned to see the hearse just going in, followed by a plain black carriage. Carr Mallory in that, he supposed. It was all very plain — no mutes, no plumes, no professional mourners. Dickens disliked the showy pomp of many funerals. This was as it should be, though he imagined that anyway Mrs Volumnia Mallory would not sanction any display for her disreputable son.

He followed at a distance. "Man equals man in dust", Jerrold had written in his poem. In one sense, of course, but for all his landed gentry background, Pierce Mallory was not the equal of a Mr Brim, nor, indeed of the living George Nimmo or Barney Dax, whose hearts had been given to their children, good or bad. He thought of the yellowing newspaper clipping which had told the story of Thomas Nimmo's debts and his suicide. His son had found the body. George Nimmo had set out to restore that child. Pierce Mallory had given his heart to no child, it seemed, but then, perhaps his mother had broken it. And it had repaired, as hearts do, but into something hard and selfish.

The carriages turned into the south-west path, away from the Egyptian monument and towards the grave, where Dickens saw another black carriage waiting at a distance with two black horses, adorned with plumes. A relative, perhaps, inclined to make a show for the dead man. The threatened rain came and umbrellas were raised. He saw Thackeray first talking to Sam Jones and Doctor Elliotson. Dickens joined them, and now he could see that there were quite a few gathered — about twenty, he guessed. Nathaniel Snee was there. Some journalists he recognised from *The Daily News*; Tom Beard and Baldwin representing *The Morning Herald*; a few from *Punch*, for which Mallory had written a few times.

Thackeray went to greet Carr Mallory, who stepped out from the carriage with another, older man. 'The solicitor,' Sam murmured. They all watched as the coffin was brought to the grave and lowered. No one emerged from the distant carriage, where the curtains were closed. Perhaps Mrs Volumnia Mallory was seated silently within, waiting to be sure that her disgraceful son was safely in his grave. Or perhaps her heart had softened. Somehow, he doubted that. The black carriage suggested something implacable. There was no twitch of a curtain and the black horses stood very still — even their plumes did not stir. Where the driver was he couldn't see, for the rain swirled about so that the carriage seemed uncannily ghostlike, as if it waited to carry off the corpse to the next world.

He turned to pay attention as the clergyman began to intone the words with which Dickens had become all too familiar. "Dust to dust" — he thought of Montague Wildgoose amid his dusty parchments. The rain spat diagonally into their faces, blown by a sudden gust of wind which lifted the clergyman's surplice. No one moved, but the faces were very white and strained in the cold and wet. *A dreary business*, Dickens thought, *and somehow wanting*. No tear shed. They had come, his colleagues, out of duty. Only Pierce Mallory's brother looked moved at the words "We brought nothing into this world, and it is certain that we can carry nothing out." And Thackeray — remembering Cambridge and the "wild Irishman", regretting the waste of a clever man who might have done much. He glanced at the carriage and wondered if the occupant could hear the closing words which asked the Lord to raise man from "the death of sin", and asked for hope that the departed brother should find his rest in Him. Mercy for the erring son? He thought of her icy words. Unlikely.

Then it was over and he made to speak to Thackeray, but he had immediately gone to Carr Mallory with some of the other mourners. He saw Beard and Baldwin turn to go — what a story it would make for *The Morning Herald*. Baldwin would relish it. Sam Jones was approaching. He'd have to see Thackeray another time. Jones didn't speak, but held his umbrella over Dickens and they moved to the path which would take them to the entrance.

The air cracked with a sound that was too sharp for thunder. Some black birds rose into the air, cawing raggedly. Jones whipped round. Carr Mallory was falling, someone was shouting, the horses rearing and plunging wildly, the undertaker's men struggling to control them, their neighing filling the air with panic, the horses of the third carriage bolting away, the mourners scattering, and Sam Jones running. Carr Mallory was lying on the ground. Dickens ran forward. Doctor Elliotson was kneeling, Thackeray holding his umbrella over him. Sam Jones was kneeling now.

Silence followed. The horses were still now. Only the clergyman's white surplice fluttered. That sound — a shot. Carr Mallory had been shot.

Doctor Elliotson had opened Carr Mallory's coat and waistcoat. Dickens saw the blood pumping out. Elliotson used a scarf to try to stop it, but the blood soaked the silk and Elliotson's hands were dyed red. Carr Mallory's eyes were open in dreadful surprise. And in the frozen silence Dickens could hear a horrible bubbling at his throat as if he tried to speak, but the sounds were indistinct. Jones stood to take Thackeray's umbrella and he knelt down to take the dying man's hand. The clergyman knelt, too. The mourners were frozen in various attitudes of shock and horror; some in pairs, a few huddled together, several alone — all motionless in the places to which they had fled.

Then it was over. Doctor Elliotson stood up, shaking his head. Thackeray stood and the mourners began to move uneasily like a picture coming to life, but they remained in their places, waiting for someone to tell them what to do. Dickens turned to Jones, who asked, 'Do you know who they all are?'

'Some, but they all know each other. Thackeray will know — that carriage, Sam —'

'Which?'

'There was a third, but no one got out of it — the horses have bolted.'

'Go and have a look while I sort things here.'

Dickens hurried along the path past the place where the carriage had been standing. He saw the kicked-up stones and the marks of hooves and wheels where the carriage had careered away. He followed and there it was amongst the trees where it had come to rest, the sort of private carriage that an undertaker might have for mourners, but there was no sign of any undertaker, or mute, or other attendant. The horses were placidly nibbling at grass round the graves. It looked exactly as it had looked not far from the graveside. The doors were closed, the curtains still drawn, and no sign of a driver.

Someone must be in there, Dickens thought. A dead someone? An elderly lady died of shock, her icy lips pursed in disapproval, her frozen eyes staring into eternity? He'd have to look. Supposing she wasn't dead? He hardly dared, but he couldn't just leave to get Sam. She — or whoever it was — might be injured. The horses looked at him briefly and incuriously as he approached. The rain didn't bother them — they were intent on their surprise dinner — but he could hear it drumming on the carriage roof. He approached the door to listen, but there was no sound from within. He put his hand on the door handle, listened again, and wrenched it open.

It was empty. He looked about him, but there was only the rain beating its tattoo and the horses munching. He went into the trees, wondering if someone had left the carriage — but the door would have been open, surely, if someone had been tossed about in terror as the horses bolted. No driver. Someone had driven to that graveside and remained inside until the moment came. That someone had shot Carr Mallory. And the question was: why?

Beyond the trees, there were more graves, and he saw a veiled woman in mourning of the deepest black standing up from a grave with the figure of a child on top. There was a splash of colour on the grave — flowers, perhaps, for a never forgotten child.

19: POST-MORTEM

Another bullet — not much to look at, but as dark and deadly as the first. And, by its size, surely not from a pocket pistol at that distance. Another duelling pistol? Sam Jones put it down on the table between them. 'We'll ask Henry Egg tomorrow.'

It was late, almost ten o'clock. Dickens and Jones were sitting in the parlour of Jones's house in Norfolk Street. They were warm at last and well fed by Elizabeth Jones with hot soup, cheese and newly baked bread. And they had a glass of wine each.

The funeral carriage had taken the solicitor, Doctor Elliotson, and Thackeray to the Hampstead Workhouse infirmary. Dickens and Jones had squeezed up with the undertaker and his driver on the hearse. The body of Carr Mallory was inside — laid in the place where his brother had made that last journey. Jones was dropped off at the police station to report the death and to ask for the abandoned carriage, left guarded at the cemetery, to be taken to Bow Street. Then he had gone on to the infirmary.

The surgeon at the workhouse infirmary conducted the post-mortem and removed the lead bullet which had entered Carr Mallory's left breast about four inches below the nipple, had passed through the liver and lodged in the lung on the left side.

By the time Dickens and Jones had returned to the cemetery, it was too dark to see very much. Dickens had shown him where he had found the carriage, but even by Jones's bull's-eye lamp there was nothing to be found. At Bow Street, they had examined the carriage, but the murderer had left nothing behind. Jones would send his men to search in daylight.

Neither the undertaker nor his men had seen anything. They had assumed that the carriage belonged to one of the mourners, and they had been too busy calming their horses to pay attention to anything else.

'Mr Arthur Ellis keeps a carriage,' Dickens said.

'We'll check, of course.'

'What did Thackeray and Doctor Elliotson tell you?'

'Mr Thackeray was shaking hands with the doctor, who was going home. Carr Mallory had turned to go back to the funeral carriage. The solicitor was shaking hands with the cousin of the Mallory family. They heard the shot. Next thing, Carr Mallory fell and we saw the rest. None of the other witnesses said anything different. They weren't looking at the carriage. They were shaking hands and in groups until they scattered.'

'Did Elliotson hear him say anything?'

'He couldn't really tell — he thought Mallory was making a "K" sound, but the poor man was choking.'

'A name, maybe? His wife? I'll ask Thackeray. He — I mean, the murderer — was waiting for that moment, but someone could have been walking with Mallory, Thackeray, for example. Good God, he might have been killed.'

'I know. What a risk he took. The question is who? And why?'

'Mrs Volumnia Mallory was at the hotel, I presume.'

Jones gave him a half smile. 'The solicitor went to tell her, but I'll have to see her. Dread thought. I doubt you'll be welcome, either. I'll take Inspector Grove with me.'

'She'll blame Pierce Mallory — say it's whoever murdered him.'

'Which it probably is — Ellis? Caroline Dax and her paramour?'

'Though why Caroline Dax should want to kill Pierce Mallory's brother, I can't work out — unless she had a dalliance with him, too.'

'Maybe she wrote to him asking for money, and he refused. A woman scorned? I feel I'm clutching at straws.'

'There was a woman.'

'Where?'

'At a distance — at a grave — just standing up. There was a stone figure of a child — and flowers, I thought. A child's grave — I wonder —'

'Why she didn't rush off — she must have heard the shot — you'd surely —'

'You would — mind, Sam, think of Pierce Mallory's death — no one took much notice of that shot in the middle of the night. Was she so lost in grief?'

'We'll have a look in daylight — see what name's on the grave. But Wigge? For Caroline Dax's sake? I don't know. However, I can't help thinking about what James Wildgoose said about shooting — it might have been gossip, but —'

'I know — one of those little bells that ring with a rather loud echo. He'd have to be a crack shot. That carriage was twenty yards away — twenty paces or more. A duelling distance, I suppose, or, Sam, a rifle — a sporting gun — country houses, Wildgoose said.'

'Mr Egg will be able to tell us. And then there's anyone else — the anyone else we don't know about.'

'Nemo — Mr Nobody — or Mr Nimmo.'

'The rag-picker? What's he to do with it?'

Dickens told him about staunch, upright George Nimmo, whisky and wine merchant, who had adopted his nephew, the boy, Richard Nimmo, after his father's suicide, and how the fine young man had gone to ruin and that Miss Fanny Hatton never wished to see him again.

'Remember, Thackeray told me about Pierce Mallory and a girl called Fanny — some young lawyer's girl he'd stolen and abandoned, but George Nimmo seemed to think that Fanny Hatton had been offended by Richard Nimmo, as if he had abandoned her, or done something dreadful. I was going to ask Thackery if he remembered anything more about them at the funeral, but, of course, I couldn't, and the infirmary was hardly the place. He was shattered. It happened practically at his feet. I'll see him again and ask about Nimmo and whether the girl's name was Fanny Hatton. Nimmo might have been a crack shot in his day.'

'Where'd a man as poor as he get the guns?'

'Good point, but it's worth at least asking about Fanny Hatton.'

'Pierce Mallory seems to have had no conscience where women were concerned. He's left a trail of destruction. You might as well ask Mr Thackeray while I instigate a search in daylight and see the mother and Henry Egg. I'll send Stemp to the Ellis house first thing.'

'Divide and conquer.'

'If only … but I do wonder what his brother has to do with it. Why kill him?'

'Something in the family?'

'Carr Mallory has a skeleton in his cupboard?'

'Apart from Mrs Volumnia. She won't tell. Perhaps Thackeray knows something about Carr Mallory. I'll try to see him tomorrow.'

'That would help. I'll come to Wellington Street about five o'clock.'

'I'll be there — staring hard at a blank quire of paper, no doubt. Cudgelling my brains over a story I've committed to for a magazine. Rash promise, I made — story about a haunted woman — a woman who dreams of a face looking at her fixedly out of darkness. The face of a man she does not know.'

'Well, while you're at it, dream a murderer's face for me.'

Dickens walked back to Wellington Street. *Faces*, he thought, recalling the scene at the graveside. Those figures scattering at the terrible sound of the gunshot, then stock still, hands raised, mouths open, eyes on the scene by the body. He conjured it again, his mind's eye travelling over the faces. Something not right — someone not right. After he had looked in the carriage, he'd gone back to the graveside. The figures had moved, huddling in little groups, some under umbrellas, whispering together. Except for one. A figure leaning against an angel. Leaning, almost casually. Who was it? The face of someone he did not know.

20: ASHES

Dickens looked down at the list of names — most he recognised. Thackeray had known the rest, even if distantly, including the cousin who lived at Chelsea — the elderly cousin who had not been able to tell Inspector Grove anything — except that he hadn't seen Pierce Mallory or his brother for many years. Twenty names. Impossible to say if there had been more than twenty people at the funeral. The mourners had arrived severally, most in cabs which had dropped them at the gates, and they had come to the graveside in dribs and drabs. Then there had been the rain and the umbrellas, and everyone had watched as the coffin was laid in the ground. As for the closed carriage, Thackeray had assumed that some had come in that. He hadn't really noticed.

Nevertheless, that figure leaning against the angel. Not that the detail was clear, but that sense that he was not horrified. A figure without an umbrella, an impression of dark hair, a top hat dangling from the hand. Casual — that was the word, or he seemed so. Black coat, of course. Standing by a grave with a very large weeping angel looking down. Alone, but then some of the others were standing alone where they had fled from the sound of the shot. But when he returned, the mourners had naturally moved together. One single figure. And then not. He remembered speaking to Sam again about the carriage and the mourners walking away down the gravelled path, still shocked and silent now. But there had been no figure by the angel.

Someone had come and gone — slipped away when everyone started to move, because whoever it was didn't belong. It would have been easy. That tall angel with its large wings — how simple to move behind that and steal away when everyone was preoccupied. But who? Not Ellis. He would have been noticed. Many of the people there would have known him. Wigge? Caroline Dax in the carriage? Caroline Dax, the shooter? The woman by the child's grave? But why Carr Mallory? Just because he was Pierce Mallory's brother? It seemed so unlikely. What would they get out of it? He had imagined Caroline Dax shooting Pierce in a fit of anger and jealousy, or even in revenge — that dish served cold, but not this.

Carr Mallory? Dickens had asked Thackeray, who had called at Wellington Street in the morning in response to a note from Dickens, if he could think of anything? Thackeray hadn't really known him. Not a Cambridge connection. He'd been in Ireland for several years. Ran the family estate. Wife an invalid — that's why he went back to Ireland. There'd been some scandal about the wife's father — debts, Thackeray thought. He couldn't imagine why anyone would want to kill Carr Mallory — only that it had to be connected to Pierce. He was baffled.

However, he had remembered the name Richard Nimmo as the lawyer connected with the young lady, Fanny. Yes, Hatton, that was the name. As far as he recalled, the young woman had fallen for Pierce Mallory and Nimmo had faded out of the picture. Pierce had mentioned her in some conversation or other, and Thackeray had just thought it was another dalliance. Thackeray hadn't known Nimmo at Cambridge — he'd left before, but Pierce had known him because of the Apostles, he assumed. He supposed there had been a dinner — Cambridge reminiscences, probably. He sometimes went to such things. He might have met young Nimmo, he couldn't recall, but the name stuck because he and Fitz had shaken their heads over

Pierce Mallory's new entanglement. He didn't know what had happened to the young lady. Pierce had probably gone off to Paris or somewhere and left her.

Did Thackeray know a Mr Estcourt? Oh, yes, Thackeray remembered him — Fred Estcourt, a scapegrace, spendthrift — gone through a fortune at Cambridge — gambler and all round bon-vivant. Thackeray had known him at Cambridge and in earlier days in London. Yes, friend of Pierce's — they went about together at some time. Not recently, he thought. Yes, alive — Thackeray had seen him. Gone to seed in Soho. Lodgings over a furniture shop in Gerrard Street. Money wanted. But, no, he didn't know if Estcourt had known Nimmo. He'd given money and not gone back. Estcourt was too far gone.

Frederick Estcourt had been a lawyer in Middle Temple. Chucked it for some reason, Thackeray had said. Nimmo had been at Middle Temple. Gone to seed in Rag Fair. Perhaps Estcourt did know something about Nimmo. It was worth a try.

Dickens knew Gerrard Street very well and the shop which had once been a bookseller's — now the premises of Roland Graveson, upholsterer and undertaker, the latter part time, he assumed. The booksellers had been subsumed into the undertaking side, the window of which was adorned in black and featured some smirking angels and other funerary accoutrements.

Dance of Death, Dickens thought. The widow of the bookseller had lent him Holbein's illustrated work with its terrifying skeleton haunting the populace from Pope to ploughman. Grim reading for a boy. He'd imagined waking up to find that hideous skull grinning at him from the end of the bed. Upstairs above the bookshop had lived his uncle, Thomas Barrow, whose leg had been amputated, which was why the young Dickens was a constant visitor. Well, Thomas Barrow had departed to marry without his leg, the bookseller's widow was dead, he supposed, and here was poor Fred Estcourt, sometime denizen of Middle Temple, amid the gravestones and angels.

A phlegmatic young man with nails in his mouth — whether for the coffins or the sofas, Dickens didn't know — jerked his thumb in the direction of some stairs. Presumably to where Fred Estcourt was to be found. The stairs, cluttered with more funereal ornaments, led him to a landing and a door through which he looked upon several fallen angels, urns of a most melancholy black marble, drooping plumes, lengths of black silk, top hats. Through another, he glimpsed a man in woollen combinations trying on a top hat from which streamed the black weepers worn for a funeral. The face in the mirror looked at him angrily. He passed by quickly.

Another door took him onto a landing into the upstairs of the former bookseller's. He recognised the narrow stair up which he had toiled to bring comforts to his bedridden uncle. And here was the very door. He knocked and a voice called him to enter.

Gone to seed — the room and the man. Uncle Thomas Barrow's landlady had kept all in the daintiest manner. The table under which Thomas Barrow's leg had been stowed — he remembered his uncle asking where it was — was still there, covered with papers, letters, all sorts of chipped crockery, half-smoked cigars, ash, wine bottles, and another black marble urn which contained a quantity of quill pens. The smell was of cigar smoke, brandy, and someone unwashed, and underlying those, the sickly, vapid smell — and taste — of laudanum.

On Uncle Barrow's sofa — now much worn — reclined the man, wearing an old silk nightcap with a ragged tassel and a shabby, ash-strewn, red Turkish dressing gown trimmed with faded gold. His feet were bare and very yellow, as were the long toenails. In all he presented an appearance of degraded raffishness. A cigar burned in a saucer on his chest. He appeared to be asleep. Dickens knocked again on the open door.

'Leave it on the table.' A tired voice, but an educated one. A voice born to have its own way.

'Mr Estcourt.'

At the sound of a stranger's voice, Estcourt sat up. The saucer fell, scattering ash everywhere, and the cigar dropped onto the newspaper on the floor. Dickens sprang to pick it up, displacing several discarded letters as he did so. He had no wish to be burnt to death.

'Obliged.' Estcourt took the cigar, reclined again, and put it in his mouth, drawing deeply, then he spoke with the cigar at the corner of his mouth. 'Wasting your time, my dear sir — I'd pay you if I could, but, as you see —' his arm gestured languidly about the frowsty room — 'I should try my friend — '

'I am not a debt collector.'

'Oh, then who the devil —' He sat up and a greyish-yellow face and red-rimmed, yellowish eyes looked at the visitor for the first time. 'Dear God, Charles Dickens. Well, well — from the empyrean heights to the slums. But you're used to it. Nothing surprises you, I dare say. Come to offer me a job on your magazine? I could turn my hand to a pretty article for the masses, I daresay.'

Dickens ignored the barb. 'I had your address from Thackeray.'

'Dear old Thack — gave me some money — generous type, but I could tell what he thought. "Oh, what a falling off is here" — Hamlet, dear sir —' as if Dickens wouldn't know — 'Prince among men, I was, when Thackeray was no better than a pauper and you were nobody. Fortune's wheel, eh?'

Not luck, thought Dickens, contemplating the coarse, ruined features, the red-veined nose, the thick lips and the sallow skin. *Damned hard work.*

'I came to ask you about Richard Nimmo.'

The eyes glinted with malice. 'Ah, this is about Pierce Mallory. Murdered, they say — well, the life he lead — and you want to know if Nimmo did it. I have no idea. Haven't seen him for years — nor Mallory, for that matter. Not since the affair with Fanny. Richard Nimmo, eh? He was cut up, but that girl was no good — as Mallory found out — bad blood there, but he didn't care. Should have been more careful, Mallory. Plenty of enemies, I daresay. Nimmo, though, vanished from the face of the earth. Gave it all up —'

'You mean the law. He was at Middle Temple — so were you.'

'Oh, I was. He was a good little fellow — moneyed. Father — or uncle — a brewer, I think. Trade, anyway. Never short, Nimmo.'

'What happened after Fanny Hatton left him?'

'The usual — drink, gambling, whoring. Debts all over. We went about a bit then — pouf — he was gone. And Mallory, gone to his grave. Some irate father or husband, I'd say. Plenty of 'em.'

Dickens was about to ask about Carr Mallory when someone knocked at the door. A girl appeared with a tray, on which there was a cup of tea and some bread and butter.

'Ah, breakfast. Close the door, Charles Dickens, as you go.' Estcourt lay back, blowing out a cloud of smoke.

Dickens turned on his heel, slid on an envelope, felt his foot crunch on something, and kicked the envelope aside in a spurt of anger. But at the door, he paused and felt the coins in his pocket. He was tempted to leave them there, but he thought about Thackeray, thought that it was, after all, easy to fall, thought about an uncle's kindness to a small boy, and left a sovereign on Thomas Barrow's little table by the door. He went back the way he had come. The man in the woollen combinations was seated on a coffin and he was sobbing, the top hat in his hands. Ashes to ashes.

21: PERCEPTION

"Never short, Nimmo." That told him everything. The prince among men had dragged down the scholar. Debts piling up, Estcourt borrowing and never paying back, creditors at the chambers, avoiding the Temple to evade the creditors, the sheriff's man — a greasy man at the door, waiting, wanting, wheedling. And underneath it all, the shame — to betray the man who had brought you up, who had loved you as his own son, and the memory of a man with his throat cut, sheets stained in red, a father who had killed himself for debt.

But what that all had to do with the two murders, he had to admit he did not know. He felt at a bit of a loss. Leaving Estcourt so precipitately meant that he hadn't asked more about Fanny Hatton, or anything about Carr Mallory. Not that he thought Estcourt would have told him anything else. The man simply didn't care. He was so much reduced — not so far gone as Nimmo, but he had no shame. Like Pierce Mallory. And somehow not pitiable. A mixture of self-pity and arrogance — never an attractive combination. Malicious, too. Not a shred of feeling for Pierce Mallory — or for the ruined Nimmo.

He was walking across Grafton Street — only a step to Crown Street and the stationery shop where Scrap, errand boy, counter deputy, great friend of the superintendent's adopted children, and sometimes amateur detective, would probably be. Now, if a person wanted cheering up, and if a person wished to find a ragged man with extraordinary eyes, then Scrap was the lad for that.

Scrap's face lit up at the sight of his visitor. *Bringin' news*, he thought, an' not before time. Things 'ad bin too quiet lately — since May, in fact, when they'd investigated the Chinese case. The Chinese puzzle, Mr Jones 'ad called it. Scrap had been in his element. Solved it — well, practically — brought a nasty cove down with the poker. That'd 'urt 'is feelin's. There'd bin that Exhibition, o' course — exciting in its way. Dinosaurs an' engines an' diamon's — an' a statue of Mr D's Little Nell — nice enough, but not a patch on detectin'.

'Wotcher, Mr D. Long time, no see.'

'Ah, well, I have been busy.'

'New book? The one about the woman wot's goin' ter do the murder?' Scrap, amateur detective, also literary critic and adviser, had, after the case in which a woman had murdered her lover, asserted that Mr D. should use the idea.

'I haven't started yet.' *And how I should like to.* Dickens thought of the chaos at Tavistock House. 'Moving house, you see.'

'Where yer flittin'?'

'Not far — Tavistock Square.'

'Knows it — delivers ter some folks there. Woz yer wantin' anythin' in partickler?' he added casually.

'Oh, just some paper. The blue slips — the usual and some of your finest blue ink.' Dickens couldn't resist a bit of teasing. Scrap's face fell. 'I've a list somewhere —' searching his pockets, finding a bit of paper — 'ah, yes — oh, something missing — or rather, someone.'

Scrap saw his smile. 'Oh, very funny, Mr D. Mind, I'm not laughin'.' But he was — grinning from ear to ear. 'Yer wants me to find someone.'

'I shall do, though I haven't spoken to Mr Jones yet —'
should have thought of that — 'but I don't think there's any
danger.'

'That's a comfort.' Scrap could be very dry when he wanted
to be. 'Since when 'ave I ter be worried about that?'

'Since Mrs Jones began to worry about you — and me —
and Mr Jones.'

'True,' Scrap conceded, 'but was ever there anyone better at
sniffin' out a villun without that villun seein' 'im?'

'Your powers always astonish me, but rules is rules. I'll meet
you at Bow Street about half past four. Mr Jones is coming.'

''Oo's the missin' cove?'

'A rag-picker, name of Nimmo. Once a scholar at Cambridge
University. Selling his wares in Rag Fair now.'

'Way o' the world, Mr D.' Another of Scrap's specialities —
practical philosophy. 'Plenty of folk wot come down in the
world. 'Ow'd it come about?'

'That's what I want to find out when you find him.'

'Villun?' Scrap rather hoped so — murderer, p'raps.

'I don't think so — but we can never be sure, so you just
find him and tell me.'

"Urgent" — a word that sent Dickens hastening from
Wellington Street to Torrington Square. Mr Ellis senior's note
requested him to come. Mr Stephen Ellis wanted to speak to
him.

The man in question was sitting in the drawing room, the
little dog at his feet, his father standing at the mantelpiece.
Stephen Ellis looked haggard, his former plumpness having
deserted his boyish face. He looked thoroughly miserable, but
there was a petulance about his mouth which suggested
another consumed by self-pity. Not an attractive man, really,

despite his youthful looks — eyes too close together. What had Mrs Ellis ever seen in him? Escape from her irascible father, probably. Another man who did not love her.

Mr Ellis senior explained. 'It is intolerable, Mr Dickens. A policeman asking questions of my groom, asking to see if our carriage is in the stable — where else would it be? Talk of robberies in the area, asking about strangers. Spying on my house.'

Dickens ignored him and looked at the man on the sofa. 'You wished to see me.'

'You came with a policeman to ask about Pierce Mallory. I didn't kill him. I didn't.'

'But you did see him at The Athenaeum and at a pub called The Lion and Lamb?'

'Mr Dickens, you may be a very celebrated man, but you have no right —'

'Mr Ellis, I am here at your urgent request. If your son prefers to speak to Superintendent Jones, then I suggest he goes to Bow Street.'

'Father, please, this is not helping. Let me explain to Mr Dickens. I made a fool of myself at The Athenaeum, but I'd only just got back from Paris. My own wife — telling me — Mallory, who'd been a guest at my table, a friend — had her in my bed —' his voice, rather nasal and high, rose even further — 'congratulating me on the coming child, and all the time he knew. Do you wonder that I was enraged? I would have killed him if he'd come to the house to see her, but, no, he wrote — had business in London then off to Constantinople — and I to deal with his leavings. And she — half distracted — writing letters, pleading with him. By God —' anger now, and at his wife; furious at his own humiliation — 'prostrating herself —

169

she disgusted me. I'd have let her go. She was like a mad woman.'

'She is mad — you're better off without her.' Mr Ellis senior couldn't stop himself.

Nor could Dickens now. 'I saw her. Most distressing. Her father has no care for her either.'

'I don't want ever to see or hear of her again. It was not a happy marriage. She didn't love me — nor I her, but I did my best.'

Dickens doubted that, but it was no use saying anything. He only asked, 'The Lion and Lamb?'

'Never heard of it.'

'It's on Drummond Street near Euston. Pierce Mallory had lodgings nearby and someone was seen with him at the tavern a few nights before he died.'

'I didn't see him after I was sent packing from The Athenaeum — damned interfering porter.'

'And you went to see a lady called Caroline Dax at Lancaster Place.'

'Another of his whores — she said she didn't want to know anything about him — never wanted to see him again.'

'What did you want with Pierce Mallory?'

'I'll tell you what I wanted — for him to take his harlot to Constantinople and his by-blow. He'd refused when I confronted him in Paris — the nerve — told me the child is my responsibility. And she — whining and snivelling —'

'The child *is* your responsibility.'

Ellis senior spluttered. His son ignored the comment. 'You think I'd have waited and followed him to kill him — after that public scene? Mallory would have told his cronies — laughed about it, I don't doubt. And Thackeray — he should keep better company. His wife's mad. He ought to know —'

'And what did you do when you heard he'd killed himself?'

'I didn't want my name in it — my dirty linen washed in court. I just waited for Father to come with the children. Kept out of the house. Then you and that policeman came and it was murder. How do you think I felt? I kept my head down. And now the brother.'

'Mr Ellis, is there anything you can tell me about Mallory or his brother that might make them victims of murder?'

'Nothing of Carr Mallory. Pierce Mallory was a devil about money — oh, yes, he borrowed from me —' his temper was rising again, his hands clenched and unclenched as if he wanted to strike out — 'and I paying him to bed my wife — my wife! There'll be others, but I'm not giving you any names. Mallory deserved what he got. His brother, too, I'll bet.'

The little dog rose to put his paws on the man's knees. Ellis shoved him away with one clenched fist. Dickens knew exactly what he was.

22: HISTORIES

It was not far off half past four. Dickens thought he'd better go to Bow Street to confess his precipitate recruiting of Scrap before the young detective appeared, swathed in rags purloined from Zeb Scruggs's old clothes shop in Monmouth Street. "Gotter look the part," he'd say.

The superintendent was waiting.

'I know I'm early, but I wanted to get here before Scrap,' said Dickens.

'Been and gone. We're bidden to gather at Wellington Street — your office commandeered for a conference at five o'clock.'

'Oh blow, I needed to tell you.'

Jones's lips twitched. 'All I know is that he's to find some ragman. Name o' Nimmo — witness to a murder.'

'Ah, not quite what I said.'

'I did wonder, but you'll have ter be a bit on the sharper side, Mr D., if yer wants to catch up with Detective Scrap. Something new about Nimmo?'

Dickens gave him the story: broken-hearted Nimmo, destroyed by debts; Estcourt — the yellowing, dissipated ruin, and ruiner, half-buried in ash — unfeeling as a marble urn; vitriolic Ellis senior; petulant Ellis minor — whining about himself — weak mouth — cross-eyed — temper, though — cruel streak — haggard as a murderer, but probably not one —

Sam Jones saw them all as if he had met them in the street. 'You have been busy. Let's start with Ellis. Probably not? Their carriage is in its stable.'

'There's logic in it. Made a noise at The Athenaeum. He might have killed Pierce Mallory in rage — he admitted that,

172

but I'm sure he wasn't the lion cub's man, not the man who watched. Ellis wouldn't have sat quietly talking. And I doubt he killed Carr Mallory. Someone else.'

'Nimmo? But you believe this Estcourt actually ruined him and Estcourt's still alive.'

'Just about. They're all linked, though, Pierce Mallory, Nimmo, and Estcourt — Cambridge and Middle Temple, the woman, Fanny Hatton — and debts.'

'And Carr Mallory?'

'Ah, I gave it some thought. That letter — he was coming to London. I wondered if he told you what for when you spoke to him after the second inquest?'

'I didn't get a chance to ask. He did say that he had sent money to Pierce Mallory for his journey in Constantinople. He was more concerned about the investigation, and suspects, of course.'

'He seemed to think his prospects would improve, though. He was coming to London before his brother's death. About a job? He was obviously dissatisfied with his petticoat regime. Did you see the Snow Queen?'

'She was too prostrate with grief. I had to accept that, but I did speak to a Miss Leaf, some sort of cousin-companion to the old dame. Poor relation, anyway. Told me that Mr Carr Mallory was out on business after we'd seen them at the hotel. Mrs Mallory rested.'

'Business?'

'She didn't say what, but, over a cup of tea, she became quite confidential — lonely, I imagine —'

'Ah, the superintendent's kind grey eyes. And?'

'Mr Carr Mallory had his troubles — as she did herself — the old lady was very exacting, and Mr Carr had somehow disgraced himself and was summoned home several years ago after his wife's father's death —'

'Ah, now Thackeray said it was because his wife became an invalid — and that there was some scandal about her father's debts.'

'He was, it seems, occasionally allowed to come to London, but not allowed to see his brother, though Miss Leaf had the impression that he did. A noticing sort of body, is Miss Leaf.'

'Did Carr Mallory say what his brother was doing in London?' Dickens asked.

'Ah, that letter again. He gave me the impression that it was to do with Mrs Ellis — naturally, I didn't enquire further, his brother having been murdered.'

'Perhaps they had some scheme cooked up for Carr Mallory — Pierce was to prepare the way. But what? And how had Carr Mallory disgraced himself?'

'Debts? That's the usual thing that prompts a man to leave town. That reference to Fagin's kitchen — moneylenders, perhaps.'

'Den of thieves — yes, could well be. Estcourt in debt, Nimmo in debt — is that the link? They're all in thrall to some moneylender? Nothing to do with Pierce Mallory's amatory entanglements?'

'I wondered about the lawyer, Nathaniel Snee — whether he'd know anything about Nimmo and Estcourt. He was at the funeral. He knew Pierce Mallory.'

'Pretty well, too. He was the man who dined with Mallory and Thackeray — and who used his influence to get Mallory his job with *The Morning Herald*. I know him slightly. He lives in Bedford Square.'

'We'll see him tomorrow. I've been to see Mr Henry Egg. As we thought, whoever shot Carr Mallory used a different gun —

could have been a sporting rifle, interestingly, good for long distance.'

'Quite the gentleman, Solomon Wigge —' Dickens repeated James Wildgoose's words — 'fishing, shooting.'

'Perhaps he and his lady love are taking a sporting holiday with a titled client.'

Dickens smiled. 'Motive, though — it can't just be that the Mallory brothers wronged her.'

'Wigge's a lawyer, and a wrong 'un, we know that, so maybe they are all connected to some nefarious money dealings. Anyway, we'd best get to our conference.'

'There's one more thing,' said Dickens. 'I'll tell you the details on the way. Thackeray and I put together a list of those present at the funeral, but I think there was someone else there — someone on his own. I saw him after I came back from investigating the carriage. Someone whom nobody knew.'

Scrap was waiting, not yet heavily disguised as an urchin fit for Rag Fair, but blue eyes dazzling. Sergeant Rogers was there, too. He had something to report.

'Scrap said you were coming here for a conference —' his eyes twinkled — 'so I asked if I might come to make my report.'

'You are welcome, Mr Rogers.' Dickens kept his face straight.

'Sir?'

'Oh, by all means, Sergeant. Tell all.'

'Nothin' at the graveyard, sir, nothin' where the mourners were standin' after the shootin', or where that carriage had fetched up, but I saw a grave nearby which had a posy on it — very fresh, I thought. A lady, I'd say — a womanly touch about it. I looked closer an' there was a little bit o' card tucked in —'

'A message?' asked Scrap. 'Maybe from the murderer — to 'is — acc- acc- whatd'yercallit.'

'Accomplice?' supplied Dickens.

''Xactly.'

Rogers read solemnly from his notebook, '"To my dearest Herbert. Your loving wife, Rosamund." I put it back, o' course.'

Dickens turned to Jones. 'Husband? The woman I saw was by a child's grave. Two women?'

'Could be — it's a public place. What else, Rogers?'

'The inscription on the gravestone I looked at tells us that it belongs to Mr Herbert Cox, died October, 1850, aged fifty-four years — a year ago to the day. "Loved and respected wherever he went" and —'

'Died happy in bed and rests content.'

'No, Mr Dic— oh, yer made it up — just like you, sir.'

'Epitaphs are my speciality — serious or comic — as you like.'

Jones interrupted, 'The death will be registered — Rogers, you can find out at Somerset House tomorrow morning. Maybe Mrs Cox — if that's who it was — did see something. It's worth a try. And we'll look at the child's grave in daylight tomorrow.'

'Scrap mentioned a Mr Nimmo, sir.'

Jones explained what they had discovered during the day, and turning to Scrap he told him, 'You know your duty — Mr Stemp will be at —'

'They could meet at St Helen's Church near Bevis Marks — where we met Mr Kaprillian,' Dickens said. 'You remember him?'

'Course I does — never forget 'im.' Mr Kaprillian was an Armenian merchant who had assisted them in the murder of a sea captain — a man with a wonderful collection of curiosities by which Scrap had been fascinated.

'Right,' said Jones, 'we meet tomorrow first thing. Now, you might as well go home with Sergeant Rogers.'

'Stemp can keep his eye on him,' Jones said when Scrap had torn himself away. 'This business of the man you saw by the angel. We should go to Highgate tomorrow — can you manage it when I've finished with Scrap and Constable Stemp?'

'As I am a man and brother. Are we to visit Mr Snee at Bedford Square?'

'Now?'

'No time like the present. He'll know what you want.'

Going into Bedford Square ten minutes later, Dickens remarked, 'Number forty-two, as I recall, next door to The Society for the Diffusion of Useful Knowledge.'

Thirty minutes later, The Society's windows were dark, but light shone from the amiable Mr Snee's hallway as he bade farewell to his visitors whom he had welcomed most cordially, and they were going away with some knowledge of matters legal and matrimonial.

He had not shed much light on the cases of murder, but he did remember that Richard Nimmo had been in chambers at Middle Temple under the guidance of Sir Mordaunt Quist, Q.C., a most eminent man — still at Middle Temple, still eminent, mind like a trap, still fat, still humorous, and very rich indeed. Wife an earl's daughter. Snee liked a gossip.

Very promising, Richard Nimmo, but not suited for the cut and thrust of the courtroom — on the delicate side, Snee thought. The girl, Fanny Hatton? Yes, there was something to do with Pierce Mallory and Nimmo. Mallory taking the girl about, but that was Pierce — well, you couldn't help liking him for all his faults. Estcourt, now — bad lot. Quist had given up on him. Lazy, apparently. Thought the world owed him a living. Debts, he believed.

Highgate? No, he hadn't remembered anything new. Ah, poor Carr Mallory — trouble there. Went back to Ireland with his wife — invalid. Her father a suicide. Gossip about debts. But, then there always was gossip. But, Carr's death — shocking business. Hoped they'd find the blighter who'd done it. Mr Dickens should see Quist about Nimmo — had a phenomenal memory — known for it. And he enjoyed a joke. Said his sister was sharp as Shakespeare's Portia in the law, but, alas, for her brother's purse, as ill-favoured as Dickens's Sally Brass.

Snee's laughter accompanied them as they went back through the square.

'You go and see this Quist tomorrow — enjoy yourself over a glass of sherry,' Jones told Dickens. 'I'd better see the family lawyer, find out what I can about Carr Mallory's troubles. Highgate first thing, though.'

23: UNDERTAKINGS

A very tall and very lugubrious man in the deepest black preceded Dickens into Bow Street police station next morning and went with a purposeful stride to the counter, his face as long as that of a man who had lost a sovereign and found a sixpence. His sepulchral voice matched his garb. He sounded as though he were made to read the burial service in some windswept graveyard on a remote cliff top. He had lost something, though.

'Black, sir?' the duty constable asked, his tone suggesting that he ought to have played the second gravedigger in *Hamlet*. Constable Doublett, a man of many parts and equal to any mood, pastoral, comical, tragical — and all the rest. Dickens couldn't help drawing nearer.

'For funerals, constable, a black carriage, vanished from my premises and needed to convey the bereaved. I've had to hire another at great expense.'

'Name, sir?'

'Graveson, Gerrard Street, upholsterers and undertakers, and Headstone — now deceased.'

'And the circumstances of the theft, Mr Grave, er, son?' A slight lift of an eyebrow.

Dickens stepped up. 'Excuse me for interrupting, Mr Graveson, but I think Superintendent Jones would like to hear this. Is that all right, Doublett?'

It was. Of course, the protean Doublett knew Mr Dickens and was quite ready to relinquish Mr Graveson and his missing carriage to a higher sphere. Dickens escorted the son of the grave, who loomed beside him like his ghastly shadow, to the superintendent's office where Jones received the victim's name and his history without looking at Dickens, whom the undertaker seemed to think was some kind of special messenger employed for the conveyancing of visitors to the rarefied purlieus of the superintendent's office.

'A funeral day, sir, and the carriage all polished — gleaming it was, and the horses, brand new plumes — ready to go, sir. Kensal Green. The hearse — four horses and two carriages — two horses apiece — ordered for the ceremony at noon — a quiet affair, but genteel, sir, very genteel — feathers, silk scarves, kid gloves. I sent my assistant out to open the gates — and they were open — the carriage gone — and the horses — the whole bloomin' lot. No time for anything, but to borrow a cab — a public conveyance and a brown horse.' His handkerchief was bordered in black. The blowing of his nose sounded like the last trump.

'When was your carriage stolen?'

'Day before yesterday.'

'And you are only reporting it today?'

'No, sir, I went straight to the St Giles's police office. Den of thieves, St Giles's — ruffians sneaking into my yard and taking my goods, hay, bridles, horseshoes, feed — but never a carriage. I know the sergeant at St Giles's. Course they've looked. I went early this morning and the sergeant told me to come here.'

'Highgate, Mr Graveson, that's where your carriage ended up — at a funeral. It is now in our yard with the horses.'

Anguish suffused Mr Graveson's already melancholy countenance. 'Tubby! That villain, Tubby. He'll have sold a funeral and had no carriage — nothing fit for more than a tumbril to the guillotine. Funerals, cheap and respectable — that's his line — cheap — and the clergyman no better than a mountebank. Some actor from Drury Lane, I'll be bound — the devil — my carriage — my horses —'

'No, Mr Graveson, I don't think so. Your carriage was used by a murderer.'

Mr Graveson appeared to be speechless; his mouth remained open, but only some strangled noises emerged.

Jones continued, 'You need not concern yourself, sir, the murder is my business.'

He escorted the still mute undertaker back to Constable Doublett who, at a glance from the chief, arranged his features into an expression of solicitous commiseration, and took him to find his carriage.

Dickens, meanwhile, was pondering the coincidence of Estcourt and Graveson's funeral premises, a thought he put to the superintendent when he came back.

'It's damned odd — Carr Mallory's murderer steals the carriage from the very place Estcourt lives, Estcourt who was a friend of Pierce Mallory, Estcourt who — as I infer — was somehow involved in Nimmo's ruin, Nimmo whose girl was stolen by Pierce Mallory —'

'It is suggestive — they are all connected, and they all have something very fishy in their backgrounds.'

'What say we make a dash to Gerrard Street,' suggested Dickens, 'see if Mr Estcourt has had any visitors who might have gone away in a funeral carriage?'

Uncle Thomas Barrow's door was closed again. Dickens knocked, but no weary voice called him to enter. They listened, but there was only silence, except that from some dim region below the stairs came the steady tap-tap of a hammer. Coffin-maker somewhere. *Dead as*, thought Dickens.

Jones tried the handle, which gave at his touch. Everything appeared to be exactly as Dickens had seen it before, even to the man reclining on the worn sofa in his shabby dressing gown, but there was no little plume of smoke, no cigar on a saucer — that was a little different.

Dead as, Dickens thought again as Jones moved over to take up the man's hand. Their eyes met. Jones didn't need to say it. He removed the handkerchief from the face. It was not the same. Something had twisted the lips into a hideous grimace so that the yellow teeth appeared as snarling fangs, and the bulging eyes were open, the film of death upon them, but not concealing an impression of a terror which had passed yet left its shadow behind.

'Poison,' Jones said, taking something from the folds of the Turkish dressing gown.

Dickens saw a little medicine bottle at which Jones sniffed. 'Opium. Anything to suggest he was an addict?'

'I could smell laudanum when I was here. He looked like an opium-taker.'

Jones sniffed at the dead man's lips and looked at the face again. 'Opium didn't do this.' He lifted the hand again and lifted the other. 'Hands clenched and —' he lifted the dressing gown to reveal the feet, which were curiously arched and turned inwards, the yellow toenails like the claws of some wild beast — 'someone wanted us to think that he had killed himself.' He dropped the folds of the gown and covered the dreadful face again.

'He wouldn't do it. Too idle, and he didn't care. I think he was quite comfortable where he was. He thought I was a debt collector. It didn't seem to bother him. He told me that —'

'What?'

'That I should go to see — and I interrupted him to give my name.'

'Someone supporting him with enough?'

'Thackeray had given him money, but Estcourt was that sort. He expected it. I left him a sovereign as I went out.' Dickens looked at the little table. 'It's still here.'

'He wasn't desperate, then.'

'I don't think he was.'

'We need a doctor to certify death. I'm certain it wasn't opium.'

'What then?'

'I look at that mouth and those clenched hands and arched feet and I think of strychnine.'

'Lord, Sam, that's a dreadful death. I didn't like him, but what a cruel thing. Oh, Lord, remember Miss Abercrombie?'

'Thomas Wainewright's sister-in-law — I remember — he poisoned half his family.'

'He got away with it because the doctors said that she had died of pressure on the brain — I once dined with a Doctor Locock, who was one of the doctors. Wainewright did it for the insurance money — eighteen thousand pounds, as I recall, but he was indicted for forgery.'

'This is not pressure on the brain. After a local doctor's seen him on the spot, I'll have the body sent to Doctor Woodhall at King's College Hospital — we know we can trust him, but before I do anything, look about you. Anything different?'

Jones knew he could rely on Dickens's powers of observation. Nothing escaped him. His bright glance would have taken it all in at first sight. And he'd remember, as he had remembered the man by the angel. Highgate would have to wait, however.

Dickens let his gaze travel along the floor — the letter on which he had almost slipped was gone. The newspaper with its scorch mark was still there. He looked up — there were no papers or letters on the table. Someone had been here. Someone who had not wanted Estcourt's secrets known.

'There were papers and letters on the table and on the floor here. I almost slipped when I was leaving.' He knelt down. The boards were bare, but just protruding from the gap between two boards was something red. A fragment of wax seal. 'This is what I felt under my boot. I thought it was a button or something.'

Jones squinted at it. 'Nothing to tell from this, except it might have been important — something official, maybe. Now, think about the letter that's missing.'

'He'd tossed it aside. Cream paper. Black ink ... from the office of ... I couldn't see anything else.'

'Tossed it aside, yet it was important to the murderer. You all right to stay here while I get a doctor?'

'There's a surgeon round the corner in Macclesfield Street. Want me to go?'

'No, first I'll send someone from downstairs with a message to Bow Street for a couple of men to bring the mortuary van. I'll say there's been an accident. Then I'll fetch the doctor.'

'Then I'll stay. I might remember something.'

Dickens looked at the remains of Frederick Estcourt. He seemed diminished under his shabby covering, though there had been only remains even when he was alive. Dickens was aware that the tap-tap of the hammer had resumed. Someone making a sofa — or a coffin. He went to close the door. Rat-tat-tat, rat-tat-tat, rat-tat-tat and then tap, tap, tap, tap like the ticking of a very loud clock or someone knocking. Someone who was not going away. Something inexorable about the sound, each tap a reminder of mortality. It was coming, the hammer said. Death at the door. Rat-tat-tat. One last loud tap — the final nail in the coffin. Then silence.

Dickens looked back at the man on the sofa. That tired voice, though, could it be suicide? He doubted it. Who had Estcourt last seen? Had he waved away that visitor to go and find that someone who might be paying his debts?

And how had the poison been administered? The murderer of Pierce Mallory — and it was surely connected — would not have engaged in a struggle with his victim, forcing the poison between his lips — no, no, he would have been cleverer than that. So, where were the wine glasses? Frederick Estcourt would have taken wine. Or brandy.

He looked at the table again. The wine bottles were still there — empty. And a brandy bottle, hardly touched. He couldn't remember if it had been there the first time. Glasses, yes, with the remains of red wine in them. Hard to tell if they had been recently used. Frederick Estcourt would probably have used the same glasses without washing them. Some dregs of brandy in one glass — perhaps that's where the poison would be found. Some bread and butter — Estcourt's breakfast, perhaps. A squeezed bit of lemon on a plate in some liquid. He sniffed. Fishy, indeed. Oysters, perhaps. Had he died of a bad oyster? And tried opium to ease the pain? But opium didn't produce those horrible contortions. And no shells. Unless the girl who had come with the breakfast the other day had taken them away. The letters, though. Someone had taken those.

The hammering had not started again. Dickens went out onto the landing and looked down Uncle Barrow's narrow staircase, which presumably led now into the undertaking part of the business. He went down. Two rooms on the left. Coffins in what had been the widow's parlour, and the front of the shop was what had been the bookseller's. On the right a scullery and a back door into the yard, where the original walls had been removed so that it opened into Mr Graveson's stable and carriage yard and there was the undertaker with his hand tenderly stroking the nose of one of the black horses; the other horse nuzzled at his pocket from where Mr Graveson took something which he held on his flat palm. A man with a heart underneath his black armour.

Dickens went back inside before he was seen. Something cracked under his foot. Good Lord, an oyster shell.

24: POISON

'You are right, of course, Superintendent Jones, it looks like strychnine. The body exhibits the most common evidence of strychnine poisoning — that is the clenched hands and arched feet you noticed, and in such a case, the body remains unusually rigid for a long period, as you see here. And those contracted muscles of the face are very characteristic — *risus sardonicus*.'

It was more than sardonic, Dickens thought. Mercifully, Doctor Woodhall had covered up that face of a cornered beast.

'Black and liquid blood throughout and the heart empty,' Woodhall continued. That was Estcourt's epitaph. So his heart had been in life.

'When do you think he died?' Jones asked.

'Judging by the process of putrefaction, I would say two days ago.'

'Mr Dickens saw him alive two days ago, so that suggests some time after he left.'

'I need to make a thorough examination. There will be signs to confirm our initial conclusion, though strychnine leaves no trace in the body. However, I can test the oyster shell and the plate and the brandy glass. Will you be able to return later? At about five o'clock, I should think.'

'Someone watched him die,' Dickens said as they came out of the hospital into Portugal Street by the old burying ground where many of Woodhall's patients ended up, despite the compassionate doctor's best efforts; a mass of corruption, bones heaped on bones where the ghostly vapours of the dead rose up to kill the living, and even the grave diggers fled from the corpse gases. Still, there might be progress. Dickens had spoken about the scandal of the overcrowded burial grounds, there were articles in *Household Words*, and Henry Austin, secretary to the General Board of Health, was working for the cause of their closure, but when, he wondered, when? Portugal Street was still a mouldering stain on the landscape with its vile smells, broken coffins and scattered bones. Highgate, though, Kensal Green, Norwood — all better places, open and green, but did it matter where your bones were? He thought it did. He thought of baby Dora in the dark catacomb.

'All right?' asked Jones, noting the silence and the sudden spasm of pain across that mobile face, a face with the life of fifty human beings in it, someone had said, and a dear face to him for its courage and bright sympathy with everything around him, and those sometimes anguished looks which revealed a darker element at work where some tragedy resided — if you had eyes to see it. And Jones did and worried about it, and told his wife too. And they were there, ordinary, they always thought, compared to Mr Lemon of *Punch*, or Mr Maclise, the artist, or Mr Forster, that formidable man of letters. But Elizabeth Jones said he needed ordinary friends sometimes, and a supper in a small kitchen where there was new bread and warm soup against the cold, and a warm fire against the dark. Sam Jones loved her for that.

'Just thinking of burial grounds — Lord, Sam, the sight of them chokes the very soul. Let's hope there's someone to bury Estcourt in the open air.'

'Inspector Grove is onto his background. It'll be Highgate, perhaps. Bow Street first, though. I want to know if Rogers has found out anything about that widow lady.'

On the way, Jones broached the subject of Dickens's comment that someone had watched Estcourt die. He thought of the man who had watched Pierce Mallory at The Lion and Lamb public house. 'The Watcher — could it be Wigge? Not that we know why, except that he's connected to Caroline Dax.'

'Whoever it is has nerves of iron — to steal a funeral carriage, shoot a man in broad day, and to stand by while another man writhes in agony. And he's cunning. He must have inveigled his way into Estcourt's lodging with a bottle of brandy and a plate of oysters.'

'But he dropped that shell, and it might not have been noticed but for you. He may have nerves of iron, but he makes mistakes. Estcourt must have known him. Pierce Mallory must have known him; therefore, Carr Mallory knew him?'

'Pity I didn't get a chance to ask about that. There's only Nimmo now. Scrap might have found him by the time we get back — though, I hope —'

'He's not the murderer, I know. Don't fret about Scrap. Stemp won't let him out of his sight. I've told them to start at Mr Dax's shop.'

Sergeant Rogers was waiting, as his message at Bow Street had said, near the pile of earth which was the newly dug grave of Pierce Mallory. Would there ever be a memorial stone, Dickens wondered, to say that he rested, lay content, and was missed by all who knew him? He thought not. No posy with a woman's touch. No child to remember. The grass would grow over until it was lost to sight. Unwatched, unwept, uncared for.

Rogers was explaining that he had found and interviewed the widow lady, Mrs Cox, at number ten, South Grove, just beyond the church of St Michael.

'Yes, sir, she heard the shot an' saw the carriage hurtling along. No driver. Then a man suddenly appeared, but he just rushed off. She thought he might be going to get help. I wondered about the church — that'd be a place to hide.'

'Any description?'

'No, just a fleetin' glimpse of a man in a dark coat. '

'What about the church?'

'I haven't been in yet — in case I missed you.'

'We'll take a look. He could have concealed himself in there. The Hampstead police made enquiries of the clergyman, but he was home at the time. However, while it's still light, let's search about Mr Dickens's angel.'

The angel still looked down at the grave he was guarding. Dickens stood where the stranger had lounged against the angel. When Dickens stepped behind the grave, he was completely concealed. More graves with more angels and then a little copse of trees. Those who had laid out the cemetery had kept the original trees from Lord Ashurst's park. Easy enough to slip in there and make his way to the catacombs where he might wander as casually as any visitor. Highgate was popular as a tourist attraction for its quiet walks and the extraordinary Egyptian Avenue leading to the great Cedar of Lebanon with its circle of twenty catacombs — even if you met a funeral occasionally.

Jones and Rogers followed him through the little group of trees, but there was nothing to tell that a man had stood here. Beyond the trees was the central avenue, across which were the catacombs. There were a few people still strolling there and some paused to peer over the wall down to the other catacombs below.

Jones looked about him. 'No one about on that day in that rain. Only a few people came running at the sound of the shot, but I got rid of them. He could have slipped away in any direction — more trees over there. Right, Charles, show us the grave where you saw your woman in black.'

They retraced their steps to where the carriage had been abandoned and Dickens pointed out the grave with its sculpture of a child. The flowers were still there. The epitaph told that the angel child had gone to the arms of her Saviour in 1836 at the age of three years.

'Fifteen years ago,' Jones said. 'Still, it's worth trying to trace the family. Rogers, you'll have to go to Somerset House again. Mr Dickens and I will try the church — find out if anyone saw anything.'

The church was outside the cemetery on top of Highgate Hill, where Dickens had put the Steerforth house where David Copperfield had watched Rosa Dartle walking up and down like some chained creature, being eaten away by her jealousy. Handsome, heedless, careless Steerforth, who, like Pierce Mallory, had left ruin and hatred behind him.

Inside, the last rays of the sun came through the high windows above the gallery from where they heard the sound of an organ playing a low, mournful strain which gave the empty church a solemn, deserted air. They stopped to listen, and when the music died away Jones went to the staircase to call out that he would like to speak to the player. A voice floated down that he would come and quick footsteps followed. A man of about thirty came down — a pleasant-faced young man with fair, curly hair and a healthy complexion who asked cheerfully how he might help.

Jones introduced himself and asked if the young man had been in the church on the day of the funeral at about half an hour after midday. The musician had, but he had not heard any gunshot, but then he had been playing very loudly — sounding

it out, loved to fill the whole place — he grinned — let it rip
— Toccata and Fugue.

'At what time did you finish?'

'About a quarter before one o'clock to go home to luncheon.'

'Was there anyone in the church when you came down?'

Now the friendly face frowned and looked anxious. 'A man was in that pew over there, sitting at the end. He was praying.' *Well, he might*, thought Dickens, though he doubted that the murderer was praying for salvation — not to be caught, more likely. 'He looked up as I passed. A face I shouldn't like to see again — a look of malevolence on a very white face; and black hair, very black against the white face.'

'You didn't notice his eyes?' asked Dickens.

'Black, I think, very dark anyway — it was just a glimpse, sir. I felt quite frightened for a moment. I think it was the contrast between the music — the place — and such a look as if he hated me. I had been so enjoying myself — the music, you see, it fills you with such a sense of the sublime. I went out and then in the company of my dear wife and my little son, I forgot him —' his face clouded again — 'but now you mention him —' he turned to look at the pew he had pointed out — 'it is as if he has left a stain there. That is all I can tell you, Superintendent; now, if you will forgive me, I shall go back to my music. You might stay and listen a while.'

The low, melancholy music came again as they walked quietly about the church. Dickens went over to the pew and opened the little door, but there was nothing to see, except the stain of which the musician had spoken; there was a darkness on that seat, as if the stranger's shadow sat there. A trick of the light, perhaps.

They came out into the porch and the music faded. They saw it was dusk and felt the wind blowing about them. They didn't speak until they were out into South Grove.

'Could there have been two men — one at the grave and one in the church?' Jones pondered as they went in search of a cab to take them back to Doctor Woodhall's mortuary.

'Unless — there weren't two —'

'You saw him.'

'I did, but the timing — those carriage horses bolted as soon as the shot was fired. There was no one in it when I got there. Mrs Cox saw him briefly; then he was away through the trees and leaning against that angel. He wanted to be sure that Carr Mallory was dead. He could have done it. Then he was gone — into the church. He has the nerve for it.'

'The woman you saw — was she in that carriage, I wonder?'

'Handy if she was — if anyone looked in, they'd just see a grieving woman — one of Pierce Mallory's lovers, they might think —'

'Well, Rogers should be able to find a grieving mother for us to eliminate — if that's what she was.'

'Or someone else — Caroline Dax, for example — slipped out of the carriage before I got there.'

'Back to her again — and to Solomon Wigge.'

'He of the glittering black eyes.'

'What's his connection to the Mallory brothers?'

'The law — it's the only thing I can think of.'

25: TWIST

'I have examined the internal organs. The poison leaves no trace, as I have said, Superintendent, but there is evidence of strychnine poisoning in the congestion of the membranes and substance of the brain, and, peculiar to strychnine, congestion in the upper part of the spinal marrow. It is what we call a spinal poison, which rarely produces narcotism as in other poisons. Strychnine produces very severe tetanic convulsions in which the body is racked and twisted into dreadful contortions, though in the intervals of spasm the sufferer's intellect is sufficiently clear to enable him to speak —'

'How long, Doctor?' asked Dickens of Woodhall.

'Two hours of the most intense suffering is usual, though it may be much shorter — as little as twenty minutes. It depends on the dose. The poison was in the oyster shell. I tested it. A complicated business, but, in brief, with a small quantity of acetic acid, water, and alcohol — a process of infiltration which leaves crystals of strychnine —'

'But the bitterness —'

'Swallowed it whole and then too late,' Jones said. 'The murderer took those oysters — and not from any nearby fishmonger; my men checked. Could be from anywhere.'

'It could be,' Doctor Woodhall answered. 'It's easy enough to get hold of. Butler's Vermin Powder, for example — three grains in a sixpenny packet. Half a grain can cause death.'

'Well, that's clear enough. Poor devil,' Sam said as they went back into Portugal Street. 'I'd better get back to Bow Street to see what Inspector Grove has unearthed about Estcourt, if anything. Someone didn't like him, apart from you.'

'A man with black eyes?'

'It's no use our haring about after him. All right, someone might have seen a black-eyed, black-coated man getting into a cab or on an omnibus from Highgate, but that's no help. We have to get at him and the other through the people our victims knew — the law, you said.'

'Sir Mordaunt Quist — I've an appointment in fifteen minutes.'

'Good — come to Norfolk Street afterwards. We'll feed you. I'm off to see the Mallory family lawyer at Lincoln's Inn.'

It was but a five-minute walk down to Fleet Street and into Middle Temple Lane, then under Christopher Wren's gateway to Middle Temple, where Estcourt and Nimmo had put up their brass plates and eaten their dinners as he had himself when once he had considered the bar as a career before rejecting the process of having an old frayed gown put on in a pantry by an old woman and going to take yet another bad dinner. Indigestible, the law, in more ways than one, though he hoped he would have done better than Nimmo or Estcourt — one in rags and the other living off hand-outs. He passed the old lath and plaster houses which had survived the Great Fire and the stationery shops where deeds and wills were engrossed and copied, and all branches of law-writing were executed, &c., &c., &c. — until the end of time, no doubt, by a legion of dusty clerks in inky sleeves — and from which the smell of dust and ink and sheepskin wafted. A turn took him into Fountain Court, where Sir Mordaunt Quist had his chambers.

A very tall, very narrow, very melancholy young man, resembling if anything a dusty gas pipe with a sharp turn in it as he bowed, doubted, looked at Mr Charles Dickens's card, nodded, changed his mind, doubted again, whispered that he would see — perhaps Sir Mordaunt would — he might — as Mr Dickens was so — could he wait?

Mr Dickens could and the whispering young man, still bent at an angle, approached a door, looked at the card, looked back at Dickens, sketched a smile on his pale face, and knocked timorously.

From within, Dickens heard the sound of laughter — a deep-throated laughter, the laughter of a big man who enjoyed his life, enjoyed the law, enjoyed company, for another laugh joined his, higher, a neighing, snorting sort of laugh, a smaller man's laugh. A man who laughed because his master laughed. A laugh with something mocking in it. *Risus sardonicus*, Dickens thought, feeling a chill at his neck as he listened.

There was no response to the tentative knock, and the laughter continued. The clerk dared to knock more loudly and a voice boomed that he should enter. When the clerk reappeared, his smile erased, he opened his mouth, closed it, and motioned that Dickens could go in.

Sir Mordaunt Quist was alone, standing in the middle of his Turkey carpet with both hands extended in greeting. There was no sign of the person Quist had been laughing with but Dickens noted another door leading out of the room. Quist was a very large man, but he wore his bulk with confidence, his bald head gleaming as if it oozed satisfaction, his smile wide in welcome to reveal very large teeth — all the better to eat you with. Brown eyes, warm in greeting.

'Mr Charles Dickens —' his voice like deep, dark velvet drew out the name lingeringly and then boomed again — 'this is an honour, indeed.' Two surprisingly small white hands took Dickens's hands. Scented hands, very soft, and somehow unpleasant. 'What delight, what charm, what joy do your books give. Even your lawyers, my dear sir. Oh, some of my colleagues sniff — guilty, you see, but I find them irresistible. Naughty, Mr Dickens, but very, very amusing. Mr Sampson Brass and divine sister Sally.'

Dickens felt as one in the teeth of a gale as the boom came in at his ear and seemed to come out at the sole of his boots, but he managed to express his pleasure for such obliging words. Sir Mordaunt invited him to sit and asked if he would take some very fine sherry, or some cake — pointing to a table upon which there were glasses, decanters, and a very large cake. Dickens declined. Sir Mordaunt asked to what he owed the pleasure of Dickens's visit. 'A matter of law, my dear sir, a suit?'

'No, indeed, my own man is Mr Loaden at Bedford Place.'

'A fine lawyer, Mr Dickens, you are in safe hands. I cannot think why we have not met hitherto — so many friends in common —' he boomed on, naming names, at each of which Dickens inclined his head, feeling like some demented puppet, and waiting for his opportunity to speak — 'a legal matter for a new book? A new character? I am at your service, of course. Sir Mortmain Twist, perhaps, of Middle Temple?' He laughed uproariously at his own joke.

Dickens laughed his appreciation — he rather liked the idea. He seized his chance. 'I am looking for someone, a man called Richard Nimmo who used to —'

'Ah, yes, I remember, a dear boy, a promising boy, but he and the law did not quite hit it off. Not cut out for it. You know it, Mr Dickens, a tough business.'

'What happened to him?'

'Gave it up, sir. A love affair gone wrong, I believe. A broken heart.' Quist closed his eyes as if he were suddenly struck by a painful memory. 'Ah,' he murmured, 'a sad young man — a dear young man. I thought the church, perhaps.'

'You don't know what became of him?'

Quist's eyes opened, liquid with regret. 'Alas, no, I am sorry to admit. I should have — but one's life is full of those who pass in and out like ships in the night.'

'And Mr Frederick Estcourt, who was here and a friend of Richard Nimmo's?'

Sir Mordaunt sighed. 'Another failure, I am afraid. I don't know what's happened to him — another who made a brief incursion into my life and is lost to sight. I liked him — a man of charm, good background, good humour, but he lacked seriousness. I like my pleasures, of course, but work, Mr Dickens, is a serious matter —' smiling now, eyes caressing his visitor — all teeth and temptation — 'as your works so ably demonstrate — comedy is not achieved by anything less than dedication — you and I are alike in that, I think. If I may presume before genius.'

Dickens inclined his head at the compliment. He was always susceptible to flattery, but this did not come from the heart. Of that he was sure. The man was an actor. He would be. He was on stage every day in the courtroom.

'May I ask, however, why you wish to know about Nimmo and Estcourt?'

'Did you hear of a man called Pierce Mallory?'

'He was murdered — I read about it. You are involved?'

'I knew him and I —' If Dickens hoped to side-step the matter of his involvement, he was aware of a sudden, hard, penetrating stare from the man opposite, the sort of stare that would have cowed a lying witness or even a truthful one. He found himself tied in a knot — he did not want to mention the police — 'Mr Thackeray wanted —'

The smile was back — self-deprecating now. 'I must beg your pardon, Mr Dickens, not my business, of course, but if you should need defence counsel, I am your man — or, if indeed, the murderer does.' He threw back his great head and laughed heartily again. 'But we must not discuss these dreadful matters at our first meeting. We shall be friends, I know it. I wonder if you would care to dine at my house tomorrow. Do say you will. My wife would be so glad to meet you at last.'

Dickens accepted and Sir Mordaunt escorted him to the door. Those hands again, and that scent of roses. 'Cavendish Square, my dear Mr Dickens, number fourteen. Quickswood House. Delighted, delighted.'

As he passed through the outer office, the whispering man was folded over his desk, scraping away with his pen. Dickens bade him good day. A pair of frightened eyes looked back at him very briefly and looked down again without a word. Frightened of him? Of Quist? What kind of a man did he work for? Exacting, probably, and capricious, perhaps. Aware of his power over his subordinates. Kept them guessing.

He went on his way. He had felt compelled to accept the invitation for the next night — not that he wanted to go. He felt he had been out-manoeuvred somehow when he tried to analyse what had just occurred. Quist hadn't told him anything. He had smoothly glossed over Dickens's enquiries. Nimmo's failure, Estcourt's failure — sorry, of course, but these things happen. People vanish from one's life. And how cleverly Quist had turned matters to flattery, to laughter and good cheer.

He thought about that sudden hard stare when he had referred to Pierce Mallory. Quist hadn't said he knew him, but, surely, he could have done. Estcourt and Nimmo were connected to Mallory. That look — brief, but something dangerous in it. Unsettling, certainly. Dickens wondered about the man behind that mask of bonhomie. The iron hand in the velvet glove? A man may smile and smile and be a villain. And who had been the man who laughed? The man who wasn't there. And a pair of frightened eyes. A man who dared not speak above a whisper.

On his way to Jones's house, his mind ran on and his footsteps beat to the sound of the words: Quist, fist, mist, casuist — egotist. Twist — that brutal synonym for hanging. He made a sharp turn onto The Strand. Twist. Quist.

26: ARABIAN NIGHTS

Supper was in the kitchen, where Elizabeth Jones was doling out eggs and bread and butter. Sam Jones was eating soup which smelt very appetising. Scrap had obviously finished his bowl and was addressing his egg. Tom and Eleanor Brim, the Jones's adopted children, were waiting for theirs. Dickens was offered the choice. 'Soup, please,' he said.

'You look as though you need it. When did you last eat?' Elizabeth asked. She liked to take care of him, knowing that his family would be in Broadstairs by the sea until Tavistock House was inhabitable.

'Breakfast,' he said, receiving his bowl and bread and finding that the smell of chicken and barley made him ravenous. He liked to be taken care of sometimes, too.

Out of the corner of his eye, he could see Tom Brim, who seemed to be taking an unconscionable time over his egg. The spoon burrowed in and out. Surely there could be nothing left unless it was Pandora's egg, an idea he was going to put to the little boy when he became aware that every spoonful of soup he ate was mirrored in the action of Tom's spoon, and the child was looking at him very speculatively. Tom Brim was waiting for him to finish and would not finish until Dickens had.

His curiosity got the better of him. He put down his spoon after the last mouthful. Tom put down his and continued to gaze at him. Those innocent eyes concealed some scheme.

'A question for me, Master Brim?'

A most engaging smile. 'A story, please, Mr Dickens.'

'Oh, Tom, Mr Dickens has hardly finished his soup,' Elizabeth said. But she saw the light in his face which banished the tiredness she had seen at first — that light which she had never seen in any other man or woman.

'No, no, it is quite all right.'

'Giants and goblins.'

'*The Arabian Nights*,' Eleanor suggested.

'Well, quite by accident, I do believe I have a story that might suit. There is a giant of a kind in it and it bears some likeness to *The Arabian Nights*. I have it about me somewhere —' feeling in his pockets, Scrap giving him a sceptical look — he had seen this performance before — 'ah, yes —' taking out an imaginary paper, unfolding it, smoothing it down.

No one spoke. They just watched the mime. You thought you could see it. It was magic.

The magician put on a pair spectacles and cleared his throat. 'This is a story about a palace not so far from here called The Great Temple — a palace made of sugar — which, rather inconveniently, has a way of melting in the rain, but it was there today. It may not be tomorrow. And in that palace lives an enormously fat prince called The Caliph Mustapha Quill —' he glanced at Jones, who returned an amused look — 'spherical like a globe. You could find out countries in him. He has a laugh that could move a mountain. He laughs a great deal and his hands are perfumed with ottar of roses — from the east, of course. He enjoys his sherry and his dinners and his cakes — he likes them best of all, and he eats a good many of them very greedily. A happy man, but a man with a secret — a secret that can never be told. And all who would find out that secret are doomed to death — sometimes by a poison that leaves no trace.

'He has an assistant — an invisible man who laughs, too. You hear his laugh — a neighing laugh, a sly laugh — in The Great Temple, but you never can see him. And there is a very tall, very narrow servant who speaks only in whispers. He does the writing for the Caliph, who is too busy eating and laughing to do it himself. The whispering servant is frightened of the Caliph and dares not disobey — he might if he could.

'One cold winter's day, a visitor came to The Great Temple in search of something he had lost — or rather someone —' now Scrap received that knowing glance and winked in return — 'a man who was known as Nemo, which means no name.

'But the great Caliph would tell him nothing — only that Nemo had loved and lost a princess, for she did not love him. Broken-hearted, Nemo had vanished from the face of the earth. The visitor had heard of the Caliph's magic lamp — rather like Aladdin's — and wondered if the Caliph and his invisible man had made Nemo disappear — perhaps the Caliph wanted the princess for himself.

'The visitor noticed a very nasty look in the Caliph's eye when he had mentioned another man named Lance, who had vanished. He thought he had better go, but the Caliph laughed and laughed, and invited the visitor to a banquet the next night.'

'An' that's all?' Scrap had been waiting for something a bit more tangible than this.

'Well, it is part of the thousand and one nights so it cannot all be told in one go, but there is an important question for the visitor which I want you all to consider. Should he go to the banquet?'

'Yes,' cried Tom Brim, 'there's cake.'

'No,' said Eleanor, 'I don't trust that Caliph.'

'Bad 'un,' Scrap was very definite.

'Ask the whispering man,' suggested Elizabeth.

'Offer him money.' Scrap knew the world.

'I shall have to sleep on it,' Sam Jones said, 'and so should you children. We'll decide tomorrow.'

'Very well, I accept your condition.' The magician's long, deft hands folded up the paper and it vanished into his pocket. But they had seen it, they were certain.

In the parlour, there was wine and a good fire. 'Bad 'un?' asked Sam, laughing. 'Very clever. I got the gist.'

'Of Quist — it's what happened, aside from a few embellishments. I went a bit far with the poison, perhaps — poetic licence, but there was something about him I didn't trust.'

'Nimmo,' said Scrap, who had slipped in behind Dickens and Jones. It was his case, too. 'That's 'oo yer meant when yer called 'im Nemo. Me an' Mr Stemp 'aven't found 'im — yet.'

'Did you find out anything?'

'Oh, a few folks know 'im. That Mr Dax thought 'e lodged in a place called Crook's Rents, but there's all sorts o' cheap lodgin's that way. We're goin' agin termorrer, but this fat cove — is 'e a bad 'un?'

'Something wasn't right — when I was waiting outside his office, I heard two people laughing. When I went in, there was only Mordaunt Quist.'

'''Oo?'

'The fat cove's real name. All smiles and jokes, but I'm not sure about him at all. I felt as though I had been outwitted, and he really did give me a hard look — very brief — when I mentioned Pierce Mallory.'

'But I gather from your tale, he asked you to dine,' said Jones.

'Yes, with his wife, too. I think he wants to know what I'm really after. I said I would go — it will give me a better idea of the man. I might be wrong.'

Sam chuckled, 'You? Never! Now, I must go back to Bow Street. I've something to check on.' He gave a meaningful glance to Dickens, who responded by standing up, too.

'Time I went. I'll walk with you. I'll see you tomorrow, Scrap, no doubt. Let's hope there's news of Mr Nimmo.'

'Tell Mrs Jones, Scrap, that I'll be back in an hour. Keep her company for me.'

In the street, Sam said, 'I wanted to tell you what the solicitor said about Carr Mallory. Before he went back to Ireland, he was a barrister in training at Middle Temple in the chambers of your Caliph.'

'Was he, by God? Well, well, Quist didn't mention that when I referred to Pierce Mallory. He must have known Pierce Mallory or of him. And Carr Mallory's shooting is in all the papers. Something odd there. He knows something.'

'It is odd. Carr Mallory married a clergyman's daughter, Letitia Spencer. He confirmed what Snee told us — her father committed suicide about eight years ago. You'd think Quist might have mentioned Carr Mallory — he must have known about his troubles and the shooting. He must read the papers.'

'He changed the subject. Very cleverly — oh, let's not talk about such matters when we've just met. Come to dinner — all very cordial. Flattering me, of course, but somehow, Quist didn't ring true. This clergyman, though, why suicide?'

'Debts.'

'His?'

'Now that I don't know. Carr Mallory and his wife returned to Ireland after the suicide and lived off Mrs Mallory. Suggestive?'

'Snee said there was gossip, but whether about the clergyman or Carr Mallory wasn't clear. What about the wife?'

'The solicitor said only that she was an invalid. I don't know in what way. I'm going to try to see Miss Leaf again on the pretext of wishing to see Mrs Mallory. I know she won't see me and I can't force her, but Miss Leaf might be forthcoming.'

'They are an unlucky family. Anything on the clergyman?'

'Not yet, but Inspector Grove found an uncle of Frederick Estcourt who hadn't seen him for a few years. Grosvenor Square — pretty well off, but had washed his hands of Estcourt, Grove gathered — always on the cadge, Estcourt, but the uncle did remember a Captain Bone, a Newmarket man with whom Estcourt was close.'

'The horses, eh?'

'Sounded like it, but the uncle didn't know where he might be except Newmarket.'

'I know a man.'

'You would. Who?'

'*Bell's Sporting Life* — the racing correspondent. Goes by the sobriquet, Pegasus. Knows all the form. Shall I try him?'

'Do. It's the inquest on Estcourt in the afternoon — it'll be adjourned like the others. No one saw you there, so no need to come. And, on the subject of inquests, Rogers saw the lion cub, but he couldn't tell him anything more about the man who watched.'

'Did he find out about the woman at the child's grave?'

'Nothing doing. Rogers found the record of the child's death and the address, but there's a different family there now — the name didn't mean anything. I mean, after fifteen years —'

'So someone else left those flowers, a convenient someone who had just got out of a bolted funeral carriage?'

'Very possible, but we can hardly go round to see Caroline Dax and ask if she's been putting flowers on a grave in Highgate Cemetery recently. That would alert whoever did it — if she's part of it. And you only saw the woman for a moment. It's not enough. Now, I ought to get back. I said an hour. I'll try Miss Leaf in the morning.'

'Fallen, do you think?'

'Give over — dried, more like.'

Dickens saw him downstairs. 'And tomorrow night's story?' asked Jones with a twinkle in his eye.

'Oddly, the sugar palace will have vanished.'

'You'd best hope for rain tonight.'

27: PEGASUS

It did rain in the night and it was still raining in the morning when Dickens wove his way to the premises of *Bell's Life in London, and Sporting Chronicle* at the top of Norfolk Street, just off The Strand — and a thick, muddy way it was under a leaden sky and rain coming down straight as knives and the world and his wife jostling, pushing, and poking with umbrellas, and the horses stock still, unable to go anywhere so jammed was the traffic, the road packed with carriages, carts, growlers, cabs, steaming horses — and steaming drivers and passengers.

The horse man he was after was Mr Francis Clarke, otherwise Pegasus, and famed as the writer of racing reports for Bell's periodical. If Captain Bone was an habitue of the turf, especially Newmarket, then Francis Clarke might well know him — or not. Mad idea, wondered Dickens, as a gampish sort of woman shoved by him, almost dislodging his hat with her umbrella. He begged her pardon for being in the way, but she was gone, and someone else shouldered by and he had no choice but to join in, barge on past Somerset House, and turn thankfully into the offices he knew very well.

He had been through that door many a time, for it was in *Bell's Life in London* that some of his early writing had been published under the pseudonym "Tibbs" — way back in 1835. The story of Miss Amelia Martin, the Drummond Street milliner was one and another entitled *Love and Oysters* — oysters, indeed. Fate at work again. He went up the familiar wooden staircase — the handrail was still rickety — and found a very inky lad to show him to the office of Mr Francis Clarke, who seemed to be all ink, too, and deeply engaged with his quill pen.

'Misserdick'ns,' the boy said and vanished.

'Charles Dickens.' He thought he ought to make it clear.

Francis Clarke looked up, astonished. 'Good Lord, that's what I thought he said. It is you. We haven't seen you up here in years. Good Lord, Tibbs.'

Dickens laughed. 'Fifteen at least, I was just thinking.'

'Racing tips for *Household Words*?'

'And lose my readers and their money. No, my dear sir, I'm looking for a man called Captain Bone, known at Newmarket.'

'You'd better sit down. I do know him — sometime race-card seller, tout, buys and sells horses, a wheedling sort of fellow, always promising the horse is worth more than he gets, whines that men don't treat him fairly, always knows a good 'un which he'd buy himself if the price weren't a bit heavy just now, but for a friend, well — and it's only fair that he makes a bit on commission. A man's got to live. Well, if the horse loses — uncertain in training — he told you that, and Chester or York, or Epsom — the going was heavy, of course. Talk his way out of a nosebag. But he survives, somehow. Has a cottage at Newmarket. That's where you'll find him. May I ask what you want him for, because if it's buying a horse, I wouldn't —'

'No, no, something else entirely — did you hear about Pierce Mallory's death?'

'Murder wasn't it? And his brother.'

'Yes, and the police are investigating another murder — it'll be in the papers — possibly connected. One Frederick Estcourt — I heard he was thick with Bone a few years ago.'

'Hm, I know the name — something shady about him. I'll do some digging. There's a race meeting tomorrow. Come down with me — I'll point out Bone for you.'

'I will. Any tips?'

'There's Prince Charley — no, I mean it — well fancied for the Criterion Stakes; Legerdemain, Perseverance, The Widow — unlikely, I think, however, and Strychnine —'

'What!'

'I know — but it's well-fancied. Owned by Sir Mordaunt Quist.'

Dickens could hardly breathe, 'The barrister.'

'The very one — named because of the Wainewright case. You know that girl, Helen Abercrombie, his sister-in-law, died of strychnine poisoning — at first it was thought that she'd eaten a bad oyster, then the doctors said congestion of the brain, or something.' Dickens could only nod. 'Quist was one of the counsel when Wainewright was done for fraud. Wainewright wrote for *The London Magazine* — Janus Weathercock. Janus, indeed. Transported for forgery, not the murders.'

Dickens managed a few words to the purpose. 'I saw him in Newgate — he looked a wretched creature.'

'He was lucky that the murders only came to light afterwards.'

'And Quist was involved in the fraud trial.'

'Yes — big man, now, in all senses. And a wag — he's always telling the story that Wainewright said he killed her because she had very thick ankles. "Neatly turned, my own," he says with that huge laugh of his. Strychnine's a good horse, though, second at Royal Ascot last year — Venom beat him by a nose.'

'Venom — dear Lord, and Strychnine — the names'd put me off.'

'Not at all —' Pegasus glanced at his paper, then grinned at Dickens — 'dead cert, Strychnine, ten to one, tomorrow.'

Ten to one, he's in it, somehow, except I don't know how, Dickens mused as he went back along The Strand, having committed himself to Newmarket. Now, Quist might be there watching his poison come romping home. Ought he to say something at the dinner? If the subject came up, perhaps.

Queer business about Wainewright — and oysters, again. Quist enjoying the story hugely. Dickens had to admit that he had laughed, too, about the ankles, but at that dinner, Doctor Locock had wiped the smiles off their faces when he had told them about the poor girl's sufferings, and about the deaths of Miss Abercrombie's mother and uncle of the same poison. Poor Locock, who had diagnosed pressure on the brain because strychnine left no trace. And Dickens really had seen Wainewright in Newgate — he remembered his untidy, sandy hair and dirty moustache. Something so mean and wretched about him. Nothing at all to laugh at.

Ten to one? What were the odds on finding out that Quist was in it? *Long,* he thought, *very long. Tonight then.*

28: STAGE

Dickens was aware of the echo of his own footsteps in the silent square; an odd feeling, as though his shadow were following him, keeping pace, a step or two behind, but always in time. He was almost tempted to look back. It was very late, night almost at odds with morning, but the dinner had seemed interminable and had not started until very late. Why, he could not tell. He had spoken to the Lady Primrose Quist, the earl's daughter, not as large as her husband, but whose voice boomed like his — a guffawing sort of woman with a plain face and plenty of money and nothing of a delicate bloom about her. She had made no move to the dining room, though he had a sense that her guests were becoming restive.

Quickswood House. A large house, naturally, a handsome house in handsome Cavendish Square. Handsome neighbours, too, a duke or two, a viscount, titled ladies — very aristocratic. The dinner — when it came — had been very handsome. A lot of money about — footmen — liveried; butler — grand old retainer; plenty of plate, branched silver candlesticks, fine crystal, the gilded earl's coat of arms on the crockery. The earl's town house, of course. Lady Quist's father, the Earl of Quickswood, was dead. The primrose path for Quist? Who was Quist?

And the dinner guests — some titles, a sprinkling of lawyers and judges, Members of Parliament, an eminent doctor from next door, some ladies — he knew some of them by sight. He had sat by Lady Soames at table, a soothing sort of woman, quietly spoken, who flinched occasionally when the booms came their way. He sympathised. His host had greeted him most cordially — "my dear friend, Mr Dickens" — repeating his joke about Sally Brass, his voice so loud that it sounded as though he were speaking through a brass trumpet.

Why am I here? Dickens had kept thinking, joining in the talk where he could. Matters of the day — the closing of the Great Exhibition — wholehearted approval of the spectacle; the knighting of William Paxton, the architect of the Crystal Palace — not entirely a matter of unanimous favour — the duke's gardener, forsooth, someone observed. *Humbug,* Dickens thought. Paxton deserved his title. He said so, and that the duke, whom he had the honour to know, had been delighted by the honour given to his architect. That shut up the purple-faced clown who had made the offensive remark. He looked away. Dickens's ear caught the marriage of Lady Henrietta Capel to a French Count; the birth of a son to Captain Cowper of the light or heavy cavalry — as if it mattered; an heir for a neighbour in Cavendish Square — there seemed to be a great deal of giving in marriage and getting of heirs — he could have read it all in the papers. Ah, death now — the Earl of Liverpool dead of a seizure. Pleurisy brought it on, opined the eminent doctor, Sir James Savage. Liverpool's title dies out, so said another — daughters inherit the lot.

He had been surprised to hear Lady Primrose's voice at that point, observing firmly that it was quite right. Quist applauded his wife with a booming, 'Hear, hear — my wife ought to be the Earl of Quickswood with her brains.' Lady Primrose acknowledged the compliment with a gracious smile, and on the talk went. Gossip. Gossip.

'He has no children,' Lady Soames murmured. Dickens felt a slight chill at his neck. Macduff's words about Macbeth. Macbeth who had murdered all Macduff's pretty chickens, but Lady Soames looked compassionate. She had daughters — and wondered what lives they would have, and he talked of his daughter Katey's artistic talent, and of Dora, the little dead one. Lady Soames looked compassionate again; then someone asked about her nephew in the dragoons and the talk turned on other topics.

At last it was over, and Dickens hadn't learned anything except that Sir Mordaunt Quist had no children, was highly respected, eminent, formidable in court, phenomenal memory, always good company etcetera, etcetera — everything that Snee had told him. By midnight, guests began to depart. Dickens was about to bid farewell to Lady Quist and make his escape when he felt a touch on his arm and looked down to see a soft white hand. He thought of slugs and almost wanted to brush it off. Sir Mordaunt was inviting him into the library to join a few others — brandy and cigars. A few young friends who came in after dinner — not all legal fellows, but he had promised them Charles Dickens. What could he say? He allowed himself to be led away — like some sort of captive animal for display.

A few young fellows — odd company for such an eminent man — about eight of them, man about town types, well-dressed, flushed with wine, who clapped as he came in. Dickens wondered if the laughing man were one of them, but he didn't hear that laugh amid the general good humour. Dickens had, as always, been very careful about the amount of wine he had taken. There had been generous helpings at the table, but he had very often put his hand over whichever glass was to be filled by the attentive footmen. He accepted a brandy for the sake of politeness. Sir Mordaunt Quist, he noticed, took only a little. The library was lit only by candles and there was a very good fire in the black marble fireplace. Deep red curtains were drawn at the windows. Dickens noted the well-stocked shelves and the large desk upon which were several of his own volumes and a copy of *Household Words*. Very flattering, he thought.

How soon the talk turned to murder, he couldn't exactly recall, but it seemed fairly soon that Quist had turned to him to observe that he had just seen Samuel Phelps acting the part of Macbeth at Drury Lane.

'Not a patch on Mr Macready — a close friend of yours, I believe. His farewell Macbeth last February — matchless, sublime.' The young men were in enthusiastic agreement. Several had seen the performance. 'And Mrs Warner, as Lady Macbeth, she rose to his heights. She acted Phelps off the stage the other night. A great loss to the theatre, Mr Macready.'

'We shall not see his like again,' Dickens agreed. 'When he came on, all that boisterous crowd became still water in a moment and remained so from beginning to end. I don't think I ever saw the part played with greater dignity and truth — or greater pathos.'

The young men agreed. Talk turned to Macready's King Lear, to his Coriolanus. 'Monumental,' someone said.

'Cold fish, Coriolanus,' Quist said, drawing laughter by his next comment, 'but what a mother — the formidable Volumnia, eh, under her thumb, I'd say. Lovely wife, though.'

'But is he a tragic figure?' asked another.

'Macready made him so,' Dickens said, 'but I don't think we feel the pathos of his downfall as with Macbeth.'

'Nor the terror,' an earnest young man joined in, 'you feel it so when Macbeth looks at his hands. "Will all great Neptune's ocean wash this blood clean from my hand?" That's the bit that gives me the horrors. Knowing you've done it and no turning back.' He turned eagerly to Dickens. 'Did you ever read De Quincey on the knocking at the castle gate? How he says that it brings home the separation of the murder from ordinary life, which restarts with the knocking at the door and —'

Quist interrupted, "'I am in blood, stepped in so far that returning were as tedious as go o'er —'"

He raised his hand and seemed to pass it under his nose. Did he smell blood — or just roses? *He has no children.* How queer that he had heard that at dinner. Dickens felt the prickle of the hairs on the back of his neck. Quist had said it with such a chilling emphasis.

'No, sir, if you'll forgive me,' the earnest young man said, 'that's not right — you make it sound as if Macbeth wants to go on — that word "tedious" should not be sarcastic. It's a terrible realisation — Macbeth understands what he has done —'

There was just a brief moment of silence as if they all waited for Quist to pronounce his verdict on the young man who had dared to contradict, but Quist chuckled.

'Ah, well, my boy, I'm not Mr Macready, of course, and must bow to your wisdom.' His tone was indulgent, but Dickens had caught a glimpse of something hard in his look in that brief pause, that look he had seen when Quist had asked about Pierce Mallory.

'Tragedy,' Dickens put in to divert Quist from the lad, 'one ought to feel the tragic inevitability and pity it.'

'A tragic murderer? Yet my experience contradicts even Mr Matthew Guard, here, and even Mr Shakespeare. Mean wretches, your murderers of today.'

'Do you mean that only a great man can inspire pity?'

'In such a murderer as a poet will condescend to, there must be some great store of passion, hatred, vengeance, jealousy — ambition —'

The young men looked in admiration — the words resonated in the room. Quist might have been in court — advocate for the defence. Quist bowed at the compliment. Dickens wasn't going to let him get away with it. 'Ah, De Quincey, again — such passion as "will create a hell within him, and into this hell we are to look."'

'Oh, yes, Mr Dickens has it right —' the eager young man again — 'Shakespeare shows us that hell in Macbeth.'

Quist was too smooth to show the slightest irritation. He simply slipped round a corner. Quist. Twist. 'Most murderers are grubby cowards — take Wainewright, I saw him in Newgate.'

'But he was an artist,' another of the young men put in, 'and a talented one, a poet, too.'

'Ah, murder as fine art,' Quist said, raising his glass to Dickens. 'De Quincey again, the connoisseur of murder. Most fascinating on the subject of the Ratcliffe Highway murders. Murder is not what it was, according to De Quincey.'

'For all that, John Williams was as sordid a murderer as Thomas Wainewright,' countered Dickens, remembering the dirty moustache.

'Wainewright, the poisoner — strychnine, which leaves no trace in the body.' Quist raised his glass to Dickens again. 'He got away with it, though, three murders. I wonder how many do get away with murder, as the vulgar tongue has it.'

The word "strychnine" led someone to ask Quist about his horse, and the talk turned to the races. Dickens thought it was time to go — he'd had enough, but he thought he heard someone mention Wigge, who liked a bet. He didn't dare move and was glad when Matthew Guard came over to speak to him. Was Mr Dombey, in his way, tragic? Mr Guard thought so, though Dombey hadn't grandeur, he supposed, but a man so profoundly mistaken as to his daughter's devotion — Dickens agreed, congratulated the young man on his perspicacity, listened to praise of Paul Dombey's death, the pathos of David Copperfield's time in the bottle factory, forbore to look at his watch — and all the time knew that he was being watched, or Matthew Guard was. He did not look at Mordaunt Quist, but he knew whose eyes were on them.

At last Dickens was able to extricate himself by consenting to receive Mr Guard at Wellington Street — with his writings — oh, Lord another author. A footman entered to tend to the fire and Dickens bade farewell to Quist, begging him not to disturb himself. The footman could show him out. He had no wish to bid a private goodbye to the man. If he saw him at Newmarket, then too bad. Quist did not move — he just raised his glass again. 'Mr Dickens, your company has been a joy — to us all.' The young men applauded him through the door.

Now in the quiet of the square, with only his shadow and echoes for company, Dickens felt a sudden loneliness and wished himself with his family in Broadstairs by the quiet sea. He thought of that fat white hand and shuddered. The man was a charlatan — "a joy", forsooth.

Fine art, he thought. *Humbug*. Yet, there was a good deal of artfulness about Quist. He had engineered the whole discussion, Dickens was sure. Why? Because he was enjoying himself, playing with his guests, young men easier to be played upon than a pipe, and Charles Dickens, too, laying the bait with talk of William Macready, knowing full well that he could turn the talk to murder. Clever, very clever, Sir Mordaunt Quist. And those references to Wainewright. Had it all been calculated? And the mention of Volumnia — did he know that Carr Mallory was under his mother's thumb? He'd relished that joke. Strychnine, which leaves no trace in the body. Were those part of some devilish plan? Quist hiding in plain sight? Cleverer, more agile, more subtle than Charles Dickens? Dickens did not like the idea at all, but Quist was a frightening man, he had to admit. And very clever.

Yet he had made a mistake. Mrs Warner had not acted with Samuel Phelps. It had been Miss Goddard. Had Quist really seen that performance at Drury Lane the other night, or had he used it deliberately to stage his own drama? What were the odds? Short.

And what had De Quincey said concerning *Macbeth*? De Quincey did not understand why the knocking on the castle door was so profoundly affective, but he felt it. Dickens had no evidence that Quist was at the centre of it all, but he felt it. He felt it.

It was in that very quiet spot by St Giles's Church that he heard it — that high-pitched, neighing, sneezing laughter. A man laughing in the dark. A borrower of the night.

29: ODDS

'Odds, 'evans, 'orrors an' 'ell.'

Jones couldn't help laughing, 'All of 'em?'

'Rolled into one. I didn't sleep a wink. I tell you, Sam, I couldn't wait to get away, but he's in it somewhere. All that talk of murder. He did engineer it, I'm certain — almost — well, you had to be there — I felt it,' he added, feeling the weakness in his case.

Superintendent Jones had listened to Dickens's news about Pegasus and about the dinner and the name he'd thought he'd heard. 'Wigge?' he asked.

'Could be — I mean, James Wildgoose said he had moved up in the world, but then I can't be sure. The law, though, Sam, it is a connection.'

'It's evidence we need, and it won't be easy to get at. The letters stolen from Estcourt could have been from Quist's office, but we've no way of knowing. That piece of sealing wax is no use — pity you trod on it.'

'The oyster shell,' Dickens countered mildly, 'I trod on that.'

'So you did. Apologies — 'umble.'

'Obliged, Mr Jones, but do go on.'

'Quist's a great man in his way. I can't go blundering in there, asking questions about murder — and, in any case, he's clever. It would only put him on his guard.'

'Matthew Guard — he was an intelligent young fellow and wants to come to see me — with his writing, of course. I wonder if he's at Middle Temple — I might get him talking.'

'Unless it was Mr Guard who followed you — and laughed in the dark. And remember, there could have been two men — the shooter and someone who drove the carriage.'

'Lord, Sam, I didn't think of that — and the woman at the grave just a genuine mourner ... but would he have asked to see me?'

'Why not? He doesn't have to come. All that flattering talk about your books to put you off your — guard.'

'Put on by cunning — and that laughter in the dark. Yet, when I think of it now in broad day, I do wonder if I mistook it. I admit he unsettled me. Perhaps I imagined it, but then —'

'What?'

'The conversation — that remark about Wainewright getting away with three murders and his question as to how many got away with it nowadays. Telling me, but not telling me, and then warning me off. Oh, I don't know — feelings, eh? Same with Nimmo, I suppose — I felt. I'm not helping, am I?'

'But, thinking — not feeling — Quist must know that you've been involved in murder cases with me. The Ferrars case — that made a splash. You there with the body —'

'You're right. I'll not forget Needle's cross-examination in a hurry. It was all in the papers. Not a warning — a challenge then?'

'Well, let's be careful about him. Don't go looking for this Mr Guard at Middle Temple — wait for him to come to you. We need your Mr Nimmo. He knows them all. Pity we haven't found that girl, Fanny Hatton, who could tell us what happened with Pierce Mallory — but let's leave his love life out of it. Go back to Quist.'

'Quist is linked, however tenuously, to Pierce Mallory through his brother, who was at Middle Temple as were Estcourt and Nimmo — all three having been at Quist's chambers. Quist keeps a horse called Strychnine at Newmarket where Estcourt's pal, Captain Bone, a dubious character, trades in horses.'

'All of them have something in their past — Pierce Mallory short of money — bad reputation about women, Estcourt living on the edge, left the law, dabbling in racing — debts there, I should think — Nimmo ruined, and Carr Mallory living on his mother —'

'Blackmail — suppose someone knew all their secrets and they've had to pay.'

'But why kill 'em off?'

'Pierce Mallory was supposed to have committed suicide, but when it was murder it led to Carr Mallory's murder because Carr knew something, and Estcourt knew something?'

'Miss Leaf couldn't tell me much about the brothers, nor, by the way, could she tell me anything about the clergyman father-in-law. Miss Leaf wasn't living with Mrs Mallory when all that happened. Mrs Mallory never spoke of it, nor did the others. Mrs Carr Mallory is a delicate lady, it seems, who lives a very retired life. I had the impression that Miss Leaf was not very keen on talking too much about her. But I'm working on it — the suicide would have been in the papers.'

'Something they wanted to forget, perhaps. I'll think about it, but I'd better be off. I'm meeting Pegasus at London Bridge Station for the express to Newmarket in time for the Criterion Stakes. Nearly three hours on the train. Pity you couldn't come.'

'Aside from what the commissioner would say about my waltzing off for a day at the races, we don't want Sir Mordaunt Quist — or his laughing friend — to see us together.'

'No, indeed.'

As Dickens opened the door, Jones asked, 'What's the odds on Strychnine?'

'Shortening all the time — I hope.'

'Not a winner,' Pegasus had declared, 'twenty to one.' Odds and Ends, owned by a Mr Gamble, looked all right to Dickens, who had declared that was the one for him. Strychnine did look good, all black and gleaming, but there was a wild look in his eye. The odds had shortened — four to one.

'One pound ten to a bob.' 'Thirty to one taken an' offered.' 'Fifteen pun to 'alf a quid.' So the different, raucous voices called, all honest men, no doubt, despite their uniformly cunning, covetous, calculating faces. Yahoos, Dickens thought. How noble and innocent the horses seemed.

But he hadn't been tempted to put money in Quist's pocket, despite the assurances of Pegasus. Prince Charley was scratched. He considered Lord Stanley's Legerdemain, remembered he hadn't liked Stanley much; thought about Perseverance; considered Lola Montez, last won at Whitby, owned by Mr Pearson, against whom, he reflected, he knew nothing. He thought of Pierce Mallory. No, then. Definitely not Hecate after last night. The outsider then, Mr Allen's Magic Wand, out of Sleight of Hand, at thirty to one. Five shillings to win. Pegasus looked very doubtful as they left the betting room for the stand at the end of the Rowley mile — actually nine furlongs.

'They're off — it's Strychnine.' 'Red cap! Green cap!' 'Here they are — it's Perseverance!' 'Red cap — it's Strychnine!' 'By jingo, blue jacket — it's —' 'Strychnine has it!' 'No, it's — by jingo — it's green cap —' 'No, Strychnine's in front —'

Strychnine led the whole way — dead cert, as Pegasus had said, until Magic Wand, by the jockey's sleight of hand, no doubt, came up on the outside, passing Legerdemain. Perseverance fell back, Strychnine faltered and green-capped Magic Wand came in by a head to a roar and uproar of disbelief from the crowd. Long faces in the betting room. Grinding of teeth. Blasphemy. Drink taken. Fortunes won and lost. Dickens thought of Quist. Unlikely.

'Tibbs,' said Pegasus, ripping up his ticket, 'you always were a lucky dog. That horse is for sale — buy him, pay the deposit with your winnings.'

Dickens laughed. 'Don't tempt me, but what about Bone — where's he likely to be?'

Pegasus explained that Bone would be somewhere in the betting room for the Cambridge Handicap Stakes. 'Thirty-three runners. If he has an owner in that, it's easier to disguise the horse's poor showing — too much bunching — couldn't get free — the horse would have done better with a smaller field — or unfair weight, of course — should have carried lighter — that sort of thing, but he'll be betting on his own account, you can be sure. Having a go?'

Dickens thought not, until he saw that Mr Frankum's Dolly Varden, out of Muley Moloch, by Pocahontas, was running. 'Dolly Varden?'

Pegasus laughed, 'No more chance than Bone's nags.'

Dickens protested that Dolly Varden had won at Newmarket in '49, only to be told that she had gone downhill since then — fifth last November in The Hopeful Stakes. Over nine furlongs for the Cambridge — hopeless. Pegasus was probably right — a good few horses had been named for his characters — Sarah Gamp, Betsey Prig, even Newman Noggs, and not much to say about any of them. Not since Walter Gay had won at Canterbury. Nevertheless, he did it — out of loyalty, and for Dolly Wildgoose. Barmaid was a no-hoper, according to

Pegasus. But Dolly Varden wasn't in the mood; she unseated her jockey and gave up the idea of winning. Fat as His Master took it. Oh, he would. Dickens lost his five shillings.

Pegasus nudged him. 'Over there — Bone — back to us.'

Captain Bone was in earnest conversation with a bandy little man with a head like a Dutch cheese, dressed in a fustian stable suit, who looked like a gone-to-seed jockey. Dickens noticed that he pocketed something, and the two shook hands. Bone started like a guilty thing as he felt the touch of Pegasus's hand on his arm. The bandy man faded away. Bone looked as if he would have done likewise had not Pegasus kept a firm grip on his coat. He gave a wary look at Pegasus who, of course, he recognised. 'Mr Clarke — good to see you.' A smell of whisky, a red-veined nose, watery, cowardly eyes, and a general spindliness of build — nothing but skin and Bone — suggested that the captain had probably never even been a corporal. He wore a cutaway coat, a speckled cravat pinned with a horse's head, and white trousers, the tightness of which was meant to be dashing, but proclaimed only his elderly leanness. The dirtiness proclaimed his time in a variety of stables.

'Mr Charles Dickens — the writer.' Pegasus introduced his companion. The wary look vanished under a spotted handkerchief and the face emerged again, all cordiality and delight in meeting Mr Dickens — bad luck about Dolly Varden. Mr Dickens had a bet, no doubt? He sympathised, but he had business to get on with if they'd forgive him. The wary look reappeared when Pegasus explained that Mr Dickens wanted to ask him some questions.

'Not about horses,' Dickens explained, 'about a friend of yours.'

Now Bone looked distinctly uncomfortable. Probably didn't have any friends, or, if he did, they were as untrustworthy as he. 'Oh, yes?'

'Frederick Estcourt, who has recently died. His friend, Mr William Thackeray — you'll have heard of him — *Vanity Fair* —'

'Good little horse.' Captain Bone on surer ground, brightening.

'Indeed, she is. Mr Thackeray and I are trying to find any next of kin.' Dickens had noted the relief on the mean little features when he'd said that Estcourt was dead. 'Your name was mentioned by Mr Estcourt's uncle. Are you able to help?' Dickens clinked the coins in his pocket. He had money to spare, thanks to Magic Wand. 'I wonder if we might go somewhere for a drink.'

Tempted by the promise of a drink and a tip, but cautious about giving anything away about himself or his connections, Bone weighed the odds. Dickens saw the conflict and kept a benevolent smile upon his own face. Pegasus kept a hold on the cutaway coat. Bone consented to go with them, not that he could have escaped, given that Pegasus and Dickens were either side of him like two gaolers. A refreshment booth provided whisky for the captain, beer for Pegasus and Dickens.

It cost him more than the price of the drinks — half-crown by half-crown, sip by sip — to tempt the information he wanted. Bone talked freely enough about Estcourt's fondness for the races, grew confidential — he, good old Boney, had put Estcourt in the way of a good horse or two, how they'd bought and sold at Tattersalls — grew wistful — good little partnership, money made until —' Another drink.

'What?' Five shillings on the table.

'A third party —'

A leap of faith. 'Sir Mordaunt Quist?'

Now Bone looked frightened. It took more money down — another five shillings on the table and a nearly full glass for Bone to answer with unconvincing vagueness. 'Quist? Quist? Oh, him as owns Strychnine — used to come down —'

'With Estcourt?'

At last it came out. Ten shillings more. Dickens didn't mind the expense — he'd got the money for nothing.

Quist — very free with his money — drinks, dinners, hotels — everything the best. 'T'was Quist who advised Estcourt to give up the law — use his talents in the horseflesh. Estcourt was glad to — easy money to be made — the law was damned hard grind. Went in for big things — connections, see, Estcourt — didn't forget his old pal, Boney. Then, somehow — he didn't know — Estcourt was in trouble. Quist sorted it out, paid off old Boney — decent of him, but Quist didn't know him now — Estcourt back to London — never saw him again. He didn't know, but Quist, he —

Another glass. Not driven snow — never claimed — old Boney an' Fred were all right. Fred overreached himself — no need — the watery eyes spilled over.

'No need, Mr Dickens, sir, no need. Quist never spoke to me again, not even when he comes down. Old pals. No need.'

Dickens put a sovereign on the table. It was time to go. The express was at 7.00 and Pegasus was fingering his watch. Laughter at a nearby table — a high-pitched, snorting laugh. Dickens didn't turn round, but he put his hand in his pocket again.

'Get out, Mr Bone.' He placed two more sovereigns on the table. 'Go to Ireland. Plenty of horses there.'

He and Pegasus left. He hoped the captain understood. He saw the little fustian jockey coming towards them and stopped him. 'Your friend, Captain Bone, look after him. Get him out of here. He has enough money.'

'Good of you, Tibbs.'

'Ah, well, it didn't cost anything. Poor devil.'

'Any use at all, what he said?'

'About evens.'

The train was crowded, even first class, but they squeezed into two seats among the mostly long faces, the smell of spirits, horseflesh, soot and oil. Some laughter, but nothing he recognised. Pegasus took out his notebook, jotting down his ideas for tomorrow's paper. Dickens sat and thought.

30: PLOTTING

Dickens was still thinking when he arrived at Wellington Street at almost eleven o'clock, exhausted and wide-awake. He prowled about his rooms, trying to make sense of what he had heard. On the train he had pondered. A novel without a plot — as if you had laid the ground, introduced your characters and didn't know what to do with them. A familiar experience. Very often you couldn't get the people of your imagination to do what you wanted. They would insist on working out their own secret histories in their own way. Secret, indeed.

He sat at his desk, listening to the windows rattling. The rain had returned, lashing against the panes, and the wind whistled in the chimney. It was the time of year for high winds and storms. An unruly night. The night of King Duncan's murder, a storm prophesying confused events. What was to come? He felt cold suddenly and put some coal on the fire. Macbeth again. Quist again. And a drama of his making.

A play whose plot was so obscure that no ending could be discerned, leaving the audience completely mystified by the end of the second act. How many acts were there to be? Here were the leading actors. He pushed about the pens, the inkpots, rulers, sealing wax, seals. Here was Pierce Mallory, next to his brother; here was Estcourt and here Nimmo, and Bone, and Quist all in a row. Leading ladies? Add Fanny Hatton, Caroline Dax. Two mistresses. Jealousy? Revenge?

He moved fat inkpot Quist front of stage and pounce pot Estcourt with him. Quist, who had spent freely on Estcourt and his pal. So what had happened that had ruined Estcourt and left Bone out in the cold? Estcourt who lived off someone,

Estcourt who thought Dickens was a debt collector and almost told him to go to — let's call him Quist. Money?

Treat a man, indulge him and his shady pal, advise him to go in for horseflesh. Wait for the crash? Bring about the crash? Then you have him by the hip — because he was a threat to you? Another motive: to remove an object dangerous to the murderer's peace?

Dickens moved them about like puppets on a toy stage — inkpot Quist now in the centre; pounce pot Estcourt; quill pen Carr Mallory; small inkpot Pierce Mallory; sealing wax Nimmo. Dickens muttered to himself: motive, motive — murder, money, debts, reputation, scandal, love, law. Were they all a threat to Quist's peace? He thought of the earl's handsome house and the gilded crests, the silver, the servants. A lot to lose, Sir Mordaunt Quist.

He picked up his last character — a little seal. He'd almost forgotten him. Wigge — cheat and fraudster. Wigge was no longer at Doctors' Commons. Legal adviser to prosperous men. Wigge set up with Caroline Dax. And here she was. He put a stick of wax next to Wigge. He stared at them for a moment or two. Thought about possibly hearing the name Wigge at Quickswood House and put them both in the circle that surrounded Quist. Twist.

"Neither twist Wolf's-bane, tight-rooted, for its poisonous wine." Keats had written that.

News came the next morning after a restless night, during which Dickens had dreamt of horses ridden by Sarah Gamp and Dolly Varden and all the rest. A race that never ended and was never won. And the oddest thing of all was that all the horses laughed and snorted as they went by, showing their huge yellow teeth to him. Laughing at him.

Two letters arrived first thing. One from Thackeray, who asked Dickens if he knew of a barrister called Sir Mordaunt Quist — Pierce Mallory knew him because his brother had been at Middle Temple. Quist might be able to tell him about Carr Mallory. It might be worth seeing the man...

Too late, thought Dickens, but then he read on and felt a good deal better, for Thackeray seemed to recall that it was through Quist that Pierce Mallory had taken up with Caroline Dax. Caroline Dax who was connected to Solomon Wigge, whose name was mentioned at Quist's house. Wigge, the legal adviser.

The second was just a short note from Pegasus: *Found the details about Estcourt. Come to see me about the Trueboy affair.*

Dickens was up the rickety stairs in ten minutes. Pegasus wasted no time.

'A betting scandal back in '47.'

'Trueboy was a horse, I take it.'

'He was, well-fancied for the Derby, trained at Newmarket by one Tom Dunning, whose son, William Dunning, was a jockey — won the Criterion Stakes. In brief, William Dunning was to ride Trueboy. He and another man — and this is why I wanted you to know — one Frederick Estcourt — cooked up a scheme to bet against the horse. The buzz went round that Trueboy hadn't a chance of winning. Of course, others — names not known — took bets against. At the same time, the two conspirators got up a rumour that Trueboy was in with a very good chance — this to make certain that the considerable betting against didn't look suspicious. There'd be betting for the horse, as was expected, given Trueboy's form.'

'The jockey knew it would lose because he'd be riding it.'

'He and Estcourt stood to make two thousand pounds apiece, and the others a decent profit, too.'

'Tempting.'

'Very. However, anonymous letters were sent to the owner of Trueboy about the scheme. The owner told his friend, Sir Robert Bascombe, a big man in the Jockey Club. An enquiry ensued. William Dunning and Frederick Estcourt were banned from any Jockey Club premises or any place where the rules of the Jockey Club were in force. The two bookmakers who took the bets were exonerated.'

'What happened to Dunning and Estcourt?'

'Dunning went to Australia. Nobody knows what happened to Estcourt. Just vanished.'

'Was Bone in on it?'

'He probably knew about it — probably had a bet, but his name didn't come up.'

'And Bascombe?'

'Dead, I'm afraid — heart attack in 1849, but he's interesting as far as your matters are concerned. First, his reputation, his absolute commitment to making improvements in the racing business. He introduced stringent rules against defaulters and any corruption — betting rings, sudden injuries to horses, drugs — that sort of thing. A martinet — any sniff of cheating and he'd be onto it and no quarter given, anonymous letters or not.'

'And second?'

'Family — fifth son of the Duke of Mortland, only two left now, but the Duke, still with us, and Bascombe married the sister of the Earl of Quickswood.'

'Quist's father-in-law.'

'Oh, yes, very high connections, Quist.'

'And some low ones. But, whoever sent those anonymous letters knew there'd be an enquiry and knew his man in Sir Robert Bascombe.'

Dickens thanked Pegasus and swore him to secrecy on the matter of Quist. 'I'll give the information to my policeman friend, but it's too delicate a matter for anything to get out prematurely.'

'You have my word, Tibbs. Don't leave it so long next time. I'll bet on the outsider next time we go racing. Sleight of Hand, eh?'

Going by Wellington Street on his way up to Bow Street, Dickens was surprised to see Betsey Ogle hesitating on the doorstep. She turned at his approach.

'Miss Ogle, anything wrong?'

'Somethin' wrong about the doctors' rooms, sir. I can't get in. I didn't know what to do fer the best.'

31: DUST

Superintendent Jones made short work of the locked door with his skeleton keys. Betsey Ogle had told them on the way that she hadn't been in for weeks — them noises, see — and then her conscience pricked when she thought that Doctor Sage's son might come to inspect them. Do a bit o' dustin', she'd thought, but her keys was gone from the hook in the kitchen.

Betsey was shooed back to her kitchen while Dickens and Jones went in. The doctor's office first: a desk clear of any papers, some cabinets and sets of drawers, but nothing of any note. However, an open door led into what had been a small library judging by the shelves, though there were not many books left. A circular table with drawers, open and empty, and dusty except where it had been brushed away to accommodate some cutlery on a plate, on which there was some congealed gravy. A dirty napkin on the floor. An easy chair of old leather by the fireplace. Ashes in the grate — cold, but there were some loose matches on the mantelpiece, a full coal scuttle, and an empty wine bottle on the hearth and a glass with the lees of some dried-up red wine.

'Wigge?' whispered Dickens.

'Someone has stayed here and not so long ago. Who else? Very secret and convenient — but why?'

'Keeping an eye on Caroline Dax. I was coming to tell you. I had a note from Thackeray this morning. He seemed to think that Quist had something to do with introducing Caroline Dax to Pierce Mallory.'

'Quist knows Wigge. Quist knows Caroline Dax?'

'Thackeray seemed to think so. I wonder if —'

'He put Wigge onto her — and she's been missing for six days.'

'Someone else who knows something about Mordaunt Quist?'

They went through another door into a little room with a water closet concealed behind a screen, and a sink and tap. A cake of soap, not recently used, and scum in the bowl, and a dry towel on a roller. Sam unlocked another door, which led into a small garden. Beyond the gate, there was an alley and some mews.

'He could come and go as he liked. Out the back, round the front to call on Mrs Dax,' said Jones.

'Unless she knew, and he sneaked up there at night when Betsey was asleep.'

'Maybe she did. Betsey said she heard noises in the doctor's rooms — she'd have told Caroline Dax, I'll bet.'

'And Caroline would have agreed it was best not to go in there. Perhaps they consulted Mr Wigge on one of his calls and he agreed that it wasn't safe to go in there.'

'It doesn't matter if she knew. I've had a thought. Since Caroline Dax vanished, you've seen Quist at his office where you heard that laughter, and you thought you were followed from his house —'

'And I heard it at the races, when I was questioning Captain Bone.'

'Go and ask Betsey Ogle.'

Dickens came back within minutes. 'Queer laugh, it was, very 'igh-pitched fer a gentleman, but always in good-humour, Mr Wigge. Dark hair and eyes. Very charmin'.'

'So where was Caroline Dax when Wigge was on your tail?'

'Lurking down — oh, God, Sam, the last we heard of her was when she left her child with her father. He didn't know

where she went. Six days ago. A stolen key — a locked door —
'

Jones looked down at the dirty napkin and then at what looked like sooty footprints coming out from the kitchen. 'Coal dust,' he said, 'coal cellar.'

Outside, there was a trapdoor under which there was a chute where the coalman emptied the sacks. There would be a door from the kitchen scullery into the coal cellar, where Betsey would fill her scuttles for the kitchen range and the upstairs fires.

Sam squatted and shone his lamp down. He could see the heap of coal glinting. The coalman wouldn't look. He would know from the order how many sacks to empty. Jones ordered a ton of coal every month for his house and he never looked down the chute. He leant in as far he could. There was something white, something revealed when the coal had slipped as Betsey had taken her shovel to the pile near the door to the kitchen. But it wouldn't have mattered, because a new ton of coal could have covered it up again.

Jones looked back up at Dickens. 'Find a stone, if you will, something heavy that I can throw down.'

Dickens looked round the garden, found a largish stone and handed it to Jones. They heard the rattle of the coals below as they shifted on the impact. Jones leaned in again. His lamp picked out the white, bigger this time — something edged with lace. It looked like a woman's petticoat.

Constables Stemp and Feak dug her out from the kitchen end. Doctor Woodhall's assistant cleaned her up. Dickens and Jones stood with the doctor in the mortuary at King's College Hospital, looking down at Caroline Dax's dead, bruised face.

'She was last seen six days ago,' Jones told Doctor Woodhall.

'I can't tell you anything yet, though the bruising suggests that she was thrown down there. She would have suffocated.'

Dickens felt the familiar choking sensation which sometimes afflicted him — it was thought of entrapment, imprisonment in the dark. What a dreadful end. He did not dare ask how long she might have lain there, knowing that she could not get out.

'She might have been unconscious, of course.' Doctor Woodhall lifted her hand. The hands were still blackened, but he observed that there were no signs of any struggle to get out. 'I might expect the hands to be wounded if she had —'

'Yes, I see,' Jones interrupted. He had seen Dickens's face. 'The man who put her there knew when the coal delivery was to come — that was five days ago, according to Miss Ogle, who is the housekeeper at Mrs Dax's lodgings. The day after Mrs Dax was last seen. Miss Ogle had ordered one hundredweight. He knew she would be covered up. The coalman would just empty the sacks down the chute and Miss Ogle would have no reason to look — she just shovelled the coal from the door that led into the kitchen.'

32: GRIEF

'Where to start?' Dickens asked wearily when they were back at Bow Street. 'Dear God, Sam, what a terrible thing. Worse than the strychnine poisoning, if she were conscious.'

'I know. Put it aside for now and start by telling me about the races.'

Dickens gave his account of his day and ended with the possibility that Quist had sent the anonymous letters to Trueboy's owner, knowing that the matter would come before Sir Robert Bascombe.

'Ruined Estcourt yet supported him — a bit contradictory, though.'

'Suppose that Estcourt did know something about Quist — as we thought. And Quist turned the tables on him, but kept him close, so to speak. Did they all know something about Quist and somehow he ruined each of them, so that they could never tell for fear that their own stories would be told — held in mutual fear until —'

'Carr Mallory's debts. I saw the solicitor who told me that they were gambling debts. His father-in-law, the Reverend Spencer paid them and ruined himself in the process — borrowed heavily, couldn't pay back — committed suicide.'

'And Carr Mallory's wife doesn't know that they were Carr's debts, but Quist does? Because Quist was behind those debts. Carr Mallory leaves London, but Quist has that hold on him. Mrs Carr Mallory could never know that her husband caused her father's suicide. That suicide which maybe turned her into an invalid.'

'Then something happened that meant that they had to be got rid of. Pierce Mallory is the first victim. He is the key, and the man at The Lion and Lamb who is not Quist. The lad would have remembered Quist.'

'Wigge? He wasn't laughing that night, I'll bet.'

'I should say so. Carr Mallory asked his brother to act for him — that's what he meant in the letter. Remember, Charles, he wrote that he'd be glad if Pierce would prepare the way — but carefully. Was that because he knew Quist was a tricky customer? Let's say Pierce wrote to Quist, who sent Wigge to find out what Pierce Mallory wanted.'

'Immediate expenses, Carr Mallory said. It would have been to tide Pierce over while he took the first steps. Carr was coming to London before his brother's death, and that's why Pierce Mallory came from Paris instead of going straight to Constantinople, and why he was living in that out of the way place, and why he met Wigge — as we surmise — in the pub.'

'Pierce Mallory made demands — we don't know what about — but they signalled danger to Quist.'

'They found out something about Quist? Fraud? Legal chicanery? Quist lied on oath or summat?'

'If he has done something shady, then he has a lot to lose. Pierce Mallory told Wigge that Carr Mallory was coming to London — another danger, especially when the murder was found out.'

'And, after two murders, why not finish off Estcourt, too? Quist quoted Macbeth to me: "I am in blood stepped in so far" —'

'No turning back. What the devil is it that they knew?'

'Something pretty serious — for murder. Did Caroline Dax know something about Quist?'

'Which is why, perhaps, Wigge took up with her at Quist's instigation.'

'I wonder if she made a mistake by sending for me — she was meant to keep her head down, but she was greedy and overreached herself. Boasted to Wigge that they could make something from Pierce Mallory's rich friends.'

'And famous ones — drawing attention to herself and Wigge. She went to Pierce Mallory's house a few nights before the murder. I'll bet that wasn't intended. And, Charles Dickens, suppose she was your woman at the cemetery. Now that would make her a danger.'

'And I walked straight into the whole thing by going to see Quist at Middle Temple — and Wigge was there. He must have been. I heard him laughing, but there was only Quist in the room — Wigge was somewhere, I'll bet, and he overheard my asking about Pierce Mallory. He followed me, and I was at the races. Dear Lord, Sam, is Quist one step ahead all the time?'

'He's keeping an eye on you. We need to find out more about Quist — on the quiet.'

'I know a lot of lawyers —'

'Only someone you can trust — with your life. I mean it. If he's at the centre of these murders, then he's ruthless. And Wigge is, too — think what he's done already.'

Dickens nodded. 'The daring of it at the cemetery, and the cruelty of it — Caroline Dax in that heap of coal. He knows no bounds.'

'We need to come at them by very crooked ways.'

'Talfourd — he's a bencher at Middle Temple. You know, one of those that run the place. A parliament, they call it. Anyway, that doesn't matter. He'll know Quist. Bound to. Judge Talfourd. I know him very well.'

'Good idea. I've met him. Remember the police constable, Cole, who was had up for murdering a man called Cogan in Plum Tree Court?'

'Den of thieves, as I recall. Talfourd was the judge.'

'Every witness had been had up for something — pickpocketing, assault, theft — the lot. One man didn't even know his own name. Thought it was Burke, but he usually called himself Sullivan. They made the whole thing up, but Mr Talfourd summed up very fairly, and the jury listened. Cole was acquitted.'

'He is fair, and as good a man as you could find in the law. He'll tell me what he thinks about Quist and he'll keep it to himself. I'll go round to Russell Square this evening.'

'I'll go to see Montague Wildgoose again,' said Jones, 'find out about Wigge's frauds. You'd better keep away, and away from James and Dolly Wildgoose. I'll send Rogers to warn them to be on their guard about Wigge. No mention of you to anyone.'

'And Nimmo? Any news?'

'No — Scrap could be looking until doomsday. I think that's a dead end.'

'Unless I go — I've seen him. I'd know him again — oh, Lord, Sam, Mr Dax. He doesn't know.'

'Good God, we'd best get along there and tell him.'

'What a thing, Sam, to have to tell him that his daughter was found dead in a heap of coal.'

Barney Dax seemed to be looking at some imagined distance down which, Dickens knew, he would see a child, a little girl with golden curls, wearing a pinafore and looking at him with wide, trusting eyes. Barney had said nothing as yet, only stood absolutely still as if to brace himself against a terrible wind.

Sam Jones stood still, too, near the back of the shop. Dickens had offered to tell the news. He had broken it as gently as possible, but nothing, he thought, could prepare a man for such a horror.

'Someone — put — her — there?' His voice seemed hoarse suddenly. He sounded like a man who had been silent for an age, for whom words were unfamiliar and had to be tested, as if he did not know what they meant.

Dickens sat him down on a rough stool and offered his brandy flask, but Barney Dax did not recognise what it was. He tested out more words. 'Someone — killed — her?'

'We think so — the doctor thinks she may have been unconscious. There were no signs of a struggle.' Dickens mentally crossed his fingers, hoping that Woodhall would say that was true.

'Who?'

'We don't know. It may be connected to Pierce Mallory's death.'

'She was such a pretty child — so — the only one — so innocent then. I wish —'

Dickens offered him the brandy again. 'Please, Mr Dax, take some. It will steady you.' Barney Dax took a gulp and shook his head, and then he looked at Superintendent Jones.

'You'd best tell me the truth. You must know something.'

Jones came forward. 'There was a man she was involved with — a Mr Solomon Wigge —'

'She never said. Oh, what mess has she got herself into? She never told us anythin' an' I knew it wasn't right — the life she chose — but rags, see — rags — yet we still loved her. She was our daughter — flesh an' blood — an', oh, the boy — the boy —'

242

'He is very young, Mr Dax, and he has you and Mrs Dax to care for him now.'

Barney Dax looked at Dickens, and in that look there was a painful recognition of a truth. 'He never asks where she is. I don't think she cared —'

'It might be so,' Dickens said, divining his meaning. 'Pierce Mallory didn't care for her and little Alfred is his child. I can understand, in a way, that Caroline resented him — a reminder, perhaps, of what she had lost, of the chances she might have had.'

'Mebbe, Mr Dickens, mebbe. I know you mean to be kind, but she found another fancy man and left her child behind. She wasn't comin' back. I knowed it. Married, is he, this Wigge?'

'We don't know — we don't even know whether that is his real name, but we do have some information about him, and we will find him,' Jones said.

'There'll be an inquest?'

'Tomorrow at the hospital in Portugal Street, near Lincoln's Inn. Do you know it?'

'I'd like to see her. It's fittin'. I don't know what I oughter think, but she was my girl, an' I hope, Superintendent, that you'll find out who did it. She didn't deserve any man to do that to her.'

'She did not, Mr Dax. Come tomorrow morning at nine o'clock. I'll be there.'

Barney Dax stood up. 'I'd best tell the wife. Thank God we have the boy. It'll be something — it'll be everything now.'

They left him still standing in his shop, looking again into an imagined distance. Dickens glanced back and saw him square his shoulders, run his fingers through his hair, and turn towards the door at the back of the shop. *Thank God for the boy, indeed*, he thought.

33: ON GUARD

Jones went off to see Montague Wildgoose and Dickens returned to Wellington Street, where he found Matthew Guard was waiting to see him — which might be providential, Dickens thought. He looked the earnest, serious, scholarly young man as he had at Quist's house, and he certainly could not be Wigge, but he ought to be careful about discussing Quist. The young man might be as guiltless as a naked new-born babe whose tears might drown the wind, but — and that talk of Macbeth came back to him — he might well be the serpent under the innocent flower.

They squelched through the rain for a late lunch at The Rainbow in Fleet Street, and there Dickens learnt of the young man's ambitions. Like Simon Jarvis of The Athenaeum and a dozen others who showed him their works, Mr Guard wanted to write — as well as rise in the legal profession. The law was, however, extremely dull at times, but he had to keep at it — his uncle demanded it. A Dean, did Mr Dickens see? Mr Dickens nodded to show that he did. An Uncle Dean of wherever might well make demands on a young man.

Mr Guard continued — many men wrote as well as practising law. Judge Talfourd was his ideal — poet, playwright and writer on the law. Naturally, the Dean admired the latter, but to have written a tragedy performed at Covent Garden — had Mr Dickens seen it?

Mr Dickens had read it — a copy given to him by the author—

Oh, of course, Mr Talfourd would make a present to his fellow author — and Talfourd's sonnet to Lord Denman in *Household Words* — such noble sentiments —

Dickens let him rattle on about poetry, and the more he heard, the more he believed that this young man was not a creature of Quist's making. He risked a question. 'And Sir Mordaunt has an appreciation of the drama, has he not? Another literary lawyer.'

'Oh, yes, though I still think he was wrong about Macbeth the other night.'

'Ah, yes — you know him well.'

'No, not at all — I had heard of him, of course, and I was invited by a fellow lawyer from his chambers — it's open house, apparently. And Sir Mordaunt had invited some of his young men to meet you. My friend, knowing my interest, assured me that Sir Mordaunt would welcome me — and he did, sir; he was most affable to us all.'

'You are not at Middle Temple?'

'No, no —' Matthew Guard blushed and took a sip of his wine — 'I'm in training — to be a proctor at the Court of Arches —' Dickens hardly dared speak — Doctors' Commons again. The mysterious Mr Wigge. He let the young man go on in his bashful way. 'You know all about it, Mr Dickens, I know — er — David Copperfield, you see. Training to be a proctor like me, though I think he had a better time than I am having. Your stories of old ladies in mourning being pounced on by touting clerks never seems to happen to me. It would certainly break the monotony. Sir Fabian Ramsey — the chief, you know, is very severe.'

'Keeps you at it, I daresay.'

'Indeed. I am deep in Waddilove's *Digest of Cases* — baptism, bonds, brawling —'

Dickens laughed. 'Ah, I know the sort of thing — quarrelling, chiding, or brawling are offences if they occur in any churchyard? But, oh, the vestry is tricky —'

'Just what I've to give an opinion on now. Suppose a meeting of the vestry committee takes place in a public house, are the blows exchanged an offence subject to ecclesiastical jurisdiction?'

'Is a public house consecrated ground?'

'Not this one.'

'Only to the drinkers. Was it The Angel?'

They spent a few moments exchanging potential consecrated grounds at The Mitre, The Cross Keys, The Lamb and Flag or St Bride's. Dickens congratulated Mr Guard on his ingenious suggestion of The Jerusalem Coffee House and finished with The Crutched Friars. Dickens liked Mr Guard, he thought, and now he was relaxed and laughing, it was time to ask a question about Doctors' Commons.

'Did you ever come across a fellow named Solly Wiggins — sometimes called Solomon Wigge?'

'The man who they said stole the wills.'

'So I believe — someone told me about it when I was doing a bit of research into Chancery cases —'

'For a new book, Mr Dickens? You're investigating the law —'

Mr Guard was looking at him, awestruck. If Dickens were not careful, the talk would go along paths that he had no wish to tread just now. 'Yes, wills and so forth — mysteries, legacies, that kind of thing. Did you know him?'

'No — he was in the Prerogative Office, but I heard of it. He's not there now, but I came across him with my friend — the one who took me to Sir Mordaunt's house the other night.'

'He wasn't there that night?'

'I didn't see him, but I met him at The World's End — a pub near Doctors' Commons. It's popular with the clerks. My friend introduced me to Mr Wiggins — said to call him Wigge. A nickname, he said — Mr Wiggins was known for his skill in the law.'

'Your friend from Sir Mordaunt's chambers?'

'Yes, he knows Wigge pretty well, I think, though —' Matthew Guard's face clouded — 'I didn't really take to him, and after what I'd heard about the fraud — well, he seemed very sure of himself. I wondered —'

'I haven't met him,' Dickens said reassuringly, 'you can speak freely if there's something worrying you.'

'Well, it is. I should like to confide in you, Mr Dickens, if I may — if you have time.'

'All the time in the world, Mr Guard, if it would help.'

'I'm not — that is — I don't — my uncle, the Dean, supports me — it was he who wished me to study ecclesiastical law — he found me the place at the Court of Arches. I was eighteen — it takes seven years, Mr Dickens, to become a proctor. I am twenty-three now and it's dull work at times, as I've said.'

'Except for the brawling — livens things up a bit, I hope.'

Matthew Guard smiled as Dickens hoped he would, but became serious again. 'I'm a dull dog, I suppose. I've never been one for going about. I lodge with my great-aunt, but Henry Porter, my friend, thinks one should see a bit of life. We were at school together, and he persuaded me to have a night at The World's End. It was all a bit much — a lot of drink, and I spent money that I don't have. There were cards at a casino—'

'And you find that you owe Mr Wigge?'

'I don't quite know how it happened, but Henry said not to worry. Mr Wigge wouldn't press me, and then the invitation came to Sir Mordaunt's. Henry said he would be a fine contact to have if I wanted to rise — and I do, Mr Dickens. I thought it was a fine thing to meet Sir Mordaunt — and it was. All the talk of the plays and so on, but —'

'Something happened.'

'It was decided that a group of us should go to — a club. I didn't want to, but Henry insisted. Sir Mordaunt encouraged us — we ought to have a good time, he said, all work and no play etcetera. He seemed to think I ought to have some fun. Never mind the Dean, he said, and he'd —'

'He knew your uncle is a Dean?'

'Henry told him, I suppose. Anyway, they all thought it a huge joke — all sorts of puns on apron strings — you know, the bishop's apron and all that —'

'I do.' *Oh, I do*, he thought, and Matthew Guard was to be tied up in another kind of string, no doubt. He didn't know why, yet, but the story was very like Nimmo's. Matthew Guard looked thoroughly miserable now. There was more, Dickens was certain.

'I had not meant — I never thought I would be able to tell anyone, but to be telling you, Mr Dickens, I don't think I can. What will you think?'

'I will think that you have been misled, that mischief has been done, and that you have been taken to where you did not want to go. Now, tell me, and I promise to advise you honestly.' Dickens looked the young man in the eyes, where misery and guilt contended and the blush flamed in his cheeks again.

'There were girls — of a type I hadn't met before. Flashy girls, confident girls who liked their drink, too. Most of the men paired up. I wanted to go home — I don't know many girls, except my cousins at the Deanery, and they are — they tease me, but only gently —' Matthew Guard swallowed hard, blushed even more deeply. 'Henry and his girl introduced me to another, and, I don't know — I didn't wake until the early hours. I didn't know where I was. Somewhere off Drury Lane — in a bedroom. The girl said I'd — she was so distressed. I couldn't bear to think that I'd —'

Dickens had a sudden thought. 'The young lady — did you find out who she was?'

'Henry seemed to know her — but I don't know her name — I'm so ashamed. Henry said I wasn't to worry. He told me Wigge would see to it all — I thought he meant that Wigge would give her money.'

'And the bill has come in. Your Henry, no doubt, advised you to borrow from Wigge on the Dean's security.'

'How? I see, of course, you know about life, Mr Dickens — you know about borrowing without the means to pay —'

'I do indeed. I have met Mr Micawber many times, and his youthful counterparts.' *Brother Fred, for example*, Dickens thought. How much he knew about debt and its miseries, but Matthew Guard was speaking again.

'I feel such a fool. The Dean can't know — what am I to do?'

'Firstly, let me have your writing and I will see whether I can publish any of it. Second, you can write something for me — about the wills, the wives and the wrecks — perhaps about your brawling cases. See what Mr Waddilove's *Digest* has to say, but brighten it. A touch of humour and fancy is wanted — perhaps a story of two brawlers, their wives, their children. See what you can do —'

Matthew Guard cheered up. 'Oh, I will — it will be the greatest pleasure, but —'

'I know. I will lend you the money you need to pay Mr Wigge, but you must do it through your friend, and you must ask for leave of absence from your work. You must escape the clutches of Wigge, or he will ruin you, of that I am certain. I doubt you are the first. Now, the next part of my advice must be taken on trust. I cannot explain my reasons for what I am to advise you, but, Mr Guard, you came to me. You have told me your woes and I will help you, but on the condition that you obey without question the injunction I am going to place on you.'

Matthew Guard stared at Dickens. He felt almost afraid for the first time in his company. He seemed so genial, so full of humour, but now there was a force in his eyes — a kind of fierce blaze which compelled him to feel that he must obey. 'I will do as you ask.'

'You must leave London. Where have you friends or relatives?'

'I have a cousin who lives in Manchester.'

'Excellent. You will send your friend the money, but you will not say that you are going. He will believe, perhaps, that your disappearance is to do with the shame and guilt you felt —'

'He won't care, Mr Dickens. Of course, our friendship is an old one, but I know now that we are poles apart. In the telling of my story, I see that I was his dupe as well as Wigge's.'

And Sir Mordaunt Quist's, Dickens thought, but it was safer not to mention that name. 'And you must never mention my name in connection with this matter, nor must you discuss any of it with anyone, however close your connection. There is danger at the heart of this — grave danger. You will hear from me in some weeks, I fancy. Now I will return to my office in

Wellington Street. Call in half an hour's time and ask for Mr Wills. He will advance to you the sum that you need. You will write to Sir Fabian at the Court of Arches, and you will take the train to Manchester this very afternoon. Have we a bargain, Mr Guard?'

Matthew Guard took the proffered hand and felt the firmness and warmth of its grip. Then Charles Dickens was gone.

Dickens did not even glance at the papers Matthew Guard had given him. All that mattered was the lad's safety. He might be a writer, he might not, but Dickens had no doubt that he would pay back the money somehow. In the meantime, most pressing was the question of Mr Wigge and Sir Mordaunt Quist, who were bound together in wickedness.

Quist. Setting aside whatever it was in the man's past which had prompted the murders — and he could understand that motive which desires at all costs to remove an object dangerous to the murderer's peace or good name, or that which he has gained through fraud or treachery — why should Quist risk his gains by ruining young men?

He thought of Lady Primrose, that large, plain lady, daughter of an earl. No children. So there was an obvious reason for Quist's liking for the company of young men. Such things happened. He thought about the admiration and the deference of those young men at Quist's house. Perhaps that was all it was — that Quist basked in the attention of his audience, and ambitious young men were prepared to give it. How far would any one of them go? Lady Primrose had not looked at her husband with anything but good humour — no adoration there. None of the women at the dinner had seemed particularly drawn to Quist, but then there was the idea that he had passed Caroline Dax on to Pierce Mallory. Men and women to his taste? To Wigge's taste? A little line in blackmail? Wigge and Quist? He'd have to ask Talfourd if there were any rumours about Quist's love life.

But suppose not. Matthew Guard had contradicted Quist — there had been that moment when Quist's eyes had shown that malevolent look. "Mr Dickens has it right," Matthew Guard had said, and Quist had watched them. Quist, whose dramatic flair in court was well known, Quist whose friends and neighbours thought highly of him, Quist known for his wit and his learning. Quist who had tried to best Charles Dickens over the matter of De Quincey's words on murder, Quist to whom all must defer. Suppose it was simply power, the power to raise or to cast down. When a man spent his life ensuring that another man — or woman — went to the gallows, then that man might well enjoy such power beyond the Central Criminal Court.

Stepped in blood so far that he had no idea when to stop. All causes must give way to his own good. Egotist. Intensely self-absorbed, like every murderer. That's why they never saw the consequences of the act, why they never gave a thought to the victim — beyond the victim's threat to that monumental self.

'Quist,' he said out loud, putting on his coat to set out to see Judge Talfourd. The very word was like a spell, as if the man were an enchanter weaving his unholy charms around his followers — those young men, and Nimmo, Carr Mallory, even Estcourt. Even Wigge. Caroline Dax. Fanny Hatton? 'Quist?' The name was like a question. 'Who?' you wanted to answer. Wist. Who wist? Who knew? Hist — a warning. Danger. On guard.

In Russell Square, a woman was selling matches, a poor ragged tiny girl on her arm. He stopped to buy some. The child looked at the coins and formed its little mouth into a kiss. A sweet little face, and innocent. He thought of Mrs Ellis's baby and dropped another sixpence into the woman's hand. 'Thank you, sir,' she said. 'Kiss,' the baby said, looking at Dickens, 'kiss.' And he obeyed, taking the tiny hand in his — it was just bones.

He walked on. That little thing, so innocent and hopeful of kindness from strangers. Your heart could break. Just a kiss. Kissed. Quist. Good God. Doctor Elliotson had heard the letter 'K' on Carr Mallory's dying lips. His wife was Letitia. Or Elliotson thought he heard the 'K' — not so fast, he told himself. But still. Quist?

34: LEGACY

He hurried up to Bow Street. Sam needed to know all this, and fast. Talfourd had not been able to tell him anything much about Quist's character — except that he was a clever, clever lawyer whom Talfourd did not much like. 'It's all about him,' he told Dickens. 'He enjoys it too much. The power of it all.' And no, nothing said about his sexual proclivities — if there were any. Plenty of young men about him, that was true, but then you didn't always know about a man's private life. Often, you didn't want to know. Many a blind eye and a deaf ear in chambers when it suited.

However, Talfourd had pointed him in the direction of a retired lawyer living in Bedford Square, whither Dickens had sped on that advice. An old lawyer, a very old one, infirm in body, but with a memory as long as a three-volume novel. And he had remembered Quist from twenty years ago. As he walked, Dickens tried to put his thoughts in order for Sam. He had been so astounded that all thoughts of Matthew Guard had fled, but he did remember to call in at Wellington Street, where Wills told him that he had advanced the money and that Mr Guard's message was that he was leaving for Manchester that evening.

Superintendent Jones's response was not disappointing. 'Ireland!' he exclaimed at Dickens's first hurried sentence. 'Quist came from Dublin?'

'County Dublin, Talfourd said, a place called Loughlinstown. Of course, I thought of the Mallorys. That envelope told that they came from Dublin County — Kiltiernan. Talfourd had a map, so I ventured a look —'

'And the two places are near?'

'Near enough, my boy, for it to be suggestive. Now, let me try to tell all succinctly. Talfourd knew that Quist had studied at Trinity College Dublin, and that he had been married before the wood nymph — Lady Primrose,' he added, seeing Sam's raised eyebrows. 'More about her in a moment. The first wife died, it seems, and Quist came to London with all the right credentials — money, I mean — and bought himself into the chambers of William Langton, well known at Middle Temple —'

'When are we talking about?'

'Twenty-odd years ago. Langton's dead, before you ask — wealthy man, but enormous debts. Paying two thousand pounds interest on them, but no one seems to know what he spent his money on.'

'And Quist his partner — very interesting.'

'So it is. Anyhow, Quist takes over, moves in high circles, marries the Earl of Quickswood's daughter. Older than he. Quickswood dies. London house and other property go to Lady Primrose. Quist's luck was the general feeling, but Talfourd put me on to an ancient lawyer who did business for Quickswood and remembered Quist, of course. Shrewd old body. Did wonder about the marriage, but Quickswood wanted her married and getting an heir, otherwise the title would go to some distant cousin. And there was talk that Quickswood had debts.'

'Quist had the money — the lady had a title.'

'They live in style now — not the case, apparently, before Quist married her but, here's the interesting thing. The earl did have money to leave as well as the London house to his beloved daughter.'

'Ah, a will.'

'Indeed, surprise all round, so the lawyer said, the old earl having a tidy sum to leave — must have forgotten it.'

'Not in his right mind?'

'Invalid, certainly after a lifetime of drink and cards, but died peacefully in his own bed underneath the heraldic shield of his forbears, his devoted daughter at his side. No questions asked.'

'The abbey and the title?'

'In the event of no direct heir, Quickswood Abbey — Surrey seat of the earls thereof from time immemorial — would go to the new earl, the distant cousin, in some distant future. Not much to write home about, the abbey, it seems. Falling about their ears, which seems to suggest that there were money troubles. However, Quickswood's will was very clear that all other property and monies should be inherited by his devoted daughter, and then the heirs of her body — male or female. If male, then, of course, the remote cousin would be out altogether, and the abbey would go to the infant of her union with whomever came galloping along on his charger.'

'How old was she when she married?'

'Nearly forty.'

'Optimist, the earl.'

'The will found and proved in Doctors' Commons. Unusual for a woman to inherit everything except the family seat. Women do inherit sometimes. I heard at that dinner that Lord Liverpool's daughters inherited his property and fortune, but that title dies out, which is not the case here. Lady Primrose approved heartily of daughters inheriting.'

'I'll bet she did.'

'However, no one could gainsay the will.'

'And how easy it is to practise a fraud. Mr Montague Wildgoose, under some persuasion, told me all about it. As we saw, you pay to see the will — easy enough to substitute another if, perhaps, you have some inside knowledge.'

'Quist has plenty.'

'Wigge? Mr Wildgoose told me about the frauds that his nephew mentioned. A few years ago, there were letters in the papers from a man who had been one of the chief clerks at the Prerogative Office. He was complaining that over a period of years, wills had been lost after they had been copied — no proof of what the original wills actually said, but the correspondent pointed to the scandal of lost wills involving property and estates to the tune of thousands and maintained that the losses had been concealed from the public. It seems that the registrar and his deputy in those far off days are now dead, but a scapegoat was needed now to answer the charges made by the former senior clerk. One clerk was censured for his carelessness after enquiries were made about the present situation and he left — and Wildgoose admitted reluctantly that, and I use his words, "If it was the object of any person to purloin a will or substitute a will, such a thing might be accomplished."'

'And the clerk was…?'

'Mr Wildgoose confessed that it was Solly Wiggins, our Mr Solomon Wigge, who, as Wildgoose was at pains to point out, left of his own free —'

'Will, indeed. When?'

'Wiggins departed in 1845, but the scandal of the wills had been going on for years and years.'

'Something shady about the earl's will?'

'We'd never prove it. That is, if somehow a substitute was provided for the earl's true will. But why would there be? Quist had money.'

'Quickswood House, though — he wouldn't want to give up that to some distant cousin — a magnificent house in Cavendish Square, and all those aristocratic neighbours — neither would Lady Primrose, I'll bet. And think how the earl's daughter, the house, the portraits, the earl's crested plate and china would be the signs and seals of probity and integrity. A very good bargain for both of them. She gets her legacy and he gets an unassailable position in society.'

'And no case against Wigge, either.'

'Damnably not. Of course, it might not have been him and Quist, but the connection between them is there. Wigge and Caroline Dax, and Wigge was instrumental in introducing Matthew Guard to Quist. I'll tell you all about him later. Wigge went quietly because they didn't want any more enquiries into missing wills, and he knew he'd be looked after by Quist.'

'Speculation, I might remind you. We can't go forward without evidence.'

'What about Ireland? Something fishy about the first wife? Quist, the grieving widower, comes to London with his pockets full of gold —'

'So what? Same trick — no evidence.'

'I tell you what struck me. The old lawyer remembered all about the property — as lawyers do, but he couldn't tell me anything about Quist the man, as in his background, nor could Talfourd for that matter, except that he didn't like him; only the Trinity College part and the first wife — all very vague for a man of such substance.'

'The law directories for Ireland — where'd we find them?'

'Lincoln's Inn Library,' Dickens answered, already turning to go.

'Who do you know?'

'I blush modestly, Mr Jones, but Mr Spilsbury is the librarian and I have dined with him. Moreover, I have praised his treatise on the history of Lincoln's Inn and its library, of which he is rightly proud. A few words of humble astonishment and eulogy from you and he will give you the moon.'

The moon, however, was not in Mr Spilsbury's gift, and neither was the name of Mordaunt Quist. Mr Spilsbury, having heard Mr Dickens's close friend, Mr Jones, express his awe at the magnificence of his library and its windows, its shelves, its busts, its thousands of volumes, was quite prepared to allow Mr Dickens to consult The Irish Law Directory. Just a brief look was all he needed — a mere checking of a detail for something he was writing. Oh, no, he did not need Mr Spilsbury's assistance, but he was obliged.

And it wasn't very speedy, for they had to trawl through all the barristers and the solicitors. There were several Quains, two Quartermans — should that be men? Dickens couldn't help asking, nor being distracted by Mr Fetherston Quartermass. Queales aplenty. Dermot Quick — and dead, alas, Dickens observed. Peter Quince, a comic turn, no doubt, but not worth knowing at the moment. However hard they looked for the name in the years they thought might be applicable to the young Quist, he was not there. No one in the lists of practising lawyers went by the name of Quist.

'He was someone else,' Dickens speculated. 'Maybe he took his wife's family name when he married — people of property, maybe. It's not uncommon. No need to put his nose to the grindstone of the law. Changed his mind when he came to London — with a fat inheritance from the dead wife?'

'Unless he wanted to leave himself behind when he came to London.'

'Something disreputable in his own background? Oh, look there.' Jones looked to where Dickens's finger pointed at the last of the names under the letter 'P'. 'William Mordaunt Purefoy.'

Jones read on. 'Entered in 1820 — so practising when we think Quist was about. *Who's Who* gives Quist as fifty-two years, so we're assuming he would be practising in the 1820s. Perhaps he knew this chap and stole his name.'

'Unless Purefoy's a relative.'

'Not much use. There's no address given. We could find your Fetherston Quartermass in Merrion Square — we could find most of 'em, but we only want Mr Purefoy.'

'Dead?'

'Knowing our luck, probably.'

'Yet, Talfourd definitely said Trinity College. He must be in their records — he must have trained in the law. He can't be masquerading as a lawyer and really be a waiter, or something.'

'And I'm not waiting to find out. It's time Mrs Volumnia Mallory answered some questions. She must know something about our Quist. Carr Mallory was in his chambers. Nearly neighbours, according to your map. Perhaps she can tell us who Sir Mordaunt Quist was before he married into the family.'

'Quist. Kissed.'

'His wife?' Jones asked, astonished.

'Why do I doubt that? No, it was something I was saving up if the moment came. I can't get his name out of my head, and every time I think it or say it, I rhyme it — with twist, or fist, or something, and I came up with kissed. Elliotson thought he heard the letter "K" —'

'As Carr Mallory was dying.'

'His last breath on earth — the dying man's gasping accusation —'

'Or just choking.'

'If I'd written it —'

Jones grinned at him. 'Stranger than fiction — but not evidence, I'm afraid. Elliotson can't swear to it.'

35: DROWN-DEAD

Mrs Volumnia Mallory regarded her visitors with icy disdain. She looked exactly the same in her deep black. She sat perfectly still and straight as before, and Dickens wondered in what way she had been affected by the murders of both her sons. There were no tell-tale signs of weeping, no falling in of that marble countenance, no softening of her freezing gaze. Miss Leaf, somewhat desiccated, seemed to tremble beside her as she put down her teacup with a slight rattle.

Superintendent Jones showed Mrs Mallory the last paragraph of Carr Mallory's letter. He had thought that it would be too insensitive to show her son's words about "her claws" and the "petticoat rule" he had chafed beneath. After all, she had lost both her children, and to find that her favourite son had betrayed her to the loathed one would be too cruel.

'Human heart, eh?' Dickens had said, quoting Mr Lion's words.

'She probably hasn't one, but —'

'Yer niver knows what lies beneath.'

Now, Sam Jones wondered about that heart as he watched her scan the words. When she had finished, he asked, 'I wonder if you have any idea what is meant by the words referring to Mr Carr Mallory's intention to come to London and his asking his brother to pave the way?'

She was sharp, too. 'Where is the rest of the letter?'

'I do not know,' he lied. 'This portion was found in an envelope addressed to Mr Carr Mallory, poste restante in Kiltiernan.'

'You have been through my son's letters?'

'It is my job, Mrs Mallory, to find evidence in the pursuit of whoever killed your sons.'

'And will it bring my younger son back? Are we to have our family's name dragged through the courts, my older son's disreputable life blazoned in the newspapers, his debts, his love affairs, his illegitimate children —' Her eyes blazed now, and Dickens saw the red spots on her cheeks. She felt something, then. 'What good will it do for my grandchildren? Pierce's son will inherit my estates. He has been protected from his father. And is his name to be defiled? They have brought it upon themselves — both of them.'

'Why both?' Jones was quick.

But she wasn't to be caught. She had gone further than she had wanted to in her anger. Dickens thought of Thackeray's words about Stephen Ellis and his children — the inheritance of a notorious name was a burden, but Pierce Mallory was a victim. His reputation and his illegitimate children would be forgotten. Mrs Mallory would see to that, but surely she saw that Carr Mallory deserved justice.

'There are other victims,' Dickens said.

She ignored him and addressed Jones. She had recovered her poise. 'Then investigate those, if you must.'

'I am doing so, but I must ask you again if you can shed any light on Mr Carr Mallory's intention to come to London.'

'I have no idea. I imagine that he had come once more under the malign influence of his brother, who, no doubt, had some dishonest scheme for raising money.'

'Mr Carr Mallory had debts?'

'I supported him and his invalid wife. He had no need for money. It would be his brother's notion.'

She had probably known that he'd wanted to escape her, but she wasn't going to admit it. Nevertheless, Jones pressed on. 'I would like to know if you are familiar with the name "Quist"?'

Miss Leaf uttered a brief exclamation.

Jones turned to her. 'You know the name?'

'Of course she does,' Mrs Mallory interjected. 'Mr Quist was the barrister to whose chambers Carr was engaged when he had a mind to pursue a career in the law. Carr was recommended to Mr Quist by his tutor at Oxford. I have not heard the name for years.'

'Miss Leaf?'

'It's just that people named Quist lived at Loughlinstown. You remember, Volumnia, Mr Lawrence Quist owned the lead mills at Ballycorus. They had a daughter — there was a tragedy —'

'Lead mills, Emmeline, how would I have anything to do with lead mills? I don't remember any Quists, but then we would not have connections with such people. In any case, how would you know about them? You hardly go anywhere.'

'No, no, but Miss Frances Quist was a pupil when I —'

'I doubt that the superintendent is interested in your modest scholastic career, and it can hardly be anything to do with a barrister in London.'

'It may be, Mrs Mallory,' said Jones. 'I should like Miss Leaf to tell me what she knows.'

Miss Leaf blushed and trembled under her cousin's frosty glare, but the policeman looked like a man who was going nowhere until she answered. 'Miss Quist was a pupil boarder at the seminary where I was employed — gracious, it was in the 1820s — but I do remember — a dear girl, but rather spoilt by her wealthy parents. She eloped with a young man from Trinity College, a friend of her brother's. They both studied the law.'

'Do you recall the young man's name?'

'William Fagan.' Fagan — Fagin, thought Dickens — the thief and fence, and corrupter of young boys. Good Lord, Carr Mallory had written about Fagin's kitchen. 'He was a poor young man who was supported by a connection of his father's. His father had been a draper in Dublin — or, perhaps it was his grandfather — but he had fallen on hard times, so the connection —'

'A name?'

'Such tittle-tattle, Emmeline — other people's business is not yours. It is just the kind of thing I hate.'

Jones was firm. 'A name, Miss Leaf, please.'

'I remember, you see, Volumnia, because my colleague, Miss Fitzgerald, spoke of it when she came to tea some weeks ago — she lives now by the sea in Dalkey, Superintendent, and Volumnia was kind enough to let me invite her — and, of course, we spoke of old times. There had been a death in Miss Fitzgerald's family — a bride, you see, drowned only a few days married, and it reminded us of that old tragedy. We were all so shocked at the time. Such a pity — so young —' Here she faltered and dabbed at her eyes. Mrs Mallory remained unmoved.

'And the tragedy of Miss Quist?' Dickens asked quietly, seeing her distress.

'Oh, well, Miss Quist and Mr Fagan ran away together. The Quists were very angry, for they believed that Mr Fagan was a fortune hunter,and even Mr Mordaunt Purefoy cut him off —'

Dickens didn't look at Jones. He merely asked as if in general enquiry, 'Mr Mordaunt Purefoy was the young man's sponsor?'

'He was the lawyer, you see, but he would have nothing to do with the matter. When Miss Quist and Mr Fagan were caught up with — in a hotel in Meath — well —' Miss Leaf blushed even more deeply — 'her father had to agree to the marriage because —'

'He'd ruined her. A foolish girl, no doubt, with the romantic notions of her class. I suppose the draper's son became a bad husband,' observed Mrs Mallory with characteristic acidity.

'Oh, I don't think so — there was the tragedy, you see. Her parents, Mr and Mrs Quist, and their son were drowned in a yachting accident. Very dreadful, and it was very complicated, for Mr Quist's will left a good deal of property and money to his son, and money in trust to his daughter, but, of course, it wasn't clear who had died first — in the drowning, I mean. They were all buried together, you see, in Loughlinstown. In any case, I don't suppose the young man made a will, though he was betrothed. I can't quite remember all that, but fortunately it came out that Mr Lawrence Quist had made another will after he had become reconciled to his daughter's marriage to Mr Fagan.'

'Another will was found?'

'I don't recall exactly, but Miss Fitzgerald seemed to remember that Mrs Fagan, who was Miss Quist, found the paper in her father's prayer book. Her father was a lawyer.'

Patience, thought Dickens. 'Miss Fitzgerald's father?' Miss Leaf nodded.

'What a lot of nonsense you talk, Emmeline, what paper?' Even Mrs Mallory wanted to know the end of the garbled tale.

'A deed — that's what it was — a deed which was signed by her father and dated, and in which he revoked the first will. As it was in his prayer book, I suppose he meant it. A man wouldn't —'

'Really, Emmeline —'

'The original will which established a trust for Miss Quist.' Dickens interrupted to clarify the matter.

'Oh, yes, Mr Dickens, very kind — that is so. This new deed, so Miss Fitzgerald said, made Miss Quist heir to her brother if he passed before her and died childless — which, of course, he did — being only betrothed, you see. And Miss Fitzgerald said that it was quite correct — she thought that Miss Quist had every right, for Miss Fitzgerald's brother had always come before her, just as my brothers came before me, and if it were not for Volumnia —'

'Never mind all that, Emmeline. I should like to know, Superintendent, what on earth any of this has to do with me? It happened nearly thirty years ago and such an incoherent tale —' here Mrs Mallory fixed poor Miss Leaf with a withering look — 'can hardly assist you in a murder enquiry, if that is what you are about.'

'I do not know, Mrs Mallory, if it is of any use, but, with your forbearance, I must ask Miss Leaf something more. Miss Leaf, did Miss Fitzgerald remember if the deed was signed by a lawyer?'

'Oh, yes, her father was quite sure of that. Being a lawyer, you see, he would remember. Oh, it was all very satisfactory, and Mrs Fagan, who was Miss Quist, was able to sell the lead mines to the Mining Company. They should have been very rich and very happy, but, of course, Mrs Fagan —'

'Died?'

'Oh, no, Mr Dickens, no, it was worse. You see, they were not aboard the yacht because Mrs Fagan was expecting a child. She lost her baby when the news came that her family had perished. She never recovered and — well — she had to be confined to the asylum.'

Dickens thought he hardly dared hear any more. Good Lord, if that was Quist's secret — fraud and bigamy — no wonder. Jones was asking about Mr Fagan.

'I don't know, Superintendent. Miss Fitzgerald said that he was so grief-stricken that he went away. People said he'd gone to America — or Australia — or was it Africa? A long way, anyway. The house was sold and that was the end of the story.'

Mrs Mallory rose. 'And that is the end of my patience, Superintendent. I am returning to Ireland tomorrow, and I will thank you to remember my family's reputation as you go about your trade.'

She swept out, leaving Miss Leaf to gather her sewing and her wits in preparation to follow, but not before Jones shot in another question. 'And the asylum? Is Mrs Fagan still confined?'

'It was St Patrick's in Dublin — it's called Swift's after Dean Swift, you know, *Gulliver's Travels*. You wouldn't think a Dean would write — oh, but I don't know if she is still there. It is a long time ago, and we didn't discuss it because Letitia — that is Carr's wife — was rather exhausted by all the talk — she is very delicate — and then it was all rather sad, and she might have remembered her father, who committed —' Miss Leaf blushed — 'a clergyman — I mean, he was — Lemuel, you see — he was Lemuel like Gulliver, but he was Goddard, of course — so Carr took her upstairs, and then it was time for Miss Fitzgerald to go. Indeed, Carr came back and very kindly offered to drive her to the railway station instead of Malley — he's the groom, you see.'

'Oh,' Dickens said casually, 'Mr Carr Mallory was present at the tea?'

'He came in to see if Letitia was managing, and we were just talking of Miss Quist so he joined us — not that he usually cared for ladies' teas — but he knew how much I valued Miss Fitzgerald, so he stayed and showed great interest in the story.

Now, was that not kind?' She put her handkerchief to her brimming eyes. 'Oh, I shall miss him. So kind.'

'One thing more, Miss Leaf, and then we will leave you in peace. Did Mr Fagan have a sister?' Dickens was remembering Nathaniel Snee's reference to Quist's joke about his sister.

'Oh, no, Mr Dickens, he was an only child.'

'To Fagin's kitchen,' Dickens raised his teacup. 'Quist knew the name "Mallory", I'll bet. Took Carr Mallory on, knowing who he was. Keeping him close.'

'And Carr Mallory only had to mention idly one day that there had been Quists in Loughlinstown, and did Sir Mordaunt know them,' Jones said, taking a gulp of his tea. They had repaired to Dickens's rooms in the office at Wellington Street — a quiet place to mull over what they had heard.

'So, the debts — the net drawn about Carr Mallory. He had to be got rid of back to Ireland, with his own secrets and in such disgrace that he would hardly want to mention Quist again.'

'And then, years later, he finds out that Quist is a bigamist. He must have learned more when he kindly offered to take Miss Fitzgerald to the station, so he wrote to his brother about it all.'

'No more danger from Quist and Carr Mallory can come back to London, a free man, so to speak. Mrs Volumnia and the wife neutralised. And Pierce, always impetuous, never heeding the consequences, approached Quist — Quist sent his henchman to The Lion and Lamb, and Pierce, in drink again probably, said more than he ought. We'll keep your secret and you must swear never to reveal Carr's.'

'You knew Pierce Mallory. Would he ask a price for their silence?'

'Oh, Mr Jones, that letter —'

'Carr Mallory seemed to think there was money coming.'

'And Pierce had his money worries. Blackmail to the blackmailer — Quist wouldn't like that. A threat to his power.'

'So they had just found out that which could ruin Quist. What about Estcourt?'

'Estcourt knew the Mallory brothers, and that was dangerous. Pierce Mallory murdered. Carr murdered. It's what Brutus says about Caesar, "and lest he may, prevent." Equivocation, they call it —'

'Of the fiend, in his case. However, fiend or not, we need proof, so who do you know in the lunatic line?'

Dickens spluttered over his mouthful of tea. 'Elegantly put, Mr Jones,' he said when he had recovered. 'I take it you mean someone sane enough to find out what we want to know — that is, if Quist's first wife is still alive, and, if dead, when she died — before or after the marriage with Lady Primrose.'

'And, if he was, in another life, Mr William Fagan, the student of law at Trinity College.'

'Where in the records anybody interested in Quist's university career would find him, because Mrs William Fagan's brother, the bona fide Mr Quist, so to speak, will be there — conveniently at the time William Fagan was there, and, equally conveniently, dead. How can we find out?'

'Mr Mayne — he's a Dublin man —'

Dickens laughed, 'Sure he's Mayne? Any skeletons in any cupboards?'

Jones grinned back. 'Locked tight as the Bank of Ireland, I should think. I was going to say he could write to whoever's in charge there. I shouldn't think there'd be much change for a Superintendent of Bow Street. I wonder how many Fagans there are, though.'

'It'll be easier to find out if Mrs Fagan is still confined.'

'How so?'

'Mr Bryan Procter — otherwise the writer, Barry Cornwall — in the lunatic line — Commissioner of Lunacy.'

Jones looked at him consideringly. 'A commissioner, is he? And, of course, you know him.'

'Yes, to both. I'll go round to Lincoln's Inn later. I can ask him if he will write to St Patrick's to ask about Mrs Fagan.'

'On what pretext?'

'He's a playwright, he'll think up a plot.'

'So, those two birds can be set to flight. In the meantime, what about these wills — the second deed? I'm inclined to believe it.'

'Wainewright was a forger as well as a murderer — forged signatures to power-of-attorney documents to get hold of a legacy. Mind, he didn't get away with it.'

'Quist cleverer?'

'It takes nerves of iron, I should think, but we know Quist has those. That clergyman, William Bailey, Sam, remember him?'

'I do — forged a promissory note by tracing a signature on a receipt he'd got hold of. He might have got away with it, had one of his witnesses not admitted that he'd been part of it.'

'Highly respectable, too — eminent, in fact. Very popular with his congregation. Who'd have thought a clergyman? And, as I remember, of Trinity College Dublin. There was the Ricketts case, too. Who'd have thought the admiral's son would have forged his father's will? And Lady Ricketts in it, too. Who would think an eminent barrister — wife an earl's daughter etcetera —'

'Audacious, though, but then you have to be, and in Quist's case, the circumstances must have been very fraught.'

'Yes, here's a girl mad with grief at the loss of her entire family. Here's a young husband, accepted reluctantly into the family. Family drown-dead. But, the father's will leaves all to the brother — who maybe made a will in favour of his betrothed — but that young husband knows the law, and hey presto, here's a deed — or another will — in a prayer book, leaving the lot to his wife. Who'd have thought?'

'I wonder, though, who signed the deed — Miss Fitzgerald's father said that a lawyer had signed it.'

'Quist got away with it — someone must have been paid off, perhaps.'

'We'll never know. It's the possible bigamy that's the important thing, and proving that Sir Mordaunt Quist is William Fagan — and that won't be easy.'

'Because those who knew, or might have known, have been eliminated, except Nimmo — Nimmo, by God, is he in danger?'

'You'd best take a look tomorrow with Scrap after you've seen Mr Procter. I've thought of a Trinity College man I know — similar age to Quist, and Irish as they come.'

'Who?'

'Queeley O'Shea.'

'Diet of shamrocks, is it?'

Jones laughed. 'I know it sounds improbable. O'Shea's a lawyer, lives in Bolton Street — or lived. I met him years ago. He'd not long come from Dublin. Case of fraud. He might know something — that story of the elopement and the yachting tragedy. There must have been talk in Dublin. I'll try him tomorrow — I can leave Mr Mayne out of it for now, thank the Lord. But first I'll see Mr Dax at the mortuary.'

'Am I to come?'

'If you will.'

'He knows what she was, and yet all that is cast out by her death.'

'Unlike Mrs Mallory. She knows all about Carr — prepared to support him — to use him to run the estate for the heir, but not to forgive him, even after death. I don't think I've ever had a case in which a victim's relative does not want it investigated. Barney Dax, rag-dealer, asks for justice for the girl who abandoned him, but land-owning Mrs Mallory cares only for her name.'

'Pride — so inflexible that she didn't even ask who the other victims were, though, if we were to be charitable, there are Pierce's children to think of. Thackeray said what a legacy Stephen Ellis would leave if he had murdered Pierce, but — what are you thinking?'

Jones was frowning. 'Could the Mallory brothers have known about the Quist tragedy? That would make nonsense of everything. If they knew, they wouldn't have waited all these years —'

'They might have known the name — it's not a common one. As you said, Carr Mallory might have mentioned it in passing, in a casual way, but they were children at the time. Pierce would only have been about six. Quist was long gone to England by the time those boys were taking notice of anything but their toys. Mrs Volumnia didn't know them. Suppose Quist did put it about that he was going to America — or Australia — very convenient, if you want to be forgotten.'

'Thank God for that — I had a horrible thought that we'd got it all wrong.'

'And that possible casual question, which, no doubt, Carr Mallory would have forgotten, but which was like an unexploded bomb in Quist's life, led Quist to Pierce.'

'Ah, yes, Mr Thackeray thought that Quist introduced Caroline Dax to Pierce Mallory.'

'Keeping his eye on him — and trying to find out what he knew about the Quists of Loughlinstown. He couldn't ruin Pierce, though. Pierce was quite capable of doing that himself.'

'And that question you asked about the sister — why does Quist tell that joke?'

'Invent yourself. Invent a sister. She's a fiction — like the rest of his life.'

36: HOPE

Bryan Procter, Commissioner of Lunacy, had promised to write to St Patrick's Hospital in Dublin to find out if a Mrs William Fagan was a patient there still. Mr Procter told Dickens that St Patrick's was a public asylum, but they did receive private patients. That made Dickens think as he was making his way back to Wellington Street, where Scrap was to meet him for their excursion to Rag Fair.

Suppose that Mrs Fagan was still confined after all these years. Did someone pay for her? Did Quist? He thought not, because payments would leave evidence, though he might have used a third party — in London? He would have severed all his ties with Dublin and the Quist family, and with the Fagan name. Dickens knew that when families ceased paying for their confined lunatics, the patient would become the responsibility of the state or charity. He thought of Mrs Ellis. Would she, too, be abandoned at Guy's Hospital while her husband and father wrangled over the bill?

And what about that poor little baby at Mrs Flax's? He would have to find out what could be done for the baby. A solicitor, he supposed. What a tangle. It was bad enough that poor people abandoned their children in the streets — he remembered a nurse in one of the workhouses weeping over what she called "the dropped child", a poor infant simply left in the street which she had nursed devotedly and which had died. He would never forget the great tears which choked her, and yet these men of substance saw the Ellis baby as a disgrace to their names, and a means by which to punish poor, mad Mrs

Ellis. Mrs Ellis, senior, though. She was a pleasant woman — she might do something. He'd have to ask.

Scrap was waiting — early, of course, his bright face turning to Dickens as he went in. Scrap, another abandoned child, whose mother had died, and whose abusive father had vanished with some other woman, but, he thought, Scrap had found a family in Sam Jones and his wife, Elizabeth. They wouldn't let go of him, nor of Eleanor and Tom Brim. Love was what counted, not blood. Richard Nimmo was not George Nimmo's son, but he was loved as such, and he needed to be found.

Scrap was looking at him critically. 'Coat's all right. Where's them gloves — the fingerless gloves yer keeps? The ring needs coverin' — Rag Fair ain't no place fer diamon's.'

'Indeed not. In the pocket, I expect.' Out they came with the green spectacles he kept for deep disguise.

'I don't think so,' Scrap said, 'yer can't see properly with them, an' no one's goin' ter notice us in Rag Fair.' Scrap was becoming very much in charge these days. Course, Mr Dickens woz only an amateur. Not in trainin' fer the professional life, as he was himself. To be the superintendent's right-hand man was the lodestar of Scrap's ambition. 'Mr Dax, first — mighta seen 'im.'

'Only if the shop is open. He's just been to the mortuary to see his dead daughter —'

Scrap gave him a look — a look which told that he understood. Scrap knew all about death. In the time of cholera, men, women and children had died in the streets; that dropped child in the workhouse might well have died where it had been left. Accident, disease, poverty, all Death's servants. Scrap had seen the thousand natural shocks that flesh is heir to. He had seen grief, too. The death of Mr Brim, father of Eleanor and

Tom, had taught him that, and he handled Eleanor Brim as if she were a fine piece of porcelain. 'Get yer,' he said, 'we'll see.'

Dickens smiled inwardly. That was what he so often said to an importunate child, often more than one. Eight pairs of very round eyes. The zoo? The toyshop? The seaside? We'll see. And, fortunately, often nobody saw in that unspecified future. He'd be bankrupt else.

The shop was open. Mr Dax stood at his counter, patiently waiting for the rag-picker to empty his sack. It wasn't Nimmo. Barney Dax looked the same, though Dickens knew what he had felt at the mortuary where his only child lay, all her sullenness and bitterness departed, her face white and peaceful as if she were sleeping and would wake at the kiss of a prince. But she did not wake at her father's tentative kiss on her brow. He had touched her cold cheek, wiped his eyes, and thanked them, and away he had gone, slightly round-shouldered from his burden.

He went away before the inquest, which was to be held that morning. Superintendent Jones told him that it would be adjourned until more evidence as to the circumstances of her death had been found. Dickens had not stayed, either. Scrap was waiting.

The rag-picker left with his money, and Barney Dax saw that his visitor was Charles Dickens again. Barney just shook his hand, the pressure telling Dickens that there was nothing more to say. He recognised Scrap, and Dickens explained that they were still looking for Nimmo. 'I've found out something about him — an uncle. Have you seen him?'

Mr Dax had. Nimmo was in the London Hospital along the Mile End Road, where Mr Dax had kindly conveyed him. Nimmo had been attacked and left for dead in a yard off Cutler

Street. Someone had found him, and knowing Mr Dax's benevolence, had fetched him. Mr Dax had brought his horse and cart, caused the unconscious man to be loaded onto it, and with the neighbour's assistance had sought medical assistance in the shape of a doctor.

'He ain't dead, Mr Dickens, not yet at any rate, but I don't know — he looked very bad.'

'Attacked in what way?' Dickens asked.

'Stabbed — don't know who done it, but it'd be for a few pennies, that's all I know. Some low thief from the lodgin's, but Nimmo had nothin'. I ain't seen him since you came with the superintendent, so I ain't paid him for any rags. Told your lad that.'

'I'd better go and see,' Dickens said. 'What's the name of the doctor? I need to know who to ask for.'

The doctor at The London Hospital looked at Dickens's card and was very willing to answer his questions. 'He is in a bad way, sir, but I think he might live. He lost a lot of blood, and he's not in good shape — half-starved, well nearly starved. It will depend if he wants to live —'

'He doesn't?'

'I don't think he has much to live for — except the streets and the rags, but there's something about him. I don't know — as if he's fallen from grace.'

'That he has, Doctor, but I know someone who wants him back. I'll fetch him, but first can we see him?'

The ward was a cavern of a place, with a vaulted ceiling and long rows of iron beds facing each other. Coal fires at each end gave out a good deal of smoke, but not much heat. The smell was of smoke, ammonia, and an underlying sickly smell of drains, but the nurse who came to meet the doctor was a young and pretty woman who looked neat and clean. The doctor took them to the bedside.

Richard Nimmo lay still as a waxwork, his remarkable eyes closed, and his thin hands still on the blanket. He might have been dead, Dickens thought, were it not for the faintly perceptible rise and fall of his breast. His breathing seemed easy enough and someone had cleaned him up, though his nails showed the grime of a life in the streets, and there was ingrained dirt in the creases of his face. He looked young still, very thin, and very pathetic.

Dickens took one of the thin hands. 'Mr Nimmo — Richard —'

The eyes flew open at his touch, at first bewildered, and then Dickens saw recognition in them.

'I know you.' Nimmo's voice was very faint.

'I saw you at Mr Dax's shop, sir, and I have come to ask if I might do anything for you.'

'A gentleman — no, sir, no. It is too late. I only want to sleep. And not to wake up.' The very pale green eyes closed, but he was still breathing. There was hope, he thought.

He turned to the doctor. 'I am going to fetch someone who will want him to live. I will have to go up to Pentonville. I beg you — keep him alive until I return.'

'There is no more I can do, Mr Dickens,' the doctor said. 'Nature will take her course.'

'Sit with him, Scrap, hold his hand, keep him alive for another hour — or two.' The City Road was a long walk.

Scrap nodded and took Dickens's place by the bed. The doctor brought him a stool. Dickens squeezed his shoulder as he left. At the ward door, he looked back to see the doctor and nurse with another patient. Scrap was holding Nimmo's hand. He'd not let go, and if, God forbid, Nimmo died, there would be a pair of bright blue eyes watching and a warm hand on his dying one.

George Nimmo was not at his warehouse. A clerk told him that Mr Nimmo was at the canal basin, supervising the unloading of casks.

And there, standing in the bitter wind, by the sluggish, leaden water of the canal, and under an equally leaden sky, Dickens told George Nimmo the news for which he had waited for years.

'Alive?'

'Yes, but we must hurry — the doctor fears for him. He says that all will depend on whether Richard wants to live.'

They went back to the hospital in George Nimmo's carriage. Dickens had walked up to Pentonville at his usual swift pace, anxiety lending wings to his feet. He had seen the traffic on the Whitechapel Road and known he could be quicker, but George Nimmo looked fragile suddenly, his face drained of colour, and his breath coming in quick spurts. It would take too long to walk. On the way, he told him the danger that Richard might be in, and of the murders of Pierce Mallory, his brother, and of Frederick Estcourt.

Scrap was still at his post, his hand still clasping the other man's. He nodded at Dickens's unspoken question, and made way for George Nimmo. They heard him say, 'Richard, my boy, I've come to take you home.'

Home, magic word. Dickens saw the eyes open. George Nimmo clasped his nephew's hand. 'Home, Richard, home.' And he saw the tears on the older man's cheeks. Richard Nimmo must live for him. Shame, humiliation, guilt — all nothing to this.

They crept away. Dickens would contact George Nimmo later. This wasn't the time to be asking questions about Quist.

'Uncle, yer said.' Scrap was thoughtful. He often was after something important happened.

'Yes, he brought him up after his father died, but then something went wrong with his life, and he thought he could never go back. I think he believed that he deserved his miserable life as a rag-picker.'

'No one deserves that — 'cept a murderer.'

'You kept him alive. You've given that man his hope back.'

'Opened 'is eyes once. Told 'im 'is uncle woz comin' — told 'im ter 'ang on.'

'And he did, thank God.'

'What now? What's 'appenin' about that caliph, whatsisname?'

'Ah, Sir Mordaunt Quist — we're waiting for news. Mr Jones is out on enquiries. Let's get back and find out.'

'The whisperin' man,' Scrap said, after a while, 'wot yer doin' about 'im?'

Dickens stopped suddenly in the street and stared at him.

Superintendent Jones looked weary. His fine grey eyes had a touch of red about the rims. Nevertheless, he put down his pen and smiled to welcome Dickens and Scrap, and was delighted to hear that Nimmo had been found. The stabbing, however, made him ask, 'You told George Nimmo to be careful?'

'I told him Richard might be in danger. I said we'd have to come back to see Richard. I didn't go into too much detail, but I warned him about Wigge. He looked very grim, but he has a lot of men working up there — rough types, all muscle, used

281

to hefting barrels, and loyal. They are very familiar with rogues and vagabonds after the drink.'

"Opes they throws that Wigge in the drink if they sees 'im,' Scrap said.

'Ah, the drink,' mused Jones, 'Queeley O'Shea's a man for the whisky.'

'Have you the drink taken, Mr Jones?'

'More than is good for me, I daresay, and Mr O'Shea certainly wetted his whistle. Talk about talk.'

'William Fagan?'

'Oh, yes, he remembered, and so did his wife — naturally, she could tell me all about the tragedy. Not much more than Miss Leaf told us, except for one nugget. Mrs Fagan went mad when she lost her second child.'

'There was another?'

'Indeed, there was, and it was assumed that Mr Fagan took the first child with him when, broken-hearted, he sold the Quist property and vanished from sight. O'Shea believes he went to America, so he wouldn't connect Quist of Middle Temple with Fagan. Oh, his departure to a new life was understandable, of course, after such a dreadful turn of events —'

'But he has no children now — I heard that at the dinner.'

'Not that anyone knows about. He could have placed the child in an orphanage for all we know — in Ireland — anywhere.'

'I wonder, did Miss Fitzgerald mention the child when Carr Mallory so kindly drove her to the railway station? And did he tell Pierce, who let slip that he knew to Wigge at The Lion and Lamb?'

'Dangerous knowledge, that.'

'Scandal, indeed — a child abandoned. And suppose money was left to that child by the grandfather. Maybe the child was a son.'

'Easy enough to destroy wills, deeds, papers in all the upheaval after the tragedy, and Mrs Fagan's breakdown.'

'The man's a monster.'

'So he is, but we're no nearer getting to him.'

'Did Queeley O'Shea say anything about Trinity College?'

'Yes, he knew Fagan had been there, but he didn't know him, and only took an interest because of the tragedy, but it doesn't prove that Mordaunt Quist is William Fagan. However, I did ask him about someone else — a shot in the dark, so to speak —'

'Who?'

'One Mr Mordaunt Purefoy, who, I discovered, had his chambers in Merrion Square, Dublin, and to whom I have just written, enquiring about Mr William Fagan. Mr O'Shea knew of him —'

'A hit, a very palpable hit.'

'Not quite yet. O'Shea thought he'd be retired by now, but was able to give me the name of a lawyer whose chambers are at the same address. I'm hoping that if Mr Mordaunt Purefoy is still alive, this other letter will get to him by the request I have made to the lawyer at the address in Merrion Square. In the meantime, we have to work out how we might get closer to Quist.'

'The whisperin' man.' Scrap had been waiting for his chance. Sometimes they woz that slow in gettin' ter the action.

'Who?'

'In that story wot Mr D. told about the caliph — there woz a man, 'e said, wot whispered an' woz frightened, but Mr D. said 'e'd disobey if 'e could, an' I said —'

'Offer him money — my word, you did listen carefully.'

'Yer'd both forgotten. Not me,' Scrap said complacently, 'so wot about 'im?'

'What, indeed?' asked Jones. 'We need to get at him by some means.'

'Doublett,' Dickens said, 'pastoral, comical, historical, tragical — clerical, perhaps?'

37: CHAMBERS

Mrs Matilda Crutch, laundress and general provider, went down the stairs from the chambers at the top of Garden Court in Middle Temple. Well, a day, she was muttering to herself, mind, Mr à Beckett was an odd cove, 'ad 'is fancies, 'im bein' a lawyer an' a writer — bound ter know queer folks, but them as was up them stairs — peculiar an' no mistake. Up from the country an' wantin' rooms for the young man. Old 'un woz a queer fish, them starin' eyes lookin' at everythin', askin' a dozen questions, askin' about damp — course there woz damp. 'Adn't 'e seen the river? Still, they'd took the rooms, an' it was Mr à Beckett's business. An' sixpence fer the trouble. An' more, judgin' by that young man's face — simple, 'e looked.

She bustled off to her cubby hole under the stairs. She'd erran's ter do.

Them three upstairs, were of course, Charles Dickens, the father of the would-be lawyer, Constable Doublett, and Scrap, a stray lad who'd carried up a portmanteau and a box. Mr Gilbert À Beckett, barrister-at-law, playwright, contributor to *Punch*, and therefore possessed of a sense of humour, had not turned a hair when Dickens had asked him if he might borrow a couple of empty rooms in Garden Court for a few days, rooms which gave a good view of Fountain Court and the gardens thereof.

Constable Doublett, with his very ancient father and the stray boy, had been assured that the rooms were comfortable — not that they looked it, and there was damp. Dickens could smell it. The laundress had sniffed and referred him to the river, which was just a step away. 'Ad 'e not noticed it? The last gentl'man 'ad found the chambers to 'is liking until he'd passed. When Dickens mischievously enquired as to whither, he was answered with a reddened finger pointing skywards.

'Dead as?' he asked.

'A doornail,' she replied predictably. ''Ad the 'orrors, see, dreadful. Took away, 'e woz, but it want ter do with the chambers. The law, I daresay, lots o' mad folk hereabouts.' She gave her interlocutor a significant look and stumped away. They could hear her muttering to herself as she shut the door, after which Dickens turned the key.

'That bundle of animated rags will fleece you,' Dickens told Doublett, 'and you let her. Don't get up a mystery with her. Guileless, Mr Septimus Doublett, an innocent abroad — nothing to hide.'

Doublett grinned at the name "Septimus" — he was merely a Jack — and then his face took on an uneasy expression of bewilderment, his mouth slack; even his shoulders seemed to shrink so that his nearly new black jacket appeared too big. Just a lad setting out into a world of traps for the unwary.

Dickens chuckled. 'Very good, my boy. Now, remember, hasten to Mr à Beckett's chambers at Inner Temple Hall from time to time — for the look of the thing. Someone will give you some large books to bring back for your extensive studies. Keep your eyes open for the whispering man. And listen out for that distinctive laugh.' Dickens had demonstrated the laugh to chilling effect at Bow Street. 'Remember the face, but don't go near.'

They looked out of the little window. The idea was to look out for Quist's whispering man, who must surely emerge from Quist's chambers at some time during the day. They had come in the morning so as to get the advantage of light. It was also possible that the clerk might come out the back way into Essex Street, and that was where Scrap would wait, but only after he and Doublett had seen their quarry. If the clerk came out in Essex Street, Scrap was to follow and return to inform Doublett, who might scrape an acquaintance in a chophouse or pub. It was up to him to use his wits.

They waited. And waited. Various people came and went. They saw the laundress go into Fountain Court Chambers and come out again with her mop and bucket. Eventually, in the afternoon, the whispering man appeared. Dickens knew him. He was still curiously bent over, like a man who was looking for something he'd lost, but they couldn't see his face. Then he turned and made his way along in front of the Garden Court houses when he looked up and glanced behind him. Dickens thought he looked like a frightened man, but so he had appeared that first time. Naturally timid, perhaps, or afraid of someone at Fountain Court? Then as he turned his head forward, they had a good view of the thin, anxious-looking face. They watched him turn right at the end of the court. Then he was lost to view.

'Got 'im,' Scrap said.

'Me, too.'

'Good. Now Scrap and I will leave you, Doublett. Lock the door behind us. Unpack that portmanteau and then have a stroll about the gardens and Fountain Court, and go over to à Beckett's. Scrap will be in Essex Street on watch. I suggest you meet — by chance — at five o'clock. Give the lad a penny, Doublett, and Scrap, come back to Wellington Street after to report.'

Scrap went off whistling — just a messenger boy. He slipped down Essex Street and found a convenient doorway in which to lounge, somewhere between the back of Fountain Court and the lane which led into Milford Lane, from which vantage point he might catch a glimpse of the whispering man if he came up that way. A little later, Doublett's elderly father went halting down the stairs and out into Garden Court, where he turned right, following in the footsteps of the whispering man. That way would take him into Milford Lane. The clerk could have gone that way.

Dickens stopped at the archway into Essex Street and looked up the street. No sign of Scrap, but he'd be concealed somewhere, and he'd be able to see if the whispering clerk came up by him. He glanced down Essex Stairs, which led to the river, though the whispering man would more likely use Temple Stairs. It was a gloomy little spot with the misty vapours rising in a sudden squall of rain, and the light fading, and nothing much down the greasy steps but water. He could hear it running fast. *High tide later,* he thought. He looked along at the warehouses abutting Essex Wharf, from where he heard a shout and then hammering. Probably from the blacksmiths' works down Tweezer's Alley. An oddly magnified and haunting noise heard just here, as though a funeral bell were tolling.

He went into Milford Lane, a narrow thoroughfare leading to the Strand, from where it was no distance to Waterloo Bridge and Wellington Street.

The cobbled lane was lined with some very old gabled houses with leaded windows, and was crowded with people coming and going from the various coal merchants, beer shops, bakers and pubs so that he couldn't see far enough ahead in the gloom to discern the stooping figure of the whispering clerk. Perhaps he had gone up Essex Street. Well, Scrap would see him and follow. Dickens came abreast of one of the seedy little pubs and the crowd parted momentarily, and he saw his quarry just turning into Tweezer's Alley. He made to hurry, but someone shoved him from behind. His stick caught in the wheel of a passing cart. Dickens stumbled and fell, losing his hat in the process, and his spectacles as he hit the cobbles hard. He lay, winded for a few moments, and aware of a press of people about him. 'Oughter look where 'e's goin', the old cove,' someone said. 'Shouldn't be out on 'is own.' There was laughter and rough hands pulled him up. A calloused hand gave him his stick, and his hat, rather dented, followed. A gloved hand held out the broken spectacles, and a pair of very dark, glittering eyes caught his. There was the impression of a cruel mouth and pockmarks about the chin. The spectacles dropped again; the eyes and mouth were gone. Someone else handed him the spectacles, and the rough voice said, 'On yer way, old 'un.'

The people milling about the pub swirled around him. No one paid attention to the old man fumbling with his spectacles. Dickens felt shaken, and the street suddenly looked all awry through the broken lens. Tweezer's Alley? He took a step forward, and then he heard it. That unmistakeable, high-pitched, snorting laughter. Those glittering eyes had known him. Wigge.

He limped on — not acting now. Now what? Risk it and go back, assuming that Wigge was going back to Fountain Court? Go on and risk being followed? That didn't matter. Wigge knew very well where to find him. But — frightening thought — had he already been followed? Right into Garden Court.

Dickens walked on up to Little Essex Street. His intention was to work his way back down Essex Street and find Scrap. There was nothing to be done about Doublett — he'd be safe enough in Garden Court for now, and Wigge could hardly attack him in broad daylight as he was on his way to Gilbert À Beckett's chambers. Not that it was broad daylight now. Dusk was descending into Little Essex Street, but there were plenty of people about.

Essex Street was busy, too, with its pubs, its tobacco shop, bakers, tailors, lodging houses, and solicitors' chambers from where clerks and messengers hurried about the business of the law. He glanced in every doorway, but no sign of Scrap. He risked a glance behind, but there wasn't enough light to see. He was nearing the end of the street and could see the archway. He thought about that dismal little dark spot just above the steps where the river vapour rose and the water rushed.

''Ey, mister,' a voice said at his elbow.

'Where were you?'

'Follerin' you. Saw it all — an' that cove wot picked up the specs.'

'Let's get out of here before he sees us again.'

''E went down Tweezer's Alley — watched 'im an' then follered you. Knew yer'd be lookin' fer me.'

'In here.' They took refuge in the doorway of The Essex Head pub.

'How come you followed him?'

'Sees yer just at the archway an' then 'e came. I dunno, Mr Dickens. Sees 'im look up toward where I woz an' then 'e looks the way you'd gone. Dunno, I jest thought 'e want right. Felt it.'

That was good enough for Dickens. 'He wasn't. Did you get a good look at him?'

'Clear as day. Not the whisperin' man. 'Ard-faced cove. Nothin' special about 'im, but I'd know 'im again.'

'Back to Bow Street — separately. I'll wait here. Go back up the street to the Strand.'

38: WAITING

Dickens had agreed to Superintendent Jones's plan of campaign. He had spoken confidentially to Judge Talfourd, who had agreed to speak confidentially to a Very Powerful Somebody of Middle Temple — *a very big wig*, as Dickens observed to Jones. The bigwig, being on the side of the law, and like most law-abiding citizens, not very much in favour of a fraudster who might be a murderer, and equally not much in favour of the reputation of The Temple being tarnished, had also agreed. *Little did he know*, Dickens thought.

The Very Powerful Somebody, bencher of Middle Temple, knew only that a clerk, possibly connected with Middle Temple, was suspected of the murder of his mistress. Naturally, the Very Powerful Somebody had demanded a name. Superintendent Jones had given the name "Wiggins", entreating that it must remain absolutely secret. He had been uneasy, but at least the name of Wigge had not been mentioned. The Very Powerful Somebody had pondered a while, and had agreed to speak to the Treasurer of the Honourable Society of Middle Temple, an even greater power in that land, who had also agreed. However, since the grindstones of the law were slower than the mills of God, as Dickens put it to Sam Jones, these agreements took some days. All they could do was wait.

Superintendent Jones had also been very cautious about any reference to Sir Mordaunt Quist, Q.C., husband of Lady Primrose, daughter of the late Earl of Quickswood. 'Hard evidence,' he had reminded Dickens. But, having heard of

Dickens's brush with Wigge, he had been very ready to see if they could find him, providing steps were taken.

The result of these somewhat tortuous agreements was the engagement of a gardener at Middle Temple and a general handyman. Constable Stemp and Sergeant Rogers had hardly needed telling that they were to keep watch and ward on the ragamuffin hanging about the purlieus of Middle Temple. Scrap, now the wretchedest of urchins, had a blackened face, the filthiest of ragged clothes and the shabbiest of boots which, however, were firmly tied with string. A lad might need to run — very fast. Constable Doublett, hard at work in his garret, was to keep his eye on the whispering man who might prove useful in revealing the whereabouts of Mr Solomon Wigge.

All this left Superintendent Jones looking anxiously at Dickens. 'Could he really have seen you all go into Garden Court?'

'He could. He must have followed me. It was Wigge in Milford Lane, I'm sure. My hat fell off, and the specs. He must have seen me then. He made to hand me the specs and then dropped them deliberately. It was only a few moments after that I heard the laughter. He was near, that's certain. And he knew me.'

'And only Scrap got a good look at him. That worries me.'

'I know, but he'll not be recognised. Just a lad that carried the stuff up to Doublett's rooms. Now he looks as if he's been swept up on the charwoman's shovel and thrown on a dust heap. What now?'

'We wait. We wait for your Mr Procter to find out about the first wife.'

'I should find a time to go up to Pentonville to see Richard Nimmo — he might be well enough to tell me something about Quist and the rest of 'em.'

The bewigged and Very Powerful Somebody was presiding at the Court of the Queen's Bench away in Westminster; the Treasurer was in his counting house; the Solicitor General was busy; The Philazer's Office was mysteriously occupied in threading writs; and The First Fruits Office, no doubt, harvesting its profits. No one from The Seal Office, The Crown Office, The Surveyors' Office, or any office at all, paid the slightest attention to a scruffy lad, or the gardener with his broom and spade, or to the general handyman with his canvas bag of tools which rattled meaningfully in the halls and passages of the various courts and chambers. Their business was with the labyrinthine passages of the law — and with the making of money.

Only Mrs Crutch saw. Her little eyes, as sharp as two pin heads, and as piercing in any number of gloomy chambers, missed nothing. Sharp ears, too, small enough for any keyhole, and if you were kneeling with your bucket at your side, then who would notice? No one did take any notice. Mrs Crutch, her mop, and her bucket were all inanimate objects in the eyes of the law. However, Mrs Crutch liked to know — and to take her news to Mr Crutch, the bargee who worked on the river and whose barge was always moored at Essex Stairs at about nine of the clock, late evening, when Mrs Crutch came to sleep in the connubial bunk aboard the barge which they called home. And she always had at least half a nice jug of wine or beer, a good half a loaf, and the legs or wings of a roast chicken or partridge. Mr Crutch often had a fancy for a nice bit of partridge. Fish he couldn't abide.

There were rich pickin's in Garden Court, Essex Court and Fountain Court. Tips, too. Information was worth somethin' an' there woz them as liked ter know the comin's an' goin's, specially when them as came woz new.

An' Mr Doublett — simple soul — woz quite ready with 'is tip and 'is bit o' roast fowl. Nothin' much ter tell about 'un, she had told her interlocutor. Oh, the lad, jest 'elped with the baggage. Saw 'un run off. There woz allus lads about. An' the old pa? 'Adn't seen 'un. Gone back ter the country, she dared say. The nosey old fool. An' no, she 'adn't 'eard tell of any Mr Dickens, an' as far as she knew that Mr Doublett 'adn't 'ad no visitors, 'cept 'e seemed ter be thick with that clerk, the bent 'un — the one that couldn't 'ardly speak from Sir Quist's chambers. Oh, aye, sir, she'd let 'im know wot woz wot an' if anyone came ter visit Mr Doublett. An' yes, she'd be sure ter tell if she 'eard that name, Dickens. And away she clattered with her sixpence.

In the interests of detection and verisimilitude, Septimus Doublett had found himself purchasing paper and ink in the stationery shop in Middle Temple Lane. In the interests of Sir Mordaunt Quist, the whispering man was doing likewise. And Septimus Doublett, whom his old father frequently chided for his clumsiness, seemed to slip on the wet floor, drop his umbrella, and fall against the stranger, who, reaching for support that wasn't there, lost hold of his ink bottle. It went with a crash. His quire of paper broke and scattered. Septimus Doublett was mortified. His apologies were fulsome. The whispering man — a sensitive soul — forgave him, and to the coffee house they had gone. Mr Doublett's treat. How else could he make up for his ridiculous clumsiness?

Then Sergeant Rogers had a break — in Garden Court. It was there he heard the laughter. And two voices — one of them a woman's, he thought. Coming from under the stairs. He wondered about Mrs Crutch. But he had to scarper up the stairs when he heard a door opening. He only saw the top of a hat. And it was Scrap who saw the man he thought was Wigge — difficult to tell in the dark — going down Essex Stairs, where Scrap could see the lights of a barge. He could hear voices. A woman and a man, he thought. But he scarpered, too, when he heard the man say goodnight.

39: PLUNDER

'It was not uncommon, apparently, for families to incarcerate an inconvenient relative before emigrating, and to make off with their money,' Dickens told Sam Jones.

Dickens had seen Bryan Procter at Wellington Street early in the morning. Procter had been able to tell him about Mrs Frances Fagan, who had been confined to St Patrick's — that institution founded by Dean Swift for "Fools and the Mad" — since 1822.

'Nearly thirty years. Dear Lord, a life sentence — and her husband put her in there, knowing that she would never get out.'

'No feeling at all. That's my reading of Quist. Egotist, I keep saying to myself, the life of another worth nothing when it stands in the way of his desires. Like all murderers who lay their cold-blooded plans, incapable of pity and unable to realise the horror of it. Not having to, anyway, if someone else is doing the actual deeds. Same with the asylum — out of sight, out of mind.'

'Wouldn't he have required a doctor or two?'

'One, at that time, so Procter told me, but it seems a clergyman could require the admission on behalf of the family. And the signature on the admission form for Mrs Fagan is that of a reverend gentleman who would have testified to the patient's behaviour prior to the admission — the clergyman might have attended Mrs Fagan and seen that she was mad with grief. Procter says that the testimony would show that the patient had to be watched at all times, would demonstrate manic behaviour, and would show that the nearest relative, the grieving young husband, Mr William Fagan, was not able to look after her. Anyone in a dog collar, I wouldn't be surprised.'

'And she was paid for?'

'She was — and the fees were paid until five years ago on behalf of a relative — name not known — by a solicitor in London — Herbert Wing at Lincoln's Inn. The asylum received notice of the death of the relative, and that was the end of the fees. Mrs Fagan presumably became a charity case.'

'I take it she cannot speak for herself.'

'Exactly. She is not dangerous, very quiet and ladylike, it seems, but — and this is the dreadful part — many patients who are confined for years are unfit for life outside. At worst, they develop problems such as catatonia or idiocy — Mrs Frances Fagan is, medically speaking, an idiot.'

'And he just left her there.'

'And stole everything she had.'

'I wonder why he paid for so long?'

'He'd have had to at the beginning, and if the fees were being paid, no questions would be asked about William Fagan, or any relative, and by 1846, it would be too late. He'd gamble that he could stop. No one would bother to try to find William Fagan in America or Australia. Shall we try the solicitor at Lincoln's Inn — see if he knows the name of the person who paid the fees?'

'Not Quist, I'll bet. Yes, we will. Nothing from Mr Purefoy — as yet, nor, indeed, from the lawyer to whom I wrote.'

'Any news from Middle Temple?'

'Doublett has made friends with our whispering man, but I've told him to tread very carefully. However, Doublett reports that the young man isn't happy in Quist's chambers. Wigge, it seems, is very much a power there, but I've told Doublett not to rush at it — get the information naturally, draw the man out. Scrap thinks he saw Wigge by Essex Stairs talking to a woman, but it was too dark and wet to see much. Rogers heard him laughing — under the stairs in Garden Court. Again, he might have been with a woman. Rogers thought the charwoman, Mrs Crutch, but he had to vanish double-quick when the door opened.'

'That's an uncomfortable thought. Wigge and that hag-ridden creature. I told Doublett she'd fleece him. Wigge's informant, do you think?'

'I do, but Doublett won't give anything away. He'll know to come here if anything breaks. Rogers'll be careful, too. He knows just to keep an eye on the comings and goings, and Scrap, as well. He was sharp enough to scarper when he heard Wigge say goodnight.'

'Good lad. If only Doublett could find out something from the whispering man.'

'He will, if something is to be found out. In the meantime — '

'On the wing, then?'

Mr Herbert Wing had roosted at the top of number eight, New Square, Lincoln's Inn, in the usual gloomy set of chambers since the beginning of old time, it seemed. In his rusty black, he resembled a rook hunched over his dinner, from which position he unfolded himself in a rather creaking way. A pair of beady eyes looked at Dickens very closely. 'Molloy,' he said.

'Indeed, sir, I was downstairs with Mr Molloy — more than twenty years ago.' It was twenty-three years since Dickens had entered the building where once he had clerked for Mr Molloy — for ten shillings a week — and considered his vocation as a lawyer. It had not taken him long to find the ways of the law a very little world and a very dull one. He had not remembered

Mr Wing, but there had been a Mr Gull at that time — taken flight, presumably, heavenwards, perhaps.

'Never forget a face — knew you at once, Mr Dickens. My word, just a boy then. Who'd have thought, eh? Ah, Mr Molloy — gone, of course —'

'And Mr Gull?'

'Departed — to Margate. He liked the sea. He'll be sorry to have missed you, but I am very glad to know you again, Mr Dickens, and Superintendent Jones, a pleasure, sir. What am I to do for you?'

'I'm looking for information about the fees paid for a patient, Mrs Frances Fagan, to St Patrick's Asylum in Dublin.'

Mr Wing sat down again, took off his spectacles and rubbed his eyes. 'Good gracious, I never thought to hear of that again. The money stopped coming —'

'Who did it come from?' Jones asked, thinking of Quist, and hoping the answer would be Fagan.

'Mr Dermot Barbary.'

'Would you oblige me by telling me about him and how he came to be connected with the asylum?'

'May I ask what this is to do with?'

'A serious crime, Mr Wing. I cannot reveal the details, but there is fraud involved, and possibly murder.'

'Good gracious, that is alarming. However, I cannot tell you much about Mr Barbary. I met him but once —'

'Was he Irish?' Dickens asked.

'He was, but I cannot tell you much more.'

'A lawyer, perhaps?'

'I'm afraid I don't know — a retired gentleman, I thought,'

'Can you describe him?'

'A man of middling height, thin face. Nondescript, really. Very reserved. I can't tell you anything about him. He told me that a friend had recommended me and that he wished to arrange the payment of fees to the — er — hospital where a relative was confined. I was given the name of Mrs Frances Fagan —'

'When was this?' asked Jones.

'Oh, a good many years ago — 1823–24, as I recall, and instructions to pay the fee yearly — it was eighty pounds, which was sent to me every December. I always paid on January the first.'

'And had you a written agreement?' Dickens asked.

Mr Wing gave him a very beady look. 'Mr Dickens, you know the law and lawyers.'

'I beg your pardon, sir, of course you had.'

'May I see the agreement?' Jones asked.

Mr Wing rang a bell for his clerk, who was instructed to bring the Barbary box. While they waited, he asked if they knew that the money had stopped at Mr Barbary's death.

'Yes, we have that information.'

'I wrote to the director there to explain that Mr Barbary had left no instruction — I must say I thought it odd that no provision had been made. I only knew about his death because the payment did not arrive in December. I waited, of course, until January and then enquired at the house to be told that Mr Barbary had died. The young lady could tell me nothing about any arrangement, nor, indeed, about any Irish relation —'

'Young lady?' Dickens asked.

'His daughter, I assumed. I enquired if there were any lawyer who could help me, but she could not say. She said she knew nothing of Mr Barbary's business affairs. A young lady, you see — she would hardly be expected to know — if you see what I mean. And that was it — there was nothing more I could do.'

'Where was the house?'

'Mary Place. I remember because it was the name of my dear wife. It's off William Street — a terrace of a few houses, as I recall. The last house. You can get to it through Charles Street off the Hampstead Road. You know the area?'

Dickens nodded. He did. It was not far from Drummond Street. 'And the young lady's name?'

'Miss Barbary — oh, I see, I did not get a first name. The meeting was but a few moments — and, as the young lady was so recently bereaved and rather — well, upset, of course — I hardly thought it was decent to persist.'

The clerk came in looking as if he had been down some mine, so dusty was he. He handed the box to Mr Wing and departed.

'This is the agreement — it is very straightforward.'

Dickens and Jones looked at it. It was very simple — Mr Dermot Barbary of number five, Mary Place, William Street instructed Mr Herbert Wing etcetera, etcetera. It was signed by both parties and dated: December 12th, 1824.

'And, to confirm, Mr Barbary died in 1846?'

'Yes. Prior to that, I gave Mr Barbary all the receipts from the hospital and I have copies of the receipts I gave to him for the money paid here.'

'They may be of use to me, Mr Wing, as evidence, so if you will oblige me, I should like to take them away for now. Of course, I shall return them.'

'Well, I think we can guess that Mr Dermot Barbary had a lawyer — not one who wished to be consulted, however. A fellow Irishman, though,' Dickens said when they were out in the square. 'From Dublin, perhaps.'

'Quist, I'll bet. Let's try William Street. See if we can find out anything about Barbary's daughter, or whoever she was.'

'Mistress?'

Jones laughed. 'Then she'll be long gone.'

They found the passage in Charles Street, an undistinguished thoroughfare with modest houses, and went down towards Mary Place. At the end they could see the terrace of equally modest houses. Just before they crossed the road to the last house, the front door opened. As one they shrank back into the passage, but Dickens risked a look. There was a woman at the door, and a man was coming down the steps. He stopped to put up his umbrella and to look up and down the terrace, and in that brief moment, Dickens knew who it was. The front door closed and the man made his way in the opposite direction towards William Street.

'It was Wigge. A woman at the door,' he whispered. 'He's gone up towards William Street.'

'Miss Barbary, I wonder?'

'William Street. William Street,' Dickens said, as if remembering something.

'Wait a minute — I sent Inspector Grove to William Street to find Fanny Hatton. No one knew of her.'

'By Regent's Park — that's what Mr George Nimmo told me — where Fanny Hatton's guardian lived. It's just round the corner. It leads to Albany Terrace by the Park. I assumed he meant that one, rather grander than this one. Who the devil gives the same names to two nearby streets? That's what comes of too much toadying to dead kings —'

'Never mind that, Mr Radical. Think. They are both near enough the Park — it's not possible, is it? That she could be Nimmo's girl.'

'Anything's possible in this labyrinth of connections, and Mr Wing only assumed that his young lady was Barbary's daughter. If she were his daughter, she knew precious little about him. And Wigge there. Quist in it? Oh, Lord, Sam, the name — Fanny — from —'

'Miss Frances Quist who became Mrs Frances Fagan?'

The Post Office Trades Directory gave them the occupant of number 5 Mary Place, William Street.

'Mr Solomon Wigge — well, well. I'm gormed.'

'So am I. Could she be, do you think? Nimmo's girl and Quist's daughter —'

'Married to Solomon Wigge? Nothing now surprises me in this case. Nobody's who they say they are. Remember Lola Montez —'

'Right at the beginning. I should have known.'

'An omen, Sammy, my lad. And she was a bigamist, too. Why can't people be satisfied with who their benighted parents wanted them to be?'

'Burke who thought he might be Sullivan — in that Cole case.'

'Stemp, Rogers, Doublett all disguised, too. I'm beginning to wonder who I am. You are Samuel Jones, ain't you?'

Jones laughed. 'I think so.'

'I remember what Estcourt said about Fanny Hatton — "bad blood there". I wonder if he thought Fanny Hatton was Quist's illegitimate daughter? "Bad blood" — just the sort of thing Estcourt would say. He told me I was a nobody —'

'Or, he knew about the mad wife — and that was the bad blood.'

'Lord, Sam, that could be it. Estcourt knew. Dangerous, and he struck me as a reckless devil and arrogant — thought he was safe, knowing he had Quist's secret.'

'But Quist didn't trust him any longer — drink, drugs — he didn't dare rely on him not to spill the beans.'

'What do we do now?'

'We can't knock on the door at Mary Place — too risky. You should go to see Richard Nimmo. Find out if he knows anything about Mr Dermot Barbary and his relationship with the girl — and if there was anything to link her with Quist, anything at all.'

40: WITNESS

The whispering man was a lonely man — and an unhappy one. He liked the new young lawyer whom he had met in the stationery shop. Someone to talk to. A good-humoured fellow, Mr Doublett, and no airs and graces. He didn't think the law would be the right profession for him, though — a hard, dry business, especially for a humble clerk. It was drudgery, really — nothing but copying until your eyes ached, and you were always on the outside — looking in, so to speak. Looking on, more like, because you couldn't look in on Sir Mordaunt, whose hard eyes belied his jovial manner to his clients and his visitors. He heard the laughter behind that sealed door. It was the laughter of Mr Wigge he hated the most — that snorting, high-pitched, sneering. Wigge laughed at him, he knew. 'How's tricks, Micks?' he would ask. That wasn't his name. The whispering man's name was Micah. No doubt Mr Wigge thought it very funny. Sir Mordaunt called him Mr Reed — but he sneered on the "Mister". And he hated Mrs Crutch, too, always cadging leftovers — cake, bread, wine, anything she could get her greedy hands on, and he knew that Sir Mordaunt thought he had taken them. Not that he said anything. And what was it that Mr Wigge gossiped about to Mrs Crutch in Garden Court? He'd seen money change hands. And Wigge had seen him.

He was glad to meet Mr Doublett, who had just been talking to the handyman — wanted something doing in his rooms, perhaps.

Doublett looked at him sympathetically. 'Come and have a chop somewhere, old fellow. You look thoroughly worn out.'

Mrs Crutch came out of Garden Court with a basket. She smiled at Doublett ingratiatingly. "Opes yer don't mind, sir, I've took that bit o' bread yer left at yer breakfast, an' there woz a bit o' bacon. Don't want it ter go ter waste, sir.'

'No, of course not, Mrs Crutch. I don't mind at all.'

'Greedy creature,' Doublett observed as she stumped away towards Fountain Court. He saw the handyman follow at a distance.

'You don't like her?' Micah asked.

'She's a grasping liar, Mr Reed. There'll be more than bread and bacon in that basket. I left half a bottle of wine — that'll be gone.'

'Won't you tackle her?'

'Would you?'

'No — she frightens me, somehow. They all frighten me.'

Doublett stared at him, astonished as he saw the tears pool in his eyes. Here was a chance. 'Something happened?'

'I've been sacked.'

'Lord, what for? No, don't tell me here. Come upstairs. I'll give you a drink — if she hasn't taken it all.'

Upstairs, there was only tea, which Micah Reed accepted gratefully. 'Now, tell me. It will do you good to get it off your chest.'

'Work not good enough — too slow. Too many mistakes. It's true, Mr Doublett. I make mistakes because he scares me — Sir Mordaunt, I mean, and Wigge. I've been there two, nearly three years. I thought it was a step up — where else can I go? Without a good word — no reference for another post. Wigge will see to that. But, I like the place — here, I mean, The Temple, the quiet, the church, the gardens, but Sir Mordaunt's chambers — there's something rotten. It's Wigge.

I think he's wicked — there's nothing he wouldn't do for Sir Mordaunt. And the young lady —'

'What young lady?'

'Mr Wigge's lady friend. Miss Fanny Hatton, she's called. So cold, so haughty, and they are always in with Sir Mordaunt, always laughing, and when I knock and am called in, they look at me as if I'm the dirt under their feet, as if they know something. They don't speak. I put the papers or whatever on the table. And when I close the door, the laughter starts again.'

'And Mrs Crutch?'

'In cahoots with Wigge. I've seen them together. He gives her money. I think she gives him information about people. He likes to know, especially about newcomers. He talked about you — I heard your name. I don't know, Mr Doublett, I think he's dangerous. Mr Dickens's name, too, Mr Charles Dickens — he came to see Sir Mordaunt — I don't know why — they were laughing.'

Doublett looked at the miserable man before him. He had a good heart, and somehow, he didn't like to use him. And that reference to Mr Dickens. It was time to act. 'Then you're better out of it. I'd like to take you to meet someone — a friend of mine, and if you'll come, well, I can't tell you now, but there are things this man will tell you.'

George Nimmo had advised Dickens to take care. 'A wild wind,' he had said, 'a very high tide, I should think. I'll have to get down to the wharf.'

The moon was full and that was usually a sign of a high tide. Common enough, and sometimes so high that streets and houses were flooded, and those who lived in cellars — and there were plenty — found themselves in a deluge of filthy water and debris, and homeless afterwards. He strode on, and now he looked there were clouds thickening and the moon tossing in the restless sky as a ship in a stormy sea. Ominous.

The information from Richard Nimmo set him thinking as he hurried on. Nimmo had met Fanny Hatton at a dinner given by Sir Mordaunt Quist. Her guardian, Mr Dermot Barbary, had been a friend of Sir Mordaunt's. Mr Barbary had been a cold sort of man, apparently not much interested in Miss Hatton's marriage prospects, but Sir Mordaunt had seemed fond of her. Richard Nimmo thought that Sir Mordaunt had approved of his courtship, but everything had changed when Pierce Mallory had taken up with Miss Hatton.

Or, had Fanny Hatton taken up with Pierce Mallory? At Quist's instigation — that relationship had preceded Pierce's affaire with Caroline Dax. Had Fanny Hatton meant to ruin Pierce Mallory, the married man? But Pierce Mallory had dropped Fanny Hatton, because that's what he did. Apart from the danger of the Mallory brothers knowing his secrets, Quist would remember Pierce's treatment of the girl. That would add an edge to the murder plan. She was Quist's daughter, surely. And Wigge? No nicety of feeling to prevent him from allying himself with another man's leavings. It would be a profitable alliance, no doubt.

Nimmo, though? Richard Nimmo had only thought that Frederick Estcourt was a sympathetic friend with whom he had gone about to assuage his grief. Dickens thought of Matthew Guard and the woman who had claimed that he had seduced her. Was that supposed to happen to Richard Nimmo, followed by a nice little line in blackmail? Had Mr Dermot Barbary begun the fraud by suggesting to George Nimmo that Richard Nimmo had deeply offended his ward? And had Estcourt set out to complete the ruin, taking what pickings he fancied for himself? But Richard Nimmo had vanished from sight. No use then in approaching Mr George Nimmo, wine and whisky merchant of Pentonville, with a spot of blackmail.

The wind was rising. Dickens kept his eye on the sky where black, rain-curdled clouds seemed to be pressing upon the rooftops. *Storm and tide*, he thought. Queer weather it had been yesterday, when at daybreak a deep yellow fog had enveloped the rooftops and the wind had blustered from every point of the compass, it seemed, and back to the north-east, a sign of high water, and then rain again when he had seen Wigge putting up his umbrella. It was coming again. He ought to go to the office and tell them to close up and get home. Then to Bow Street.

In the hall, he was surprised to see Constable Doublett and the whispering man. Doublett, who had always struck Dickens as an up-bobbing cork sort of a young man, looked very solemn, and uneasy, too; the whispering man looked terrified. Good Lord, what on earth had happened?

'I've brought Mr Reed, Mr Dickens. He has information I thought you should hear. This is Mr Charles Dickens, Micah — he's the man to tell. He knows who you are. Micah Reed, sir.'

And a broken one, Dickens saw, a poor, trembling fellow, and still bent over. He looked as though he expected a beating. 'I'll just be a moment.' He darted into his sub-editor's office to tell him to close up because of the weather and the possible tide.

Up in Dickens's office, Micah Reed did not speak. He was terrified — terrified to be brought to meet a man who was a friend of Sir Mordaunt Quist, who had dined with him at Cavendish Square. He had read the books. He had believed that the man who had written about the poor, the downtrodden, the weak and the helpless had cared, and he had been disappointed, hearing the laughter from Sir Mordaunt's office. He had hardly dared speak to Mr Dickens when he came out. But now he found two eyes looking at him with such compassion and kindness that he dared hope, but he could not speak.

'I remember you, sir, you are most welcome,' Dickens said, still wondering what had frightened the young man so. He looked to Doublett for enlightenment.

'He's been sacked by Sir Mordaunt. I thought — I hope I've not done the wrong thing, but, I think Mr Reed might be in danger.'

'From Sir Mordaunt?'

'From Mr Wigge, sir. Mr Reed saw him giving money to Mrs Crutch. She gives him information — especially about newcomers. She saw me talking to Rogers.'

'Does Mr Reed know who you are?'

'No, sir, I haven't told him anything, but I thought he might find it easier to tell you first rather than…'

Dickens understood the pause. The mention of Superintendent Jones might be too much for the fragile-looking Mr Reed. He trusted Doublett's judgement. He would know his man, but, caution, he thought. He did not want to tell Sam Jones that they had spilled the beans to the wrong man.

'Before I explain, Mr Reed, I need to know, what are your loyalties to Sir Mordaunt Quist?'

The young man spoke — still in a whisper, as though Sir Mordaunt Quist and Wigge might hear him. 'He frightens me. The whole place frightens me. I did not realise how much until I began to tell Mr Doublett. I told him — it's a rotten place. That Wigge is a wicked man, Mr Dickens. He asked Mrs Crutch about you — and about Mr Doublett —'

Dickens had not taken his eyes off poor Micah Reed, and if this wasn't a frightened man, then he ought to be on the stage — acting the villain's innocent dupe. 'I will tell you that Mr Doublett here is a police constable — no, you must not be afraid — he is investigating on behalf of Superintendent Jones of Bow Street — it is murder, Mr Reed —'

Doublett caught Micah Reed, who seemed to collapse before them, his face white as paper, his mouth almost blue. Doublett helped him to a seat by the fire while Dickens poured some brandy and made Reed sip it.

'Take your time, Mr Reed.'

They saw the colour begin to return to his lips, but he still trembled as though he were deadly cold. His face had collapsed and he seemed to have aged all in a moment — it was the face of one who had realised a dreadful truth.

Dickens drew a chair and sat opposite Micah Reed. 'Tell me, if you can, what it is that you have realised. You are safe here. No more harm can be done to you by those two.'

'They know where I live — in Tweezer's Alley. He — Wigge — will find me. He's followed me. I know it — sometimes I've looked round and caught a glimpse. I can never escape, for I know now — I believe I know what they have done. I didn't understand then — but now —'

'They cannot find you, Mr Reed. You have my word. I will find you a safe place. There are two other policemen at Middle Temple keeping watch. What do you know? There is not much time, and what you tell me, I must tell Superintendent Jones.'

'Mr Carr Mallory was shot — I read about it in the paper. They talked about it — laughed about it. I heard them. I knew the name because Mr Mallory came to Sir Mordaunt's chambers. He left his card.'

His death warrant, Dickens thought. 'When was this?'

'A day or two before the shooting. Then I heard them talking about him.'

'When did you hear them? How?'

'On the day of the funeral and the shooting. It was late — I had been to the stationery shop. Sir Mordaunt has documents copied there. I was on my way home when I remembered. I collected them — I wanted them to be there in the morning. He could be — is — often vicious-tempered. The other clerks were gone. Sir Mordaunt's door was open. I heard them laughing. Sir Mordaunt said, "The murderous shaft's that shot" — as if he was acting — enjoying himself —'

Oh, he would be, thought Dickens, recognising the words from *Macbeth*, and feeling that same prickle at his neck as he had felt in Quist's library, but Micah Reed had not finished.

'He said that they had scotched the snake and killed him — and he laughed again. "Wise of you to say your prayers, Solomon." That's what Sir Mordaunt said, and they all laughed again. I stood at the entrance door. I didn't know what to do. They might see me come in with the papers, yet I dreaded the next day — and then Sir Mordaunt turned to the young lady —'

'What young lady?'

'Mr Wigge's young lady, Miss Fanny Hatton. They talked about oysters — he told her to buy fresh ones tomorrow — our friend, he said, needs a treat, and oysters is in, he said — and not to buy them in Gerrard Street — then they laughed, and Mr Wigge said they should go out to dine, so I put the papers down on a desk and went away. I saw — I saw —'

'What did you see?'

'A black bonnet — and a heavy black veil and a cloak on a desk — clothes for a funeral.'

The woman at the cemetery, Dickens thought. It was she, Fanny Hatton, not Caroline Dax, but Wigge had killed Caroline anyway because she knew too much.

'Does it mean that they killed —'

'I think it does — and I must go to tell Superintendent Jones at Bow Street. You will be safe here with Constable Doublett.'

Doublett was about to protest, but Dickens motioned him to the door. Outside, he said, 'You'll have to stay with him. Wigge followed me — you don't know if he followed you. We can't leave him here alone. Question him about Estcourt — see if he knows anything about Quist and Estcourt — or even Pierce Mallory and Miss Fanny Hatton. And ask about a Mr Dermot Barbary. Superintendent Jones will want as much evidence as you can get. Come down and bolt the door after I've gone.'

41: TEMPLE

It was raining hard now. The moon had vanished completely behind those massed clouds; there was water overflowing from the gutters, and a furious wind was sweeping down to the river from the north-east. Then Dickens was astonished to see Superintendent Jones and Constables Stemp and Feak rushing towards him down from Bow Street.

'I was just coming — what's wrong?' Dickens asked.

Jones's face was drawn into a mask of dreadful fear. 'Scrap's missing. Rogers is still at Middle Temple. And Doublett's not to be found, either. No time to lose. You'd better come.'

Dickens felt the blood drain from his own face, but he only said urgently, 'Tide coming.'

'I know — we'd best get a move on. Feak, go back to Bow Street and bring more men. Meet us at the top of Essex Stairs — as fast as you can. Give me your lamp.'

They hurried down to The Strand, intending to weave their way through the back streets which would take them to Essex Stairs and The Temple. Water everywhere, gutters overflowing already, spouts cascading, and underneath it all the ferocious rush of the river like an engine gathering power. Doors opening, people already in the street, the cry of 'Water's coming.' A man leading a neighing horse from a stable, another skidding in the water after a loose pig, and chickens flapping and scuttling about. Dogs barking and children shrieking in terror. Paper and straw, hats even, flying about in the wind. Outside a pub, a man was boarding up his door, and there were figures emerging from the mean little alleys and courts, even from underground, clutching bits of furniture and rags of bedding. The rats would be next, Dickens thought — they always deserted the sinking ship, but they couldn't stop to help anyone. Not now. The water swirled at their feet and the rain blurred distance and time. Heads down against the wind, they hurried on.

Dickens had to shout. 'Doublett's all right — at Wellington Street with the whispering man. Name of Micah Reed. Knows about the shooting of Carr Mallory. They did it, Sam, Wigge and the girl — I'm sure of it. But, tell me — Scrap.'

'Don't know. Rogers spoke to Doublett, who went into Garden Court chambers with your Mr Reed. Stemp was in Fountain Court doing his garden and keeping his eye on Quist's chambers. Wigge was nowhere to be seen, and the usual clerks were coming and going. What with the light going and the rain coming, he thought it time to rendezvous with Scrap. They'd meet halfway down Essex Stairs before Scrap left for home — I didn't want him about there at night. Stemp was all right — acting as night porter at the gate by Garden Court. He waited —'

'Oh, Lord, Sam — they've been watched —'

'I think so —'

'The charwoman, Mrs Crutch — Doublett's charwoman — Mr Reed told us that she is paid for information by Wigge. He heard my name — and Doublett's.'

'The woman at the stairs — Scrap thought he saw Wigge with a woman — Wigge saw him, perhaps. Saw him with Stemp at the stairs. They thought it was safe — no one about. The lawyers and clerks use Temple Stairs. Only the odd barge moored there. We need to find that woman — she might know something —'

'But why take Scrap — a lad — what would they —'

'Find out who he is, what he knows —'

'Good God, Sam, what they are capable of?'

There was no Sergeant Rogers at the top of Essex Stairs, where he and Stemp had arranged to meet. There was only the water surging up the steps — beyond halfway — boiling in the rushing wind and the driving rain. High tide was at four o'clock. It should be ebbing now at nearly five, but it wasn't. It was swelling with increased ferocity and would be at the top soon, and Temple Gardens would be flooded as they had been several times before. Scrap usually met Stemp halfway down — had he been swept away?

'Rogers still looking?' Jones asked Stemp.

Stemp looked about him. ''E said, sir, we agreed 'ere at the stairs. I knew I'd only be twenty minutes or so. Unless 'e's found Scrap and they're shelterin' somewhere. They'd not stop 'ere with the water risin'.'

'Where, Stemp, where do you think?'

'The hut, sir, where they keep the garden tools —'

They weren't there. 'Doorways,' Jones said. 'Anywhere sheltered. And Stemp, try Quist's chambers. Ask if they're all safe — anything. Charles, you know the place — anywhere. I'll try the church. Back to the top of the stairs in —' they heard the clock strike the hour — 'when it strikes the quarter.'

They separated. It was hopeless, Dickens knew, as he rushed about, buffeted by the wind, the rain flying at him in vicious squalls. He squelched through the water lying on the lawns. It was hard to see, but he tried any open door where there was light. Many doors were closed against the storm, of course, and there was no one about the paths to ask. He dashed into New Court, where he met a charwoman. She hadn't seen the handyman or a boy. Most folk had gone. A night porter in Essex Court hadn't seen them, either. Same story — storm had driven everybody home. He could go over to the Inner Temple, but they could be anywhere in this labyrinth of chambers and courts. The church clock struck the quarter. Back to the stairs, then.

'Nothing,' Stemp said.

'We'll try Mrs Crutch,' Jones said.

'She'll be in 'er cubby hole under the stairs in Garden Court — saw 'er go in.'

'When was that?'

''Bout an hour ago, I should think. It's 'er tea time.'

The door under the stairs was open, but she wasn't there, though the kettle had boiled and her teapot was waiting.

'Doublett's room,' Dickens said, 'I'll bet she saw him go out with Micah Reed — she'll be after a bit of something to eat.'

They went up quietly and met her coming out of Doublett's room with half a loaf and some butter on a saucer. She was as smooth as butter, too. 'Ooh, sir, yer give me quite a fright. Mr Doublett ain't about. I was jest —' But she did look alarmed when she saw Stemp, the gardener, and the other burly man step up to confront her, and she looked positively frightened when Jones introduced himself.

'Just a few questions, ma'am, if you will.'

She had no choice but to back into Doublett's room, still clutching her bread and butter.

'A lad — you'll have seen him hanging about — now he's missing, and the handyman. Have you seen them?'

She gave herself away. Her little eyes darted from one to the other, and to the smaller man who had also come in. Her face lost its usual ingratiating expression, though she tried to get out of it, whispering hoarsely, 'No, sir, I ain't seen a lad —'

'Speak up,' Jones barked.

'It's the damp, sir, what settles on my chest. I ain't a well woman —'

'The boy,' Jones said, stepping towards her.

'Ain't seen 'em. Leastways, not terday, an' the 'andyman, no, sir, 'e ain't bin about —'

'Oh, he has, Mrs Crutch, you saw him talking to Mr Doublett. He followed you to Fountain Court. A meeting with Mr Wigge, was it?'

She looked at Dickens as though he were some kind of conjuror. Her face seemed to collapse and the saucer fell from her hand. The butter had melted now. The noise of the breaking saucer made her step back and clutch for support as the two other men stepped forward. She was trapped and she knew it. She slumped against the table like an old sack, and her breath came in gasps.

'The truth, madam. We know all about you — your thieving and your spying — we have our spies, too.' Dickens was relentless.

'Where's that lad?' Jones moved forward again.

'On the barge — Mr Crutch — Mr Wigge, 'e arranged —'

'When?'

'An hour since.'

'Where to?'

'I dunno where they woz goin' — Mr Wigge wanted jest ter — take the lad somewheres — I dunno — it want important — jest an urchin —'

They left her, taking her keys and locking her in. She'd keep, Jones said, as they ran downstairs.

'There'll be a night porter at Temple Stairs gate,' Dickens said. 'Surely, he'll know the barge —'

The night porter, swathed in oilskin, was leaning on the gate, smoking his pipe and looking down Temple Stairs, where the

318

river was swirling up the steps. Mr Crutch's boat 'ad gone down about an hour since — unusual, that — moored overnight, usually, an' set off first light, but the tide —

'How far would he get?'

'He'd know the tide was comin' — wind, see — take refuge in Whitefriars Dock, if 'e's any sense. Lots o' craft go in there.'

'Where the coal is unloaded,' Dickens said.

'Right, sir, Crutch carries coal.'

'Name of the barge?' Jones asked.

'*The Lant*, sir — allus moors at Essex Stairs — fer Mrs Crutch.'

'Show us the way,' Jones ordered.

'Can't leave me post, sir.'

'You can't stop the water, man — you've a lamp and you're needed, and we're the police.' Jones's strong grip propelled him from his gate.

42: FLOOD

Whitefriars Dock, reached by a maze of dank and filthy alleys and passages full of pushing, yelling and shouting people, was a heaving mass of confusion. Jones ordered the watchman back to the Temple — he was to look out for the police and send them here — or he'd be in a cell at Bow Street by tomorrow. They pushed their way down the lane towards the dock, where they saw the collection of boats that had come in from the storm, coal barges, hay barges, lighters, wherries, rowing boats, all heaving and falling in the swelling water.

There were men with lanterns and ropes and hooks, trying to get down the causeway steps. Men were lifting women and children and passing them up the steps, which were covered in water. Jones collared a very tall, broad-shouldered man with a blackened face, in whose great black arms was a little girl, very blackened, too. He was in the act of passing her up the stairs to another equally sooty-faced man. *Coal-heavers*, Dickens thought.

'Police,' Jones shouted. '*The Lant* — seen it?'

'Yes, down there near the entrance. Tied ter the others. Bow crushed, lettin' in a deal o' water, but we brought Crutch off — shoutin' fer 'elp, 'e woz. 'E's at the top. Bit bashed about. 'E'll live.'

'Anyone else on the boat?'

'Dunno — 'as is wife, usually. She mighta bin taken off.'

'Stemp, see if you can get down — near the barge. I'll go and find Crutch. Charles, stay here and keep your eyes open.'

Dickens watched Stemp pick his way down the crowded stairs. It might be possible for him to get to *The Lant* across the other boats, which were all crashing against each other. Beyond them, he could see other barges out on the river, turning about on the swell. They'd sink, probably. Thank God, Crutch had got to safety. He'd tell what he knew. But what about Scrap? Had he been abandoned, or worse? And that fiend, Wigge?

The noise of the river was tremendous, a deep, persistent roar that spoke of the unbridled power of the water — *no engine*, Dickens thought, as he watched, no steam power, no man-made force could stop it, for nature would have her way. The river would tear on, sweeping away everything in its path, aided by its whirling partners, the wind and rain. He thought of Scrap — borne away on that surge. He'd not have a chance. And Rogers? Had he been on that boat?

He lost sight of Stemp. He only saw the water and confused lights wavering and indistinct figures trying to make fast all sorts of craft, and shadows on the boats leaping, sliding, waving, shouting. Stemp might not find *The Lant*. Which barge was Crutch's, anyway?

'Take 'er,' a rough voice shouted, 'pass along.'

Light as a feather, a little girl was placed in his arms. Her eyes were closed, but he saw the black stain on her head where the long wet hair streamed back. Her clothes were soaked, but he had no time to wonder if she were dead or alive. Someone else seized her, and then a woman was carried up, her arm bent at an odd angle. Alive, though. She was moaning in pain.

A hand grabbed him from behind and Sam Jones was there, his face running with water, his hat gone and his coat sodden, too. Behind him was the sooty-faced coal-heaver.

Jones could hardly speak, but Dickens made out the breathless words. 'Crutch — barge rammed into the dock wall — water in. No idea about the boy or Wigge — or the woman. Nothing about Rogers. Wigge had a gun. Wanted Crutch to go on. Stemp?'

'Can't see him.'

'This man knows the barge. Says he'll come with me — you stay — in case he's brought up by someone.'

'Your lad?' the coal-heaver asked Dickens, seeing only a hatless man with his hair plastered to his head and his clothes drenched. Dickens nodded. 'We'll find 'im.' He turned away. Dickens noticed the rope over his shoulder and the grappling iron in his strong hand and felt some comfort.

Dickens watched them go down, the coal-heaver forcing his way through the crush of people coming up the steps, making a way for Sam Jones. Then they were lost to view and he could only hope that they would be able to cross the decks of the nearer barges to find *The Lant* — he didn't want to think about the gun.

He helped an old woman being pushed up the steps by another coal heaver, and she was hauled beyond him by another pair of arms. And so it went on. He knew nothing but the shrieking of the wind, the pelting rain and spray in his face, the surge of the river, and the water at his knees as he was forced further down the steps as more people crammed in further up, and more women and children were helped to safety. He took whatever body was handed to him and passed it along, always looking at the face, hoping and dreading at the same time. Miraculously, a basket came to him with a screaming baby in it — very much alive. He passed it on — to whom, he had no idea. All the faces looked the same — running with water, deadly white and strained, and the clothes so sodden and black that it was impossible to say man or woman.

He felt the strong tug of water at his thighs and something clutching at his legs. Looking down, he saw that someone was in the water beneath him, a sudden swell dragging the body away. He grasped at a fistful of clothing and felt a thin pair of shoulders — a child. With as great a heave as he could manage against the sucking water, he pulled, felt himself sliding, the clothes slipping from his grip. A wave rolled over him. He was floundering under the filthy, freezing blackness, knocking against something hard, and a hand was grabbing. He caught it and his other hand found an iron ring and he hauled himself up the steps, winded and gasping, pulling the body with him so that it lay on the steps, coughing and gasping, too, but he kept hold of the hand so tightly that he felt the bones of it.

A great shout went up from below. There was a rush of feet and he was forced down again, up to his waist in the water. He crawled back up, looking over his shoulder to see that one of the barges had broken loose and was being carried back into the river. Oh, God. Not *The Lant*. He saw the barge turn and twist, and crash into the wall where it seemed stuck fast. And then there was someone standing on the little cabin roof, trying to reach an iron ring. The figure hung there. Another figure lay down on the pier, stretching its arms to try to reach him. A cheer went up. They thought he was saved, but the barge suddenly shifted again and the hand slipped from the iron ring. The figure vanished down into the water. And there was nothing to do but for the leaping figures below to attempt to secure the barge with hooks and ropes. When Dickens looked down, the clutching hand was gone.

Time had no meaning. Dickens had no idea of how long he had been there, being shoved and pummelled, almost drowned, passing people and children up, ropes and irons down those steps until he found himself sitting again and holding on an iron ring nearly at the bottom of the stairs. The wind had carried away the striking of the great multitude of city clocks, but he thought he heard a bell sounding somewhere. At the

Temple, perhaps, the ancient church clock telling him that Time was going on through flood and tempest and would always go on, even though the wild figures down below seemed to dance towards their deaths.

But he felt a change. In the wind first, which seemed to lessen as he sat, frozen to the bone, his wet clothes clinging like grave clothes. He looked down again. There seemed to be a diminution in the numbers being carried to safety, and the water seemed to be going down, the roar of the dreadful tide lessening. The flood was on the ebb, he thought.

And so it was. The tide was falling. The water receding from the steps. A man lay next to him like a thing washed up from the deep — but he wasn't the boy — boy? Why did he think boy? Because before he had looked up at the great shout, he had seen legs in ragged trousers, a boot tied with string, and a thin hand clutching his —

Someone touched him on the shoulder. 'Mr Dickens?'

He looked up into a white face with a gash across the forehead. 'Stemp? Where's —'

'I don't know — I didn't find *The Lant*, and then there was folk on other boats — I couldn't tell. Looked all over. Slipped an' bashed me 'ead. I'm all right. I'm goin' back now. Water's goin down.'

There was a wet, black strip of shore now. Stemp helped him up and they climbed aboard the nearest craft, a low-lying Peter boat, a dredgerman's boat. The water was not so wild now and they were able to slither and scramble from deck to deck until, near the opening of the dock, Dickens glanced at the barge that had stuck against the wall. It was *The Lant*, the barge from which the man had tried to escape. Wigge? And he saw the outline of a tall man, a man with broad shoulders and hefty arms.

'Mr Jones?' Dickens asked as he and Stemp made the barge and saw that the man was the coal-heaver.

Jones came crouching out of the cabin, half-carrying, half-dragging someone in his arms. The coal-heaver was first, for the other two stared in horror, but it was a woman the coal-heaver took in his strong arms.

'Miss Fanny Hatton, I imagine,' Jones said. 'She's dead. Shot. No one else on board.'

The barge rocked suddenly and seemed to turn. Stemp caught Dickens before he fell; Jones grabbed the cabin doorframe; only the coal-heaver stood still with the woman in his arms.

'Let's get off. We've searching to do.'

'There was a boy —' Dickens said.

Jones looked at him, taking in the fact that he was thoroughly drenched and that there seemed to be blood on his face. He must have been in the water. He saw, too, such a look of anguish that he asked, 'What is it?'

'In the water — I tried — and then I was sucked in — I brought him out and then he was gone — it could have been. I think it was —'

Stemp said, 'You couldn't have known in that dark — in the water — there was all sorts o' kids, families from the boats — in that crowd —'

'If anyone should have — I should — I let go — I let go —'

Jones saw him look wildly from one to the other, but there was no time. Dickens would have to bear it, as they all would. He strode across the deck and took him by the shoulder — none too gently. 'Not now. Name of Scrap,' he said to the coal-heaver. 'When we've deposited her at the top, get some men, will you, Mr — er —'

'Jem, sir, Jem Batty. I will.'

'Stay with her, Stemp. I can't afford a body to go missing. We'll deal with the shooting later, and on your way see if you can find anybody from Bow Street. I told Feak —'

'Sir.'

The coal-heaver led the way, helped by Stemp to get on to another boat and so make their way towards the steps.

'I know,' Jones said to Dickens, taking him by the arm, more gently this time. 'Come on. Let's get off this thing.'

Then they heard a shout. 'Mr Jones. Sam! Sam!'

Looking round, they saw, coming into the dock, a police galley, and standing up with a lantern was a familiar figure. John Gaunt of the Thames River Police. 'Wait,' he cried, and the boat came on as far as it could, far enough for another policeman to tie it up to a barge. Then Gaunt came across another couple of swaying barges with someone else whom they saw in his own lamplight to be their old friend, Inspector Bold.

'We've your Sergeant Rogers in our boat, Mr Jones — he's told us what's gone on. Your lad went in — we've come to help —'

'He was on the steps, I'm sure,' Dickens said. He felt sure now. It had been. The hand — he felt it now — the bones of it. Scrap's hand. And he had let go. He wanted to weep.

'Then we'll look — we know him. Go and talk to your sergeant, Mr Jones. I've four men there. Send me three across with lights. The other can help you. I've other boats coming to help and men up on top.'

'A woman's body up top with my constable, Stemp —'

'There's a dead house near St Bride's.'

'Where do you know that no one's likely to find her? I need to make sure she's not taken away with any other bodies.'

'Gas works, I'd say. Good many sheds there. I'll see to it.'

A man of few words, Inspector Bold. But he and John Gaunt would do everything right. Jones knew that. They had worked together before. A relief to see that resolute face, to hear that practical voice — and to take orders for once. And if Scrap had been on the stairs —

'You think —'

'I do, Sam,' said Dickens, 'I just know —'

'Then, there's a chance — let's get Rogers.'

There would be time to explain later. Rogers was all right. Black with coal dust, frozen, bruised and battered by the water, but standing up and ready to go. Inspector Bold's three men took their lanterns, and the fourth man led them across the boats, across the widening black strip of shore, and to the stairs. The waters were returning from off the earth.

43: EBB

After the deluge, Dickens thought, seeing the men — and some women — resting on the steps in attitudes of sheer exhaustion, some with their heads in their hands. What had they lost? Boats? Livelihoods? Children? It would be the same up in the streets and alleys: families washed out of their homes; filth and mud ankle deep in parlours and kitchens, and waist deep in cellars. Poverty and stink — and then the workhouse.

He trudged up the steps after Jones, Rogers, and Bold's constable, whose lamp paused at different faces. He saw heads shaking and felt his heart plummet. At the top of the steps all was a confusion of rope, chains, baskets, boxes, feet, heads, sodden bundles of clothes, barking dogs, chickens, another pig calmly munching at some scattered food, and policemen helping people up and directing them away from the dock. St Bride's workhouse was up the road. He saw a clergyman's collar and a shock of white hair, and arms waving. St Bride's Church, he thought, taking some of the people in. There was goodness, always — he thought of the coal-heaver who had assumed Scrap was his boy. Well, he was — and he'd let go.

Someone was talking to Sam. He hurried up the last steps. Constable Feak was there from Bow Street with Constable Semple.

'Sir,' he was saying, 'we saw the watchman at the Temple, but we couldn't —'

'Never mind that now,' Jones snapped, 'Scrap's missing. Bring lamps?'

'Yes, sir, plenty.' He had looked shocked at the superintendent's brusqueness, but he understood. They were all fond of Scrap.

'Give a lamp to Mr Dickens and —'

A cry went up. 'Body found — in the mud.'

Another coal-heaver and a mate were dragging something up the stairs. The policemen went down. Dickens followed with his lamp, feeling his legs shaking, but it was a man, not a boy. The coal-heavers turned him over. Sam Jones raised his lamp to see the dead face. No one they knew.

'Where was he?'

'By that barge — *The Lant* — saw 'im earlier try to get off, but he fell in.'

The man Dickens saw fall when he had been dragged into the water again — when he had let go. 'I thought it might be Wigge.'

'You didn't see anyone else trying to get off?' Jones asked.

'No, sir, sorry.'

'Right, Semple, Feak. I want you to get to the gasworks and find Inspector Bold — there's a woman's body. Not to be moved — Semple, you stay with her and let Bold get on with his own work.'

'Am I ter come back, sir?' Feak asked.

Jones had thought furiously. 'No, you get back to Bow Street — try going by Fleet Street, but get there and get Inspector Grove and two more men — anybody. Then you're to go to Mary Place, William Road — Grove'll know it. Number five. Get in by any means and secure the house. No one, and I mean no one, comes in. You're looking for any guns and papers, letters — tell Grove, anything that names Sir Mordaunt Quist. You might be there all night, but don't leave until I get there. Got that?'

329

'Sir.' They went back up the stairs.

Jones turned to Rogers. 'Mr Dickens thinks Scrap was at the bottom of these stairs. Go and look. Bold's men are down there.'

'The church, I'll try there. You try the workhouse,' Dickens said.

Out of the dock and into the street, shoving through the crowd, looking up, looking down, seeing faces, young, old, bruised, battered, shattered with shock, impossible to tell, listening, hoping, seeing only strangers and policemen, then hearing a voice and hoping again. Time going on. Losing Sam, finding him, hoping.

'Sam, Sam Jones! Mr Dickens!' Pushing towards them was John Gaunt, and with him someone smaller, very wet, even dirtier than the wretch who had haunted Temple Gardens, but grinning.

There was nothing to be said, but for Gaunt to go down to get Rogers. The gasworks could wait. Stemp would wait, but they'd get the news to him. Scrap stood staring at them.

Jones found his voice. 'The woman's dead. We haven't found Wigge.'

'Serves 'er right,' Scrap said, 'an' I 'opes 'e's drowned.' And Time started again. And Rogers came and said, 'Thank God, you're safe,' and Superintendent Jones said, 'Indeed. I was worried for a while,' and Charles Dickens couldn't speak.

John Gaunt went off to find Bold, and the others went up to the churchyard to find a quiet spot. Dickens was surprised to realise that the wind and rain had stopped, and up above the moon appeared so that they could see more clearly. He found his brandy flask underneath his wet coat in his jacket pocket and passed it round.

'Sovereign cure fer the gout, Mr Jones —' not Mr Dickens, but Mr Samuel Weller, whose irrepressible spirits were wanted just now — 'vich vot is known ter be caused by drinkin' too much water —'

They were glad to laugh, and the brandy was warm and welcome. And Jones gave Charles Dickens such a look — a look in which all their friendship, all their life together, all their cases were distilled — that Dickens nearly wept again.

'Now, tell us what happened,' Dickens said. 'Rogers, you start.'

Rogers told how he had been making his way to the stairs and had seen a woman carrying a travellin' bag — not Mrs Crutch — much slenderer. Thick veil and bonnet — goin' to Essex Stairs. Followed and saw her get onto the barge — the water was comin' up, so where'd the barge be goin'? It always came about nine and stayed till dawn, when Mrs Crutch came to work. Heard shoutin' — knew it was Scrap. The barge was pullin' away. Saw the rope trailin' in the water. Just grabbed it an' went in. Thought he'd get on board somehow — just held on, then a bit after — couldn't say how long — the water seemed to surge — barge spun round — found himself alongside. Barge dipped, he scrambled aboard. Saw the man, Wigge, seemed to be shoutin' at Crutch. Crutch couldn't hardly control the barge — the water was so high and so rough. Crutch pointin' to landward — wanted to go in at Temple Stairs, Rogers thought —

'Wigge wanted to go on, you think?'

'To Blackfriars, I wondered — steamer pier, p'raps. Goin' off somewhere — she had that travellin' bag, but they'd never make it.'

"'S'wot I 'ears,' Scrap piped up. 'The woman — she 'ad the gun. 'E, Wigge, asked about Mr D — said 'e'd seen us, an' why was I spyin'? An' 'oo was Doublett, 'nother spy? Niver told 'em — don't know nothink, I says. Don't know no Mr Dickens, 'cept some ancient meethoosla cove wot give me a penny —' seeing Dickens's face — 'when we woz at them chambers — yer gotter admit yer looked —'

'Elderly, I thought, but carry on, Scrap. We are all agog.'

'Barge starts rollin' an' that, an' Wigge says Crutch'll 'ave ter go on. When 'e's outta the cabin, she's got the gun on me, but then there's a big old 'eave. Barge crashes inter somethin'. She's down. I 'ears the gun go off an' I'm outta there —'

'So, Wigge didn't kill her.'

'No, I heard it, sir. Wigge was on the deck when the boat crashed, but I couldn't save myself — went right over into the water. Managed to cling on to somethin' — metal ladder, I thought, but then I was swept away. Came up against another boat — Inspector Bold, sir.'

'Scrap?'

'Sees the other barges — thinks I can jump, but I slips down in the water. Some 'ulkin feller plucks me out an' I'm on the steps, then the water's over me an' someone else grabs me. 'E's swept away — 'ope 'e woz awright — tried ter save me — an' then I'm on the steps an' crawlin' up, an' there's crowds o' folk an' I'm jest wanderin' about, thinkin' 'ow ter get back when there's Mr Gaunt.'

'What now?' asked Rogers.

'You're taking Scrap to the stationery shop,' Jones said, 'and you both get dry and get something to eat — and two warm beds — before you die of pneumonia. I'm taking Mr Dickens to Wellington Street for the same purpose, and then I've an appointment in Mary Place.'

'Wigge, sir?'

'We can't do anything about Wigge now. A man covered in mud, soaked to the skin — he could be anywhere.'

'Just one question, Sergeant,' Dickens said. 'Can you swim?'

'Never fancied it, sir. All that water.'

44: PAPERS

Dickens, swathed in blankets, his head wrapped in a towel, feet on the fender, socks and boots steaming, had stopped shivering. He was holding a toasting fork to the fire. A hunk of bread was browning nicely. It was something to eat before going to Mary Place. They had given themselves an hour. Jones had wanted to go on his way, leaving Dickens to thaw out, but, as the latter had reasonably pointed out, Inspector Grove would not leave his post, and Sir Mordaunt Quist was, no doubt, at his ease in Cavendish Square, or dining out with the great and the not so good. Jones had reluctantly agreed and had made tea.

'I'll get some clothes on,' Dickens said, having eaten his toast and gulped his tea. 'I'll be quick. Just eat something — please.'

Jones watched the steam rising from his own boots. At least Dickens was looking better — his ability to bounce back was always astonishing. But, Lord, he was weary. *No bounce in me*, he thought, taking a bite of the toast. He rested his head on the back of the chair and closed his eyes, and then Dickens was back, fastening his waistcoat.

'Dining out?' Jones asked, surveying the bright tartan waistcoat, the sight of which had brought him to life.

'Never knowingly underdressed, Mr Jones.' He dragged on his jacket and a heavy caped coat. 'I could drive a mail coach to eternity in this. No need, however, there'll be a cab down the street.'

Wellington Street was deserted. Quiet had descended. Only scattered pools of water, litter and wet newspapers showed that the flood had been. They stopped for a moment, arrested by the sound of a nearby clock striking the hour. They listened to the metal voices calling back, near and distant, resounding from towers of various heights and in various tones. *Time,* Dickens thought. *What time?*

'Only nine o'clock,' he said. 'It ought to be midnight.'

'Ought to be morning — and this all over.'

'Sorry I lost my head, Sam, back there.'

Jones touched his shoulder. 'I know. I nearly lost mine when I saw that body in the cabin. I did think — then, I'm almost ashamed to say, I was glad it was her.'

They walked on towards Bow Street, where there was bound to be a cab now that the river had gone down.

'Where were they going, I wonder?'

Jones stopped. 'Good God, Charles, that cabin — the travelling bag — why were they going?'

'They knew we were onto them. Scrap said —'

'But, leaving Quist — that's —'

'I wonder if he knows they've gone.'

'We've got time. You said Grove would wait — her travelling bag — from Mary Place — just one bag —'

'You mean passports — papers —'

'We need to go back to the dock. You know what could happen now the water's gone down — looting, thieving —'

'Or that blasted barge could sink.'

There were fewer people about by the dock, but the police were on guard — Jones recognised one of Bold's men.

'Inspector Bold?'

'Below, sir.' The man knew who he was. 'They're still lookin' for any —' He pointed down to the muddy shore, much wider now, and the river almost placid under the moonlight.

Like a dream, Dickens thought, a scene from a play where figures in shadow laboured at some pantomime task. Braziers had been lit on the mud and on some of the barges where, in the lurid glow, they could see the outlines of coal-heavers, lightermen, watermen, dredgermen, hammering, pulling, shoving, loading, scavenging for lost goods, some untying their boats, some already pushing off onto the river, making ready to sail away on the ebb tide. A little blaze seemed to flicker here and there, indicating someone moving between the boats — an enterprising purlman who normally supplied the barges and boats with grog kept hot on a little grated box, and who was sure of good custom tonight. Some of the police were helping the bargemen, and others were directing their lantern lights downwards to make circles of light. And everywhere there was the foul reek of mud and water.

'Your body is safe, Mr Jones. Gaunt's there with your Constable Semple. They won't let anyone near her. Your man, Stemp, is guarding the barge.' Inspector Bold appeared at their side as they stepped onto the mud. 'Glad you found your lad.'

'Thanks to Gaunt, and I didn't doubt your safekeeping, Inspector. Any more bodies found?'

'Two — an old woman and a child. Drowned, I'm afraid. You lookin' for someone else?'

'I am — black hair, black eyes, Mr Dickens's build. Calls himself Wigge, but maybe Wiggins — Solomon or Solly. Mind, he could call himself anything.'

'We'll keep a look out.'

'I need to get on *The Lant*. I didn't see anyone, but I'd like to be sure.'

'Easy enough. It ain't going anywhere — stuck fast.'

Bold led the way. *The Lant* looked a sorry sight, with its bow splintered and its stern at an angle in the mud. Constable

Stemp was waiting. It was easy to climb up onto the listing deck, which was awash with water and mud, and coal scattered everywhere. There was no sign of Wigge — dead or alive.

The cabin was undamaged, and there was Fanny Hatton's carpetbag on Mrs Crutch's bunk. Miss Hatton wouldn't be coming back for it. Her journey was elsewhere.

'There might be a gun somewhere, Mr Bold — the lad heard it go off when the barge crashed into the dock wall.'

'Right.'

'Give him a hand, Stemp.'

Dickens watched as Jones examined the lock on the carpetbag. He watched as Jones felt in his pocket for the skeleton keys he kept for just such emergencies. He watched as the long hands carefully inserted the key and he heard the click. He watched as one hand brought out a parcel wrapped in wax cloth. He only breathed again when Bold spoke.

'Found it.' And there in Bold's hand was a little flintlock pistol. 'It's been fired.'

'The bullet's in her, I'll bet,' Dickens said.

'Then we'll find it — without Doctor Ebenezer Garland's help, this time.' Jones was unwrapping the parcel. He handed the wax cloth to Dickens. *That smell*, he thought, lifting it to his nose. Ottar of roses.

'Quist,' he said, 'his scent.'

'Well, I don't suppose Wigge meant to leave these behind. Perhaps he was thrown overboard like Rogers.'

And all four men looked at the papers now unfolded on Superintendent Jones's lap.

45: PORTRAIT

It had seemed a very long night. Dickens supped with Sam Jones and Elizabeth, who had been very glad that neither of them had caught pneumonia in the storm. She offered a warming stew of beef and dumplings, even though it was almost midnight by the time they had returned from their rendezvous with Inspector Grove. Grove's instructions were to see Inspector Bold first thing in the morning and get Fanny Hatton's body from the gasworks to Doctor Woodhall at King's College Hospital, and to ask him to extract the bullet.

Mary Place had revealed some things of great interest, including a little cake of rose-scented soap on a wash basin in a gentleman's dressing room situated by a large, imposing bedroom. There was an old wig in a box at the bottom of a sarcophagus of a wardrobe in which, Dickens had observed, any number of bodies might have been stashed. Skeletons in cupboards, as it were. There were no bodies, but a heavy box, the lock of which had been forced — the chisel next to it telling its story. It was empty. There had been papers in there, the papers which had found their way onto a barge on the River Thames. A wax seal was broken at the bottom of the box and there was a little scrap of red tape — the kind that lawyers used.

Evidence told that Sir Mordaunt Quist had been the occupant of the bedroom — when he wasn't occupying the matrimonial couch in Cavendish Square — if, indeed, there were such an article of home furnishing. The very large-sized shirts in the chest of drawers proclaimed the very large Sir Mordaunt Quist as their wearer. The bed and its underpinnings revealed nothing but dust; the carpets were blameless, and the floorboards firmly nailed down.

Another, smaller bedroom was a gentleman's — his suits were in the wardrobe, his shirts and undergarments in a chest, his toilet bottles on top. Mr Wigge, they presumed. A single bed — perhaps Miss Hatton was not his paramour. However, the third bedroom told a different tale. The scent of violets — cloying. Two pillows with two impresses of two heads — and the sheets and blankets somewhat rumpled, and a nightgown on the floor. Her dresses were in the wardrobe, and her silver-topped toilet bottles on top of a chest with a triple mirror. A silver-backed hairbrush and mirror lay there, too. And a string of pearls — the clasp broken.

'They were in a hurry,' Jones said, opening a drawer.

'They knew.'

'He'd been following you since that dinner in Cavendish Square.'

'I gave it away by asking about Pierce Mallory, and Wigge saw me at the races with Captain Bone. You said — Quist must have known about the Ferrars case.'

'And Wigge saw us at Carr Mallory's funeral — of course they knew. And the lawyers — the benchers — they wanted the name of the suspect. I didn't want to. Oh, of course, it would be confidential, but —'

'Someone talked —'

'And someone heard — Wigge, no doubt.'

'They were running away — with the papers. No proof left of anything. Wigge would know that Quist would try to shift the blame on him, and Quist would know that they had the means to destroy him —'

Jones didn't answer. He was rifling through the drawer, taking out silk, lace, and little boxes, which he handed to

Dickens. Rings, earrings, bracelets. Expensive trinkets — for a daughter?

The deep bottom drawer contained folded petticoats, chemises, and shawls, which he lifted out. There was the scent of lavender. And then an old silk shawl. They could see the ragged fringe. Jones lifted it and felt something hard — something oblong. Inside the wrappings was a book. A leatherbound prayer book. He opened it, and there on the fly-leaf was an inscription in faded ink. The date was 1788, and the name was: Lawrence Hatton Quist, Rathray, Loughlinstown.

'The prayer book — the one where —' Dickens found he was whispering.

'The famous deed was found — pity it ain't here now with a handy forged signature.'

'Hatton, though — that's a clincher, I'd say.'

'Oh, I think so.'

'And the documents, they're enough to challenge him with?'

'I'm sure. Pity Wigge got away with his passport, though — still, let's concentrate on Quist for now — oh, wait a minute — what's this?'

This was a square bit of canvas — rather dry and cracked, but Jones peered at the writing. 'A name,' he said.

'What name?'

'Miss Frances Hatton Quist.'

He turned over the piece of canvas. And there she was. William Fagan's mad wife. Just a girl in the picture, a pretty dark-haired girl with a coronet of pink roses in her hair and a high-waisted gauzy white dress with pink ribbons at the shoulder. Looking straight at the viewer. Unafraid, almost smiling — wanting to, perhaps. A touch of mischief in the hint of a dimple at the corner of her mouth. The girl who eloped with William Fagan. Spoilt and foolish, perhaps, but a girl who lost everything and now was, medically speaking, an idiot. What harm that man had done — even to his own daughter. So much harm that she had meant to betray him in the end.

Elizabeth Jones had left her husband and Dickens after feeding them. There was nothing they could do until morning, but bed for Sam Jones was unthinkable, and Dickens swore that he could no more walk back to Wellington Street than swim against a rushing tide.

'Don't remind me,' Jones said. 'Just put your feet up on that sofa. I'm going to change my clothes. I'll come back and keep you company. Try to get some sleep. We'll be off to Bow Street first thing — Grove will have gone to Bold about the body, and he'll wait at Doctor Woodhall's mortuary. We need Stemp and Rogers for Cavendish Square. We've news for Sir Mordaunt Quist.'

Jones came back to find his guest asleep. He sat down by the fire, turned up the lamp, and began to read the letter that Elizabeth had given him when he went upstairs. It was a long letter and a satisfying one.

When he had finished, he looked at the sofa opposite. A pair of intent eyes looked back at him.

'You've been an age reading that.'

'From Mr Mordaunt Purefoy.'

'Interesting?'

'Oh, very — so much so that I will look forward very much to sharing its contents with his namesake. What you might call a clincher. Be my guest.'

Dickens took the letter and began to read. Superintendent Jones went to get ink and paper. Charles Dickens was a quick copier. Caution was the watchword.

46: IGNOMINY

They came up Holles Street to the south side of Cavendish Square by the bronze statue of Lord George Bentinck — a looming phantom presence, silvered in the grey light of the early morning, seeming to hover in the wreaths of mist about his plinth. Last night's rain had left a mist around the garden in the middle of the square so that the trees looked ghostly, too. The great mansions still slumbered, wrapped in the dream-like stillness. It seemed unreal when compared to last night's scenes at the river, the awful human suffering they had witnessed. No sign of flood or tempest here, nor poverty, nor misery, nor death.

But there were lights in some of the lower windows. Servants up and about, no doubt, heaving coals up back staircases, carrying hot water for baths, lighting fires in drawing rooms and dining rooms, firing up kitchen ranges, cooking eggs and bacon and kidneys, pouring coffee into silver pots, setting breakfast tables with silver cutlery and plates edged in gold with heraldic devices proclaiming the distinguished pedigree of masters and mistresses still abed.

Here and hereabouts the ghosts of the old aristocracy lingered, their names still echoing down the years. The Earl of Oxford's wife thrice remembered — in Holles Street and Henrietta Street; she had been a Cavendish, too; the Duke of Portland nearby and the De Vere family, who had once been Earls of Oxford, and Harley Street, named for an Earl of Oxford's heir. Lord George had been a Cavendish and haunted Bentinck Street, where Dickens had once lived with his parents while he was reporting on the wills, the wives and the wrecks at

Doctors' Commons. Lodgings — cheap enough. Genteel poverty — not quite what Lord George had in mind up there on his plinth in his spectral robes of state. He probably hadn't murder in mind, either.

And over to the north-west of the square, lights were on in the lower regions of Quickswood House, where Sam Jones hoped Sir Mordaunt Quist would be taken by surprise at his loaded table. He and Dickens had breakfasted on bread and butter and tea before making their way to Bow Street, where they had recruited Rogers and Stemp. It was time to present Sir Mordaunt Quist with the evidence of his fraud and bigamy. And to challenge him about murder.

'All set?' Dickens asked. He felt nervous. He wondered if Quist would outface them, deny Wigge, deny his daughter, somehow twist his way out of it, find a lawyer as good as himself, find a judge, a bishop, a minister of the Crown, a duke of dark corners, all of whom would hedge him about so tightly that Sam's evidence would seem but a puny blade to cut through such a thicket. Quist. Twist.

'Let's see his face when we show him what we have.'

Rogers and Stemp were to stay outside where they would not be seen from the house. Rogers would go for a cab when the superintendent's message came. Dickens and Jones ascended the steps to the house and stood under the massive portico with its Corinthian pillars. Dickens remembered the great black door from his first visit, the gleaming brass fittings, and the bell he was about to ring again. Last time, he had been invited to dine. Now, he and Sam were uninvited guests — if Sir Mordaunt Quist would see them. He didn't express his sudden doubt to Sam, but pressed the bell.

He presented his card to the powdered footman, who showed no surprise. Nor did he at Dickens's mention of

Superintendent Jones of Bow Street. After all, his master was an eminent lawyer, and Mr Charles Dickens had been to dine. A matter of some importance, Dickens told the man. They would be obliged if Sir Mordaunt would see them.

Then they were in the marble hall, watching the footman make his slow, stately way up the grand staircase with its wrought-iron banister. Dickens's card was carried on a silver salver. The dining room was upstairs, Dickens remembered, along with Sir Mordaunt's library where Quist had quoted Macbeth's words and talked of Thomas Wainewright, who had murdered his relatives with strychnine. Quist who had named his horse for a poison. And who was as good as a murderer himself — and a fraudster, an imposter, and a bigamist.

The silence seemed to congeal about them like ice, though there was a fire burning in the marble fireplace. Nothing moved. The flames seemed stilled. Dickens glanced at the paintings. The shepherd and shepherdess in their pastoral landscape had stopped to regard them curiously. The sheep gazed, open-mouthed. The lady on the swing was caught in mid-flight, her eyes wondering. Even the dead in the portraits appeared to be waiting. Above, the Roman figures on the painted ceiling stared down, grim-faced, except the one whose hand pointed to the top of the stairs. What did he know? Was that an accusing hand? Dickens felt that sense of unreality again, as if they had stepped into a dream. Middle Temple, the river, the storm, Pierce Mallory's shabby lodging, the blood blooming on Carr Mallory's chest, Estcourt's grotesquely distorted features, and Caroline Dax's blackened face all seemed as distant as another planet. It seemed impossible that they should be here. Impossible that Quist should send a message from those upper regions.

Dickens almost started when a clock struck the hour and the footman beckoned them up the stairs.

'Sir Mordaunt was breakfasting. He is in his library now. He asks if you would care to take coffee with him.'

How gracious, Dickens thought, *bidden to his presence as if we are two importunate clients. Coffee would choke me.* Superintendent Jones declined and they were shown into the library.

Quist sat behind his desk, quite at his ease. Not quite, Dickens observed. He put down his cup and stood, but he did not come to greet them with hands outstretched as he had greeted Dickens at Fountain Court. He remained behind his fortress.

'What in the world can I do for you at this early hour? You surprise me, Mr Dickens — with a policeman from Bow Street.'

Sam Jones had his hand on the papers in his pocket. 'Your daughter, sir, I have bad news.' This was what they had planned — to take him by surprise.

Quist's face merely expressed puzzlement. *Clever, clever,* Dickens thought.

His tone was equally puzzled. 'Daughter? You are mistaken, Mr Jones, I have no daughter, nor any child.'

'Miss Frances Hatton, daughter of Mrs Frances Fagan who has been incarcerated for thirty years in St Patrick's Asylum in Dublin, medically diagnosed as an idiot. A charity case, I believe. Mrs Frances Fagan, your first wife. Still alive, as this letter and these documents from the asylum show — given to me by a Commissioner of Lunacy.' Jones stepped forward to place the little square of canvas on the desk. 'Miss Frances Hatton Quist, daughter of Mr Lawrence Hatton Quist who owned lead mines at Ballycorus in Dublin County.'

Now Quist's fat face paled and Dickens saw the beads of sweat on his brow, but his voice was steady. 'My first wife is dead.'

Quist might not have spoken. Jones simply carried on. He asked no questions — there would be no accusation of police entrapment by a wily lawyer. Dickens marvelled at the hard flatness of his tone. 'Mr Lawrence Hatton Quist who was drowned with his wife and son in a yachting accident, and with whose daughter you eloped, and with whose son you studied law at Trinity College, Dublin. At which place you were sponsored by Mr Mordaunt Purefoy. Your grandfather was a linen-draper fallen on hard times. You took the name Mordaunt, and the name Quist, and the fortune from the lead mills. It seems that you found a will in this prayer book —' Jones put down the prayer book by the little portrait. Mordaunt Quist looked at the two objects with apparent indifference, but Jones continued relentlessly — 'which left Mrs Frances Fagan, the former Miss Quist, the family fortune which had, in a previous will, been left to her brother.'

'And your proof?'

'Here are the documents found in an oilskin package in a travelling bag taken on a barge by Miss Frances Hatton, who was shot —'

Quist couldn't help himself. 'Shot?'

'She was with a companion, a Mr Solly Wiggins, known as Solomon Wigge, who a witness tells me is your close acquaintance. Your daughter —'

'I have no —'

Jones interrupted, his tone unchanged. He might have been reading out the post office directory. 'This birth certificate says that you have. Frances Hatton, known as Fanny Hatton, was your first child by Miss Frances Hatton Quist, who became

346

Mrs William Fagan. Your second child was stillborn after the yachting tragedy. The shooting of your daughter was accidental in last night's flood. The portrait I found in a house at Mary Place along with other papers which prove your fraudulent dealings with Solly Wiggins, otherwise known as Solomon Wigge, who lived at the house with Miss Fanny Hatton. Evidence showed that you were a frequent visitor to that house —'

'I believed she was dead.'

'Yet the fees were paid by your friend, Mr Dermot Barbary, guardian of Miss Frances Hatton, until he died in 1846. These are the copies of the receipts from Mr Herbert Wing of Lincoln's Inn, given to Mr Barbary in token of the moneys paid to St Patrick's asylum for the care of your wife — until you stopped paying.'

'My name is not on those receipts. I know nothing of them.'

'You are Mr William Fagan, and I must take you in charge for the crime of bigamy, and fraud. You placed your wife in the asylum, sold the lead mills and property, and came to London as Mordaunt Quist, who married Lady Primrose Quickswood —'

'A point of law, Superintendent, if I may —' Ah, the law. He was on surer ground now — 'a husband, cannot, in law, defraud his wife of money or chattels, and, as to bigamy, I deny it. I believed my first wife to be dead.'

'Mr Mordaunt Purefoy has written to me. He was one of the executors of Mr Lawrence Quist's will, as well as the Reverend Mr Michael Carew, minister of the Protestant church at Ballycorus, the same reverend gentleman who signed the papers admitting your wife to the asylum. The will found in the prayer book was, it seems, signed by that same reverend gentleman and a Mr Dermot Barbary, at that time a practising lawyer in Dublin — this found will leaving half the property and fortune to Mrs Frances Fagan, and to her absolutely, in the event of her brother predeceasing her.'

'Which event occurred — in my dead wife's memory, I took the family name. My name is Quist. Her fortune, I legally inherited.'

'Mr Purefoy, who, incidentally, gives me the story of your birth and upbringing by Mr Fagan, the linen-draper, expresses doubts about the found will and its two signatories, one of which, Mr Dermot Barbary, left Dublin at the same time as you did. Mr Purefoy was summoned to the bedside of the Reverend Mr Carew, who confessed to him that he had been paid by Mr William Fagan to sign the will and to pre-date it.'

'Hearsay, Mr Jones — the reverend gentleman is dead; so, you have told me, is Mr Dermot Barbary.'

'It will be up to a jury, sir, to decide on the matters of fraud and bigamy. As to murder —'

'Oh, I am a murderer, too? Is this a fiction of Mr Dickens's invention?'

'You knew all about the murder of Mr Carr Mallory and Mr Frederick Estcourt — a witness is prepared to swear that you talked of these murders to Mr Solomon Wigge and Miss Fanny Hatton —'

'A disenchanted employee, I presume — one who has been recently sacked for his incompetence, who overheard us talking of a funeral, and of oysters, perhaps?'

'And of Gerrard Street, where Mr Estcourt's dead body was found — poisoned with strychnine. Mr Carr Mallory and his brother, Mr Pierce Mallory, were told of your connection with the Quist family, and your wife's incarceration. Mr Pierce Mallory had a liaison with your daughter, Miss Fanny Hatton, and left her.'

'Mr Pierce Mallory's amatory entanglements are nothing to do with me, and, as for the Mallory family, I knew nothing of their antecedents in Ireland. Mr Carr Mallory left my chambers years ago.'

'Nevertheless, you are connected with the principals in these cases, and you must answer questions — certainly at the inquest on the body of Miss Hatton, and about Mr Wigge, who was on that barge and has now disappeared. Mr Solomon Wigge, otherwise known as Solly Wiggins. The question of identification of these persons, and your relationship with them, must be answered by you. No doubt, questions will be asked about your identity — questions which I can answer. Mr Mordaunt Purefoy has furnished me with details of your birth — an illegitimate one, it seems. The bankrupt linen-draper was your grandfather, his daughter, your mother — dead by your birth in a common lodging house. Father unknown —'

Those two words hung in the air like blades about to fall. Now, Dickens thought, that revelation might well be worse than charges of bigamy and fraud to a man like Quist. He had connived at murder, and, he might twist his way out of it, but the ignominious exposure of his low birth — that would be poison to him. He could see it in the man's face. And two pinpoints of fury in the eyes. The sweat on his brow glistened, oozing fear now, not satisfaction, but his lips were closed.

'Rumour had it that he was a tailor,' Jones began.

'Or tinker, perhaps, beggarman, thief — a felon, certainly,' Dickens finished for him.

Quist did not move, though his glance at Dickens revealed all his malevolence. His mouth opened, but he did not speak.

'I must ask you to accompany me to Bow Street to answer the charges of fraud and bigamy.'

Before their eyes, the man whose world had shattered to pieces, gathered the remnants of his dignity — and his courage, Dickens admitted to himself — and rose behind his fortress, a big man, a formidable man, a wicked man, but a man in supreme control of himself, except that he put his hands in his pockets. To hide their trembling, perhaps, but his voice belied any fear.

'Very well. However, I ask that I may dress. Whatever you impute, Mr Charles Dickens, scribbler, I am a gentleman. I am a Queen's Counsel. I will not go to Bow Street in my dressing gown and slippers. My valet is waiting upstairs.'

Quist's coolness was remarkable. He would take his own time. He took a spoon with a steady hand, stirred his coffee, and raised the cup to his lips, wiping them with a napkin, before moving towards the door. Dickens and Jones followed him from the library and up the next flight of stairs. His step was firm and the plump white hand on the banister rail was steady. A slight, very handsome young man waited at an open door.

'The usual dress, Simpson, for court. These gentlemen will wait for me.'

Jones's hand remained on the door handle, though the valet, whose expression betrayed nothing at all, had tried to close it. It remained ajar. They could hear the sound of drawers opening and a wardrobe door, perhaps, with a faint creak, water poured from a jug, the rattle of bottles. Quist was certainly taking his time. He had not spoken since he had entered the room, nor had the valet. Jones stared at the partly open door, his face a mask of calm resolution. That silence again, thought Dickens. Waiting for the play to begin, for the chief actor to make his entrance —

A tremendous crash. The valet shouting out. Quist lying on the floor where he had fallen. The valet kneeling, staring up at them, crying out, 'A stroke?'

It wasn't. The man on the floor was in the agony of a dreadful convulsion.

'Doctor,' Jones shouted to the man. 'Send the footman. Keep everyone else out.'

47: INQUESTS

The ghastly face, the livid lips, the glassy eyes starting from the head, the hideous paroxysms of the body —

Dickens sitting by the fire at Wellington Street. Never to be warm again, seeing only the nightmarish sequence of events — Lady Primrose's face at the door, Sam Jones shouting, the door slamming shut. The valet sobbing, his hands over his face, incapable of helping. Nothing to think of but to hold the rigid body, then to be thrown back by the return of a violent convulsion. The body bent back like a bow, only the head and heels touching the floor. The face darkening by the second, suffused with blood, the mouth drawn back into that sardonic grin as if he knew that he had cheated them. Sam attempting to give him water. The jaws in spasm biting the glass and blood foaming at the mouth.

And, more horrible, if it could be so, the intervals of calm and the choking voice, robbed of its deep resonance, telling them that he would die, rather die. And then, even he, strong-willed and feelingless as he was, knowing the fit was coming, crying out and shrieking in terror. Outside the door, the cries of servants and a woman's voice commanding silence. The gasping man demanding to be held. The intermission and another horror — of being touched, for that brought another convulsion.

The doctor bursting in. Standing in awe to see his eminent neighbour writhing like a trapped beast. Pushing Dickens aside, holding the heaving frame. Knowing what it was. Knowing that nothing could be done. Yet holding him with Sam Jones, attempting to turn him over and to rub him.

How long? Hours it seemed, but one hour, perhaps, witnessing the rapid tetanic fits, one after another, longer and longer, until Dickens watched him die, and felt only relief that it was over. Nothing else said in those brief intervals of lucidity. No confession.

And Lady Primrose, unmoved, just nodding and turning away. Speaking only to the doctor. 'Do what you must.'

Dickens shook his head to banish the dreadful scenes. He sipped his tea. Strychnine. Wigge watching Frederick Estcourt die, or Wigge and Fanny Hatton. Made of adamant, if they could laugh about that. It had been in that coffee, Sam had thought. The doctor had told them that in cases of strychnine poisoning, the symptoms appear within five to twenty minutes. It fitted.

And the dead man stiffening, his hands like claws, the feet turned inwards, and the snarling mouth contorted into an expression of horror and agony. A young woman's body in the mortuary. A girl who looked like another girl in a portrait — another girl, one who had died to the world — a very long time ago. Had Quist told Fanny Hatton that her mother was dead? When had she known that she was his daughter? Those were questions that would never be answered. The only thing left was to hope that the resumed inquests on the four murder victims would enable Sam to get justice for them. Quist and Fanny Hatton had paid for their crimes. It didn't matter that they had escaped the hangman's noose. Quist had known that it was all over — he had laughed at the idea of strychnine, named his horse after it, and had faced the horror himself. Fanny Hatton had been shot, as had the Mallory brothers. Nemesis for them, but still, surely, it must all come out at the inquest on Fanny Hatton. And Wigge's name blazoned in the newspapers. A wanted man. A hunted man. Where could he hide? And the inquest on Quist — what would that reveal?

Sam Jones came, pale-faced and exhausted, and with news. 'The coroner's inquest on Quist later today at Quickswood House.'

Dickens nodded to show that he understood. It was not uncommon for an inquest to be held at the deceased gentleman's mansion. Convenient for viewing the remains, and they wanted it over. 'What did Henry Meteyard say?'

Jones had been to Lincoln's Inn to consult the barrister they knew — the barrister who could keep a secret, son of a butcher from Limehouse, who never forgot that Sampson Meteyard had pushed him onwards and upwards, the butcher who called Charles Dickens "young Charley" because he'd known him as a boy, and whose ample wife folded young Charley in her arms when he visited. Henry Meteyard, a man of good heart, and of good sense. A fine lawyer, too.

'The verdict will be an accident.'

'How so?'

'The doctor —'

'Ah, Sir James Savage of Cavendish Square — a close friend, no doubt.'

'Who had prescribed powders for Sir Mordaunt Quist — powders that were on his desk. The learned doctor is of the opinion that the deceased, upset by our visit bringing news of the death of the young lady, a young lady whose guardian had been a close friend, made a mistake —'

'And what was the deceased doing with strychnine in his pocket? That's where it was. I saw him put his hand in his pocket.'

'So did I — a servant must have carelessly left the packet of Batley's vermin powder which Sir Mordaunt removed, alas, leaving a few grains in his pocket.'

'It doesn't make sense.'

'It will do — by the time Lady Primrose, the eminent doctor, and Sir Mordaunt Quist's lawyers have perfected the story. No evidence of melancholy or illness; no troubles of any kind.'

'What does Henry say?'

'We have to let it go. A tame coroner — and they'll have one — will pronounce the verdict they want. It's likely to be Speed, and we know how he likes to get things done. And Henry tells me that to go further would be very tricky.'

'Why?'

'You're the fly in the ointment, I'm afraid. If Sir Mordaunt Quist was being interviewed about his involvement in a crime, then you should not have been there. However, if I went only to break the news of the death of the daughter of Sir Mordaunt's close friend, Mr Dermot Barbary, and to tell him that Sir Mordaunt's associate, Mr Solomon Wigge, was missing, perhaps drowned, then Mr Dickens's presence might be explained — he knew Sir Mordaunt, had dined with him, and was a witness to the flood because he was searching for a young messenger boy he employed from time to time —'

'Lord, Sam, I am sorry — and Quist gets away with it.'

'Not quite — it all depends on the inquest on Miss Fanny Hatton. There are papers to be given in evidence; there's her association with Solomon Wigge, otherwise Solly Wiggins — Lord, I'm sick of saying that — Quist's association with him — the man suspected of chicanery at Doctors' Commons; there's a gun; there's a kidnapping.'

'There are witnesses.'

'Mr Micah Reed; Mr and Mrs Crutch; Mr Dickens's messenger boy, known as Scrap; Sergeant Rogers; John Gaunt of the Thames River Police; Constable Jack Doublett —'

'Otherwise known as Septimus.'

Jones couldn't help smiling. 'Please, don't. And Mr Charles Dickens — now that'll make 'em sit up. The foreman of the jury will very likely want to ask you some questions.'

Dickens grinned at him. 'Ah, useful now, I see.'

'Very much so. At Miss Hatton's inquest, the doctor will confirm that she was shot —'

'Sensation in court.'

'Exactly. Inspector Bold will produce the gun; Superintendent Jones, Constable Stemp and Mr Dickens — looking for his messenger boy — all saw the body with its gunshot wound. That very creditable witness, Mr Dickens's messenger boy, will tell of the attempted kidnap. Sergeant Rogers will confirm all that. Furthermore, it seems that Miss Fanny Hatton intended to travel abroad with Mr Solomon Wiggins, otherwise etcetera — as her passport will show. And further papers will reveal her true identity —'

'Another sensation.'

'We'll get there because the coroner will ask Superintendent Jones to untangle this knot of evidence, and he will have to name Sir Mordaunt Quist, and he will have to advert to the investigation of four murders which are in progress — evidence being accumulated, ready for the resumed inquests on the victims.'

'Thus neatly linking him with the murders.'

'That's as far as I dare go until the murder inquests are resumed. The death of Miss Hatton on the river will be properly recorded as an accident, but the coroner will say that all the evidence heard will, no doubt, be of importance to the inquests on the murder victims to be resumed when the police have completed their investigation. And, of course, the police will be looking for Solomon Wigge — associate of Sir Mordaunt Quist at Fountain Court — in connection with the aforementioned murders.'

'Masterly.'

'Thanks to Henry.'

'What now?'

'This, for a start.' Jones held out the bullet which had killed Fanny Hatton. 'It matches the bullet that killed Pierce Mallory. Mr Egg confirms that the two bullets came from this gun. A credible witness.'

And there it was again — the little flintlock pistol — the kind a lady might use — the kind she might tuck into her innocent muff to defend herself against a highwayman — or to shoot a lover who had discarded her.

'Do you think she did it?'

'She pointed that gun at Scrap — she might have shot him. I think she did shoot Pierce Mallory. She might have shot Carr Mallory with the rifle, but more likely that was Wigge.'

'Wherever he is.'

The melancholy occurrence, as the newspapers had it, was duly reported. Dickens read the account of the coroner's inquest on the sudden death of the eminent barrister, Sir Mordaunt Quist, in *The Daily News* — Pierce Mallory's old newspaper. Not that Dickens had needed to read it. He had given his evidence.

Accident, of course, as Henry Meteyard had foretold. Mr Speed, with a wary eye on the distinguished legal representatives of Lady Primrose Quist, there to watch the proceedings, directed the jury with his usual celerity. He adverted to the testimony of the learned doctor, Sir James

Savage. To the morning call paid by Superintendent Jones and Mr Dickens which, undoubtedly, distressed his eminent colleague, Sir Mordaunt Quist, a barrister, whom everyone testified was at the height of his powers, whose success in bringing the Marylebone poisoner to justice was legendary. He doubted not that the jury remembered that notorious trial and the masterly prosecution by Sir Mordaunt Quist. The jury, like so many sheep, Dickens thought, had nodded in grave unison.

A gentleman, the coroner summed up, with a wide circle of friends among the greatest in the land — indeed, Mr Charles Dickens, the famous novelist could be counted therein — Dickens had ground his teeth at that, but he had wanted to laugh at the next tribute — a gentleman, the coroner intoned unctuously, who had, as the crowning glory of his life, married the daughter of the Earl of Quickswood, their union being of the most happy and prosperous. Lady Primrose, he was most sorry to say, was too prostrate with grief to attend. An unhappy accident, he concluded, and so did the sheep. In her goodness and charity, Lady Primrose could not bring herself to apportion blame, but, Mr Speed said, it was his melancholy duty to warn against the negligent disposal of poisons in households. The untimely death of Sir Mordaunt Quist should be a warning to all servants to be mindful of their responsibilities.

'Very neat,' Superintendent Jones had observed as they walked away from the house, past the statue of Lord George Bentinck, gazing serenely into eternity whither he had been dispatched in 1848. His body had been found on a remote country path — not murder or suicide — not the noble Lord — despite the rumours about his private life and that of his brother. Neither was married.

'The servants, of course, but how noble of Lady Primrose —
no one to blame. And me — a friend!'

'It doesn't matter. The inquest on Fanny Hatton will give
them something to think about.'

Sensation in court. That it was. Greater sensation than Lola
Montez's bigamy. It made the front page of *The Daily News* —
and that was unusual, the front pages being normally dedicated
to the races at Newmarket, railway shares, the price of coal,
books, bread, and bankruptcies. But there it was, beside the
races and the railways — the account of the inquest on Miss
Fanny Hatton, found shot to death on board *The Lant* during
the late flood.

The kidnapping of Mr Dickens's messenger boy turned out
to be the key which unlocked the metaphorical floodgates —
about which Scrap had been modestly triumphant. After all, if
he hadn't been kidnapped and made his daring escape from the
sinking barge — well, things mighta bin very different.

Through those open floodgates flowed the astounding
information about drowning, debts, imposture, fraud, forgery,
bigamy, bastardy, poison, madness, and murder. So many
aliases that even the coroner — not, thankfully, Mr Speed —
seemed at a loss at times. Quist, Fagan, Wiggins, Wigge. Solly,
Solomon. Fanny or Frances Hatton, or Fagan, or Quist?
William, Mordaunt, Purefoy, Septimus Doublett, Constable
Jack Doublett. Quist? A question which echoed through the
improvised courtroom at the workhouse near Whitefriars
Dock. Superintendent Jones, however, gave his evidence with
masterly precision and a good many "otherwise knowns" to
clarify matters. Four murders, he went on to explain, the
inquests on which would be resumed. The superintendent had
every confidence that the murderers would be named, and the

missing man, Mr Solly Wiggins, otherwise known as — a final flourish — Solomon Wigge — would be apprehended.

The coroner was relieved to be able to direct the open-mouthed jury to the simple verdict of accident as regards the death of Miss Frances Hatton.

'Whoever she was,' muttered someone in the public gallery to his neighbour.

Dickens looked down at the front page. *Newmarket*, he thought. Strychnine wouldn't have been running. The devil, though — Legal Advice had won the Cambridgeshire Stakes with Forlorn Hope second. He wouldn't mention that to Sam Jones.

Wigge. Wiggins. Or someone else entirely? Who was he?

48: ENQUIRIES

The question of Wigge's identity had exercised the mind of Superintendent Jones since the inquest on Miss Hatton. It was a question, he remarked to Dickens, to which he had not directed sufficient attention, but to which he had directed Inspector Grove, Sergeant Rogers, Constables Feak, Stemp and Doublett. Mr Solly Wiggins must have an origin. He could not have sprung fully formed from Doctors' Commons.

Mr Matthew Guard's friend had been questioned as to what he knew of Mr Solomon Wigge — a vacant young man, alas, with a head full of cards and girls. Good sort, Wigge. Good company. He had pointed Inspector Grove and Sergeant Rogers to some other young men of Quist's circle. Solomon Wigge? Oh, a good sort, always ready to help a fellow when he —

'Got into a scrape.'

'You get the picture. And, Sir Mordaunt Quist — always generous, hospitable — terrible tragedy — awful accident — greatly missed — not a word about Miss Hatton's inquest, of course.'

'They're not going to tell if there was anything untoward.'

'Not a chance. You've only got Guard's word. His friend had some cutting words to say about him — milksop — got himself into trouble — blamed his friends. A fellow's expected to face up — to what, I didn't ask. However, we've been looking very carefully at the name Wiggins — in the trade directory — not too many, I'm glad to say.'

'Good job he's not a Smith — or Jones.'

'James Wiggins, hairdresser, Old Gravel Lane, Wapping. Inspector Bold to investigate. His Constable Gaunt to have his hair cut, perhaps. Richard Wiggins, sadler, by Christ's Hospital. Constable Stemp mounted, so to speak. Samuel Wiggins, auctioneer, Cecil Street. Constable Doublett and lady friend to look at furniture for their new house. The Peacock Tavern in Gray's Inn Lane — landlord, Mr George Wiggins. Sergeant Rogers and wife to go for a drink and while thereabouts to have a look at a lodging house in Liquorpond Street.'

'That sounds low enough for Solomon Wiggins.'

'I thought that.'

'And all their purposes?'

'To watch and listen, to loiter. And Reuben Wiggins, pawnbroker, Took's Court, to examine the worthless trinkets of a poor woman and her son.'

'Feak and his ma.'

'Right. And a brother and sister to haunt the purlieus of Tavistock Square, where John Wiggins, esquire, lives at number thirty.'

'An esquire in Tavistock Square — a bit on the respectable side for Solly Wiggins —'

'You hope,' Jones said, chuckling. 'I know that, but I had to find something for Scrap to do — and Tavistock Square seemed the safest bet. I've enlisted Posy for his sister, having convinced Elizabeth that our little serving girl will be in no danger. Daylight hours only. Both decently dressed — two youngsters off to school. The beat constables will be eyeing up number thirty at night.'

'Two by two — a veritable Noah's Ark of spies, and we await the dove.'

'It's the best I can do — there are more Wiggins names further afield, so I've circulated the details to other divisions … he could be anywhere.'

'He'll lie low, I'll bet. He'll not break cover too soon. He can lie close and wait till things slacken, then try the open — make his escape to foreign air —'

'He has his passport — cunning devil. Let's hope one of our Wiggins —'

'Wigginses — like Tartes —'

'That seems an age ago. Let's hope somebody knows him — and your dove flies straight to our waiting arms.'

'With her olive leaf.'

But no dove came, nor any sign, not even in Liquorpond Street from Mrs Alice Wiggins's scullery maid, Millie Bird, whom Rogers persuaded to let him and his wife see the mean, dirty, gin-smelling rooms to let — and in so doing managed to elicit useless information about the mean, dirty, gin-smelling lodgers. Mrs Alice Wiggins had a daughter — no son or husband. The peacock did not take flight, either. George Wiggins, landlord, was a bachelor with a very hatchet-faced barmaid who seemed to give no encouragement to drinkers of any kind.

And so they waited for news, and all the while, Superintendent Jones had to contemplate the resumed inquests. Still, he thought, there would be satisfaction in laying the cases before the courts and having Solly Wiggins's name broadcast as a murderer — that might tempt him from whatever hole he was hiding in, or tempt someone to give him up.

Dickens, whom Jones did not want anywhere near Solly Wiggins, hid himself in Wellington Street and contemplated chapter ten of his *Child's History of England*, which was to appear in *Household Words*. He had only to sum up the character of that avaricious, vengeful, false king, Henry the First:

Cunning and unscrupulous, though firm and clever. He cared very little for his word, and took any means to gain his end.

It was that Henry who had died of a surfeit of lampreys. Indigestion and fever finished him off. Greed. Too fat, probably, but he died in his bed, unlike that other power-mad fat man, equally greedy and unscrupulous. Not much had changed, he thought. Power and greed were in every age, to be found in the greatest — and the least, sometimes. It was enough to make you despair.

The story of Mrs William Fagan in St Patrick's Asylum was giving Dickens indigestion, but he was pledged to dine out with Thackeray, for he had promised to tell him the truth behind it all. Thackeray had started the investigation for the sake of his old friend, Pierce Mallory. He deserved to know. Edward Fitzgerald was interested in the murderer's soul. Well, he could tell Thackeray about that. Quist hadn't had one. *Such a murder as a poet might condescend to.* Murder as fine art. Humbug. It never was. It was brutal, commonplace murder by ruffians — a ruffian married to an earl's daughter, and another, just as low, just as cunning, but, alas, still free.

49: INTRUDER

It was on his way back from the quiet pub in Gordon Square where Thackeray had been visiting that Dickens saw the light in Tavistock House.

Dickens had told the tale, most of which Thackeray knew anyway from the newspapers. It was Quist he was interested in, and Dickens's portrait of the great egotist, intoxicated with his own power. That led to the story of Mrs Fagan, at which Thackeray blanched, but he made no comment other than to exclaim, 'The devil.' And Dickens moved on to the missing Wiggins, about whose whereabouts Superintendent Jones was busy.

'Glad it wasn't Ellis,' had been Thackeray's final comment. 'I don't care for him, but those children.'

Dickens's way home took him into Tavistock Square, where he expected the wreck of the Hesperus to be in darkness, but he was surprised to see a light in Frank Stone's former studio, the room which he dreamed as his green drawing room — an impossible dream, like the dream of settling into a new study and writing his new book.

His brother-in-law working late? The rats entertaining? Queer, though. He ought to have a look. He thought of fire — someone left a lamp burning? Dear God, that would be a disaster. He had his key and hurried for the front door.

He couldn't smell burning, but he hastened upstairs, calling out to ask who was there. No one answered. The door was ajar, and in he went to see someone lying on a trestle table. Someone in a workman's apron. He called out again. And then he felt the door pushed open violently into his back — sending him almost sprawling, kicking over a paint tin as he flailed for purchase on something. Someone was behind him. The workman shot up and cried out, 'Sir, sir,' flinging himself off the trestle. Then a confusion of falling ladders, trestles, paint pots, a glancing blow from Stone's birdcage as he was propelled forward by a violent shove in his back. He went down. Someone seemed to fall on him. The workman leapt forward, swinging something. The crack of bone. White liquid everywhere. The door slamming shut and footsteps on the stairs. The workman wrenching open the door. Dickens up and after him. Splashes of white paint on the stairs. The front door wide open. The workman rushing out...

'Out the back,' Dickens shouted, feeling the cold air from the corridor. The garden door must be open.

He went out, but it was too dark to see anything except more splashes of paint, like ghostly footprints leading away from the house into the garden where an old mulberry tree still stood. He thought of the old tree on the abandoned land behind Pierce Mallory's house. Surely not. He took a step forward, then changed his mind. Not a good idea to follow if, perhaps... He turned back into the house and almost collided with the workman coming his way.

'Gone, I'm afraid. Over the wall, probably. But, thank heaven you were here, sir. I think I'm obliged to you for my life.'

'Foreman said, sir, that I was ter stay. Someone 'ad been in, 'e thought. Window open this mornin' — not us, sir, we're allus careful. I was only dozin', sir, sorry, sir.'

'No need — you woke up fast enough. What did you hit him with?'

'Pain tin, sir, only —'

366

'The lid came off,' Dickens said ruefully, looking down at his paint-spattered coat.

'Sorry, sir.'

'Not at all, my dear fellow. A little paint won't harm. It might have been blood if you hadn't been here. I think you hurt him — I heard a most satisfying crack of bone.'

'Serves 'im right. Same cove as last night, I'll bet, seein' if there was something worth pinchin'.'

'Well, he got a lot of free paint.'

'Yer'll tell the police?'

'Oh, I will, sir, I will. Now we'll lock up — I doubt he'll be back. Nothing to take anyway. The place is a wreck.'

'It'll be right as rain, sir, you jest see — we're gettin' on. I know it looks —'

'How did you know it was me?'

'Seen yer, Mr Dickens, sir — lookin' a bit down 'earted, if yer don't mind me sayin', but it'll come right.'

'You are a great comfort, Mr...?'

'Lobbs, carpenter, sir — where yer goin' now?'

'To my office in Wellington Street.'

'I'd best come, then. Two's company, eh? I lodges not far away.'

Dickens looked at the burly young man. Two's company was about right. Mr Lobbs was a very great comfort in the circumstances.

The painted footprints led Sergeant Rogers and Constable Stemp into the back alley behind Tavistock House and its two terraced neighbours, but they petered out as the two policemen went deeper into the muddy labyrinth of courts and passages beyond. It would have taken a few moments for the man to have rubbed his feet in the ankle-deep mud and to have hurried away. No one would have noticed — not the drunks in the gutters, not the tramps sleeping in the doorways, not the sneak thieves returning from their own midnight assignations. A man covered in paint? 'Dint notice, sir, jest comin' back from my work 'bout then — dint see no one,' explained the man with the shifty eyes whose breath reeked of gin at dawn and who they had seen picking himself up from a doorway. All wise monkeys down Judd's Place way. Sayin' nothin', seein' nothin', 'earin' nothin'.

'Nothin' will come of nothin', as the old king said to 'is daughter wot cheeked 'im,' Dickens observed to Superintendent Jones in the manner of Sam Weller. 'It's a known fact. It might have been just an opportunist thief who saw me go in, or someone looking for a bed for the night.'

'Lot of violence, though, shoving that door into you and hurtling in. A lad on the lurk would have scarpered when he saw someone go into the house.'

'I can't say it was Wiggins, I'm afraid. I'll admit I thought of it.'

'And I'm afraid it was. Not that it helps. Still, you'd best lie low when it's dark. Stemp had better sleep in your hall overnight. Wiggins might know you're here on your own.'

'My guardian angel.'

And Dickens did lie low. But no one came in the night to murder him in his bed. And then there was a visitor to bring tidings of a ghostly nature. Nothing angelic about the smell he brought with him, though Dickens knew well how often men still entertained angels unawares, as in the olden times — even some that were in rags.

And so down he went to his sub-editor's office to meet the visitor whom Harry Wills had not known where to put. Dickens understood when he approached the office door. A very ancient and fish-like smell first proclaimed his caller. And then the bundle of old clothes heaped on the most comfortable chair.

'Mr Tramper,' he said. *Making very free with my premises,* he thought, remembering Tramper's indignation at Duke Street.

'Sir, Mister Dickens, your honour — your health, I'd drink if there was a drop to be had now.'

'But, of course. Mr Wills can find you something, I'm sure.'

Mr Wills produced brandy and a glass, from which Tramper drank a great gulp. 'Ye see, sir, Mr Dickens, it's a terrible fright I've had, and I'd be obliged again —'

Mr Wills obliged again and Dickens asked, 'How did you find me?'

'Mr Lion — he wasn't for tellin', but I knew you'd want to know.'

'What?'

'An apparition, sir, at the house where Mr Pierce was taken to his rest. Saw it with my own eyes — a thing, sir, or half a thing — shoulders all white, I saw, an' half a head, an' nothin' else, no body at all, but it was floatin', sir, Mr Dickens, sure, it was floatin' through that doorway like the ghost of ould Finn MacCool — an' it never came out again — an' there's been a light on at night — a little ray of light through the crack, shinin' like an angel's beam — though I'm doubting there's any angel there —'

'The devil, I think.'

And it was. Dickens and Superintendent Jones found him. He didn't resist, but that may have been to do with the fact that Superintendent Jones held a gun to his temple as he was sleeping in Pierce Mallory's blood-stained chair, and Dickens grabbed the sporting rifle that was loose in his unknowing hands on his lap. The hand of death was upon him.

He knew that. Sergeant Rogers and Constable Stemp took him away, a shabby, unshaven, dirty-faced, greasy-haired, trampish figure in a muddy black suit stained with white paint about the shoulders. He had a broken nose.

'The ghost of Solomon Wigge,' said Dickens as they watched him go. 'Not the man he was.'

'Or wasn't,' Jones countered.

He snuffed out the candle. And there beside it on the table were the two inches left of a candle that had burned through the wastes of the long night in a room where a man had lain dead. And of whom nothing remained but the stain of his blood.

They went out into the moonlight. 'These houses are due for demolition in the next few days,' Jones said.

'No bad thing.' *No bad thing at all*, Dickens thought. *Burn the lot. And let Pierce Mallory sleep in the open space of Highgate with his poor brother who, though culpable of debt, stayed loyal to him, despite their steely mother.*

50: VANISHING ACTS

From Deadman's Walk to the scaffold. To vanish down that hideous trapdoor through which the hangman dispatched him. Solly Wiggins was buried in Newgate under the grim flagstones of his last walk, his body strewn with lime to hasten its dissolution, and only the roughly carved initial 'W' in the brickwork to record his time upon this earth, if that 'W' meant anything at all. No one would ever know who he really was or what made him. Perhaps another steely-hearted mother, or another fallen woman dead in cheap lodgings somewhere about Liquorpond Street or Judd's Place, or anywhere north, south, east, or west, or beyond the city, away to the hills, or the seas.

No one claimed the body of Fanny Hatton. It was a mercy, Dickens reflected, that the poor mad woman in Dublin did not know that she had a daughter whose father had corrupted her — for that was all he could conjecture. Quist had kept her close — but so he had all who might have been a threat to him, and in so doing he had made her in his own image. She was buried by the parish and lay sleeping in St James's burial ground — not a few minutes' walk from Duke Street, where she had probably killed the man who had betrayed her. And where lay also the remains of Frederick Estcourt — buried at his Grosvenor Square uncle's reluctant expense — not by Mr Graveson of Gerrard Street. Tubby, the advertiser of cheap funerals, did the honours, such as they were. Just the one carriage — empty. No plumes. No kid gloves. No stone in St James's burial ground.

Mr Dax did the honours for his daughter — simple, but heartfelt, and Caroline's grave in St Botolph's without Aldgate — not far from the rag shop — was marked as that of the beloved daughter of Barnaby Dax and his wife, Margaret. And so little Alfred was taught. He never knew who his father was. He didn't need to. Mr and Mrs Dax were all the father and mother he ever needed.

The Quickswood family vault was the final resting place of Sir Mordaunt Quist, where the grieving widow had retired to take up residence amid the decaying stones of Quickswood Abbey, seat of the earls of that name. That name, now stained beyond restoration.

She had no children, and neither had that new earl, who had not the means to live in his mansion, and who did not care to go there, nor, indeed, to use his useless, tarnished title. Lady Primrose was welcome to the place. The vault would be sealed up when Lady Primrose shuffled off her mortal coil. Dead and gone, both of them. And forgotten, the house laid waste. Dust to dust.

And the dust had departed from Tavistock House, and the parrot's cage, the paint tins, the ladders, the workmen — Mr Lobbs putting up the last shelves, and accepting his tip with a good-natured, 'Told yer so.' Even the rat and his family packed up and vanished to other lodgings, and by November Charles Dickens knew where his pen and ink were, and had written his first letter with that address at the top of the page. His own bleak house was finished and now he was at his desk, thinking about a girl brought up by a stern, unbending guardian, a girl who did not know her mother, only that she was orphaned and degraded from her birth. Esther, she'd be. Esther Summerson. Summer would come for her — eventually.

Mrs Ellis's child, another little Esther, orphaned — and degraded, according to her father and his father, but Stephen Ellis's mother had displayed remarkable firmness. He was Stephen Ellis's child, her grandchild, and should she have to leave Torrington Square to live in seclusion with the little girl, so she would. The two blustering, ill-tempered men found that they had no choice but to give in — with ill grace, of course.

Dickens was glad. He remembered the little girl's wide, wondering eyes, holding her as he had taken her downstairs, and the trust she had placed in him. That was why he had gone to see Mrs Ellis.

He heard the front door and the sound of children's voices. His wife Catherine's voice, followed by Elizabeth Jones's, and then footsteps up the stairs. They'd all be going up to the schoolroom where a children's party was to be held with a magician, and a feast of sandwiches, cakes and jellies and lemonade. Wine and beer for the grown-ups.

He went into his green drawing room through the connecting door with the sham books on the shelves. He was looking in the mirror over the mantel just as Sam Jones came in with Scrap at his heels.

'Good Lord — Wiggins!' he exclaimed at the vision before him. A figure dressed in a black robe decorated with hieroglyphics, a black moustache and heavy beard — and a great black wig.

'Rhia Rhama Rhoos, at your service — straight from the plains of Tartary, ready to perform the wonders of the East — The Great Pyramid Wonder. Five thousand guineas from a Chinese Mandarin who died of grief at parting with it.'

'Half a crown from that Noah's Ark shop, more like — seen it,' Scrap said.

'Oh, ye of little faith. Wait till you see the magic, my lad, though I do have a difficulty —'

'It don't work.'

'Oh, it will do. However, my assistant, Mr Stanfield is — indisposed, so —' Clarkson Stanfield, the artist, was usually Dickens's assistant in magic.

'Oh, no,' Jones said, backing away, 'no, no —'

'Not on yer —' Scrap retreated, too.

Dickens put his hand to his heart. 'You cut me to the bone, but I ask not for myself. Think of all those children upstairs — waiting, hoping — little Tom Brim, my Frank, Alfred, Sydney, Henry. Think of Sergeant Rogers, Mollie, Constable Feak, his ma, Constable Stemp — all deserving of a treat, and you two scurvy —'

'Not in front of my sergeant — or my constable — I've my dignity to consider.'

'Scrap? Think of it — magic tricks — disappearing hats, watches, coins, cards — come in useful when we're on a case.'

Scrap's eyes widened. Now, that was different. Blimey, Mr D. was right — serpose there woz a card sharp wot needed watchin', or a pocket wot needed pickin' —

Not what Superintendent Jones had intended. Dear Lord, the two of them in some gambling den, or worse, in the street, attracting a crowd — the police moving them on. Or picking pockets. He, having to —

Too late. Scrap was already hitching on the red robe — too long, but the chief magician had pins and belts, and eye blacking, and another beard —

'Abra —' Rhia Rhama Rhoos began, but Superintendent Jones had vanished.

He paid handsomely for his desertion, his watch purloined, a fire lit in his best hat to boil a pudding, a sovereign vanished into a pyramid of boxes — all to the great amusement of his sergeant and constables, and to Dickens, who delighted in singling him out for the dark arts of the necromancer, and to the assistant who enjoyed himself hugely. The star of the show, however, was the guinea pig conjured from a box of bran. Of course, it made straight for Superintendent Jones's trouser leg. Afterwards, he refused to believe that it had been just coincidence. 'You cast a spell on the thing. I know you.'

The audience loved it all. As they took their bow to rapturous applause, Dickens felt his assistant's small hand in his. He felt the bones of it. He didn't let go. Scrap gave him a look. He knew.

HISTORICAL NOTES

The murder of Pierce Mallory was inspired by the real-life murder of a journalist whom Dickens knew. He wrote to his sub-editor on *Household Words*, Harry Wills, about the case on October 5th, 1852:

I recollect Morton well. Met him in Fleet Street, some twelve months ago, and want to know the details — am quite amazed and shocked...

Dickens returns to the subject in a letter dated October 7th:

I never heard of such a business altogether, as you unfold in that Morton case. When I met him in Fleet Street, he told me the whole story of the Duel...

Savile Morton, the murder victim, came from an Irish landed family. He attended Trinity College, Cambridge and became an Apostle, a member of an elite society of very clever students. He became a close friend of Edward Fitzgerald (translator of *The Rubaiyat of Omar Khayyam*), who did call him 'my wild Irishman', and he was close to Thackeray, who said that Morton 'was shocking about women'.

Dickens knew Morton first when Dickens edited *The Daily News* for a brief period in 1846 — Morton was the foreign correspondent. Dickens knew the murderer, too, Harold Elyott Bower, who was Paris correspondent for *The Morning Post*.

Morton did receive a gift of duelling pistols from Edward Fitzgerald and fought at least two duels in France: one with a journalist called Forbes-Campbell; the second with Count Roger de Beauvoir, a poet and a journalist. This was to do with

Lola Montez, a dancer, and mistress of the various famous men I mention in the novel, and mistress of King Ludwig I of Bavaria, who made her Countess of Landsfeld. She was a notorious figure — an adventuress with not much talent but plenty of sex appeal. Her spider dance was regarded as a scandalous performance involving the exposure of rather a lot of flesh, and she was had up in court for bigamy.

In October 1852, Harold Elyott Bower attacked Savile Morton with a knife and killed him. Bower's wife had told him that Morton was the father of her new baby. Bower fled to England, but returned to Paris for his trial; he was acquitted on the grounds of temporary insanity.

The story was too good to miss. The newspapers were full of it, though there was a good deal of sympathy for the participants. Their journalist friends stood by them, some maintaining that Mrs Bower didn't know what she was saying when she claimed Morton as the father of her baby. Poor Mrs Bower was removed to an asylum after Morton's death. My Mrs Ellis meets the same fate, but I made up the story of her father and her meeting with Dickens. Apart from Thackeray and Edward Fitzgerald, who were connected to the case of Savile Morton and whom I link to Pierce Mallory, all the other characters related to Mallory's life are fictitious.

However, there are some 'real' characters: Richard Mayne was the rather haughty Police Commissioner; Tom Beard, another journalist, was one of Dickens's oldest friends; Augustus Egg was the brother of the famous gunsmiths, the Eggs, of number one Piccadilly; Dickens bought the house that Frank Stone, the artist, had rented; Judge Talfourd was a close friend of Dickens; Gilbert À Beckett, solicitor and magistrate, did contribute to *Punch* and write plays; Bryan Procter contributed to *Household Words* and Dickens knew him well.

You can see how useful Dickens is to Superintendent Jones — he knows all kinds of people in all sorts of professions. Oh, and Henry Austin, superintendent of works at Tavistock House, was married to Dickens's sister, Letitia.

Uncle Thomas Barrow did live above the bookshop in Gerrard Street. His leg was amputated in 1823 and eleven-year-old Dickens visited him regularly. Thomas Culliford Barrow's sister was Elizabeth Barrow, who married John Dickens in 1809. John Dickens worked in the Navy Pay Office where Elizabeth's father, Charles, was 'Chief Conductor of Monies'. However, he was suspected of embezzlement and fled the country, settling in the Isle of Man. He died in 1826. His sons, however, were fairly successful, John becoming a barrister and journalist, Edward a parliamentary reporter, and Thomas Culliford, head of the Prize Branch of the Navy Pay Office. Dickens's father was the improvident one — he borrowed £200 from Thomas. It was never paid back. And he was imprisoned in the Marshalsea for debt. Fortunately, Charles Dickens seems to have inherited the Barrow brothers' determination to overcome the scandal of their father's criminal acts. Thomas Culliford recovered from his amputation, married in 1824, and continued to prosper. John Dickens continued to borrow from his son — and his son's friends. Dickens's brother, Fred, also became a frequent borrower from his famous brother. Dickens knew all about skeletons in the cupboards of seemingly respectable Victorian families. Of course, I moved my murder case to 1851 when Dickens was in the middle of the restoration of Tavistock House, which he had bought for £1,500 in July. His letters record the delays and complications of the restoration work. In volume six of the Pilgrim edition of the letters, there is even a sketch made by Dickens of the arrangements for the shower curtains he wanted — *light, cheerful-coloured waterproof curtains*. He took a shower bath every morning. No wonder a three-hundred gallon capacity water tank was required, as Dickens writes to his brother-in-law, requesting a letterbox with a glass back for the street door, too. At the same time he is writing to Judge Talfourd about copyright, to Mr Eeles, his bookbinder, to the gardener, to his neighbour about right of way, to Miss Burdett-Coutts about a difficult girl at the home for fallen women, editing articles for *Household Words*, and trying out titles for his new book.

It wasn't until November that he was able to get into his new study and begin *Bleak House* in earnest, and Catherine, his wife, was pregnant with their tenth child, who would be born in March 1852. There were eight living children in 1851, as baby Dora had died in April 1851.

The story of the woman who was haunted by the dream of a face looking fixedly at her was published under the title 'To Be Read at Dusk' in *The Keepsake*, an annual magazine.

Incidentally, the forged will and documents cases concerning the Reverend William Bailey and the Ricketts family were true, as are the details about forgeries and substitution at Doctors' Commons, where Dickens worked as a young reporter and David Copperfield trained as a proctor. There were thirty-nine trial reports for forgery in 1845. The Ricketts case went on for years and is believed to have been the inspiration for Anthony Trollope's novel, *Orley Farm*. The case involved a deed made to revoke a trust leaving money to Sir Robert Ricketts's daughter. The daughter claimed that the new deed was invalid and Lady Ricketts was accused of forgery, and there was a question about Sir Robert's death — had he been poisoned? Would his body be exhumed? No wonder the story appealed to a novelist. It certainly did to me.

A NOTE TO THE READER

Dear Reader,

Imagine leaving a packet of Batley's Vermin Powder lying around. As my Doctor Woodhall says, half a grain could kill a man. Accidents did happen — and murder — because poisons were in every house in Victorian times, particularly arsenic. Most murderers — and there were plenty of arsenical killers — claimed to have bought the deadly white powder to kill rats. Arsenic was everywhere — in cakes, in wallpaper, in fabrics, in paint and paper, and in medicines. It was used to treat cancer, malaria, asthma, even to improve sexual prowess — as a tonic. Fowler's Solution was used for skin complaints. You could get arsenic everywhere — just as you could get opium — and you didn't need a prescription.

I don't know what was in the powders supposedly prescribed for Sir Mordaunt Quist by the eminent Doctor Savage. Or did the eminent doctor lie to protect his distinguished neighbour and his aristocratic wife? It is true that doctors prescribed all kinds of poisonous medicines. Mercury was good for liver problems, it seems, and for syphilis, presumably needed after you had taken your arsenic performance enhancer. Calomel, that is chloride of mercury, was used to treat cholera. Wine of colchium was taken for rheumatism. Colchium comes from the bulbs of meadow saffron. Sounds innocent enough, but the bulbs were deadly. Too much and that was it. The poetically named Cherry Pectoral was actually a mixture of alcohol and opium — you might die laughing, I suppose. Chlorodyne was prescribed for coughs and colds, camphorated tincture of opium for asthma. For angina, you might be given an inhalation of amyl nitrate, or steel filings in a bitter infusion — you'd choke to death, I'd have thought. It was recommended as a treatment for gout as well. Wormwood for fever, extract of henbane for colic, and coca leaf, from which cocaine is obtained, was advertised as a nerve and muscle tonic.

As was strychnine. Nerve tonics were A Thing at the time. Strychnine was a tonic for ailing appetites — the bitterness was supposed to irritate the tastebuds and the stomach lining, thus provoking hunger. It was proposed as a cure for alcoholism, too, and as a stimulant, like arsenic, and a remedy for paralysis.

Sometimes, the results were disastrous. In 1847, a chemist — or chymist, as some newspapers spelt it, and it does look rather more sinister — made up a prescription composed of two drachms of spirit of ammonia, sixteen drops of tincture of opium, four drops of prussic acid, and two grains of strychnine powder, all to be dissolved in six ounces of bitter almond water. Sounds like a witches' brew. And it did kill the patient, even though the chemist left out the strychnine. The prescribing doctor was tried for manslaughter. It was the prussic acid that killed the lady. And the chymist? Name of Daniel Coffin. I said he was sinister. However, I must admit that some newspapers reported him as Daniel Corfield. Of course, I like to think it was Coffin.

In 1849, John Jones, another chemist, was indicted for the manslaughter of Georgiana Sirgison Smith. The lady, suffering from 'a slight weakness', needed a tonic. The doctor duly provided the prescription, which was to contain a drug called salacine — you can guess what happened. Mr Jones confused salacine with strychnine. Strychnine leaves no trace in the body, but the medicine bottle contained enough strychnine to kill eight or nine people.

In 1845, a chemist in Manchester made up a prescription for Mrs Mallinson's cough. She took the powder in her tea and died of severe tetanic convulsions. The chemist had made a mistake. He had used pulverised strychnine instead of the milder nux vomica.

Perhaps Sir Mordaunt Quist's doctor had prescribed the strychnine powders. Quist might have been feeling a bit below par — trying to the nerves, all that murdering, bigamy and forgery. Handy for the doctor that a servant was blamed instead of Sir James Savage or the chemist. Trying to the reputation, if the doctor had been censured — or had up for manslaughter.

Dickens enjoyed comparatively good health — a state he attributed to taking a cold shower every day. And he walked — sometimes seventeen miles a day. However, he did suffer frequently from colds, which was not surprising given the London fogs. He recommended Justus von Leibig's beef tea and sent the recipe to a friend, declaring that it was 'the strongest and most nutritious beef tea that can possibly be made.' To another friend he sent his cold cure 'a teaspoon of sal volatile, a pinch of High Welch snuff mixed together in a tumbler of water.' I think I'll stick to paracetamol.

Oh, and as for the horse, Strychnine — in 1849, he did run at Newmarket, along with Venom and Vampyr. Strychnine came second in The Ascot Stakes and Vampyr third. Miss Nipper ran — named for Susan Nipper in *Dombey and Son*, and Dolly Varden came nowhere in the Royal Hunt Cup. All this I learned from *Bell's Sporting Life*, for whom the real Pegasus was the racing correspondent.

I hope that you enjoyed reading my novel and I thank you for taking the time to do so. Reviews are very important to writers, so it would be great if you could spare the time to post a review on **Amazon** and **Goodreads**. Readers can connect with me online, on **Facebook (JCBriggsBooks)** and **Twitter (@JeanCBriggs)**, and you can find out more about the books and Charles Dickens via my website, **jcbriggsbooks.com**, where you will find Mr Dickens's A–Z of murder — all cases of murder to which I found a Dickens connection.

Thank you!

Jean Briggs

Sapere Books is an exciting new publisher of brilliant fiction and popular history.

To find out more about our latest releases and our monthly bargain books visit our website:
saperebooks.com

Printed in Great Britain
by Amazon